PARED

A SECOND HELPING

CAMRI KOHLER

Lake Country Press
Publishing & Reviews

First published in the United States of America 2024 by Lake Country Press & Reviews.

Cataloging-in-Publication Data is on file with the Library of Congress.

ISBN: Paperback: 979-8-9889859-1-4. Ebook: 979-8-9889859-2-1

Author website: https://www.camrikohler.com/

Publisher website: https://www.lakecountrypress.com

Editor: Tara Sexton

Cover Design: Zoe Norvell

Formatting: Dawn Lucous of Yours Truly Book Services

Lake Country Press & Reviews

Lake Country Press
Publishing & Reviews

CONTENT/ TRIGGER WARNINGS

The Peachy Trilogy features dark and potentially triggering content. I hope to be as thorough as possible. Please contact me if you feel a CW/TW has not been included in this list.

- Abduction
- Alcohol Use
- Blood
- Cannibalism
- Cheating
- Death
- Depictions of Bullying
- Drug Use
- Gambling
- Gore
- References to Drug Overdose
- References to Suicide
- Self-Injurious Behavior
- Tobacco Use
- Violence

PARED PLAYLIST

1. "Back 2 Good" – Matchbox Twenty
2. "Dream Weaver" – Gary Wright
3. "I'm on My Way" – The Proclaimers
4. "Through the Valley" – Shawn James
5. "Hey Pachuco" – Royal Crown Revue
6. "Sea of Love" – Cat Power
7. "So Fresh, So Clean" - Outkast
8. "A Girl Like You" – Edwyn Collins
9. "F**k Was I" – Jenny Owen Youngs
10. "Your Love is Killing Me" – Sharon Van Etten
11. "Renegade" – Styx
12. "I Think I'm Paranoid" – Garbage
13. "Wicked Game" – Chris Isaak
14. "We Will Rock You" – Queen
15. "Another Brick in the Wall" - Korn
16. "Dragula" – Rob Zombie
17. "Let It Go" – Blue October
18. "Come As You Are" – Nirvana
19. "Sex and Candy" – Marcy Playground
20. "Stop Crying Your Heart Out" – Oasis
21. "Zombie" – The Cranberries
22. "Only Love Can Hurt Like This" – Paloma Faith
23. "Move Bitch" – Ludacris
24. "Open" – Rhye

25. "All That I've Got" – The Used
26. "My Lullaby" – Maria Mena
27. "You're Gonna Go Far, Kid" – The Offspring
28. "Black and Blue" – Counting Crows
29. "Blitzkrieg Bog" – Ramones
30. "Dammit" – blink-182

To my readers, who came back for a second helping.
This book is rough on the ticker, but please, have faith in me.
It's not over until Frankie's had her last desserts.

The juice is worth the squeeze.
I promise.

1

"FIVE MORE, FRANK."

I dragged my body up and into my knees, my measly abs shrieking in protest. I would give him *one* more.

"Nope, five," Ben ordered in response to my choice.

I curled my lip and groaned. "You are so annoying!" My irritation was beneficial, and I pushed out another three crunches off its fumes.

"You can't complain about weakness if you don't put in the effort, Frankie," Cleo chided from my right. She was pumping out crunches like a factory, her diamond-hard stomach taking each in stride. She wasn't even out of breath for Christ's sake! *I* was supposed to be the well of health.

You would think Cleo Zaher was freshly twenty, twenty-five max, but we had just celebrated her thirty-third birthday. I had gifted her several books she'd requested by email weeks prior. Cleo was the most efficient siren in North America, certainly, if not the western hemisphere.

Ben's hands gripped my toes, keeping me planted on the carpet and stopping me from running away. "Two more!" I heaved myself up, reaching my knees once in the time it took Cleo to do five. "One left!"

If Cleo was the most efficient siren, Ben Bowen was, by far, the most annoying, intrusive seer on the face of the Earth.

"I know how to count!" Against the agony of my middle, I

1

rose to my knees. I then immediately flumped to my side, clutching my gut.

Ben patted my head. "You get one minute. Then you have to hold me between those arms. You make me feel so safe, Princess. Such bulging biceps." I opened one sweat-soaked eye to see Ben's freckled face not a foot from my own. He dropped a kiss on my temple and rolled his tongue over my salty taste. "Nasty."

"You can thank yourself for that."

Ben and Cleo had been leading me through various at-home workouts for the last two months. I felt it best to prepare for the worst (having to carry another dead body) and to hope for the best (not having to).

The summer ended on a note of fortification after Paimon nearly killed us all. Cleo's magical hair was like a second carpet in this house, draped over most trims and around furniture legs. Ben blocked out an hour each morning to reinforce the unseen shield surrounding our home, but it only held while he was inside. I practiced my affinity every single day, Ben peppering in new challenges from time to time. Our physical workouts only took place three nights a week, and I hated every one of them.

Ben still lived here after a demonic fire destroyed his kitchen in July, though the repairs were nearly finished. I selfishly hoped that once he moved back home, we'd all lose interest in exercise.

Our egg-carton herb seedlings had graduated to pots, and several sprouts were scattered throughout the house like watchful gnomes. I laid my hands upon the little stems regularly, ensuring they were as healthy as can be.

I stared up at the flat expanse of white that was now our ceiling—the three of us removed the popcorn texture as soon as Ben arrived. We had not one couch, but two, both jewel-colored velvet. Thank god for fall, because those things made my ass sweat in the summer heat.

Cleo was obstinate when it came to interior design, and a much braver person than I wouldn't stand in her way. The couches were very pretty. And it was expected that we tell her how pretty they were.

We'd pushed them against the walls, beneath a framed mixed-media piece Ben completed last month, so we could crunch and squat and burpee.

"We're done for the day. I need to be at Jim's in an hour," I huffed.

"Like showering is honestly going to take you that long," Ben countered. "But fine. No more today." He put his hands in mine, his touch as familiar now as my own, and hoisted me up. I went limp and flopped like warm rubber. "Jesus, Frank."

"I need to rest for five minutes. Cool down." He set me back on the carpet and Cleo rolled her eyes into her brain. "What are you guys gonna do while I'm gone?" It was Saturday, and neither of them had anywhere to be.

"I think I'll go for a run," Cleo said as she readjusted her beautiful breasts beneath her sports bra. She ran the full circumference of Aspen Ridge daily. The spike in automobile accidents and marital spats were not her problem.

"I need to pop home, check in on the garden. It's about time to harvest. Plus, I should probably start moving my shit back there pretty soon …" Ben side-eyed me.

"Sure, yeah. Pretty soon." I didn't want to give him any sort of opinion. I didn't want to come off as pathetic. A queen bed was immense with only one person sleeping in it. Especially compared to what I used to sleep on.

Ben's eyes drifted to the wall behind me. I'd gotten used to the act, precognition hitting Ben's frontal lobe dozens of times a day. "You might get another call from Deputy Jacobs soon."

I folded my elbows over my face. The police had paid us a visit last month. My being the last client Gabriel Perez served before his untimely death was something they found "intriguing" and something I found to be "unlucky to the point of gut-wrenchingly cosmic."

The Aspen Ridge Sheriff's Department was mean in the way

most small-time cops seemed to be. They founded their bias against all of us as out-of-towners—my residence was made not born—the second I opened the door. Anyone could deduce they thought us irreverent and crude, three young people of multiple sexes under one roof. Their attitude had brought out my own unpleasantness during their last visit, and I wasn't keen to give them another reason to bother us.

"Do they have anything else?" I asked through my arms.

"No, they're desperate," Ben assured.

I nodded into my enclosure. I wished I had more to give them. I wished I could put the person responsible behind bars. But I didn't wish for it enough to confess any semblance of truth and put myself behind said bars.

Pushing up from the floor, I weaved around the various house plants and grabbed a Gold Star from the fridge, as well as a slice of white bread. I picked the spongy slice apart and shoved the bits in my mouth, suddenly full of nervous energy. Ben stretched his arms up to the ceiling and arched his back. He donned only a pair of black Nike shorts and his chest glistened with sweat in the morning light. He was beautiful, despite the volleyball-sized scar dominating his torso.

Our touching had … increased, since the unfortunate events over the summer. And with it, his scarring did appear to soften, the skin transitioning to an almost normal texture. But each time I saw his stomach and noticed the absence of the tattoos that he'd created, that belonged there, I dropped my eyes in self-hatred.

I'd done the same with Cleo, finding odd chances to touch her. Unlike Ben, she shied away when I did—an aversion to me or to my affinity—and though her scarring had ebbed slightly, she seemed to prefer her new visage. I caught her prodding the scar on her lip from time to time with an air of curiosity rather than resentment.

Ben noticed my mood. He tucked his hand around my chin and lifted my face. "Hey," he whispered as I shoved another ball of bread into my mouth. He gave his hallmark smile, half teasing and half genuine. "Don't go there, Frank. Cleo and I are just fine."

I shook my head in his fingers, squishing the last bite of bread between my lips. Ben was saying what was expected of him, being my best friend, and my *partner* or whatever he wanted to call himself (he once used the word *lover*, and I'd choke and die before saying that out loud). But my consumption of Jessamae's wounds, my gluttonous and sickening behavior, had very nearly killed him over the summer. Ben's death would have stained my hands just as much as they stained Paimon's mutated, inhuman digits. May Pamela rest in peace.

I'd gotten a voicemail a week ago from Joseph Perez, proprietor of Perez Family Funeral Home, that Pamela's headstone had been completed. The etched slate now marked her empty grave. I hadn't gone to see it. I hoped I'd never find myself there again, despite knowing that nothing slept under the cemetery grass. It was hard to separate Pamela from Paimon, considering their shared corpse rotted in a shallow grave far away from that headstone.

"I need to shower," I said again, placing a tentative hand on Ben's slippery chest. Even after all this time, it felt strange to intentionally reach out and touch him. His skin buzzed beneath mine, warming instantly. My affinity was a greedy thing; even Ben's sore muscles and fatigue were enough to trigger it. He and I had been practicing control along with everything else—I tended to achieve a contact high if he was feeling unwell, just as he got high on my painkiller magic.

I had been practicing *restraint*—the ability to turn my magic off, only healing when I willed it. It was beyond difficult, and I had made little progress. The most we had noticed is a slowness, a dragging leak of magic rather than a flush.

Ben lifted my fingers and kissed them. "Yes, you do." He wiped my sweat, again, from his lips. I held my middle finger in the air all the way down the hall.

We replaced the bathroom door within a week of Gabriel's destruction. Ben brought it home in one of his company trucks, surprising Cleo and me. It seemed mostly for my benefit, as I valued privacy more than the others. They were so blasé about their bodies. Ben had returned to his commando customs shortly after his move.

As I entered the bathroom, I remembered the night I discovered that fact. I remembered the ridges of his hips and the dip of his pelvis beneath the waistband of his gym shorts, not unlike the pair he wore today. I'd explored further and found the warmth of the soft, soft skin.

I looked up into the bathroom mirror. Even a memory made me blush.

I DUMPED my keys into the small wooden dish that Cleo assigned me. My shift had been dull and uneventful, something I'd grown to appreciate after the summer's end.

Ben sauntered out of our room in a purple sweatshirt which read, "Mama Needs Some Wine." His body ran colder than mine, and he was already bundling up for fall.

"Welcome home," he said as he bent to kiss my cheek. "How's Jim?"

"Boring. Very few people inside him today. But I think I'm up for a fifteen-cent pay raise come January. So, you know," I opened the fridge and ducked inside. "Worth it."

Ben knocked his hip into me, pushing me away from the fridge. "Don't kid yourself, Frank."

I snorted but moved to lean against the counter. "What's on the menu tonight?"

He pulled out an armful of leafy vegetables, a Tupperware storing a raw chicken breast clutched in his hand. "Soup."

I grabbed a knife from the silverware drawer. "I'll cut carrots then." Ben looked at me from beneath scornful brows. "I will cut carrots then," I said louder. He sighed and rolled them onto the counter.

My cuts were messy, but Ben was the only one who cared. I stepped away from the cutting board and he gave my work a pained expression. "Toss them in. Quickly."

Cleo strolled down the hallway in her silk robe. She waved a silent greeting in my direction. "How was your run?" I asked.

She smiled. "Mr. McCormac stopped me. Two bags of apricots, a box of jarred peaches, two jars of tomato juice, and a case of sweet peas. He gave me a ride and unloaded everything for me."

"That explains all the color in the fridge. I hope you're happy."

Her grin reached her ears. "Very. I love sweet peas."

"And I doubt you'd let that fact escape Mr. McCormac's attention."

She shrugged and moved to sit at the table.

"His goods go for a very pretty penny at the farmers' market. Nice work," Ben said as he stirred the fragrant soup. I inhaled deeply. Ben had many gifts, but his cooking was my favorite.

He ladled the dish into three matching bowls—Cleo preferred dining sets—making disappointed sounds at the sight of the floating ameba carrots.

Ben snuck glances at me as we ate. He quietly paid attention to my habits—eating, sleeping, drinking—and had yet to break his mothering proclivities. God help him if he ever tried to correct my behavior.

I stacked our empty bowls and took them to the sink before opening one of the dated brown cupboards and pulling out a box of chamomile tea.

"You know it's better fresh," Ben said from the table.

"Sure it is, but I don't feel much like pruning, drying, and bagging tonight." I set three matching mugs on the counter and tossed a bag in each. I filled Cleo's kettle with water and put it on the stove to boil. I'd been brewing chamomile tea nearly every night for over a month. Trouble sleeping. Ben offered a variety of spells to knock me out, but I didn't need him hurting himself every night just so I could get some shuteye.

I squeezed a dollop of honey in each and gave a steaming mug to both Cleo and Ben. Amir strutted from Cleo's room and leapt into her lap. As the weather cooled, he spent most of his mangey days wandering the mountains, and his nights at the foot of Cleo's bed. She stroked his gnarled fur.

"What shall we practice tonight, Frankie? The moon will be waxing for a few more days, so we can stay inside," she said, dunking her tea bag repeatedly. "We could make some charms. Your crafting is deplorable. Or we could work with fire. You struggle with that element." Amir appeared gleeful at her criticisms.

"Thank you for the report," I grunted, "but I'm tired. Can't we skip tonight?"

"I'll help you," Ben intervened. "You need your practice." He lifted an eyebrow, his eyes full of wicked promise. "And so do I. Let us adjourn to the bedroom—"

"Have you heard from Jessamae?" Cleo asked without warning.

I stopped breathing, my tea bag suspended like a hanged man above the rim of my cup. I couldn't look directly at the siren, her almond eyes intent. No one had brought up Jessamae since she left. She hadn't called, emailed, texted, or message-in-a-bottled any of us since August. Cleo knew that. "No."

Ben stiffened beside me. Though he no longer hated the vampire, she caused him great unhappiness. He certainly remembered the two of us together, particularly the moments for which he wasn't around, watching through my eyes.

Cleo shot up from the table, Amir a squashed patch of fur on her chest. I heard her door shut from the kitchen, still reeling from the unprecedented onslaught of memories.

Wandering fingers tangled into the hair at my temple. "You know what I do?" Ben asked. "I think of all the things my senses are experiencing now, in the present—the smells, the sounds. Sometimes it's the only way out of the future." He pulled me up from the table. "Or the past." He swept the hair from my forehead before guiding me down the hall. His hand was both smooth and textured, the tattoos decorating his fingers from base to tip.

It was the weekend, so the paint aroma was faint—he smelled only of herbs and soil tonight.

He led me into the room that had become ours. He moved toward me with measured, silent steps. "Control, Princess."

I nodded, swallowing hard.

His hands moved to my neck, their brush so gentle they tickled. His thumbs rubbed beneath the base of my ear, clicking against my mother's old earring. Ben leaned forward an inch at a time, a centimeter at a time. When his mouth was close enough to graze mine, he bit down on his own lip. "Control," he repeated. He had ripped the skin of his bottom lip, and there was a teeny line of blood there.

He dropped his hands to the edge of his sweatshirt, tugging it up and over his head. His bare chest dominated my vision, so much skin, scarred and inked and freckled. When my eyes fell to his sternum, to the tip of the crater, he stepped into me.

Ben lifted my hands to his shoulders. The moment my skin touched his warm freckles, I felt it. The blood, the wound of his mouth.

Resisting hurt … it was like passing on a fresh box of jelly donuts, or a steaming bowl of Ben's savory soup, and walking away hungry. It was not ignoring temptation, it was ignoring *instinct*—the instinct to sustain.

My tongue searched for that blood behind my lips. Ben's deft fingers played with the bottom of my polo, exploring the skin of my belly, around the curve of my hips. I pressed myself in closer, unconsciously stretching up on my toes. I was uncertain which impulse pushed me now, pushed me into him, into this. I wanted that lip between my teeth. I knew that much.

"Tsk, tsk," Ben clucked in disapproval, seeing my intentions as soon as I'd decided to act on them. The blood was so close. I wanted to cry at having it so close. He took my wrists in one of his hands and led me to our bed. His gray comforter and his smell enveloped me as he guided me to my back.

"Control," he whispered, but he was talking to himself now, too. His hands quivered as they made their way beneath my shirt.

I rubbed the base of his skull and dug into the shorn hair. His fingers trailed around the dip of my belly button as I kissed the edge of his jaw. I pulled him down, closer to me, more, and bit the lobe of his ear—

Then his mouth melted into mine, his tongue wet and warm. My shirt was up and over my head, my bare chest both shivering and all too hot. I'd decided to go commando too, just in case. He stared at my middle before he leaned in and dragged his bloody lip against my nipple.

My sharp intake of breath scared him off and Ben lifted himself onto his elbows.

"Don't," I whispered, my hands curling around his ribs.

He raked a thumb across his mouth. Flakes of crusty blood came away. I'd healed him. "Goddammit. We were doing so well."

"Speak for yourself." I wrenched him to me with all my strength. He resisted, stubbornly hovering above my frame. So I pulled myself up to him, finding his mouth quickly and sucking his lip between my teeth. He gave me the same intensity for only a moment before he jerked away.

"We can't get ahead of ourselves, Frank. Not until we're sure why we're doing it."

"I'm sure."

He licked the blood from his mouth. "My lip proves otherwise."

"Don't I get a say in any of this?"

"Of course, you do." He rested his chin between my tits and looked up at me from under his brows. "Shoot."

I smashed a hand over my eyes to think. I had been resisting fine until he kissed me fully. Then I lost my mind in the sensations. That didn't bother me too much. I wanted *him*. That was unquestionable and constant, whether he was injured or not. But if I lost control, the endorphins—serotonin, dopamine, or whatever it was—that I gave to Ben, might be magical and not physical. I did not like that. And he would continue to hold back until I could kiss him without the restoration taking over.

"Fine! Control, fine!" I rolled over to my side, knocking him off haphazardly.

"Come on, Frank." He folded himself behind me, tracing a lazy finger up and down my sternum. "I want the two of us to be together. But you need to trust my responses. And I want you to want me, without the pain and suffering."

"I do."

"I know. And I can't tell you how much I want you," he ran his mouth up my neck, "without your cures and your witchcraft." I felt him smile against me. "Just a little while longer. You've improved so much."

I snorted in response, facing the wall. His hand crept under my chin and turned my cheek toward him. He kissed me softly, lingering in the corners of my mouth. "Patience."

I rolled my eyes and kissed him, the naked skin of my back heating from the inside out.

"There are lots of ways to practice control, Princess." I felt him roll his shorts down behind me. He kicked off his moccasins and scooched the shorts from his ankles. Then his fingers hooked under the hem of my jeans, his skin like silk, and tugged. He slid the denim over my hips and around my bare feet. Then I felt him, *all* of him, and my breath caught in my chest. His body had me undone, loose as spaghetti. I swallowed my spit and tucked myself tighter into his chest.

Ben draped an inked arm over my ribs, his long finger drawing circles around my belly. "Goodnight, Frank."

"Night," I mumbled and coughed. I hadn't been breathing. And with his fingers so low, so close, I didn't think I'd ever sleep again.

MY EYES POPPED open in the night. I saw nothing but black at first, but my heart sped like a jackrabbit caged in my ribs. I searched for danger and my temple bumped against Ben's face. He snored peacefully.

I sat up on my hips, Ben's arm falling to my lap. He snored on, despite my shaking, my overwhelming, inexplicable fear. I looked to my snake—my familiar, my Betty—across the room. We'd turned the giant cabinet I used to abhor so much into a maze-like terrarium for her, the doors replaced with squares of glass. She was woven between two old drawer slots, her focus intent on the adjacent wall. I followed her stare with dry, painful eyes.

In the corner of the room, the darkness was taking form, shifting into something other. The shadow twitched and clicked as it developed its limbs.

Hello, piggy. Miss me? It asked, solidifying further. *Ooooh, naked under there, piggy? Never thought you for a little slut!* Yellow smeared across the oily black like the moon's reflection in a dark pond. A smile.

The wind was knocked out of me. I struggled to push a single spoon of air past my tonsils. A suffocated squeak squeezed from my lungs.

Blinding sliver lights shone above the yellow slash. *Do you think she'd be sad? The white-haired witch? Remember her?*

I looked down at my lap. The arm around me wasn't Ben's. It was shorter and sinewy, not a single tattoo to mar the skin.

White hair splayed over the pillow as if floating in water. Jessamae lay next to me, her sea-glass eyes open in horror, her cheek pale and cold as milk.

I leapt from the bed, my ankles catching in the sheets. She was dead, Jessamae was dead. I backed into the corner, away from the monster and the corpse. I wasn't breathing. I was suffocating. I flattened myself to the wall.

My visitor was gone. Silence. Complete silence.

I waited for an attack. For fire. For flies.

The silence inflated and called me an idiot. There was nothing there. There never was.

I held my breath as I inched away from my huddled position.

Then a ball rolled its way across the floor. It toppled into sight, slow and lopsided. It finished one final spin and stopped.

Silver eyes blared open like glowing coins. The eyes were stuck in Pamela's rotting, decapitated head. Brown sludge poured from her nose and puddled on the floor. The lipless mouth stretched around a slimy, purple tongue. Spit and blood webbed her teeth together over her infected, stinking gums.

"Where's your girlfriend, Peachy?" she croaked.

I raced for the light switch as it laughed at me. The thing chortled in my ear, braying, screeching. I flipped the switch, and as light flooded the room, Ben shot up from the bed.

"Frankie!" He searched frantically before his eyes homed in on my naked form. "Another nightmare?"

I tripped to the nightstand, opened the drawer, and pulled out my cell.

I would call her. Finally, I would call her.

1 New Message lit up the screen. I unlocked the phone and opened my texts, intuition forcing my innards into new and uncomfortable shapes.

The message was from an unknown number. The area code wasn't of Utah origin. The text contained a single word.

"Pioche."

2

"PIOCHE, Nevada. Six square miles. Population, fourteen hundred. Known for mining in the nineteenth century," Cleo read the webpage over a mug of black coffee.

"Could it mean anything else?" I asked. Betty White was draped around my shoulders. She had grown so much since she arrived on our doorstep that her weight bowed my neck. She was longer than was normal for her species, around four feet, and I thought my constant touch may have had a hand in her size. I held my mug to her snout and her tongue flicked out for a sniff. She wasn't a fan of the taste. She liked the smell, though.

"Pioche is French for 'pickaxe.' But that only brings us back to Pioche, Nevada again. As I said—mining town."

I teetered on the edge of her massive walnut bed, my coffee held far from my body out of fear of spillage. I was wearing the purple sweatshirt Ben had worn last night and some boxer shorts. Ben was in the shower. He woke up late because I kept him up all night. Tossing and turning. Scanning the darkness for headless ghosts. The neck of Pamela's phantom head had been cut messily, as if from inside a shallow grave, with a pocketknife, one nick at a time ...

"So what's in Nevada? Anything mystical or supernatural that could potentially ruin our lives?" I asked as I gulped my coffee.

14

"Nevada?" Ben said, leaning against the doorjamb with a towel around his waist. "What's in Nevada?"

"Pioche," I grumbled.

Cleo spun her chair around and crossed one long leg over the other. "What's the plan?" She took another sip from her mug and licked her magazine lips. I focused on the scar there to keep myself from ogling. Every time I thought myself immune to her appearance, I'd be struck dumb and put in my place at the smallest gesture. "I couldn't find the number that texted Frankie anywhere. It was sent from a burner."

Ben rubbed his head in agitation. It had been a while since I'd seen him do it. "Give me the day. I'll be on the lookout for possibilities." He gave the door frame a slap and left the room.

I stared at the dregs of my coffee, willing it to fill without my having to stand and take all those steps to the kitchen.

"Want to go on a run with me?" Cleo asked.

"No."

"Will you? Ben needs to focus if we're going to have any idea what to do with that text. And you are," she looked like there were a dozen things she wanted to call me, "a distraction." She raised a brow, asking me to contradict her, and I couldn't. As astounding as it was, Ben was frequently focused on me, especially if I was burping or scratching or falling down drunk.

"Fine." I tipped my mug high over my mouth, catching drips on my tongue like snowflakes. "But we aren't gallivanting all over town. Two miles, tops. And with a ten-minute break halfway through."

Cleo perked right up. "Want to borrow a running outfit of mine?"

I threw her a glare from the hallway. "You're hilarious."

MY CHEST ACHED with heartburn and what I thought might be actual fire. I clutched the stitch in my side, sucking air through my nose and blowing it out through my mouth. Though I could run farther and faster than I used to, my restoration wasn't the only cause. The other factor was good, old-fashioned, miserable practice. We had jogged together, the three of us—me always bringing up the rear—at least once a week since Ben moved in with us.

"Stop! Stop, we have to stop." I bent over my knees, a budding puke tickling my throat. Cleo's legs were stronger than mine, and she had shown no mercy.

"We haven't even completed a mile." She stood tall, her hands on her hips. She looked so stunning in her electric yellow bra and leggings that I was at an immediate disadvantage. Her dark umber skin contrasted magnificently, and the only two cars we passed had swerved into the ditches lining the road, spewing rocks and dirt before returning to the pavement. "But we can break, I suppose. Follow me," she instructed, and without waiting for a response, hiked into the surrounding aspens to the east.

"Why? What are we going to do now?" I followed, pitifully swampy in an oversized t-shirt and a pair of biker shorts.

"You need to practice. Something about this thing—that text, that town—it's abnormal. And I doubt it's good. We need to prepare. Especially you, Frankie."

"*Especially you, Frankie,*" I mocked as we trekked up the hill along the roadside. Cleo moved quickly, her pristine white shoes traversing the terrain as if it were a dancefloor. After I stumbled the third time, I began kicking everything in my path, puffing dirt around us and shredding the brown fallen leaves. I wore the same sneakers from Payless that I bought that day in the mountains, the day we faced Paimon. They were ugly.

Once we were high above the lonely road, Cleo turned to face me, and her beauty was blinding. "Jesus, turn it down, Cleo!" I covered my eyes. She was using her magic and I was weak in the knees.

"You need practice. I'm giving it to you." I heard her moving over the dry sheet of leaves that stretched across the ground, and I backed away in a sweat. The few times Cleo unleashed her affinity on me, I lost myself entirely. My identity, my intentions, my hopes and fears, were all pushed aside in order to see and be near her. "You can strengthen your defenses just as you do your offenses. Try recognizing the magic for what it is. I'll just do some low-level enchanting. Look at me."

"No." I shook my head with my hands over my eyes.

"Frankie." My name kissed my neck and my hands fell away.

Cleo wasn't a foot from me. Her gooey, honey eyes reflected the sun, and they were the sweetest things I'd ever seen. I wanted to drown there, between her lashes. I would have been thankful, joyful, to die there.

"Resist," said her full mauve lips. They seemed to harden, as if sculpted from rose quartz. They might cut me if I kissed them. I would grate myself bloody to hold her. I'd shred my body to confetti on her curves. I leaned in to take her mouth in mine, and my gaze latched onto her scar …

Concentrating on that minuscule imperfection, I suddenly remembered I didn't want to die.

She moved, swayed, and I couldn't see her mouth anymore. My stare flicked to her nose, her strong nose with the dandelion scar above one nostril. Paimon gave her those, and we fought him side by side. Because she was a person. The markings were human. I took a step back, focusing on the crunch beneath my sneaker, the feel of my moist shirt clinging to my back. These things were real, and I didn't want to die.

She said, "Good. Now, brace yourself," and I immediately covered my ears. "No, you need to hear this. Ben has been practicing for years. If Ben can improve, so can you." Cleo gripped my wrists like shackles and yanked them from my head.

She opened her mouth and began to sing. She didn't speak in

any language; she didn't need the words, her voice merely dipped and climbed like a feather in an autumn breeze. Without thinking, without care, I lurched on wobbly knees toward the magnificent music. I reached for her, but my vision blurred, and I was angry I couldn't see her clearly. I was crying. Cleo restrained my wriggling fingers, and the act made me want to hurt her. I swung my hands around wildly to get at her. And I would, one way or another.

A second Cleo appeared over the shoulder of the first. She was nude, her skin shining in the light like a galaxy, like she was made of desert stars. "Resist, Frankie," she whispered. But my name was a song. I fell to my hands. Tiny planets pushed into my palms. It was almost pain. I looked down, momentarily returned to my body and mind.

I focused on the sting in my hands.

"Look at me," she sang, and my head cracked like a whip. There were two glowing Cleos behind the first now, and the three began dancing in unison. Their hips rocked from side to side in a hypnotic cascade. I crawled to them, honored to be on my knees here. "Resist, Frankie."

I would do something terrible. I couldn't resist her music. I needed a way out, any means of escape. I dragged my body across the planets and stardust toward a flat rock. I clutched its rough edges until I thought my nails would snap off. The music swelled in a torturous symphony, and I couldn't stand it anymore. I couldn't fight it. I pitched myself forward, but before my head could meet the stone, Cleo was there with a hand on my face. The song ended.

"Enough, Francesca. Breathe."

Her use of my legal name helped shove me back in my shoes. I did as she said. My arms shook over the rock. I'd come perilously close to smashing my skull like a mid-November pumpkin.

"Couldn't have taken it a little easier for my first time?" I choked.

She stood and backed away, though not as far as I'd like. "That wasn't your first time. You've seen my illusions and you've heard me sing. It will get easier with exposure, trust me."

I looked away from her yellow radiance and into the sun, preferring the pain it offered. "How 'bout I just take your word on that?"

Cleo made an irritated noise—incapable of undignified sounds like snorts—and began hiking back to the road.

I followed sluggishly, my strength not yet returned. I needed some space to catch my breath and reacquaint myself with my mind and my priorities. I doubted I could ever throw her spell completely, or even get to a place where I didn't want to slam my head into a rock.

I was heaving myself back onto the raised pavement when a shining white blur whizzed by, nearly splattering us both like a pair of squirrels.

"Jesus!" I pin-wheeled off the hot asphalt.

The car hadn't seen us, or it hadn't cared. Either way, those things didn't happen to Cleo. She hightailed it back to the middle of the road and watched the car shrink in the distance, saying, "That wasn't someone from town."

"So?"

"So. No one from Aspen Ridge has family who would drive a Tesla." She hopped forward at a jog, then accelerated into a sprint. "It's someone else!" she called back as she kicked it into turbo drive.

I forced my legs into a million-pound jog. "Who cares!"

"Something isn't right!" she shouted with overly controlled exhales.

She became a yellow beacon on the horizon within half a mile. After I lost sight of her, I didn't see the point in running anymore. I walked the last leg to the house with my hands around my aching ribs.

Cleo's distress made no sense. Anyone had the right to any car they could afford. Maybe someone from town robbed a bank recently or invested in cryptocurrency. It didn't concern me, so I didn't give a damn who was behind the wheel.

The stink of death slithered up my nose. A crow carcass, around a hundred yards to the west. My death radar had grown exponentially over the summer. It was inevitable after so much craft practice, not to mention having two witches I'd bonded with in my constant personal sphere. And, as I'd experienced with Ben last night—much to my embarrassment—an injury I wouldn't have even sensed in July now got my stomach growling.

But the most annoying quirk of all since my affinity had supersized: it was much harder to get drunk.

The sun bounced off a shining white Tesla sitting garishly in my driveway. Cleo was right—she was always right. Something was very wrong here. I launched forward. Faster, faster. Someone had come for us, and it wasn't the cops. I never cared for strangers, but after this summer, I feared them all.

Throwing the door into the wall, I was blinded by the sudden darkness. I swiveled my head around as my eyes adjusted. "Who's here?"

Ben sat on the couch, perfectly at ease. Cleo stood by the window, arms folded across her chest …

Nothing was amiss. I hated when nothing was amiss. People died when nothing was amiss.

I jumped at the sound of aluminum jangling. The fridge was open, and a person was bent down behind the door. The magnets were all wrong. The picture of my mother and I that clung to the freezer was missing. I backed into the living room, into the protective circle of my friends, and steeled myself.

Our visitor straightened. He was big, taller than the fridge, with a cap pulled down low on his head. He had two beers cradled in his elbow and the missing photo in his hand. He stared at the image with a shake of his head. "Mm, mm, mmm. Such a shame."

"Those are my beers!" I shouted.

He Frisbee'd the picture to the counter and popped the top of one can. He chugged half and wiped his mouth. "Hey, baby girl!"

Patrick.

 ᘡᓍᓍᓄ

HE LUMPED himself down on the couch next to Ben, taking up most of the loveseat, and double-fisted my beers. "I can be very intimidating, but don't let me stop you from getting comfortable. If you need to shower or change out of those sweaty clothes, then please." He gestured to our bathroom with a grin.

"How kind, inviting us to use the amenities of our own home." Cleo was not a happy camper. Sweat rolled off her body in glistening torrents, but I thought now that Patrick had *invited* her to do so, she would put off showering for years.

"I'm a kind man." Patrick beamed. I admired how little Cleo's rage affected him. I would have quailed under such a blistering glare.

"I called him," Ben announced. "Told him to get here ASAP. There's something dangerous in Pioche. When I envision us traveling there, everything goes dark if we get too deep into town. In one possibility, we had this mammoth with us." He slapped Patrick twice on the cheek. "And we made it across the black spot."

"Pioche?" Patrick seemed to sober as he turned to Ben. He rested my Gold Stars on each of his knees. I used his preoccupation and swiped one of the drinks for myself. "You said Pioche? Nevada?"

"Right." Ben slapped him once more for good measure.

Patrick watched the beer in his hand, which looked like a toy in his bratwurst fingers. "There's only one witch in Pioche, Nevada, and he shoots strangers on site." He finished his drink in one swallow. "Your futures went dark because that's the moment he blew your heads off."

"*You* know him; therefore, you are not a stranger," Cleo emphasized.

"I know him, yes. I do. But the thing is ..." Patrick took a deep breath. "Jack fucking hates me. He wants me dead even more than most."

* * *

I PUT a stop to the discussion then and there. If we were marching toward the reaper, yet again, I wanted a shower before we planned our attack.

I ducked into the flannel I regularly wore to bed and slipped on a pair of Ben's boxer-briefs—he never wore them, and it was an unspoken agreement that they belonged to me now. My wild hair was wet and dripping down to my lower back. I worked out some of the knots with my fingers, plucking several strands and wincing in the process. It would be a foot shorter by the time it dried.

Ben had mitts on each of his hands and peered into the glass door of the oven. It smelled mouth-watering. Blueberry muffins.

After a resigned sigh, I said, "Okay, what's the game plan?"

Patrick shrugged. "Stay here? Drink ourselves stupid?"

That sounded marvelous, but this Pioche person knew something about Jessamae, and I wouldn't move on until I did, too. Ben knew that. He said to Patrick, "You said he doesn't answer phone calls or emails, so we can't reach him from here. And he clearly doesn't kill you in some possible futures or I wouldn't have seen it."

Patrick gritted his teeth. "How good are these chances of yours? Cause I need to be honest here, Benjamin, I'm not going if my chances of getting shot are higher than five percent."

"That seems low," Cleo stated from the corner of the room.

She skulked in the shadows like an overbearing chaperone. She still hadn't showered.

I continued raking my fingers through my hair. My pinkie got stuck in a particularly stubborn knot.

"Stop, stop, stop," Cleo chastised as she hustled over. She untangled my hands and sat me down on one of the four dining chairs. She wove her fingers through my hair, and as much as I was accustomed to her and Ben's touching now, it still twinged my spine. I batted at her until she took my scalp in a death grip. "Your hair is a rat's nest. I'm just going to braid it. Stop acting like you're about to be waterboarded." She thrust my head forward and took control of my hair, winding strands expertly and wrenching my head around in circles.

Ben opened the oven and set a dozen beautiful brown muffins on the counter. "Why does Jack hate you, Patrick?" He waved a hand through the rising steam.

"Who knows."

"I do," Cleo muttered from behind me with a particularly vicious yank.

"He's a rune witch," Patrick said.

Ben's lower lip jutted out from his chin, impressed. He turned to face me and explained. "He's like magic radar. He can sense the affinities of other witches around him. He'd be a valuable commodity for the Vegas covens." He sprinkled sugar granules over the muffin tops.

Patrick raised his beer for emphasis. "He knows that. Which is why he lives in a glorified outhouse in the middle of nowhere. Annnnd." He drained the can. I glared at him from the dining table. If I hadn't drank all his tequila over the summer, he'd owe me six bucks. "He can do more than that. Much, much more. He can amplify or," he scrunched up his face in confusion, "de-amplify?"

"Reduce, weaken, subdue, suppress," Cleo snapped.

"Okay, okay! He can amplify or reduce, weaken, subdue,

suppress affinities." Patrick's eyes darkened. "He can trigger my change. Or stop me from changing. For a while, at least."

We all froze, Cleo's stiletto nails plunging into my scalp. After having seen Patrick struggle desperately with his affinity firsthand—and lose—it was horrifying to know that a stranger could set it off. If he could control a magic as explosive as Patrick's, what could he do to the rest of us?

"When'd you see him last?" Ben asked as he plated four muffins and spread butter on each in turn.

"The nineties, give or take an election cycle."

Cleo finished my braid and patted my shoulders before taking a seat beside me. I reached back toward the disaster and wasn't surprised to find it unreasonably tame and smooth.

Ben placed a muffin in front of me and brushed my knuckles with his thumb. "Thank you," I said, and picked at the pastry, putting a juicy chunk on my tongue. "But we're going, right? We're going to Nevada?"

"Just for my knowledge, let me summarize," Patrick started before shoving half a muffin in his face. "You got a text from an unknown number in the middle of the night. Last night. That text said one French word and now you want to go to Who-Gives-A-Shit, Nevada, towing the three of us along with you, where we may or may not be shot?" I didn't know how to respond to that, so I didn't. "Did you text back? Call?" Patrick asked before he licked the muffin wrapper.

I nodded. "Obviously. No response. But if it's the guy you say it is, then he wouldn't respond, would he?"

"That's the whole issue here, Carrot Stick. Why would a recluse in Nevada be texting you at all?"

I put the last of my muffin in my mouth and let it sit in there until it was mostly spit. "It has to do with Jessamae." Ben hung his head and leaned against the counter. "I can feel it."

"Oh, you can *feel* it. Thank god." Patrick ambled to the counter for another muffin. "Who is Jessamae?"

"She blew up your window over the summer," Ben said, his eyes on the ground.

Patrick's eyebrows jumped under the brim of his hat. "I see. Looks like she owes me a few thousand dollars then. Do you know *why* she blew up my window?" Ben looked my way, but I couldn't meet his stare. Cleo cleared her throat and averted her attention. "Oh, do I sense trouble?" Patrick asked. "Fox in the hen house?" When no one answered him, he loomed over the table, crumbs trickling down over its surface.

"What the hell happened this summer?"

3

"WELL." Patrick was now stretched out on our velvet couch, his feet propped on the armrest for the second time. Cleo had slapped his sneakers away the last time he dared set his feet to the furniture, but preferring not to touch him again, she glared from the kitchen. "You witches had quite the adventure. I almost wish I could have been there—"

"No, you don't," I said. Narrating the entire morbid week that had changed my life—that had changed all our lives and will haunt me into my grave and after—had not been pleasant. Pamela and Paimon both tormented me mercilessly. Gabriel's blood would never leave my hands. The memory of his melting face permeated my dreams, painted the backs of my eyelids. I hadn't revisited those memories willingly since I put them all in their graves.

"So, the vampire who killed Grandma Hughes, who is yin to Frankie's yang, went west weeks ago and you haven't heard from her since. And we give a shit because Frankie gives a shit?"

"She saved our lives," Cleo interjected. She'd been quiet while I shared our story, and I still wasn't certain how she felt about all of it.

"Right, after she endangered them all in the first place," Patrick concluded.

I titled my head in acceptance. He wasn't wrong. "But the yin/yang is true. I need to know she's okay."

"Have you called her?" Ben asked from across the table. It was the first time he asked me about contacting her after two months, and I knew it pained him to do it.

I nodded. "I called five times today. Texted twice."

Patrick said, "Let's give her a day or two before we get on a plane."

"We should drive," I said. Plane tickets to Vegas were more than I could afford.

Patrick stood and booped me on the nose. "You're adorable. I'll buy the tickets if it means I can get some retribution for my window. And if we are borderline certain I won't be shot in the face."

Ben rubbed his head. "I think I can manage that. But Frankie's right, we should drive. Pioche is too far from any airport."

Cleo frowned. "What about Amir?"

"And Betty?" I added.

Ben said, "Both will be fine if we leave them for a day or two."

"And I'm not sharing a seat with a bunch of farm animals," Patrick bitched.

I met his hypocritical stare. "If we all agree I can take Betty in her carrier, I'll heal whatever wounds Jack inflicts on you."

He appraised me over the table. "You would do that either way."

I shrugged, calling his bluff.

"You need to call Scott, Frankie. But—" Ben interrupted, his eyes fading to a distant place, "Your excuse needs to be a hefty one. He's grown tired of your frequent truancy, dead granny or not."

"Like what?"

He squinted. "Let's see. You're lucky he's a slow talker. I'll try to read ... his lips." He looked like he was working to read a far-off highway sign. "Sickness won't do it. He won't buy a dead family member again, not that you have any more." His pupils shrank and stretched, the effect was both disquieting and expected. "He'll only give you a day for a dead pet. You're looking at a broken ankle or appendicitis."

I slapped my head on the table. "Does it have to be an ankle?" The wood muffled my question.

"A tibia will do ... or your back."

"How much time will I get?"

"Too much. Months."

I sighed and lifted my head. "I'll think about it. I have tomorrow off at least."

"Do you need to stop at your place for clothes?" Ben asked Patrick, uncertain how long we'd be gone. Ben couldn't see much until Jack decided how to handle our visit.

"Nah, I always keep an ensemble with me. For emergencies." He gave me a wink, but his mouth tightened as he did so, giving him an air of sad arrogance. Patrick hated his affinity more than any other witch I knew. But no one was exactly cha-cha-cha-ing over their own gifts in this house.

"Who's driving?" Cleo asked, more ill-tempered than usual.

"I am not. I'd need to charge my baby in the desert," Patrick said.

Ben's car had a shady transmission and wouldn't last the journey. The bank still hadn't looted the Honda, and though I wasn't sure if Pamela owned the thing outright or if she had been making payments, it had made for a reliable vehicle. I would have to drive I realized, a slight tremor in my hands. Though my phobia had steadily improved, I hadn't driven farther than Jim's since January. I opened my mouth—

"I'll drive," Ben said. "But we'll take the Honda. We'll leave first thing. Before the sun drags its ass into the sky."

BEN DROVE the four of us past Salt Lake City, Utah Lake, and through Delta before we saw much of the sun's ass. I was in the backseat with Cleo, primarily because Patrick needed the leg room but also because Cleo forced me in beside her, refusing to sit next to Patrick for four hours. I sporadically slept, my neck aching and bent at a right angle against my shoulder, my eyelids heavier than our bags stashed behind the seat—half of which belonged to Cleo.

I stroked Betty's head—she squirmed between my fingers like spaghetti, unhappy at being so confined—and stared out the window. There wasn't much to marvel at in this region of the state. Most of Utah's wonders existed south of our current route, but it was made more interesting by fall colors and a light drizzle. The weather was finally showing us Utahns mercy. I dreaded the upcoming heat of Nevada.

"Halfway mark! Or something like it!" Patrick shouted from the passenger seat. He and Ben had been fighting over the radio for the last two hours, smacking each other's hands and debating the merits of oldies vs. new age. I stopped paying attention to them while it was still dark. "And considering we won't find a decent bar within three hundred miles … Drinks?" Patrick pulled a bottle of tequila and a quart of orange juice from a bag at his feet.

I'd missed him these last two months.

Ben glimpsed at the dash. "It is 8:23 in the morning."

"I know, I would have started earlier but I didn't out of respect for your driving." Patrick spun the cap from the liquor and took a long pull. He followed it with a mouthful of orange juice straight from the carton. "So what are the chances of my annihilation this morning, Ben?" He reached around his seat to hand me the two bottles. "I don't have any cups." But I was already tipping the lip to my mouth. I chased it with juice. Too sweet.

"Patty. I can't check right now." Ben gestured to the boring stretch of road before us as if explaining the fact to a toddler.

"Guess."

I held out the drinks to Cleo. She took the tequila but turned down the juice.

"Impatient asshole," Ben muttered, massaging the bridge of his nose. "Maybe between ten and fifteen percent."

"That … is too high."

Cleo dropped the bottle back in my lap. I took another swig.

Ben groaned at Patrick's unwillingness to die. "It's hardly high. Chances are overwhelmingly in your favor. And," he plucked the carton of orange juice from my hand, "I told you—we just need to make ourselves and our intentions known before we reach Brent and Sons Hardware." He drank as Patrick held the wheel steady.

Patrick said, "No, you haven't told me. You haven't told me how we are supposed to do that. I doubt my habitual ways of making myself known will keep me alive in this situation."

"I'm sure you'll be fine," Cleo assured with an amused smirk that made me laugh.

Patrick whirled around in his seat. "You think this is funny? Might I remind you that I'm risking my life for a strange woman that not only killed your relative, but broke my window?"

My smile dropped, though I still found it funny. "She isn't strange to us."

Ben barked out a laugh.

"And she didn't mean to break your window. Though, yeah, I guess the other thing is true."

"You guess." Patrick smiled at that. "Alright. But you're leading the charge into the Pioche shithole." He threw the liquor to me and tipped the carton in my direction.

Hoping that Ben would stop me from stepping directly into the line of fire once we reached the awaiting threat, I clinked my bottle against his carton.

AFTER WE'D CROSSED the Nevada state line, we stopped for gas. Patrick filled the tank and Ben went inside the set-of-a-horror-movie gas station for coffee and snacks. I walked a few yards from the car, kicking rocks and enjoying the cool air.

I had never been to a national park before—I'd only seen the Great Salt Lake at a distance—and we were on the outskirts of the Great Basin, surrounded by snow-capped gray mountains. Green triangle pines climbed their peaks, interspersed with the yellows and oranges and reds of crunchy fall leaves. The sky was bluer here. I thought it had more room to stretch than it did back home.

"Enjoying the view?" Ben approached my elbow with a tray of thin paper cups.

"Thanks." I took a coffee from the tray and turned back to the vista. "It's big. Pretty."

Ben nodded before taking a sip of his own. I watched steam escape the small slot in the lid. I smelled his hazelnut creamer. "Aspen Ridge is pretty, too."

My brow pinched. The aspens were nice to look at, for the week or two before snow coated the earth like four-foot-deep dandruff. "Parts of it, I guess."

Ben leaned down and kissed my cheek. His lips moved to the corner of my mouth. "Parts of it."

I stood on my toes, pressing my mouth to his. He leaned his weight into me, doing his best to mold his body around the cardboard tray of coffee between us. I grabbed the front of his shirt, bringing him in closer. He was so tired, full of physical fatigue. Tasty.

"Oh! Kiss him again."

I jumped away, embarrassed, and saw Patrick leaning against the Honda's tailgate, rubbing his chest with an eager glow to his Windex-blue eyes.

Cleo popped her glossy head out the window. "Can we all get back in the car, please? Or should we wait for you two to finish?"

I stumbled away from Ben with my coffee dripping down one hand, the stinging red skin fading away in an instant. I blinked away the hunger for Ben, feeling better than I had all morning, as if this was my third, or even my fourth, cup of joe.

Ben sparked with energy. He ruffled my hair. "Alright, show's over. Anyone want to take a driving shift?"

Cleo rolled up her window and disappeared into the darkness.

Patrick bit his lip before registering Ben's question. "Don't look at me, I'm buzzed."

I'd had somewhere between four and six drinks, but whatever buzz I'd felt at the time was already gone. I took a deep breath. "I can—"

Ben grabbed my non-coffee hand and kissed my knuckles. "Shut up." He loped toward the driver's seat and slid inside.

A couple of hours later, the township appeared beside the road. Small as an RV park and just as unassuming. Pioche defied time, preserved in another century like fruit suspended in Jell-O. It was smaller even than Aspen Ridge, made up of one single-lane road lined with old-timey wooden businesses that could have been brothels or jail cells or general stores. The area was surrounded by mold-like sagebrush and nothing else save for dirt, bugs, and coal-crusted depression. The few cars parked diagonally along the street were coated in the gray-brown dust and were raised high off the ground—trucks and SUVs. If it weren't for the vehicles, I'd have thought it empty. There wasn't a single soul on the street. Making ourselves known would not be a problem in this place.

We hardly entered the town proper when Ben pulled our conspicuous Honda to the side of the road. "We need to walk. The car will be an issue."

Patrick was up and out the door before I'd unbuckled my seatbelt. It was chilly outside, much more than expected, and I kept my flannel on. It smelled like Ben out here—smoke and soil. The Honda was like a flashing neon sign reading "INTRUDER!"

amongst all the sand and stone. The slamming of our car doors was as loud as anything I'd ever heard.

There was no sidewalk, only curbs of cement that introduced the peeling porches of the homes and establishments. I couldn't discern the difference between residential and business. We walked around each in turn—Betty nestled in her pouch at my hip—following Ben's lead, our hackles raised. Ben moved cautiously. His eyes fell closed again and again, predicting the safest possible route.

It reeked of death—literally and figuratively—swirling in the stink of animal shit and hard living. The deeper we delved into the so-called town, the stronger the urge to flee. It was unnatural, almost painful, the sensation of something brushing against me. Like the wings of a cockroach, the prickly spine of a cactus. My skin tingled under the fingers of unseen ghosts. "I don't like this, Ben. How far do we have to go?"

Ben said, "It's a ward. A warning. Pushing people away, both witch and non." Halting in his tracks, a small puff of dust rising into the air from beneath his boots, he added, "Even animals."

He cocked his head abruptly and Patrick dropped to the ground with his hands in the air. "Don't shoot!"

The three of us watched him cower through twenty seconds of silence.

Cleo backed away from him, as if stupid were contagious. "Jack must know we're here by now. With this clown."

"Timing's good. Look." Ben pointed to a rusty sign on our left. It was hung above a white structure with a slate-colored roof. It used to be black, but the sun had bleached it, possibly over centuries. I couldn't see through the cloudy, brown windows, and could barely read the sign's lettering: *Brent and Sons Hardware.*

"Do we go inside?"

Ben surveyed the building through narrowed eyes. "Yes." He stomped toward the storefront with sudden and intense purpose. We all huddled near him to squeeze through the rickety screen door. There were dozens of finger-sized holes in its black netting.

Darkness. My eyes took a moment to adjust. Swords of light broke through the covered windows, illuminating dust mites drifting through the air. Several basic tools lined the slatted walls —hammers and handsaws, screwdrivers and socket wrenches— none were free of dust, and none were over twenty dollars.

A door was propped open behind the counter, leading into a black backroom. A man emerged from the shadows and stepped up to the register. He had a white mop of hair and a mustache you could sweep the floor with. His pointy jaw was clenched in instant distrust. He braced his hands on either side of the register as if we were about to rip it from the counter, and he didn't say a word.

I wasn't sure if this was Brent or Sons—the store must've been open for decades, if not millennia.

Patrick nudged me toward the counter, and I stumbled. I was about to spin around and start yelling when I remembered the deal I'd made with him in the car. Breathing in a lungful of musty, desert air, I pushed loose hair from my eyes. The proprietor made me nervous, and I stood as tall as I was able.

"Hey." I tugged at my clothes and took a step closer. "Nice place."

The man stood immobile. His lush mustache twitched in greeting.

Ben laid a hand on my back. He wasn't throwing me to the wolves, he was encouraging me, silently stating it was safe to continue.

"We're looking for someone. A … friend of ours." The mustache danced again as if hiding moths in its brush. The tension was palpable. "Jack." I didn't know the mystery man's last name, which might count against us, but I thought in a town this small, a first name would be enough. "He asked us to visit—"

"Name."

I tripped backward in surprise, expecting gunfire. Ben steadied me, his hands moving to my shoulders. The man still hadn't moved, but I heard a new set of boots touch down in the backroom. "My ... my name? Frankie. Frankie Hughes."

The walking push-broom vanished back into the shadows as if he'd never been. I looked to my friends in terrified uncertainty. Patrick was all but hidden behind a standing shelf of nuts and washers. Cleo could compete with the shopkeeper in a living statue competition. Ben smiled, extending a finger into the air. *Wait.*

I heard the clack of a screen door banging in its frame before the shopkeeper reappeared. "Follow the lane west, on foot, to the elk. Then stop. It ain't far." He turned on a dime, leaving us alone, and shut the door behind him. He didn't come back.

We left the shop without a word, and with nothing else to do, followed his instruction. I, having never been navigationally sound, fell to the back of the herd as we faced west. The structures eroded away from the road until only sagebrush and dirt dominated the landscape. I scanned the horizon for an elk, though we hadn't seen anything alive since the shopkeeper. How an elk acted as a sentry for Jack was beyond me.

The magic he surrounded this place with was suffocating. I could hardly bear its pressure. It was like being squeezed through a tube, tighter and tighter the further we walked—if a tube had a million legs that tickled the skin inside your ears and behind your knees as you pushed through.

I sensed and smelled dozens of animal carcasses at once, snakes and mice and birds, even a fox. I gagged on them. It wasn't until we'd walked a mile that I paused. I smelled it—an elk. I was the only one who could smell it, as it had long since decayed.

It sprawled before a fork in the road, one side paved, the other dirt. Its antlers were immense, splitting over and over in a sharp, yellow web. Only bones remained; even the fur had been eaten away. Its teeth were enormous, too big for its delicate, porous jaw.

Ben crouched down. He ran his fingers along a rib and closed his eyes. Only seconds later, he pulled his hand back from the elk and raised all ten fingers above his shoulders. He straightened gradually. Painfully so.

Then I heard it—the cocking of a shotgun behind me. Felt the punch of metal against the back of my head. With shaking lips, I followed Ben's lead, my hands high over my head.

The barrel knocked into my skull, hard enough to rattle my teeth.

"Shit!" a man exclaimed from behind the gun. "Jessamae didn't say you were an angel."

4

"Jessamae? You've seen her?" I asked in a rush, jerking my chin over my shoulder.

The man shoved the barrel into my cranium. "Turn right."

Ben and Cleo walked without speaking, though Cleo hadn't raised her hands as the rest of us had. Patrick raced out in front the second we were given permission to move.

"Don't go running off, Pat," the man said, and Patrick froze. "Think I missed your giant ass?"

"Missed as in didn't see me, or missed as in you wished I were here?" Patrick peeked back at the gunman.

"Answer's the same either way."

Patrick took a tentative step forward. "Nice to see you alive and well, Jack."

A dirty cough sounded behind me before evolving into a sardonic chuckle. "Yeah. Bet it is."

The four of us spread out as we moved up the path, Cleo and Patrick brushing the shoulders on opposite sides of the road. Patrick kicked dried desert blooms and big rocks as he went, each the size of a Chihuahua. He swung his leg back for another whack when Ben swiftly snatched Patrick by the elbow. He whipped the man back into the middle of the lane before a small explosion ripped a sagebrush and the surrounding earth to shreds. I fell back into the gun behind me, scraping my scalp on its barrel, as dirt and bush and one hundred pulverized bug husks rained down on our heads. A dull ringing echoed inside my head. I shook my fingers in my ears until my hearing returned.

"Well, look at that," Jack said. He had yet to step out from behind me. He hadn't even moved the gun when I stumbled. "We've entered mine country." Cleo side-stepped into the middle of the path. Patrick bent over his knees, his breaths pumping hard in and out of him. "Lucky you had a psychic with you. Anyway. Fifteen steps north. Then stop."

Jack led us on and off the road—around woven trees, over petrified bones, and through trenches—one direction at a time. The sun beat down on our heads with a hammer, and the metal Jack pushed into my skull had soldered to my scalp. The sand was covered in crispy animal hides, but I could hardly smell them over the salty sweat under our arms and between our shoulder blades. Dirt clung to our dripping bodies until every motion felt grainy.

We couldn't see anything beyond the barren stretch of nothing. Not only was the acreage riddled with explosives, but the magical barriers Jack created were stronger than ever. Sweat beaded my upper lip and my insides jittered. I bristled at the hot moisture under my clothes as my eyes darted across the horizon. We were trapped.

We crested a hill I hadn't seen from town. I was both relieved and sick as an old shack came into view. Scattered around the dinky hut were several rusted mining carts, each filled with random, dusty junk: bricks, bottles, garbage, animal skins. The building—if you could call it that—was every shade of brown imaginable, the two-by-fours bleached and cracked in some places but dark and warped in others. The foundation listed to one side like a drunk, and the roof was missing half its shingles. It smelled like mold and sawdust.

"Homey," Ben said, to which Patrick shot him a panicked glare.

Jack grunted, "I don't live here, dipshit. Workshop." I

couldn't ignore the torturous implications of a dilapidated shack in the middle of the desert being called a *workshop* and stood closer to Ben. "Inside."

We stumbled up the perilous steps, rust-brown nails sticking out every which way, to the front door, which hung crooked. Ben paused at the threshold, slightly dazed, trying to see the future.

"Open it," Jack ordered. And without any other option, Ben pushed in the door.

I couldn't see a thing. It was a different kind of dark than that of the hardware store. This darkness was thick, and my itchy skin shrank tight. Despite the gun at my back, I searched the darkness for silver-dollar eyes and started to shake. I feared the dark as much as a bullet to the brain.

Bright lights switched on with a *choo* sound. Giant fluorescents lined the ceiling in its entirety and blinded us all. "Take that bag off, Curly, nice and slow." He nudged Betty's pouch with the end of his gun.

"It's—"

"Nice. And slow."

Jack stepped around to face me, the shotgun level with my heart. He appeared to be in his forties or fifties with a stain of graying hair on his head. He was barrel-chested with a thick neck and a scraggly beard. His skin was like the hut around us—varying in brown tints depending on sun exposure—his nose and cheeks red with heat. His dark eyes were yellow around the edges, caustic, and his fingertips were black, the type of sully that was impossible to scrub away. The collar of his t-shirt had been cut off, and his simple black shoes had holes in the toes.

"You hear me?" He tipped the gun up against my chin.

I nodded against the steel and gradually lowered my arms to the strap around my shoulder, pulling it carefully over my head. Jack held the gun in one hand and extended the other for my bag. Remembering the cart of dead critters outside, I tucked the bag close to my stomach.

"What you hiding in there?" He stole the strap from me.

"It's—"

Jack silenced me with another nudge from the shotgun before he pulled the zipper, his arm bent around the bag awkwardly. Once the zipper opened an inch, the desert-person squealed in surprise, dropping the bag at his feet.

"It's Betty," I said before he could shoot me.

Betty slipped her beautiful head through the opening, her tongue sampling the foreign space. She zigzagged from the bag and wound over one of my shoes as Jack caught his breath. He huffed and puffed like an old woman.

"Hiding a familiar. Would have known if I weren't busy herding all four of you."

"Happens to the best of us," Patrick chirped, his hands still above his head.

Jack's mouth pinched in annoyance while he crouched down on the balls of his feet. He offered his hand to Betty as if she were a dog. Betty prudently extended herself toward him, her tongue batting against his soiled skin in evaluation. He lowered his hand to the floor and Betty wrapped herself around his wrist, her heavy tail twisting in the air. I relaxed. If Betty trusted Jack, then he wasn't a danger to me. Not right now.

"I won't hurt the snake, simmer down. She just spooked me." Jack lowered the barrel to the ground but kept his finger near the trigger. He met each of our eyes in turn, holding on Patrick the longest. Patrick stared at the floor. "But if I knew you would bring the ape, I wouldn't have contacted you."

"If we didn't bring him, you'd have shot first and questioned later," Ben said as he lowered his hands. "You aren't exactly welcoming to newcomers. Even the ones you ask to come."

Jack watched Ben as he tongued the inside of one cheek. "I guess I should take your word on that, Psychic. Unsolicited visitors bring nothing but trouble." His eyes moved to Cleo but skirted away instantly. "Ma'am."

The respect was unmistakable. I curled my lip. She didn't get a gun to the back, chest, and chin. *Must be nice.*

"So, an angel. Figured you were a mage—Jessamae doesn't deal with anything else. But an *angel*. Never met one. He pointed the gun at me in acknowledgment. "Nice to meet you."

"I'm a healer, not an angel. And would you lose the fucking gun, please?"

"Nope." He crossed the room, which was essentially the whole hut, with Betty snoozing in his hand. He stood the shotgun against the wall and reached under the edge of a grimy foldable table. The table's surface was black and slick with old oil. It was piled with rust-red metal shapes—cogs and blocks—that looked like they were pulled right out of a landfill. He removed a pistol from the underside of the table. "But I will downsize. How's that?" He leaned beside the shotgun. "Back to you. Frankie. You can resurrect the dead, correct?" He stroked his trigger finger along Betty's head.

Was Jessamae friends with this lunatic? Had she swapped stories with him over tea and biscuits?

I said, "Once. A bird," but wasn't going to mention the grandmotherly abomination I created. I didn't need to give him more information than he already had.

"Do you know anyone else who can do that? Even if it was 'once, a bird'?"

I crossed my arms over my chest. My sleeves were wet and sour.

"So …" he said, rolling his arms. "Angel. There you go."

"No." What I'd done to Pamela was the furthest thing from angelic.

"I can call you Frankenstein, would you prefer that?"

"Yes."

"Ha!" His shrewd eyes considered me again. "Alright, Frankenstein. Do you know why you're here?"

My eyes flickered between his gaze and the pistol in rapid succession. The gun was the less threatening thing. I looked away from both, a twitch in my fingers.

I could see stripes of daylight through the walls. There was

41

no insulation or plaster, there were only thin, peeling planks between us and the world. It was the same for the floor. Gaps of dark air peeked up at us like the spaces between a set of teeth, catching wisps of sand in a room downstairs. There had to be a cellar door hidden somewhere around the shack.

The room was filled with those mysterious, clunky metal pieces. They slumped against the walls and huddled in mounds on the floor. It smelled like gasoline in here—something that made me very nervous.

A door faced me from the opposite side of the room. I don't know how I missed it before now, it was so conspicuous. It was steel, thick as a tree trunk, and equipped with three deadbolts along one side. It belonged in a bank, protecting buttloads of cash, so why was it hiding out here, in Pioche?

"Don't look at that. That is none of your goddamn business. Any of you." Jack shot us all a scrupulous glare.

"It's his life's work," Ben told us, ignoring Jack's rage. "Every time he comes across a new witch, he keeps all their information in there. It's his databa—"

A blast blew through the workshop, and dust exploded around Ben's head. I covered my ears again, searching frantically for the mine, my heart in my throat.

A jagged, star-shaped hole now existed in the wall next to Ben's head, where a bullet just exited the room. "SHUT! YOUR! FUCKING! MOUTH!" Jack yelled, his pistol smoking.

"Jesus Christ," I whispered, forcing my knuckles to pop.

"Drama queen," Ben muttered, rolling his eyes to the ceiling. Patrick's hands were crossed over his head, and his face was smushed on the ground as though an atomic bomb were about to drop. Cleo was entertained.

Jack turned to me, resting the pistol back in his lap. "Now. Answer my question."

I stared at the gun as I answered. This man was completely insane. "You texted me. You know where Jessamae is."

Jack raised a brow—a spot of which seemed to have been

singed off—and ground his teeth. "She was here. A while ago. She required my services. But she's never left an emergency contact before, and she gave me your number before she went her way."

"Why would she need an emergency contact?" Cleo spoke for the first time since we met this man.

Jack held out my languid snake and I eagerly accepted her with both hands. "Because. She was headed to Vegas," he answered. "Abandon all hope, ye who set foot on the Strip."

JACK SLID to the ground in the corner, the shotgun like a docile terrier across his lap, and pistol in hand.

Cleo watched him sprawl in the dust with visible aversion to the squalor. "Do you have chairs?" she asked.

"All due respect, ma'am, but a chair is just a place to put your ass. So," he gestured around the room, "take your pick."

Patrick sat fast enough to jiggle the floorboards.

I asked, "What's in Vegas?"

"Everything you could ever want and all the things you never would." Jack scraped his pistol against the wood of the floor, peeling away a few chips. "Mages get a lot of play on the Strip. Can't swing a dead cat without hitting a witch in the ass … witches probably killed the cat in the first place."

I waited for him to go on. When he didn't, I surmised, "Lots of bad guys in Vegas. Got it. And that's why Jessamae needed an emergency contact. So where can we find her?"

"Oh, you're just gonna charge in there, guns blazing?"

"Then tell us what you brought us here to tell us!"

"I'll take my time, thank you very much. Either she's already dead or you'll need to mind your manners. Testy people on the Strip. Very testy."

"Yeah, cause you've been nothing but a gracious host—"

"Shut your mouth and I'll keep talking."

I pulled my upper lip between my teeth and waited.

"Mmhmm. As I was saying," Jack said pointedly. "Vegas is run by a very old mage, a fairy. Can't get within ten feet of the thing without ... disappearing. Gone for good. They work in gluttony, and lust, and envy, and greed. Glamours and enchantments so strong you forget who you are. Makes what your lady friend here does look like a party trick." He turned to Cleo. "And no offense, but you scare the bejeezus out of me."

Cleo's mouth quirked. She moved further into the room, mollified, it would seem.

"Is the fairy the reason you're hiding out here?" I asked.

"I'm not hiding," he said. "Believe it or not, I like it here. People who matter know where to find me. But there are certain individuals, and covens, matter of fact, who see me as something to own. And if I lost control of my mind," he aimed another furtive glance at Cleo, "well ... I'd rather be dead."

Remembering what he could do to Patrick I found that hard to believe. "But you're a rune witch. Can't you stop them?"

"I can hinder them, if I have mind to. So. No." He licked the edges of his mouth. "One of you go around back. There's a fridge with some waters." Patrick jumped up in one fluid motion and bolted for the door. "Don't go too far, now. There's fifty-six mines from here to town." I wondered which Patrick feared more—getting shot or being forced to change by Jack's hand. And I wondered if he would come back.

"Can you stop doing whatever you're doing to me?" Ben asked abruptly.

Jack tilted his head in Ben's direction and licked his teeth. "Why?"

"I'm not a danger to you. I'm just trying to see our options."

"You're trying to see through my door and we both know you can do more than that! But no. Can't have you knowing my every move. That would be quite *advantageous*." He stretched the word out until it was a mile long.

"Now *you* have the advantage."

"It's *my* workshop."

Ben rubbed his head as Patrick kicked open the door, his arms weighed down with water bottles. Patrick tossed them around to each of us. They were brown with dust but ice cold on my skin. I didn't open it. I didn't trust him.

"Plastic?" Cleo asked with a grimace. She hated the stuff.

"It's the best I got," Jack said. He noticed my hesitation. "Hydrate. You could have been dead ten ways to Tuesday by now, and water's too precious to poison." He tilted his head and chugged.

I twisted off the cap and took a timid sip, my defiance inhibiting me more than my fear. "What's the plan? Do I talk to the fairy or what?"

"That's funny," Jack said, water glistening in the hair around his mouth. "No. As I said earlier, if you meet them, you're gone."

I started banging my head against the wall behind me.

"Stop, stop it! This place is fragile." I looked to the heavy metal door across the room and didn't believe him. He hung his hands over his knees. "When Jessamae came here, she said she was looking for someone. A man. Said she didn't know if he was mage or not, but if he had any magic in him, his affinity would be something in the restoration field." He took his chin in hand in mock consideration. "Does that track?"

I didn't answer him. I scratched at the skin of my inner arm enough to hurt. My father. Jessamae was looking for my dad.

"There's a place. Underground bar," Jack continued. "Witches are always gossiping there. They know who's in town and how they're gettin' by. But. They're a suspicious crowd. Everyone in Vegas is. And for good reason. A lot of power trading hands. You'll need to be discreet."

"You coming with us?"

Jack stood and brushed off his jeans. "Why would I do that?"

"Because you care about her. Jessamae," Ben said with big pupils.

"Fuck you, Freckles!" Jack yelled, pointing the pistol at Ben. "Keep the eyes in that bald head of yours shut."

Ben grinned at his annoyance. "I knew it before I saw you. I knew it in town."

"You know nothing! Seeing isn't knowing. Jessamae has been coming around every few years for some time. But she was always looking for the same person. A girl. Woman. Until now." His gaze fell to the floor, and his muzzle fell with it. Without the threat of his stare or his gun, he seemed sad. Even vulnerable. "She's my only regular customer. Never been unreachable for so long before." He strode outside without a word, and we all waited a beat in his workshop until we inevitably followed.

Jack searched for the sun through the heavy cotton clouds that had materialized in the sky. Even squinting, the yellow ring around his irises glowed. "She told me to contact you if I hadn't heard from her by November first. But that's too long for anyone to be alone in that city. Even someone like her. This whole thing might be somewhat premature, but …" He still hadn't looked at us, and in that moment, I recognized something of myself in him. I didn't want to touch him, and I doubted he would allow it anyway, but Ben was right. We were both worried about Jessamae.

"You coming with us?" I asked again.

He hung his head and rubbed his eyes as if to erase them away. "One night. I'll be there one night to show you the ropes. The rest is on you, Frankenstein."

5

By the time we got back to the car, it was almost one in the afternoon Nevada time. I was getting very rude, having not eaten anything but a teeny bag of pretzels on the ride over. I muttered insolently as we retraced the lengthy path around all the landmines. Jack split from the group as we approached the hardware store, grumbling that he would meet us tonight. He wrote down an address on an old price tag and shoved it at Ben's chest. He clearly didn't want to rely on us for transportation.

We didn't eat in town—the whole place was magically rigged and threatening. It would be like trying to enjoy a meal while a team of masked gunman watched you do it. We drove for another hour before we got lunch from Chuck's Chicken on the side of the road in Alamo. I got breadcrumbs all over the backseat. The chicken was good. I fed Betty a nugget through her bag's zipper.

When the skyline of Las Vegas appeared in the bowels of the Nevada wasteland, I was immediately terrified—violently reminded of our fight with Paimon, in that tight, uncanny copse of aspen trees. Because the towering buildings were like an oasis in the Sahara, like a mirage appearing in the midst of nothing. Sudden and hyperreal. Unnatural. Just like those watchful aspens that were still painted in our blood. It wasn't until the billboards advertising steak dinners, lady shows, and motels began popping up like desert daisies that my fear eroded.

"Thar she blows! Oh, how I've missed you," Patrick cooed with his hands against the windshield.

"A fresh take on this city," I pointed out.

"Jack and I are very different people."

Ben said, "True. One has the gun and the other is pissing his pants."

"What can I say? I've grown addicted to life, and I'd prefer to keep living it for another lifetime or two."

An unexpected perspective from a man who spent most of his time alone in a big house drowning in tequila. But I understood his inclinations. I, too, had been comfortable alone, in my dark room, with no plans to speak of and no obligations to follow. But my instinct to live had been as strong as anyone's, even from the nest of my sheets and hungover from the night before.

"Where will we be staying?" Cleo asked from beside me. She had been more reserved than usual today. Having something to do with entering a city that did nothing but profit off an affinity like hers, I assumed.

Patrick picked at the blond hairs sprouting from his chin. "I was thinking the Bellagio."

Ben made a sound between a snort and a hack. "What's wrong with Circus Circus?"

"I'm not going to answer that," Patrick replied.

Ben had been to Vegas before—he found the right casino without asking for directions or checking his phone. The biggest and the brightest hotels were all clustered around a single boulevard, everything beyond that line was colorless, dirty, and made me feel seasick.

Even at this daytime hour, the sidewalks teemed with people, the herds of them eclectic to the point of bizarre. Lone hooded figures were scattered amongst the smiling masses, despite the heat, slapping cards against their wrists and offering them to passersby. Palm trees stretched taller than streetlights, of which there were far too many. The city was a shocking juxtaposition of paradise and slum, constructed from illusions.

Ben pulled into the parking structure attached to our casino, which I found confusing and overly complicated, then we traversed multiple elevators, bridges, and staircases to reach the lobby. The moment we stepped through the automatic doors, the smell of cigarettes and cleaning fluid blew into my face along with the powerful air conditioning. The ubiquitous lights bounced off the marble and the entire first floor was ringing with tinny alarms and celebratory tunes. There was a stripe of color along the ceiling—it looked like a three-dimensional mixture of flower petals and fish scales, and it made me feel like I was inside a kaleidoscope. The hotel was gaudy, aggressive, and captivating.

The number of people overwhelmed me. I'd never been in such a crowd. I was shoved and blocked repeatedly until I crept in close to Ben and Patrick, their size clearing a decent path across the flashy carpet. Cleo did not experience the same issue. Guests and gamblers froze in their tracks in her vicinity. It was as if time had stopped and she walked freely through living statues.

We waited inside a hive of grumpy people hovering around the registration counter. Cleo flipped her hair a few times and the sea of people divided, making way for the shiny-haired queen.

"Hey, how's it going. We need a room, please." Ben slapped his tattooed hands on the counter.

"A suite. Three beds, three baths." Patrick shoved his way in.

The brunette behind the counter typed like a fiend. "We can offer you a tower suite, one king, two queens."

"Is that the best you have?" Patrick asked.

"That's great," Ben assured, elbowing Patrick.

Patrick turned to glare at Ben, "Fine, but I get the king, it's only fitting."

"There will be two of us in one bed!"

Blood filled my cheeks though I already lived with the man.

"Nice try, Benjamin, but you'll have to buy me a drink first." Patrick slapped Ben's arms away before he plucked a thick black card from his wallet and held it like a cigarette. "Thank you, kindly," he said as the woman took it.

We made our way across the shiny beige stone of the hotel lobby to a bank of elevators and rode up dozens of floors. The hallway was cramped and windowless, but the room itself was enormous. It was bigger than my house in Aspen Ridge. It was opulence that I only seemed to experience in Patrick's presence —walls of windows, oversized white furniture.

"I'm showering. We aren't meeting Jack for a few hours," Cleo called over her shoulder before shutting a set of French doors.

"That's not a bad idea. I smell like Honda." Patrick flapped his hands around to dissipate the imaginary smell and shut himself into a second bathroom. Ben and I were alone.

He took Betty's pouch from my shoulder and set it on the couch. He opened the zipper, giving her a wave of fresh air, which she tasted before blending into the leather of the sofa. Ben closed the distance between us and trailed a finger down my neck. "If we scored three bathrooms, I would have asked you to shower with me."

"Do I smell?"

"A little. But that's not why." He held my jaw delicately between his hands, his fingers tickling the spaces beneath my ears. He bent down and kissed me. He felt no pain, so I stole no pain. The kiss was just a kiss. My chest lightened until I was weightless from the sweetness of it.

Ben pulled back an inch. "Interested in learning to play black-jack?" His lips rubbed against mine with each word.

"Are you asking if I can count to twenty-one?"

"Can you?"

I shoved him hard in the chest and he laughed. "Fine. Not much to learn there, I guess. Poker?"

"*That*, I'd like to learn."

"Take a seat." He gestured to the glass dining table next to the wall of windows and pulled a pack of playing cards from the back pocket of his carpenter pants. "I got these at the last gas station. Just in case." Though there were few just-in-case moments when it came to Ben. He licked his lips and grinned at me. I sat down, my stomach full of centipedes.

He shuffled with deft hands, backward and forward with a graceful whisper. "The rules are simple. Each time you lose a hand, you take off an item of clothing. Socks count as a single item. Shoes count as two." He divvied up the cards.

"That's bullshit! I don't even know how to play!"

"Great motivation. Ready?"

Imagining all the skin Ben kept hidden under his windbreaker, I picked up my cards with raw determination. Ben seemed confident and casual on the surface, but there was a tightness to his mouth. A rippling. His tongue rubbed against the inside of his cheek.

"Ready."

I WAS DOWN BOTH SHOES, both socks, my flannel, and pants. Ben lost his windbreaker, shirt, and one shoe. He assured me he wasn't precognitively peeking, but I knew he was only throwing certain hands so I wouldn't have a tantrum.

I watched the sun dance across his collarbones and hit the ink of his chest before I appraised my cards. I wanted to feel those tattoos under my hands, to trace every word and image, and the way his eyes dropped to my fluttering fingers, I thought the future looked very bright indeed.

Ben picked up on my fixation and reached for his throat. He

51

followed the raised lines of tattooed text there with his long middle finger—*I'M OK*. He ducked his head until I had to look at his eyes instead of the fingers at his neck. He held his tongue between his teeth and smiled. He'd seen what I wanted to do. And more. My mouth popped open.

"We playing strip poker?" Patrick boomed from his room. I jumped, peeling my bare skin from the seat painfully. He dashed into the dining area, hurtling over the back of the leather sofa and scaring a snoozing Betty. He yanked down the zipper of his jacket, tossed it across the room, and sat happily in his crewneck next to Ben.

"You know you only strip when you lose a hand?" Ben asked, an eyebrow raised. A flustered sheen dewed his cheeks.

"The cards aren't why I love this game," he answered.

Cleo strutted into the room on skyscraping black stilettos that clacked against the tile. Her dress was crimson and velvet and hugged her curves in a way that every onlooker wished they could. She was so beautiful my middle ached to look at her—immediate heartburn—but the pain was preferable to looking away.

"Look at Frankie," she ordered with a wave of her hand.

"Yes ma'am," Patrick said, and he took in my missing attire.

I flipped him off with an instinctual curl to my lip and Cleo made a disgusted noise in her throat. "I mean," she glowered at Ben as if he were responsible for Patrick's behavior, "she will stick out like a sore thumb in that outfit. Witches are always showing off, bodies included." She picked my flannel up off the floor with an unhappy scrunch to her nose. "You need to dress like you want to be there, like you want people to see you there."

"I'm not your Barbie, Cleo."

"That is more than obvious. I am my own Barbie. However, I'm also right."

I scowled at Ben and Patrick. "What are you two wearing?"

"It doesn't matter what I wear. I have a reputation in this town. And I always look good enough to eat," Patrick said.

Ben shrugged. "Something black." Which, for Ben, was about as dressy as it got.

I hung my head.

"You'd look dashing in a suit, but I didn't bring one," Cleo said with pursed, candy lips. "I should have had the foresight to know I'd have to dress you. Again."

She glared at Ben until he apologized.

•

IT WAS BLACK AND SLEEVELESS, with a high neck that pushed against my throat. It contrasted starkly against my strawberry hair, which had gotten paler since I started practicing my affinity. I used some of Cleo's makeup—a dark red lipstick, almost brown, that made me look spooky in a way that I liked, as well as some eyeliner and mascara. When I saw myself in the mirror, I thought I was almost pretty enough to be an escort. But I had no heels, which didn't bother me. Cleo, however …

"Stuff some toilet paper in a pair of my shoes!"

"I will break both ankles walking all night!"

"You need to break something to get work off this week anyway!"

I made an ugly face at her and flumped down on the sofa. Cleo was repulsively practical.

"Let's all just calm down. Shoes are a non-issue," Patrick said before picking up one of the phones in the room. He sat beside me with the phone to his ear, slapping an enormous hand to my leg and making me flinch. "Concierge. Yes, I need a pair of shoes. Heels. Size—"

"Seven," I mouthed.

"Seven." His eyes flashed to my outfit. "Black. Strappy—"

I lifted my legs and kicked him in the thigh.

"Ow! Hell! Not strappy. Boots, booties, boobies whatever those things are … Yes. Thank you." He hung up the phone and held his arms out as if simultaneously implying how stupid we were and waiting for applause.

"Thank you, Patrick," I drawled, my eyes dead as a doornail. "You are so smart."

"And?" he asked.

"Tall?"

"That's right."

Ben entered the living room. He'd showered and smelled like the hotel bar soap. Water droplets clung to the baby bristles on his head. He was wearing a black, short-sleeved button down that was half-buttoned—you could barely discern the thick scarring of his stomach—black jeans, and Doc Martins. His infinite freckles and tattoos stood out spectacularly.

"Who died?" Patrick asked.

"We'll see," Ben answered ominously. He watched me sitting on the couch with a heavy focus that draped over me like a fur coat. We matched.

I stood and moved behind the counter in the kitchen, sensing his eyes on my bare skin the whole way. I was self-conscious with the others around, self-conscious of how he looked at me and what I'd do if they left us alone. It felt safer to put a barrier between us. Still, I rubbed my legs together. Imagining him between them.

When my shoes arrived, everyone was anxious to get moving. We didn't need to meet Jack just yet, but the others looked like housebroken dogs crying at the door—cocktails and gambling awaited.

Ben watched as I tied my laces. Ben watched everything.

I slung Betty's leather pouch over my shoulder. I fed her already, but I snuck a packet of dead crickets in the side pocket for emergencies. Cleo glared at the accessory, not because of Betty, but because of the color, which didn't match my dress. Cleo respected Betty, Ben adored her, but Patrick avoided the bag and its legless occupant unequivocally.

I studied the mirrored wall of the elevator. Unable to look at

Cleo without crying or Ben without salivating, I looked at Patrick's reflection. Though he said his wardrobe didn't matter, he exuded casual wealth in his topcoat and expensive hoodie. When I felt Ben's fingers brush up the back of my arm, my ankle popped sideways, and I fumbled into Patrick's well-dressed torso. "Easy, Carrot Stick. At least wait until Ben leaves."

I elbowed him in the ribs.

After we stepped off the elevator, we targeted the casino. "Since you're so great at counting, want to try your hand at blackjack?" Ben whispered in my ear. I worked to ignore how close his tongue was, flicking against my lobe with each word.

"Can we get drinks first?"

"They bring drinks to the table. For free."

My face nearly broke under my smile and I dragged him to the nearest blackjack table like a caveman would drag a dead puma. There was only one seat free, which Cleo slid into as if it were a throne. The rest of the table froze to watch her nestle into the leather cushion, her shifting weight the most interesting thing in the room. She leaned on her elbows until she was a touch away from the woman on her right. "Could my friends sit here, please?"

The woman hopped out of her seat as if it singed the seat of her pants, dropping her cigarette to the floor in the process. The man on Cleo's left jumped away yelling, "Here, take my seat!" The offers worked in a domino effect until the entire table was empty, save for Cleo, though they all hovered nearby to observe the beautiful woman play. She patted the cushion next to her, which I took. The dealer hadn't moved, his eyes glued to Cleo's mouth.

"Here." Ben offered me a grip of twenties.

"I don't want your money." I frowned and turned to ask the dealer if they'd run my credit card.

Ben said, "Cash only. Take it. I won't be losing any money tonight."

I narrowed my eyes but took the cash and arduously crossed

my legs under the table. He trailed a hand up my thigh, over my hip, to rest at the small of my back. I couldn't stand it. His touch was hot and electric and ticklish in a near insidious way. I hoped he never stopped touching me. My heartbeat descended lower and lower …

"We're ready," Cleo announced to the stupefied dealer, who speedily put a new deck into play. Sweat beaded across his forehead, which glistened in the lights of the nearby slot machines. He exchanged my twenties for chips, and I pushed one forward.

"You need another, Miss," he instructed.

"What?"

"You need to put in twenty dollars. Minimum," Ben said.

"For one hand?" I said, aghast, pushing a second chip forward. And the game began.

I lost my money, of course, but Ben doubled his in one hand. He cheered, clapping like a seal before sliding a matching bet forward. "I'm feeling lucky," he said as he put forty bucks on Royal Match and winked at me. His fingers rubbed circles in the fabric against my lower back.

"Why don't you spread some of that luck around?" Patrick asked with too-wide eyes.

Ben laughed and drummed his fingers on the green plushy mat that circled the table. "Absolutely not."

"Can I get'cha drink, hun?" rasped a voice over my shoulder. A bottle blonde woman with long legs and an elaborate up-do stood with a tray at my elbow. I got a beer and Ben got a daiquiri before once again hooting in celebration. Cleo had somehow already procured her own cocktail, which was stuffed with so much decoration and garnish, the proprietor had essentially given her an alcoholic bouquet.

Though I lost more often than not, as did Patrick who was throwing back tequila and cursing under his breath, Ben doubled his money ten times over. He lost once or twice on purpose, but after one particularly profitable win, he looked around nervously and gathered his mountain of chips in a frenzy. "We gotta go. Don't want to be late."

Patrick and Cleo were eager enough to leave. Patrick had repeatedly retrieved additional cash as he'd lost whatever he put down, but Cleo made a moderate profit. There were times I thought I saw the dealer pantomime taking her lost chips, waving his hand over her bet and leaving it on the table.

"I'm having fun." And I actually was. "Let's play one more hand." I sipped from the tiny red straw swirling in my White Russian. I'd never had one before and now seemed as good a time as any. Its milkiness was weird but delicious.

"Sorry, Frank. We play much longer and we're going to attract the wrong kind of attention from the wrong kind of people." He took my cocktail and threw back its remains, dropping the empty glass on a passing drink tray.

I stood and burped under my hand. "Your fault."

I lost count of how many drinks I'd had while we played, but I had managed to finally tip my sober scales. I teetered behind Ben to the cashier counter where he exchanged only half of his chips, again to avoid attention. It was still in the thousands. I felt hot waiting behind him. Hot from the bright colors and the mob of people. Hot standing so close to Ben's left arm.

"You're buying my drinks at the club," Patrick whined.

Ben asked, "Will you stop crying?"

"If I get a steak, too."

We stepped onto the Strip, and I patted my shoulder pouch, finding relief in Betty's weight. I dropped a few bugs in the slat for her as we walked, accidentally smushing one and smearing it between my fingers.

There were even more people outside than in. The entire city was both too dark and too shiny. The sheer number of humanoids shoving themselves like paste through doorways, over bridges, up stairwells, and around cars felt like the end of the world.

Once Cleo heard the address Jack had given us, she took the

lead, strutting impressively in her very high heels. She never winced or displayed any discomfort. I, on the other hand, lagged and toddled. Ben held my hand, playing with my hair and observing my clumsiness with an annoying charm. I wanted to pull one particular freckle on his bottom lip into my mouth.

I didn't understand how there was still Strip left to see by the time we made it to the meeting place, and our destination was a popular one. There weren't entry doors as much as the entire façade opened to the street, spilling partygoers onto the side-walk like a tipped box of cereal. Four stone pillars held a dark balcony above where I watched shadows twist and tangle. Leather-clad dancers of all genders twirled around the pillars and were seen floating through the crowd inside, giggling and blowing kisses, appearing gossamer rather than flesh in the pulsing purple lights. There were just as many bouncers as there were dancers, clad in black t-shirts with "SECURITY" across their shoulders. Hypnotic trance music stained the street like wine. It smelled like bodies, hundreds and hundreds of them.

A sign glowed above the balcony, shifting colors every few seconds. Its title was spelled out in flames.

"The Harvest," Ben read. "How fitting."

"Tempting, isn't it?" Jack traipsed from the alley beside the club and into the light wearing an army jacket and the same shirt from this morning. I made a gross phlegmy sound in my throat. *He* didn't have to dress up. "But we won't be going in the front," he said. Patrick giggled at the phrasing and Jack glared. "This way." He turned around and dipped back into the alley from which he'd materialized.

My friends hurried after him. In my haste, I tripped over the curb, barely keeping vertical. A man stopped me before I could enter the alley, extending a card, his face hidden beneath his hood. It was instinct to take it, so I did. The moment the card left his fingers, he moved on.

I stared at the card in my hand. There were naked women on either side. They each sparkled, seeming to move and change in the glittery illumination. I nearly dropped it to the pavement, but instead put it in the side pocket of Betty's pouch with the crickets. The notion made me squirm inside, throwing the women to the ground like trash.

I hustled after my group, meeting Ben who was waiting patiently beside a dumpster. As we rounded the back corner of the building, we found a woman. At least, I thought it was a woman. She donned dirty clothes, layer upon layer of them. If she sat on the ground, I'd have thought she was a pile of blankets. Her eyes were fierce, sharp, and dark beneath her ratty black hair.

"Jack? The hell are you doing here?" she asked. Her voice was full of sticks and stones.

"Showing some customers around. They're interested in the talent downstairs."

"They must be paying the prettiest penny I've ever seen. How long's it been?"

"You think I'd be here if they weren't?"

I held my poker face—if we were paying for Jack's time, this was the first I'd heard of it.

The woman's eyes swung like a mallet to Patrick. There was such hatred in those irises, I thought they might boil over. "He's not welcome here."

"I fuckin' agree," Jack said. "But he can go in. We can't make business personal, Maize. You know that."

Maize hissed like a stray but stepped aside. Behind her stood a black door, painted in the same color as the rest of the building, the frame almost undetectable. "Go on!" she barked, spit flying into Patrick's face, which he kept miraculously controlled.

Jack pushed Patrick from behind, and we moved in a single-file line into total darkness.

6

THE MUSIC WAS SLOW, low, and sinister. It gripped my heart and shook. There were several black platforms at different elevations —they matched the floor and walls, making it appear as if people were floating around the room—with intimate tables from which to choose. The few people dancing were alone in inky corners. Undulating and panting. Watching felt like an ugly thing to do, but I couldn't stop.

A long onyx bar gleamed along the back of the club. The bartender was alarmingly pale, anemic; she practically glowed in the dark. Her hair was either blonde or gray and wispy, like a cotton ball that had been ripped apart. She was helping a patron, and as she turned to fulfill the order, she vanished, reappearing at the other end of the bar. She plopped a cherry in a glass and returned in an instant, as if dropped from the heavens.

"Ghost," said Jack. "Witches with an affinity for apportation and invisibility. Some can walk through objects and walls. Lack object permanence, them things."

Something scuttled out from under a barstool, snapping and chuffing. It chased after the patron's ankles, swinging its too-long head, until the man threw some cash on the counter and darted away from the bar. He fell over a table in the back and clutched his heart on the ground. The thing whipped its tail like a pendulum as it grumpily revolved back around.

"Don't tell me ... that's not a crocodile?"

It groaned and moaned like an old floorboard as it dragged its scaly ass back into the shadows.

"Alligator, I believe," Jack answered. "Bartender's from Louisiana. That's her familiar, Herman. He ensures customers pay their tab. Plus a generous tip."

Now that I'd seen the alligator, I noticed other animals watching their humans in the room—a Siamese cat wound through a chair's spindly legs, a camouflaged crow perched above thick, unnecessary curtains, observing us with a cocked head. I considered letting Betty mingle with the other familiars, but I didn't want to chance a physically temporary bartender apporting right on top of her.

We hadn't moved to sit or order drinks and I could feel the sting of curious stares. I approached the bar, exuding false confidence, desperate to keep my ankles steady despite the monstrous jaws swimming beneath the barstools.

The woman was a literal blur, and her hair was softly translucent. Though the rest of her was uncertain, her eyes were solid black. She didn't greet me.

"Can I get a beer?" I asked around the welling spit in my cheeks. "The strongest you have in a bottle."

"Plus, a New York Sour, a double margarita, and a raspberry daiquiri." Ben took three twenties—an insane amount of money for four drinks—from his thick roll of cash. Only after he slammed them on the counter did she get to work, and she was something to see—if I could see her. It was like watching the wind use a blender. All four of our drinks appeared on the counter as if from nowhere and she poured a fifth glass for Jack. I hoped I was mistaken, and he didn't drink straight vodka with a celery stick floating inside.

Jack raised his swill to the bartender. "Beau," he said before taking a gulp. He turned around and gestured to a raised platform on the other side of the club. There was a single large table atop it, which offered some privacy.

We passed several greedy, distrustful expressions, and Jack

provided quiet commentary. "That's Ray," he said, nodding to a brown-skinned man with a goatee and hawkish features. "Revenant. Scary bugger. He can't be killed, or at least, he can't stay dead. He almost seems to like it. Dying. And if he *is* dead, he can control the bodies of the living until he returns."

"Fuck," I said.

"Fuck indeed." He nodded.

"Her over there," he indicated a pale teen dancing with evident glee, "Madison. Leprechaun. Rich, young, happy," he spat the last word. "She has the affinity of luck. Things always seem to go her way, and anyone who tries to get in the way … well, they aren't around to talk about it. The universe will try to balance the scales if you so much as look at her. Best avoid her if you can."

I all but skipped past her dance party—my luck was bad enough as it was.

"Hello, there," said a woman at a small table, one of three blondes pressed tightly together. The one who spoke was older than the other two, but not by much. She wore a too-friendly smile that made me uncomfortable. The woman on her right was also smiling, but her teeth hid behind glossy lips, slightly subdued. The woman on the left was not smiling; she gazed through me, completely aloof. The three women embodied different volumes of invitation, and they had the bluest eyes I'd ever seen.

"I'm Melissa, and these are my daughters, Alexa and Alaire. I haven't seen you before. I'm sure you could use a friendly face. Why don't you join us?" The surliest of the three kicked a chair out from the table. The mother placed an empty glass at its setting. "You must be thirsty." The glass filled with water. It looked violet in the strobe lights of the club.

"Um—"

"Yes, please," Patrick said, shoving me out of the way and taking a seat. He shot back the weird water and licked his lips. Then, taking one of the drinks from Ben, he sipped the margarita

with heavy-lidded eyes. The three women enjoyed his enthusiasm, even the grump.

Jack took advantage of the distraction and steered us away
from the trio. "Kelpies. Water witches. And they're a rare group
of mages—a blood family. Melissa plowed fields of men to culti-
vate those two psychos."

Patrick was talking animatedly, waving his arm around and
drinking from the gifted glass, which had filled with water once
again.

"What about Patrick?" I folded myself into a chair across
from Jack at the corner table.

Ben stifled a smirk. "He'll be fine." He pulled out a chair,
which Cleo took, and he sat beside me. I felt his every move as if
he were right on top of me. His thigh brushed mine, so slowly it
could have been unintentional. Then he scooted in another inch
until it couldn't have been. Why now did he suddenly feel so
close?

Jack's glass was nearly empty, and he munched on the celery
stick. "Whelp. This is where I sent Jessamae. And she follows
direction like a soldier, so we know she's been here." He pulled a
celery string from his incisors.

Ben asked, "Why did you send her here?" and ran his pink
tongue along the rim of his daiquiri. So pink.

"Because of who she was looking for. There was a feller, in
Vegas, some years ago who practiced a form of restoration. I lost
track of him after he left one of the covens that camped here. But
the head mage he served is still around—we'll find her here. I've
never managed to pass through Vegas without running into the
bitch." He stretched the torn neck of his shirt farther away from
his throat. "Chances are good Jessamae tracked her down, talked
to her."

"How do you keep track of all that? How do you know
everyone?" I asked. "Did you memorize your entire databa—"

He held a finger to his lips, and I stopped talking.

"It's what I am. I know affinities, I know how they can be

used. 'Specially against me. I found it in my best interest to catalog my findings. I probably have the biggest mage ... memory," he said, avoiding the word *database*, "in North America. At least dating back through the last century."

"Don't forget, Jack. You can also affect the affinities of others. Turn them off or blow them up? Correct?" Ben said before sucking a nodule of frozen purple pulp through a straw.

Jack glared at Ben. "Patrick always did run his fuckin' mouth."

"Why do you hate him?" I asked, peeling the label from my bottle. Barry's Blood Orange IPA. "The lady at the door, too."

"The lady at the door is Maize, my cousin. Patrick ... spent time with her, like the scumbag he is, and never called her again. But that's not why I hate him." He picked more green celery threads from his teeth. "He killed my dog."

The lip of my bottle clapped my teeth. "What?"

"He changed and went roaming the desert after a bender. My dog was out hunting when he came across him." His countenance was both vengeful and sad. "That's why he's afraid of me. I took a little justice that night. But that doesn't bring Driskill back."

I wanted to argue that Patrick clearly hadn't intended to kill Driskill, though I had no defense against his fucking of Maize. But he had nearly maimed Cleo in his alternate form, and if he had killed Betty, even after shifting, I doubt I could ever forgive him.

"I'll get the next round," Ben said after slurping the dregs from his glass. I thought credit cards must be accepted here, and I turned to hand him my card, but instead met a gigantic chest only inches from my face.

"Look what the dirty, old cat dragged in. Hello, Jack."

I backed into the table until my eyes weren't directly aligned with the nipples of her heavy breasts. This woman was large, both tall and wide, with bright white skin covered in cinnamon freckles.

Her hair wasn't the orange I expected from a ginger, it was blood red. She wore a skin-tight dress that molded beautifully around her curves, but her strange eyes compelled my gaze upward—they were brown, mostly, but with the russet tint of Utah sand.

"And you have friends, how unlike you."

Jack sighed and looked longingly at his empty glass. "Frankie, Ben, Cleo." He gestured to us each in turn. "Meet Nicola. She runs this place. And the club upstairs."

She extended a hand, her fingers tipped with long, sharp nails painted black. "Wonderful to meet you."

Cleo gave a polite shake. Ben kissed her knuckles like a goddamn knight. I shook last. Her hand was hot and tacky. So this was the fairy—the Queen of Las Vegas. I feared her immediately. I was no rune witch, but magic gushed from her and flooded the room.

She took a seat at the head of our table and crossed one shapely leg over the other, the muscles of her calves standing out as if their own appendages. As soon as she sat, the bartender appeared behind her.

"Usual?" she asked Nicola.

"Yes, thank you, Beau. And another round for my new friends." The bartender disappeared.

Nicola leaned back in her chair and assessed the rest of us as if we were talentless actors, animals even, auditioning for a Broadway production. Her self-assurance rivaled that of Cleo, who now sat up straight with a stony slash for a mouth.

"Jack," she deigned to address him. "Is there a reason you broke your thousand years of solitude?"

"The price was right," he answered pragmatically. "They wanted the VIP tour of the city."

Ben swung the leg touching me, and going by the way Cleo rearranged herself, I thought he might have kicked her. "A friend of mine mentioned The Harvest. Raving reviews," she lied, steady as a river. "But it's not exactly wise to walk the Strip without a guide." She trailed an elegant finger along the rim of her glass. "At least, that's what I've been told."

Nicola replied, "How interesting."

Beau returned, by foot this time, with a tray on her arm. I wondered if there was some sort of weight limit to her craft. She placed each of our drinks in front of us and silently vanished once again.

"And who is this 'raving' friend who told you to stop by? So many new friends in my city. I wish they'd come by and see me." Nicola ran a black claw around her lips as if it were a tube of lipstick.

"Her name is Jessamae. Ash-blonde with a scar through her brow. Certainly, you've seen her loitering. She loves it here. It's been difficult to get her to leave." Cleo's heavenly smile ripped me to shreds and tears filled my eyes. Ben reached below the table and crushed my hand in his until I looked away. He didn't let go.

I hated the way Nicola summed us up. Her face said that she knew where Jessamae was, and that she suspected just how much we wanted to know. "Oh, yes. She's been staying a while, blew in with the breeze." She sipped from her martini glass. The liquid was green. "She comes around the club from time to time ... But, of course, *you* know that." She stared at Cleo, daring her to lie.

Though I was dying to ask about the witch Jessamae was searching for, my father's former coven leader, I wouldn't speak, and neither would Cleo. I sucked down some beer, grateful for something to do with my hands and mouth.

Ben turned in his seat to face Nicola. "We—"

Nicola abruptly spit into her glass before a tower of flame erupted from the green pool, dancing eerily in her eyes. "I like it hot." She smiled before downing the cocktail one gulp. The empty walls of her glass were scorched black.

"You're not a fairy," I whispered.

She cocked her head and smiled like a crazy person. "Of

course not." Putting her glass on the table, she held up her hands and completely derailed me by making two L's with her thumbs and forefingers, then twisted them into a W. *Whatever.* Her index fingers ignited like candles.

"Dragon, honey."

ಊ

My brain churned, the alcohol draining from my guts into my butt in one fell swoop.

A dragon. A dragon in Las Vegas, where someone who shared my affinity for restoration resided for many years—my father. Patrick's tome. The tome written by a dragon documenting the violent behavior of a pain junky that I'd read over the summer. The words flashed behind my eyes and took root inside my head. Was that him? Was this her?

Nicola seemed put-off by my mix-up. She wanted to rule, that was obvious.

"I'm sorry, I heard about a fairy in Vegas, and you seemed—I don't know, in charge."

She whipped her waterfall hair over her shoulder. "An understandable mistake." But she glared at my beer bottle as if she wanted to set it ablaze. She rubbed her fingers on the inside of her glass, effectively snuffing the flames out. "The vampire, Jessamae, she doesn't come in on Saturday nights. She tends to loiter on Sundays. Come back tomorrow and I'll show you a night you'll never forget."

It felt as though we'd been both threatened and dismissed, so I drank the rest of my beer and stood up from the table.

"Looking forward to it. We'll be here at nine," Ben said with a curtsy.

"I'm going to skip it, if that's alright. Our agreement doesn't extend past midnight tonight," Jack said to Ben, Cleo, and I.

"Nicola, always a fuckin' pleasure." He pushed his second empty glass to the center of the table.

"Isn't it?" She sneered.

Jack shrugged and made his way toward the exit without further ado.

I moved quickly behind him, hurrying back to the table the three water witches occupied earlier. They were gone, and so was Patrick.

"What the fuck?"

"He's a grown man, he'll find his way home," Cleo snapped as she grabbed my elbow and towed me away.

My feet sporadically ached and eased as we walked the distance back to our hotel. I was offered several more naked lady cards, which I refused to take. As we crossed the carport, I retrieved the only card I had from Betty's pouch. The shimmering effect hadn't diminished. If anything, under the bright lights of the casino, it became more pronounced. As I stared, the woman ran her hands up her sides and knotted them in her hair. She looked right at me, into my eyes, and ran a slippery tongue over her lips.

"Where did you get that?" Ben asked.

I tore my eyes from the brunette. "Someone gave it to me outside the club."

"The glittery cards … they're not witches. They're regular people who've gotten sucked into our world. Available for our use. We, us. You know. For a fee."

I flipped the card to the other side. This one was a blonde opening and closing her legs. I noticed a tiny phone number in the frame of the card. "Use how?"

He put his arm around me. "However we want." If I wasn't so revolted, I would feel tingly as he rubbed up against me.

We rode the elevator up, one of Ben's arms over my shoulder, the other tracing patterns on the back of my hand. Cleo threw her clutch on the counter of the suite's kitchen and closed the doors to one of the bedrooms, though she knew we had to sleep in that room, too. I heard the tub running. Cleansing was Cleo's way of dealing with stressful situations.

I set Betty's pouch on the ground and unzipped it, stroking her flat head. She immediately wriggled inside the side pocket, sniffing for the rest of the crickets.

"Since Patrick is biding his time elsewhere, might I offer you a shower of our own?" Ben said as he led me to one of the dining chairs. He ran his fingers down my bare calf before he untied my boot.

"Both of us?"

"It's a big shower."

He pulled my second boot from my foot and set them both aside. He slid my cheap ankle socks down my toes as if they were stockings or pantyhose. And taking my hands, he walked backward through Patrick's room, leading me through the shadowed opulence.

The bathroom was gold and marble, too glamorous. But Ben was right, the shower was gigantic, equipped with two heads and a bench. Ben reached in and turned on each showerhead. He tested the water, wiggling his fingers beneath the spray, then removed his shirt without warning. Though I'd seen his chest a thousand times before, including this afternoon—his visage left me stunned. My knees wobbled and I collapsed on the toilet.

Ben held my eyes, despite my evident nerves. It took every ounce of courage I'd grown to meet his stare.

Until he unbuttoned his jeans. Then my gaze plummeted downward. His jeans hit the floor, and he stepped out of them. No underwear. Not a single shred of underwear.

A whimper tickled the back of my throat before my mouth opened with the sound of a bubble bursting. I'd felt Ben, known his naked body to the touch. But I'd never seen him. Not all of him. Not like this.

Freckles dusted his mouth, his broad shoulders, down to his slender fingers. Only the scar of his stomach was free of them. I wanted to run my fingers through the grooves lining the muscles of his torso. His tattoos framed him in a captivating intimacy, fanning out from the angled bones below his abdomen. His legs were covered in ink, his thighs strong and thick.

I stood. Somehow, I stood on shaky legs and turned my back to him, facing the wall-length mirror. Then I pulled my weighty brass hair away from my neck and found his face again in our reflection. He drifted momentarily into the future, and his answering smile was radiant. Glorious. The most beautiful thing I'd ever known. I smiled, too.

He approached me from behind, and the skin along my spine rose at his nearness, as if the bones of my back were reaching for him. I watched his every expression in the mirror above my head.

His nimble fingers clasped the zipper below my hair, spreading goosebumps to my neck, and tugged down. His knuckle dragged from my shoulder to my tailbone, and I shivered. He pulled the dress away from my collar and it piled atop his discarded clothes. Then I felt his velvet fingers dip under the fabric of my underwear and slide them down, his hands tracing my legs all the way to my feet. The next thing I felt on my calves, my thighs, was his mouth. His kisses dressed me all the way to my shoulder.

Ben leaned into the curve between my jaw and shoulder. His breaths were soft against me, and they tickled so deeply I could feel them in my stomach. "Ready?" he asked.

My jaw quivered against his cheek. The sound of my swallow embarrassed me. "Are we going to practice control?"

His finger traced the same path along my spine that the zipper had. "Not tonight."

His lips pressed gently to my jaw, and I wanted nothing more than to feel it. To slam my body into that kiss. Then he stepped away from me, his eyes on mine in the mirror, and moved under the showerhead. I watched the water shape him, following one gleaming drop trickle down his chest, dip into his sternum, roll over the scar tissue of his stomach, and disappear ...

I moved through the glass door beside him. The water was perfect. Steam billowed through my hair, frizzing it out around my shoulders. Ben wove his wet fingers through the mass of it, around my ears, down to the roots, and pulled me in closer. I felt only a small insecurity, nothing big enough to stop me. My body couldn't be a bad thing, because having it meant I could feel what I was feeling right now—his warm, dripping chest against my cheek, his lips at my temple.

The length of him pressed into my belly, near my ribs. Slippery. A delicious wetness spread between my legs, and I kissed the edge of his scar. He titled my chin up and molded his mouth to mine. Raspberry daiquiri.

I grabbed the back of his neck and stood on my toes. He wrapped his arms around me and spun, turning us one step. Two steps. Until my back was plumb against the marble siding. One of Ben's hands trailed lower, over my hip, under my thigh, and lifted. And suddenly Ben was as close as he could get. *Almost* as close as he could get. The combination of soft and hard made me light-headed, and I turned my chin away for some air. He bit the skin of my jaw. My gasp made him laugh. His mouth explored my throat. Lower. He kissed my sternum. Lower. His lips touched my belly. Lower.

My hips jutted out to meet him and he tenderly set my leg on his shoulder. The kisses. His tongue. His teeth. I couldn't breathe. I turned my face from the water and closed my eyes. But I was drowning. And it was exquisite. Exquisite.

"Oh my god." I held his face tighter against me.

He moaned and I felt it. "God … yes." His words pooled from his trembling lips and nimble tongue. My legs shook. My hands dug into the skin of his scalp. I began to fall. Ben stood before I could topple, pressing me into the wall to steady my weight. His eyes were wild, the specks of brown and yellow and black dancing only for me. The hair on his face had sprouted in abundance. It scratched me as he rubbed his cheek against mine.

He'd kept hold of one leg, and I wrapped my ankle around

his hips, doing my best to jump into his skin. Ben wouldn't take his eyes off mine. He cupped my face, his thumb on my bottom lip, and waited.

I nodded beneath his finger, pulling his thumb into my mouth.

His breath was loud, almost choked. He lifted me, my back sliding higher against the wall. He only used one hand to hold me up, and it appeared effortless. But it was Ben lifting me nonetheless. I was floating. Ben had created a magical shield beneath me.

He pressed into me. Slow. Pushed.

The pain was immediate. I raked my hands down his shoulder blades and gritted my teeth. I looked past his skin to the bathroom mirror and saw the two of us within it. My eyes were so bright they glowed, radioactive. My fingernails stabbed into his back like daggers. They left eight clear paths in their wake, welling blood. As I watched, his skin closed silently, inevitably. Healed. In seconds, the redness vanished. As did my pain.

He pushed again. This push was good. My hips surged forward for another. Good. So good.

"Frank," he growled, "Frankie." My name was beautiful when he said it, roughly, desperately. Roses. I'd lost control of my mouth. But his name sprinted through my head, faster and faster as we moved together.

He pushed. His free hand slithered below my hips, his thumb circling between my thighs.

The pleasure was unfathomable.

BEN WRAPPED me in a fluffy white towel, his cheeks a vibrant pink and his hair long enough to hold in my fist. Which I'd discovered first-hand. My own hair was a mess, nearly down to my ribs, and curling crazily from the steam.

Ben held me close, kissed the top of my head. "How you feeling?"

"Good." In truth, I felt better than I ever had. Alive. Strong. "I lost control, though." I licked my mouth, hoping to find something of him there.

"And I may never forgive you."

I snorted. He opened the door and cool air rushed in. I knew Cleo wouldn't be bothered by my nakedness, but I was still embarrassed at the visible intimacy between Ben and me. I tucked the towel around my chest and gathered up some of the damp clothing from the floor. I had a knack for damaging Cleo's pretty dresses.

Ben hung an arm over my shoulders as we crossed the hotel room to our bed, playing with my hair.

I was happy.

A beep sounded from the suite door before it opened. Patrick tiptoed inside and through the kitchen, but gave up the discretion once he saw the two of us stock-still in the living room.

Patrick was soaking wet. Drenched completely from head to toe, he held his sopping shoes in one hand and his topcoat in the other. His mouth flattened at the awkward encounter before he gave us a small salute.

"Evening," he said, and squelched off to his room, shutting the double doors behind him.

7

THE FOUR OF us rode the elevator to the lobby. It was late in the day, and we were starving. None more than Patrick, who claimed to have "worked up an appetite that may never be satiated."

Cleo bordered on chipper, unbothered by Patrick's complaining. She flashed conspiratorial grins at Ben and me.

This morning, she'd manically ripped the comforter from the two of us, both naked as the day we were born, before throwing a still-soaked shoe at Patrick, splattering dirty water all over his pillows. Patrick sputtered awake gutturally, bellowing like a drowning bear. She scolded us all for our late awakening then returned to her unsettling glee.

I'd dressed in a pair of familiar jeans and an old baseball jersey. The sport was dull as dirt, but the shirts were loose and soft. I got it from a garage sale in town, and it took three washes to get the smell out.

"There's a café nearby. Vegetarian friendly." Cleo scrolled through the map on her phone.

"How terrible," Patrick said. He scratched at his beard, his eyes bleary and red.

"Vegetarian *friendly*, not vegetarian. There will be more than enough carcass on which to gnaw."

As blissful as she seemed, no one could compete with Ben. He was overjoyed at being pushed out of bed, beamed indulgently at Cleo and Patrick's bickering, and he sprang up and down on his toes while he played with a strand of my hair. He'd been whistling what was either a show tune or a popular R&B song all morning, skipping around the suite as we dressed and groomed. My own mood reflected his, albeit subtly. I smiled at his buffoonery. Cleo certainly knew what we'd done last night, and though I preferred privacy to her knowledge, I felt buoyant. It was wonderful.

Patrick ordered three different entrees at the café, his sunglasses nailed in place above his nose though we were indoors.

"Have fun last night?" I asked him.

His grin grew until I could see all his teeth, which, even as disheveled as he appeared this morning, were whiter and sharper than I thought was acceptable. "I had more than fun." He leered at the three of us, coming off creepier than usual due to his scruffy appearance. Cleo gagged. When hers was our only response, Patrick supplemented. "Sex."

"Thank you. That was quite the riddle," Ben said, gulping his coffee. The restaurant didn't have cinnamon, but his disappointment was short-lived. He smacked his lips loudly and smiled. He side-eyed me from behind his mug and spilled coffee down his chin. I mashed my mouth to the side to kill my school-girl smile.

Patrick followed our exchange through his shades, racking his head right and left. He raised an eyebrow so high, it poked above his lenses.

"What time are we going back tonight?" I blurted.

Ben flicked a pink packet of sweetener against the table while he concentrated. "Nine is still a good time. But I don't see Jessamae until later." He poured the white powder into his mug, the coffee nearly gone. Imagining the sweetness of it hurt my jaw.

"Should we wait?"

He shook his head. "I already told Nicola nine. She's expecting us."

"Going back two nights in a row," Patrick interrupted. "We'll need to keep a low profile. I don't want to give the water witches the wrong idea."

"But you already slept with them," I said.

"One. I slept with one. Or two. But that's not what I'm talking about. I mean commitment. I don't want them to think I'm buzzing around, looking for a relationship. They must be *pining* this morning."

Cleo chimed in, "If they are, they deserve what they get."

I DIDN'T SEE the point in dressing up twice, but Cleo turned terrifying when I expressed that sentiment. She hauled me shopping, somewhere expensive with a cursive name that was so elaborate I couldn't read it. While I suffered, draped across an uncomfortable aesthetic chair like a pair of too-tight pants, Patrick and Ben hit the casino, adding to the group piggy bank. I wished I were with them.

I didn't feel angry at Ben's offered cash today. The money felt like ours. It was as if we were all in on the heist just by existing in the city.

I tried on a few suits, but all the pants were much too long, and the sleeves bunched around my palms. I looked like a child with drug money. I tried on too many dresses until I found one that made me tilt my head. It was green, spaghetti strapped, and the fabric over my boobs crisscrossed across my chest before joining the fabric of the skirt, exposing a tiny triangle of my midsection. It reminded me of the dress I'd worn on my first date, or the closest thing to it, with Ben in the mountains. It was the only one I liked.

My jersey and jeans were back on in a flash, and I took my

dress to the counter. The snooty cashier had snooty hair and a puggish nose, which she looked down at me like she thought any cash I had was stolen. She could keep her accurate assumptions to her goddamn self.

"Six hundred twelve dollars and thirteen cents," she drawled.

I froze with my hand in Betty's pouch. "What?"

"Six hundred—"

"I'm only getting one dress."

She stared at me like I was a booger stuck to the wall. "I am aware of that."

"It's missing some of the fabric! Look, there's a piece—" I tried to snag the dress and show her how much fabric would actually cover my body, but she pulled the dress away as if my hands were covered in my own shit.

"Excuse me!" she said.

"Excuse me." Cleo appeared at my elbow and the cashier's disgust seemed to stall. "Is there a problem here?" She spoke as if she were the manager, and the cashier responded as if that were exactly the case.

"I'm sorry, this … girl, appears to have a problem with the amount. This dress is out of her price range."

"It's on sale."

I surveyed the room. Nothing was on sale. I doubted anything was ever on sale in this place.

"Um … I'm sorry, but no, I don't believe it is," the goblin responded with glazed eyes.

Cleo pursed her lips at the woman, then smiled. A smile that rivaled the beauty of the moon. I leaned in closer, but she held me at bay. "The salesman here, the one with black hair, told her it was on sale. Fifteen percent off."

We hadn't encountered any other salesperson in the store. The cashier struggled with that fact and Cleo's bewildering confidence.

After the cashier floundered in silence for nearly a minute,

Cleo continued. "The only reason she decided to buy was because of the promised discount. So that's what we'll be paying. You may as well just ring everything up together." She piled a stack of items she'd picked out on top of my dress. "Thank you so much for your help."

The woman nodded stupidly, trying to regain control of her limbs. Once she managed to figure things out, she scanned everything with alacrity.

As we walked back to our hotel, I shook my head in awe. Cleo was going over the receipt, and most of the bags were in my hands. "Ha! She gave me a discount on everything. She is going to be in a lot of trouble."

"Is this how you have so many clothes?"

"Of course not. I only take from those who deserve to be knocked from their high horses. I didn't like the way she spoke to you."

I stuttered a step, tripping over a break in the sidewalk, touched. "Well. Thanks."

"I spent more than I'd budgeted. Hopefully the boys got a big haul. Oh, who am I kidding? Hopefully *Ben* got a big haul."

Turns out Ben had seen trouble brewing in the casino almost the instant he found a table downstairs. Playing it safe, he and Patrick went to three surrounding casinos to spread Ben's winnings around. Patrick was overtly proud that he didn't lose all his money again.

"I made a profit today, ladies. Please keep your hands to yourself. Let me dress in peace!" He sauntered into his bedroom wearing nothing but a feather boa and a towel.

"He made forty-six dollars. On the slot machines. That I told him to go to," Ben supplied, taking the bags from my hands. "All these yours, Princess? Is Cleo controlling you?"

"Like it's hard?" Cleo did a cute little bob for us and tossed her hair. "That stuff is mine. But you are going to *love* what she did get. You'll want to rip it right off her." She gave my arm a squeeze before she left the room.

Ben stared at me. "Hey, Frank."

I pulled my long hair forward anxiously. "Benny."

He took my hands away from my hair and kissed one. "You still okay?"

Taking a deep breath, I said, "I'm great. Really. But … I am curious. Why last night? You've been such a stickler for control."

He rubbed his head, looking confused and sheepish. "Frank. I'm not entirely sure why last night. Maybe it was the city, or the winning buckets of cash. Maybe it was the drinks or the strip poker. Maybe—and don't get me wrong, I love how you dress. I could have posters hung of you wearing my shirt and a smelly pair of boots. But, maybe," he stepped closer to me, his stomach brushing against my chest, "it was your skin. There was so much to see last night." He smiled his trademark smile, and I got weak in my stupid knees. "And I saw *a lot*. Up here," he tapped his head. "Over and over and over—"

I punched him in the chest, and he coughed out a laugh, rubbing his sternum. "I'm kidding … I'm not kidding."

I hit him again.

"Stop! I just …" His humor drained away as he kissed my knuckles. "It was our last night to be us. Just us, you know? Without Jessamae around."

I winced at the implication, but I couldn't say he was wrong. A part of me hated that Jessamae had anything to do with what happened. But I'd wanted him so badly, the other part of me was glad he acted on his impulses for once. He was being very honest with me.

"And last night … I just wanted to. I wanted you. No maybe about it." He squeezed my hand. "But I need to know you wanted to as much as I did. In all seriousness, Frank, you're okay?"

My cheeks warmed. His charm was almost embarrassing there was so much of it. But I was climbing over this hump of self-consciousness, and I didn't feel so unworthy today. "Sure. Very much. I'm in excellent health. As are you." I pulled his hair.

He nodded. "I'm going to shave it before we leave. You always want to play your cards close to the chest when you're with unfamiliar witches. Knowledge is power. Not as much as *power* is power, but the more they know about you, the worse. And if my hair has doubled in size … Nicola is said to be a very sharp woman."

"I get it. Plus, your hair doesn't feel right anymore."

"Well, now I'm not doing it." He shook my chin, and his pupils grew. "You didn't call Scott, did you?"

"Shit! I forgot! Why didn't you remind me?"

"You said you put it in your phone!"

I pulled my phone from my pocket and fumbled to dial. "I lied!" I hissed as I put the phone to my ear. Luck was on my side; it went to voicemail. "Hey Scott, sorry, I know I didn't make my shift today. I had an emergency. Urgent. Can't talk now, but I'll explain later." I hit *End* and glared at Ben.

"You aren't allowed to blame me for this," he said with a finger in my face.

"I'm allowed to do whatever I want." I squeezed the bridge of my nose. There was no helping the situation now. "I'm turning off my phone, so he'll have to leave a message."

"Way to be proactive."

If I lost my job, I'd make him tell me my chances at every place I applied. He wouldn't be so high and mighty when he was my personal Help Wanted ad.

"I guess I'll get ready," I said, picking up my shopping bag. The woman had even put tissue paper on top, almost like a present.

"Same." He pulled me to his side, his mouth at my ear. "I'm feeling much more colorful today." Then his teeth clamped down on my earlobe, his tongue sliding against it. He leaned into my neck. "Mmmm," he purred.

"Um." I couldn't feel my legs. I leaned back into him, and the bag fell from my hands.

Ben stepped away and picked up the bag. He offered it politely. "You dropped this."

My lip curled in indignation. "Why do you do that!"

"I'm going to shower and shave in Patrick's room. See you in an hour." He blew me a kiss.

THE DRESS FIT NICELY, and because the new boots were black, I figured they went with everything. I did my makeup the same way—I liked that it made me look more mature, worldly even. Tired of my hair, Cleo sat me down in a chair in front of the mirror. "Just let me put it in a bun. Quick and painless. I promise."

I grumbled and squirmed but let her go about it. I felt like I owed her after she made the snooty lady pay for her attitude.

Cleo's hands in my hair were like spiders in a web. I watched the dark digits weave in and out, disappear and reappear, with such speed and agility that I watched for extra fingers in there, counting whenever I could. My hair was gathered into a large, perfectly askew mass in minutes. I couldn't understand the engineering behind it, how it stayed in place like that. It defied physics.

"There. Look how pretty you are."

I wasn't sure about that, but I did think I looked slightly more middle-class. Clean. "It's nice."

Cleo nodded and patted my bun.

I thought she was very dressed up for a shady club—not that anyone would complain. She was wearing a mind-melting silk ensemble. It was a two-piece dress, gold, with a plunging cropped top and a full-length skirt slit up to her thigh. Her skin was like black satin, and I caught myself staring more than once. Drool slithered over the bump of my lip. I sucked my cheeks into my mouth and turned away as she buckled the strap of one heel. Her hair was in an elegant chignon, her makeup soft and warm. She was lovelier than any princess, than any queen or king.

"You look … you know. Great. Even for your standards," I stammered.

"Thank you, Frankie. A woman feels the need to dress up every now and then." As if she didn't find a reason to blow us out of the water every single day.

Patrick and Ben were lounging on the couch watching a TV sitcom, Betty curled attentively in Ben's lap. She loved TV, and I hadn't been able to watch with her since we'd arrived. Patrick, too, was invested in the program, leaning forward and complaining about character motivations. But Ben's attention waited for me to walk through the door.

He hadn't been lying about his mood for color. His shirt was a nice fabric with a thick collar, and it was covered in tiny threaded palm trees, toucans, and tropical flowers. His chinos were green, his dark boots were untied.

I knew when Cleo stepped behind me because Patrick did a double take, but Ben's eyes held on me. He piled Betty beside Patrick's thigh—Patrick hopped to the end of the couch—and stood, extending his hand. Though I reviled public displays of affection, I couldn't help myself. In such vibrancy, wearing his favorite colors—which were all of them—it was like we'd never left home.

"Hey, Frank," he said again. For some time, he merely held my hand, eyes on my face.

"Benny."

"Get a room you two," Patrick said as he turned off the television, his eyes repeatedly straying back to Cleo. If I couldn't smell the soap on Ben's skin, see the bead of water trail down his neck, my eyes would have done the same.

"Everyone ready?" Cleo asked, clicking her heels across the kitchen.

"One sec." I took one of the bedside lamps from Patrick's room and set it on the carpet. It was the kind that bent like a pipe cleaner, so I rigged it closer to the floor, warming the carpet. If she got sleepy, Betty could spiral in this spot, and she'd be warm. I bent down to tickle her throat, and she flicked her tiny tongue, closing her eyes.

"She'll be fine if you leave her," Ben said. "You've spoiled her with all those bugs. She won't be hungry for a while, Princess."

Though I hated leaving her, apprehension squatted in my gut. We were going back into the lion's den, and I didn't want Betty in danger. I stroked her head, soft as a feather. "Be safe."

⸎

THE HARVEST WAS JUST as busy as it was yesterday, the scene eerily similar, as if time stood still. The wave of déjà vu made me feel afraid. Without Jack I was vulnerable. Our entire group was vulnerable. Even with Ben, I felt blind.

Maize was missing from the backdoor. This seemed irregular to the point of freaky for such a seedy establishment. She'd acted as a magical sentry. How could they be seedy without a sentry?

Cleo pushed but the door didn't open. There was an ornate bronze knocker I hadn't noticed yesterday, shiny from oily fingers. Cleo knocked three times and the door swung open. It seemed too easy, but Nicola had been expecting us.

The moment we crossed the threshold, I felt it. The long-dormant cords in my chest hummed as if plucked. A weak vibration between my ribs. She was here. Jessamae was here. I wasn't afraid anymore. I was in a hurry.

"Hello there, my besties!" Nicola boomed, strutting across the floor in our direction. She wore shiny leather pants that clung to her voluptuous hips and a high-neck red top. She looked like she slayed vampires for a living, and I knew it was intentional. She kissed Cleo on both cheeks, then Patrick, who was theatrical in his smooches. Ben let her greet him but made no effort to return the kiss. When she got to me and leaned in, I flinched back instinctually from the foreign touch. She was instantly affronted. "Problem? Francesca?"

I straightened my spine. Only one living person liked to call me that … and a couple dead ones. "No. No, how are you?" I leaned forward and kissed her cheek. It was at too straight an angle and it felt like I was making a pass at her.

As my lips made contact, I sensed a burn in her. It stung my mouth. Her back was sore, too much pressure on the spine after a long day with a large chest. Small aches didn't have the same flavor that bloody, spurting injuries did, but still had a pleasant effect, almost an aroma. I could sense when Ben and Cleo were fatigued, were hungry. It was the most perfect scent. I assumed it was because of our bond, that they affected me more than others. But I had no bond whatsoever with this woman, so that didn't explain how I could sense such small doses of pain. I felt myself inhaling. I inhaled until I was dizzy, my mouth pressed against her sweltering cheek.

Nicola pulled back and appeared content enough. She didn't smile, but she didn't scowl either. Then she whipped her head, and her eyes grew until they took up half her face. I had done something. I had done something, and she knew it.

Her shocked expression jerked to something behind me, over my shoulder. My curiosity turned me around.

Pale, phantom eyes zeroed in on me like dual pistols.

Jessamae Mori was here.

SHE COULD HAVE BEEN an illusion under the pulsing multicolored lights, as unreal and unsettling as a night terror. She belonged outside, in the natural, beautiful places. We both knew that. She hadn't dressed up much, though her white blouse was clean and billowy. She resembled Peter Pan, her olive pants tight around the ankles. Her hair, which I'd always known to be tangled if not ratted, fell in soft, straight lines over her shoulders.

She mouthed my name. I knew it to be mine even across the club and through the darkness. Her face gave away her joy, but it morphed into sadness so quickly I couldn't be certain if she'd been happy to see me at all. She crossed the room like a hawk who'd spotted a rabbit, ignoring a man who wanted her attention.

"Francesca—Frankie. It's so great to see you." She took my face in her hands, though her fingers were as stiff as a corpse. She, like me, felt Nicola's lobotomy eyes on the two of us. She pulled me in close, and the cords eased at the contact. She held me in a tender embrace, her hand tracing the strap of my dress. "I didn't know you were visiting."

"Yeah, I know, but, um, when we heard how much you were enjoying yourself, we thought we'd stop by." I strived to sound casual, but I'd always been a terrible actress. I played the line-less reindeer in elementary school and line-less Juror Number Two in my junior high production.

Cleo saved me from saying more by gliding forward and clutching Jessamae's elbows. "Jessamae." She held her out as if needing a good look after years of absence. "It's been so long!"

Jessamae scanned Cleo from toe to crown, and her eyes became two blue planets. "Cleo. You are …" She swallowed. I'd never seen her at a loss for words before. "You're beautiful." She brought the siren in for a squeeze. "I've missed our talks. I got caught up in the city. So much to do." Jessamae gave the group a small smile, but her focus was sharp as a razor. "Let's sit down."

"Actually," Nicola piped in, "I thought we'd regroup upstairs. There's tons of fun y'all have yet to experience." She looked at each of us in turn and stopped on Jessamae. "Except for you, sweetie. I know you've acquired quite the taste."

I resisted the urge to gawk at her inflection. What had Jessamae tasted? And would I have to sample it?

"Frankie, can I speak with you for a second?" Ben tugged on my arm.

A blush filled my face. Ben. I was acting as if he wasn't even here. "Course." I followed him to the corner, past Patrick who was staring daggers at Jessamae.

I didn't want to lose track of the vampire. I thought if I didn't pin her down, if I didn't keep up with her all the time, she'd vanish like a dream into the recesses of my head. But I didn't want to hurt Ben. Not like I did over the summer.

Ben bit both his lips. "I don't think we should stay here."

"In Vegas?"

"No. Well yes, probably, but no. The club. There are a lot of possible paths branching tonight. Too many. Something bad is coming."

"Bad how?"

"I'm not sure. Nothing is certain, too many decisions to be made by too many parties. But something. Something very bad." He rubbed his hands together before raking them across his shorn hair and pulling them down his cheeks. His eye sockets stretched down like a ghost's.

I looked back to the group. Patrick stood behind Jessamae, his eyebrows creating a dramatic sinkhole in his face, though she'd taken no notice of him skulking above. Cleo ignored us completely—her self-control was outstanding. Jessamae spoke politely with the two women, her eyes flicking to us.

Ben's resentment seeped through the room, acrid and bitter. I could almost smell it.

"You only saw something bad after Jessamae showed up? Sort of ... convenient."

Ben's hands fell to his sides and his chin jutted forward. "You could call it convenient. I'd call it inevitable."

"What's this really about, Ben?"

"What is *this* really about?" He threw his hand out at me. He'd flipped from calm to irate in a heartbeat. "Since when haven't you trusted my precognition? Because *she's* here? You just don't want to go back because you—" he clamped a hand to his mouth and took a deep breath. He closed his eyes before he spoke. "Because you missed her."

I crossed my arms and stepped back. I didn't want to draw Nicola's attention, but I didn't want to get into this again. Throughout Jessamae's absence, I *had* missed her, but it was a manageable void. Now that I was here, now that I felt the cords grow taut inside me, the void was starved for her. He *knew* she and I had this connection. "I thought you didn't hate her anymore."

Ben cocked his head like the crow watching from the curtains. "I don't hate her. I'm not trying to fuck with whatever is going on between you two." He cringed in distaste. "I'm telling you the truth. Something's wrong. Something's shifting. Horrible things are about to happen."

I scratched at the exposed skin of my stomach, my lip curling. I didn't want to do this. I didn't want to say, "You've always manipulated my life to fit whatever future you wanted. How do I not know you're doing that now? How can I trust your visions when everything you see happens to suit you?" My voice was cold, and I hated to hear it. But these mean ideations had entered my head from time to time, when my mood was black. And here we were. We'd come all this way to find Jessamae and now, because he said so, we were turning around? Giving up? "Why didn't you see any trouble in the hotel room? Or at breakfast? Or in the shower?" He flinched as if I'd slapped him. "All we're doing is going upstairs for Christ's sake."

Ben straightened. He'd been bending over me, now he towered above me. "You know there's nothing I can do about that. I still can't control everything—"

"Then what good are you?"

I regretted it the moment I said it. Faster even. He seemed to empty completely. It was *worse* than if I'd slapped him. I turned on my heel and stalked toward our group, easing the cords in my chest. I didn't look back, unable to face what I'd done to him. I wanted to cry.

"Let's go then," I snapped, arching against the burn in my chest. How could I have said such a thing to my best friend?

When I saw Jessamae's glass eyes pique with worry, I put his devastation on the back burner. We weren't here on some sort of honeymoon, we were here for her, to make sure she was okay.

But Ben was right about one thing—something wasn't right on the Strip. And just as we were in danger, so was Jessamae. I wouldn't leave without her. All I had to do was convince her to go back to Utah with us, then we'd avoid whatever Ben saw coming. Win/win.

"Let's," Nicola agreed. She turned unexpectedly toward the bar, and Jessamae grabbed my hand, towing me along the correct path to the club upstairs. Cleo kept up with Jessamae but seemed ill at ease. The tension had turned, spoiled like milk.

Next to one side of the bar—Beau was busy fussing with drinks for a group of loud men—there was a black curtain. Nicola moved it aside and revealed a second staircase. The walls were lined with sconced candles, and the gothic aura felt both theatrical and genuinely creepy. Patrick fell in behind me and I hoped Ben brought up the rear. I couldn't stand it if he left without saying anything. I couldn't stand how far this might go. I didn't want to apologize, but I wanted to say *something*. I wanted to fill the grave I'd dug between us.

Nicola stepped off the staircase into a dark room with no furniture. The only light source was the same small candles that illuminated the stairwell. Our shoes clacked loudly on the black floor—it felt like plywood beneath me, and I bounced a little with each step. The room was perfectly circular.

Ben appeared from the depths of the stairwell and our group was complete. I couldn't look at him and couldn't look away. His face was impassive and hard. I'd done that. My hand lifted to touch his arm—

"Ready?" Nicola asked, taking my hand.

"Yes." Even in the midst of whatever this was.

Nicola guided me to the wall, better to see, and reached up for one of the sconces. It was copper and green from oxidation. She pulled.

The flame sputtered but continued to burn as the sconce righted itself against the wall once more. Then the walls rotated around us.

They revolved gradually, but I stumbled with disorientation. It felt as if the ground was spinning instead of the walls. All the candles remained alight as they moved, and eventually, an empty square appeared in the walls beyond them. An arch led through the circular space into The Harvest.

The entire ground floor was covered in writhing, serpentine bodies. Throngs of dancers hung above the floor in cages, circled pale Greek pillars scattered throughout the room, and stomped across lacquered tabletops. The music pulsed under my ribs like a second heart. The lights were blinding. The smoke was suffocating, and it coated the ground as thickly as a moor.

Two bars lined adjoining walls, four bartenders behind them. The women wore what looked to be corsets or tuxedo vests, and the men were bare-chested. That was more than I could say for the patronage.

People were wrapped in translucent ribbons of tulle or wore painted-on scales or wore nothing at all. I smelled the sweat. I smelled the desperation and the longing and the spilled cocktails. I wondered how many witches mingled amongst the crowd, and—remembering the sparkly card I'd been given yesterday—how many regular people knew the witches for what they were.

"There is an incredible VIP section right over there." Nicola pointed to a roped-off corner full of cushy booths and sofas. "Just say my name and you'll be let through. Working girls and guys regularly come around offering their services." My eyes dropped to the floor. "The bar serves any refreshment you can dream of—shaken, stirred, blessed, cursed. It's all to die for." I cleared my throat of sticky mucus, burping into my clenched teeth. "Now if you'll excuse me," she said, giving a wave like a baby would—clapping her fingers to her palms—and waltzed through the crowd, a head above most of the guests.

Ben stalked past me, leaning away to avoid touching me, and stopped at one of the bars, his fingers white against its edge. A woman leaned across the counter, and he gave her a bouquet of twenties. She smiled too widely at him and nodded. In seconds, he had a drink in his hand, not the daiquiri he normally preferred, but something dark. He stormed to the VIP section and whispered to the large, neckless, security guard there, who let him through the velvet rope. He then folded into an elegant leather armchair in a secluded corner, held his drink in both hands, and drooped his head over his elbows.

Tears welled in my eyes, angry and ashamed. I'd hurt him so much. I'd done it again.

"Dance with me," Jessamae interrupted. Her expression was serious.

I stared wanly back at Ben. If he felt my gaze, he didn't care to return it.

"I'll talk to him," Cleo whispered in my ear. Whether she knew the details or not, you didn't need to be as clever as Cleo to see the wilt in our demeanor, his and mine. Her mouth was pinched, her jaw set, as she sashayed toward the velvet barricade.

"Well … I'm thirsty," Patrick added flippantly before pushing around us to the same busty bartender who'd served Ben.

"Dance with me," Jessamae said again, yanking on my hand. "We need to catch up." I spared one last regret for Ben, alone in the dark, then followed her onto the dance floor.

The trance music was not to my taste, and dancing was something I don't think I'd ever done in public, so when we found a small space free of swirling bodies, I stepped side-to-side like a nervous goon.

"What are you doing here?" Jessamae growled. She draped her wrist over my shoulder and swayed to the beat. "I told Jack to call you November first."

"He was worried about you. I think. Why haven't you called?"

"I was worried that you would come, Frankie. That you would bring your whole household with you. I disposed of my phone. I'm getting quite close to some extremely vigilant mages." She leaned in and watched my friends over my shoulder. Her lips brushed my cheekbone, softer than a makeup brush. "It's not safe here."

"Then I was right to come."

Her eyes took on a familiar, insane gleam when she looked at me. She reached out and stroked my collarbone. "I've missed you." I leaned into her fingers. Just an inch. She tickled the skin along my chin, near my mouth. "It isn't that I'm not glad to see you. The witches here are incredibly secretive and suspicious. I've only gotten as far as I have because Samhain is on the horizon and celebration equates to amiability. A love for our fellow kind. I'm close, Frankie. Very close."

So the mythical connection between Halloween and witchcraft wasn't entirely hokey. My curiosity simmered, but I ignored its heat. "Why are you here? Who are you looking for?"

She continued to dance, albeit resigned. "You met Jack. You know who I'm looking for."

Dear old dad. "But why? What is finding him going to do?"

She surveyed the bar, her hand clasped around my shoulder. "Fine. If you insist on conversation. Come on. They have anything you could possibly dream of."

A dark-skinned man with long braids waited for us, his eyes on Jessamae and his hands planted on the bar. "Evening, darling. Whiskey with a twist?" He grabbed a short glass.

"No, thank you, not tonight. I'll have whatever my friend's having."

He looked expectantly to me. I was distracted by his bouncing pectorals. "Um. I don't know. Just a beer, I guess. Whatever."

His mouth turned down, disappointed. He glanced at Jessamae with a tattle-tale air. "Really?"

"Is there a secret menu or something?" I asked.

"This isn't Starbucks. However, be it blood, bone, or essence. We got it." He gave me a condescending smirk and danced off to get our drinks.

I looked to the VIP booth. If what the bartender said was true, Cleo could be in even more danger than the rest of us. Her hair and teeth—even spit and fingernail clippings—equated to currency on the magical side of the planet. I didn't want to think of what the rest of her would be worth, or the means a witch would go to get it.

She leaned intently toward Ben. He wasn't looking back at her, but I saw his mouth move begrudgingly, answering whatever questions she had. I hoped she'd get through to him. We needed to stay together, and he clearly had no interest in being here. I should apologize. I knew I should. But I wouldn't. Because I was afraid he was right about me.

The bartender returned with our drinks, two bottled Coronas with drooling lime wedges poking out the top. "Twenty even."

"What is it with this place!" I shouted without thinking, reaching for my money pouch. I grasped at nothing. "Shit, I left all of my stuff at the hotel!"

"Here." Jessamae put some cash on the counter and grabbed the bottles.

I shuffled to the VIP section, but she grabbed my arm before I could make it. "No. Not up there. She wants us to sit up there. It's quiet. Easy to observe and overhear the attendees." She led us to a minuscule table meant for standing, mere steps away from the gyrating sweat sacks. It hardly held the two bottles on its surface.

Jessamae didn't waste time. "You need to leave, Frankie. I mean it."

"No."

"Frankie."

"Jessamae."

"I'm safe. I promise you. I'm being very careful."

"If Jack is worried, I should be worried." Her mouth puckered with guilt. "He said you were a regular customer of his? That you've never been gone so long?"

She nodded. "He's been helping me track my sister's whereabouts for years. He contacts me when he gets any leads, but so far, they've all been dead ends."

"And now you're searching for my dad."

She sucked the juice from her lime and smacked her lips. "I am."

"Have you found him?"

She paused with her mouth open, lime juice glossing her chin. Avoiding my question, she looked around the bar.

I needled her, "If you found him, then where the hell is he? Why are you still here?"

"It's complicated. It is very complicated. It will take more time, but now, with you here, I can't—" She closed her eyes and wiped her chin. When she opened them again, they'd dulled dramatically. She tipped her head to the side, toward the VIP's. "What's wrong with your friend?"

I didn't want to accept her change of subject, but her words only added to my bitter feelings. She knew Ben. Had fought alongside him. Had saved him. And she knew we were more than *friends*. "He thinks something bad is going to happen tonight."

She raised a brow, distorting the pale scar there. "Should I be worried?"

I shrugged. "Maybe. But I'm not sure if he's being, I don't know, *unbiased* in his sight."

She tilted her head, chewing on the lime rind. "I don't know how much you should hold that against him." She took a swig from the bottle and the humanness of it caught me off guard. Her eyes still held the fantastic and the strange. If she closed them, we could have been at a pool hall or a bowling alley. "Our affinities are evolutionary in nature, accelerating in ways that help us, *the individual*, specifically. It would make the most sense if his second sight revolved around that which helps or hurts *his* condition."

"You're taking his side?"

She raised her translucent eyebrows. "I am only telling you what I believe."

I made a fart sound with my mouth and finished my drink. I wanted to wallow, and I wanted to be angry. I didn't want to feel worse than I already did for saying what I did. Especially at Jessamae's hand.

"You look lovely tonight," she said. It sounded like a whisper, but it couldn't have been with the thumping bass. My eyes remained on the scuffed surface of the table, but I felt a fingertip trail across my temple. "Elegant. Though I admit, I wish your hair were down. I've missed your curls. So much." She wound her finger around one loose tendril at my ear, and a tremor overtook my hands.

"Thank you," I mumbled. I couldn't look up. I wouldn't. Not when Ben's misery stabbed me like quills from all the way across the room. And meeting those sea glass eyes had thrown my bones right out of my skin in the past. I'd missed Jessamae, how she made me feel, but I refused to lose myself in her and hurt Ben.

Jessamae took her hand back, sensing my reluctance. "You aren't happy." I didn't say anything, because it was obvious. "I know," she said with a tap of her knuckles on the table. She loped toward the bar and the same bartender hurried to fill her order, abandoning another patron. Jessamae must tip well, or he knew her for what she was. She turned around carrying two shot glasses, each filled to the brim. The liquid was faintly yellow and off-putting. It looked like healthy, hydrated pee. "Here." She set a shot in front of me.

"What is it?" I dipped my finger in and sucked the juice from my nail. It burned my gums but soothed my throat. Excruciatingly sweet.

"Joy."

I rolled my tongue around in my mouth, enjoying the tingle. "What?"

"It's called Joy. I'm not privy to the ingredients but I know the fairy of Vegas contributes something of their own making. I've only had it once, but it's an unbelievable feeling." She held her shot glass up and waited.

I turned to the VIP section. Both Cleo and Ben had new, neon-colored drinks. Ben was looking at Cleo when he spoke to her, and that was something. Before they'd finished their glasses, Nicola appeared. She squished them both farther into the booth and took a seat, not with a round of fresh drinks, but a tray. She would get them hammered within the hour.

Cleo, feeling my eyes on her, gave us a quick scan. Her gaze bounced between Jessamae and me a few times until she returned her attention to Ben, grabbing one of the dozen drink options Nicola brought over. Ben drained his glass and took another without a thought or word of thanks. Nicola laughed and drank happily beside them.

"Alright." I clinked my glass against Jessamae's. Real glass. Classy.

"To you," she said with a primal smile, and threw the urine-like liquid back.

I resisted the unwelcome, commercial instinct to say *to us*, and did the same. My head rolled at the warring sensations. My tongue grew fuzzy in my mouth, both numb and crackling. My cheeks burned and cooled intermittently. I licked my teeth, which stung from the chill. The lining of my throat felt like electrical wiring. And finally, a pleasant taste. Floral, spring roses. "Wow."

"Wow," Jessamae repeated, beaming. She reached for my neck and wrenched me in close, kissing my cheek. Her fingers continued to brush along my skin. She pulled a few more curls free from my bun and spun them.

Her touch was warm and rough—it rattled me, literally rattled me. My teeth chattered against the vibrations of her.

I combed through her straight locks. "Your hair is so straight. No wind." I giggled at my gibberish, and Jessamae threw her head back in delight.

"Now, we dance for real! No pretending this time!" She grabbed my hand and skipped to the middle of the dance floor. People floated out of our way like the most beautiful tufts of seaweed, and gravity lost its hold on me. I danced. I moved with nothing but the desire to move. I laughed that I was afraid of these people and this music before now. Their nakedness, their hair and their thighs and their cheeks; I wanted to touch them.

Jessamae's hands were on my shoulders, and I felt her waves in my skeleton, like the sea had entered my body. I moved in closer to her, wanting more of the ocean inside.

A figure approached, wiggling in like a caterpillar. They had no face but their shoulders were wide. They thrust into our hips until they pushed their way between us. Jessamae's calloused fingers hung over the wide shoulders, dangling before me like balloon strings. I pulled them and they sprung back into place. They made me laugh.

The person sandwiched between us was rumbling like an earthquake. No pain, no hurt. A useless happy thing, a shimmying obstacle and nothing more.

Jessamae released my hand and put it on the figure's waist. It was a human man, I realized with a smile. He was dancing with us. I watched Jessamae from around his bicep. She put her free hand on his chest. She was hungry. I felt it snap its teeth. And then I felt something else, a seeping, leaking, sickness grow in the stranger between us. It grew and grew, like steam above a juicy steak. I wanted it. I licked my mouth and static sparked across my lip.

I touched a ridge in his back directly across his innards from Jessamae's hand. I sucked at the sickness she created. It was foreign, a new flavor outside of any pain I'd tasted before. It was thick, cloying, no blood for the salt. I slurped at the flavor until it shrank to nothing, and I rejected the alien impulse to wipe my mouth. But as soon as my treat emptied, it returned, blossoming like budding fruit. I drank him dry again. And again.

Jessamae and I passed his pain, his life, his weakness, his strength, between us like a cigarette. It ebbed more loudly than the music beating the air. Until I couldn't even hear it anymore. I only heard her and the meal we shared.

I was wobbly. I was full. The walls were spinning. I was spinning. The man between us crumpled to the ground like a bag of fresh cut grass. Green. I stumbled over the hill of him, and Jessamae cradled me in her arms. She held most of my weight and the scene changed in an instant. I was again at the wall, my back pressed against it. It was warm as bath water. Jessamae had two new cups with two new colors in her hands. The surface of the colorful liquid twinkled. Galaxies. I floated away, far away, all the way up to space. I drank what I was offered.

Sour, so sour it hurt. I gagged. I couldn't feel the racking of my gut from the outside, but I felt it behind my eyes. My head plunged forward violently. Without warning, a blast of energy ignited from my feet up, and I was capable of anything. Everything.

Jessamae put her hands on either side of me, rolling her hips like boulders down a mountain, imminent and devastating. I danced with her.

She took my face. Those eyes found mine. Sea-glass.

She kissed me.

And through her, past her skull and brains, sparkly neurons, I watched Ben in the VIP booth, surrounded with dots of colorful liquid, crumble with the most appetizing agony I'd ever seen.

9

I HAD NEVER FELT WORSE in my entire pathetic existence. I was afraid to open my eyes, afraid of what I'd see. I groveled to my body, to the universe, to fall back asleep. To unconsciously eradicate the nails in my brain, the nausea in my gut, and the prickles of my sensitive flesh. I wanted to die. I was angry that I hadn't already. This was hell. I'd gone to hell.

I pried open one eye—miraculously without a crowbar—and cringed. An overhead bulb hung naked and bright above me. I covered my face and dragged my ruined mass onto my elbows. I almost vomited right then, but swallowed the bile and peeked between my fingers. I thought I was still in the club, but in a room I didn't recognize. The floor and walls were the same, though they had lost all their glamour and mystery in the harsh light. Crude drawings covered the walls, and the floor was warped and wet.

I looked down at myself. I was still wearing my dress, even my shoes. I reached up my skirt and huffed a breath of relief when I found underwear.

I'd been sprawled on the floor like a factory mannequin. Jessamae was in the corner, bent at a forty-five-degree angle on her side, and I felt another wave of relief. We were both alive. I wasn't entirely sure why that came as a shock, but it did. Glittery foreign bodies littered the room, like the card I'd been given come to life. Some were naked, some were covered in tarps or sheets. All were unconscious.

I heaved my body to my hips and, steeling myself, got to my feet. I tripped into the wall but roused no one. My feet were heavy as I careened out of the body room and entered the main dancefloor of the club. I looked back, and for the first time, noticed five identical doors behind me—private rooms. There was a cleaning crew mopping and wiping at multicolored stains around the place. They paid me no mind.

Exiting through the main entrance, the open front wall, I shielded myself from the sun with my elbows, wishing I had my gas station shades with me. Tourists paid me no attention because I wasn't the first one to appear from a club like a ghoul into the light of day.

I couldn't remember exactly how far the hotel was from The Harvest, but began walking the distance, pitching forward and falling back at random intervals. I stopped down a gray alley to vomit behind a dumpster, sticking my fingers down my throat until I was satisfied at the puddle. I almost felt better, though I could smell myself now.

By the time I saw the Bellagio, my headache had quelled to a dull hum and my nausea was gone. I rubbed the mascara from my eyes as I entered the building, leaving black smears on my knuckles.

Stepping off the elevator, I realized I didn't have a key. I didn't have a phone. I didn't have anything. I hoped the other three were okay and that they were all together. I had no idea what happened to them after that shot. That Joy. And then the second shot, the Energy, plus a third shot and a fourth.

I knocked on our door. I waited. When no one answered, I knocked again, assuming they were as hungover as I was. Crawly anxiety entered my chest cavity. It dug at my tissue and veins, trying to break out. I knocked again and put my ear to the door. I heard something. Steps. The door flung open into the room.

Cleo rushed past me in a blur. She was wearing sweatpants and a hoodie. I didn't know she owned leisurewear outside of her workout attire. She wiped her face as she sprinted for the elevator bank. "Cleo! Hey, Cleo!"

She didn't turn to my voice.

"Where are you going?"

The elevator arrived and she disappeared within it. For an insane moment, I wondered if I actually *had* died last night. That I was a ghost.

A monster sigh came from the hotel room. Ben stood in the center of the living space, his feet bare on the marble. He had no shirt, just a pair of loose Nike shorts. His eyes were red. "Hey, Frankie."

"Frankie ..." I whispered. Why did my own name hit my ear wrong? The awful memory of Ben, furious Ben, on his back porch after Pamela's funeral. He had called me Francesca then.

Ben's pain seeped into me though we were a good distance apart. It was overwhelming. A wave of regret and resentment and betrayal. Emotions. But still, I felt them as if they clobbered his body. I smelled them. I tripped forward, ready to apologize for ... something. Something had happened with Jessamae, something I couldn't quite remember. I would explain. The drinks ...

But as I opened my mouth, I took in Ben's wounded pallet more clearly. Self-hatred. Chalky and strong self-hatred. I knew it like I knew my own emotions. "What—" I turned back to the elevator, expecting Cleo to return with a coffee or a scone. But she had just left. Why was I anxious for her return? Now, right now.

Ben's arms hung at his side. Not rubbing his head, not crossing his chest. The stance made him seem thinner, smaller. "What happened? Is everyone—" I met his eyes. I wanted to vomit again. I didn't understand the awful, nightmarish anticipation. "Okay." My brain painfully connected the narrative—our fight, Cleo's intervention, Jessamae, Cleo fleeing the hotel room in rare tears. Ben's face now. Ben, above all else, terribly heart-achingly afraid.

I didn't want to say it. I didn't have to say it.

"No." I lost my balance and hit the wall. "Please, no."

I fell. I was surprised the ground rose to meet me, to catch me. That I didn't plummet down, down, down.

ॐ

BEN KNEELED BESIDE ME. He didn't touch me. I didn't want him to. I planted my hands on the tile—ice cold—ready to run from this place. From Ben. From my worst fear taking form and beating me to death. The mental picture of them—of Cleo and Ben together, as he and I had been only two days ago—made me want to scream. To explode. To be nothing.

"Frankie, please. Let me talk to you. Let me explain."

Just what I had said, all those months ago, when I'd hurt him. When I *spent an afternoon* with Jessamae … not while I fucked her.

"No."

"I didn't mean for anything to happen! Neither did she! I don't think we actually slept together. Everything is all … fuzzy. I can't see anything. I can't think. But I didn't want this, I didn't—"

"Then what did you do?" My voice was as cold as the tile. Colder. Cold as a body in the ground.

"What?"

"If you didn't sleep together, what did you do?"

He didn't answer, his mouth hung open as if he hoped answers would crawl inside it.

"God," I said, covering my face with my hands. It was like I could see it happening right in front of me, like he was kissing her neck right here on the floor. They were alone. Not like

Jessamae and me. They had the hotel all to themselves. They could have done anything.

Ben reached for me.

"Don't!" I scuttled backward on my hands and knees, too dizzy to stand.

"Come on! Stop, just stop." He grabbed my wrists fiercely. "Do you think I liked watching you with Jessamae? Was I just supposed to ignore that? Accept that? How do you think it felt to watch you choose to be with her over me? You kissed her! You fucking kissed her … after how we'd spent the night before."

Despite my aversion and renewed stomach pain, I tried to sort through the fog of the evening, after I'd swallowed the yellow stuff she'd bought me. We were dancing … with a man … he'd collapsed. We had used him to the point of collapse.

"Oh god." He hadn't died. I would have known. But he'd collapsed. Then … we kissed. Ben saw us kiss … Ben's delicious pain. I'd said those horrible things, then I kissed Jessamae while he watched.

Did I do this? Did I do *all* of this? "Oh my god." I yanked at my wrists, but he only tightened his grip on me.

"When I saw you with her at the bar, I just—I couldn't do it! I hated the possibilities for you. And for her. I didn't want to see." Our arms were shaking. I didn't know which one of us caused it. "I drank. And I drank more. Anything to blind me to what might happen between you. Nicola brought me more. The drinks were … different. They tasted so good. And I felt better. Then she wouldn't leave us the fuck alone! And Cleo, she—we left. We came back here. We were so … drunk. But I didn't feel like drunk is supposed to. And we were both so … sad."

"You were both sad. That excuses it? It's okay now?"

"That's not what I'm saying, I'm just saying I wasn't looking to … sleep with her."

I started to cry. I had known what we were yelling about, of course I did, in my bone marrow I knew. But to hear him say it. If I thought I'd been empty before, he had dug so much deeper.

"I kissed Jessamae. I did, and I'm sorry! But nothing else happened! And you—" Two beautiful bodies writhing together, undulating in our sheets. His breath. Her moan. "You just—" a hitched sob cut me off.

"I'm sorry! I'm so sorry I hurt you. But Frankie, it was *killing* me. I can't pretend you aren't breaking my heart every time you're with her! And to kiss her right in front of my goddamn face!"

"I didn't know what I was doing! I was ready to reject any advances from Jessamae in that club! And it was working! Then I had this drink! It wasn't normal. This yellow drink—"

"That's bullshit, Frankie!" Ben stood and threw my hands down in the process. "That's bullshit and you know it. You might have been swayed, influenced, uninhibited, whatever, but don't lie to me and tell me that your relationship with Jessamae is platonic! Stop lying to us both!"

I got to my knees and wrapped my hands around the back of my neck. "I was drunk, high, I don't know!"

"And what if I said the same? I have no idea what that bartender gave me, what Nicola gave me—"

"But I didn't fuck Jessamae in the same hotel room where you and I—" a wave of embarrassment struck me like an arrow. "Where we were together for the first time." In the shower. Which meant … "Was it in our bed? Ben?" As much as I wanted to hurt him with the question, I couldn't bear that answer. I heard Ben's name in Cleo's mouth, in her beautiful voice … I summoned my strength and met his eyes. Then I shattered all over again. I folded into myself and shattered.

Ben pulled me out of the position, forced me to look at him though I fought him and screamed. He gritted his teeth before his lip began to quiver. He eventually bit down on it hard, but his eyes shone with unshed tears. "Frankie … I only want you."

A strangled noise escaped me. I wanted to hear those words from him. I needed them. It was as if he were reading a script I'd written, a script I created when I'd played out this very moment in my head. My worst nightmare. In my imagination, I knew it would hurt. I practically fantasized about how much it would hurt in the horrible Cleo/Ben scenarios I'd conjured when I couldn't sleep. But such a pain was unimaginable. How stupid I was to think I could predict it.

"Please, Frankie." He reached for my hands again, and without thinking, I let him. My attention was on my own hollowness. On each breath moving in and out of my mouth. On surviving this. "I drank to ease what was eating me alive! Then I drank to dull my sight. I couldn't stand the possibility of seeing you together. I drank everything I was given. I didn't care who gave it to me or what it was. And Cleo—" he clenched his jaw, looking to the ground. "We were both so hurt. I would have done anything to just … stop. Stop feeling the way I did! I can promise you, I *promise* you, it will never happen again. We don't want to be together! I want you." He kissed my fingers. Over and over. "Tell me there's nothing between you two. Tell me again. You're done with her. Say it. Please, Frankie."

I shook my head. I couldn't stand it. But I couldn't stop him from what he was about to say.

"I love you."

The strangled noise burst from me in a shriek, and my lungs nearly popped with its release. That he would say it now—for the first time, in the dead center of such turmoil—was the cruelest thing he could have done to me. I took my hands from his and scrambled to the leather pouch on the carpet. Betty was circled beside it, as if she knew we were leaving. I guided her inside between my pitiful cries, then put a hand to my chest, as if to soothe them from the outside.

"Frankie! We need to talk about this!"

Unable to resist, and following some twisted masochistic tendency, I whispered, "Why did you even tell me?"

He faltered a step. "What?"

"Why did you tell me?" I hooked Betty's pouch over my shoulder. "You knew how this would go. There is," I swallowed the lump in my throat, "zero chance it would have gone any differently."

Ben moved closer, and his body heat stuck to me. I was sick at the comfort he offered. "You had to know. I can hardly live with myself having done it. I couldn't live with myself if I kept it a secret. I want you. I want you more than anything and it's the only way. To tell you. I had to!" A tear finally escaped, it dripped down his cheek, striping his face in a shimmer. He dropped to his knees at my feet. He held my hands to his forehead before kissing each of my knuckles in turn.

His princess.

I couldn't fend off my undoing much longer.

"Frankie, I love you. I love you so goddamn much. Please." He was the one shaking. Sobbing. The ridges of his tattoos rubbed against my fingers. "We can do this, Frank. It's you and me."

Unleashed tears curved around his jaw, and I remembered the single drop of water I'd followed along the topography of his body in the shower. A body Cleo had seen. A body she'd tasted and felt and loved. A flash of her face made me flinch. A woman, to which, I could never hope to compete. I never had.

And to know that I had all but shoved Ben into her arms …

I took my hands back with a broken heart—a broken spleen, a deflated lung, with all my insides spoiled and bleeding. I stepped around his kneeling form, and his hands clawed at his face. I nearly made it to the door when the room erupted.

The dining chairs flew back from the table, battering the walls and skidding across the tile. The cushions of the sofa soared near the ceiling like large leather birds. The framed paintings whipped to the ground as if caught in a hurricane. The doors slammed open; the television cracked against the living room rug. And all the while Ben kneeled, in the eye of the storm, his head bowed.

I shut the door softly behind me.

IT WAS HARDER than ever to get drunk—human drunk, not that blessed/cursed shit I was last night—but I was up to the challenge. I still had the cash Ben gave me yesterday, and I tucked it into the top of my dress with a small well of shame. I raked a forearm across my dripping eyes and found my way to the hotel bar. I yelled at the woman across the way, "A shot!" And with my mind on Cleo, added, "Bourbon!"

The woman gave me a nod but returned to the customer in front of her. I pounded my hand on the bar, "Hey!" And when she threw me an offended glare, I waved my stack of cash in the air. She excused herself with a finger and arrived promptly with my drink.

I tossed it back with a wince and a gag. "Another."

She raised her eyebrows but said nothing as she poured a second. After that was gone, I pushed a ball of money her way. "Keep it coming, but mix something in this time." She was efficient, and for that, I dropped another twenty on the counter. She put a bourbon and Coke on a little green napkin and slid it forward.

I had nine more before Patrick showed up. "Oh. So you're alive then."

He must have been trying to call. I found my phone in the pouch after I got to the bar, but it was dead. I also sensed Betty's need to be held, to comfort me, but I didn't deserve anything like that.

Patrick must be out fucking his latest fancy or drinking himself stupid to have found me down here. Not that I had any room to talk. He sat his were-ass next to me and I wanted to kick him.

"Can I get ya' a little somethin'?" I asked, wagging my glass in the air.

He shook his head. "No, I'm alright." His refusal made me

feel pathetic. I finished my glass and pounded my hand on the wood under it—the signal the bartender and I had developed for more, please and thank you.

"What you want? A dance?"

Patrick was dressed annoyingly well, his dark topcoat accentuating the blue sweater underneath, though he still wore a baseball cap.

"I don't want anything. Well, that's not true." He smiled. "I want everything. But, right now, I want to ask a favor."

I spread my arms in invitation.

"That you stay here. In the hotel. As far as the casino and as high as the rooftop bar. But *here*. I know your phone is dead—"

I barked out a mean laugh. "Yeah? How you know that?"

"Look." He took a sip of my whiskey, and I did kick him. "I'm not here to convince you to talk to him. Though I can be very convincing." He winked at me, and I almost smiled. He was treating me like I had never fallen apart inside that room, like I hadn't dissolved like sea foam. His kindness burned my throat in the same way my tears had. "He'll drive me crazy if he doesn't know where you are, so please, for my sake. Just stick around." He slid a hotel key across the bar. "The room's been cleaned up. You won't have to worry about that. And I'm getting a different room for him and me, so Ben won't be there. I swear."

Hearing his name was a bitch of a charley horse and I cringed against the ache. Patrick took my hand gently. "Take care, baby girl. I mean that." He covered both our hands with his other and gave a subtle bow before leaving the bar.

Fresh tears started building in my ducts and I slapped my hand on the counter.

I would decide if I stayed in the hotel or not, and I would leave whenever the hell I felt like it. But the thought of a toilet to pee in was too enticing a possibility to walk away from just yet.

I took my glass with me and left some money on the counter without bothering to count it. I fumbled around in my heels until I felt confident in my footing and roamed in the general direction of the lobby. Missing the elevators somehow, I wound up in the casino. I circled what I thought was the same herd of green tables multiple times until I grew tired of the practice and hunkered down on the floor. Pouring my latest drink over my open mouth, I spilled a bit down my neck and dropped the glass to the heinous carpet beneath me.

Cleo. Why did it have to be Cleo? "Because how could it not be?" I asked. "You're the biggest ... idiot ... in all of Las Vegas. Of all the idiots in Las Vegas!"

I questioned every moment I was apart from them for the last few months, for the last six years. Every shift at work, every long shower. One quiet voice in my head argued that it was last night and only last night. But I felt a sick and savage satisfaction at the possibilities. The attraction, the desire, had to have been there all along. Vindication. "Right?"

How could he ever find me beautiful now?

～～～

"Excuse me." The voice came from above. God, maybe. I must have closed my eyes. "Do you need some help?"

A waitress in a short skirt bent over me. She had a tray of drinks balanced on one arm.

"Um, yes, yes I do." I used the wall to get myself back on my feet. I kept one hand against it until I was sure everything would stay put. "I am looking for the elevators. Would you show them to me?"

The waitress nodded with a nervous smile and gestured which way to go.

It wasn't a long walk, and I felt a tiny bubble of pride at getting so close on my own. "I'll give you twenty dollars for two of those." I pointed to the drinks on her tray. She didn't think long before she handed me a mimosa and a glass of clear liquid with a lime. I peeled a twenty from my chest. It was wet with my sweat.

I watched my own eyes in the elevator mirror as I rode up to our floor. My visage was so terrible, it competed with only one other night in my life—after I'd been in a kitchen fire and nearly burned alive.

Mascara spread from under my eyes to my cheekbones. Lipstick was on my teeth and smudged into the corners of my mouth. Though the bulk of my hair remained in its elastic, just about all my ends had escaped and were sticking out from my head like a grungy tiara. But that wasn't why I looked awful. My defeat was something you could see. My loss weighty and big, like a hiker's backpack. I was alone. "Not very pretty, Princess," my mouth said.

The elevator slid open with a dingy sound. As I flopped down the hall, I remembered my night with Jessamae. I'd wanted her to kiss me. Denying it was a pointless thing. Despite the club, despite the shot, I'd wanted it. Ben was right. Everything was always my fault.

It took a few tries to get the door to accept the key. Finicky. Both drinks were squished in my elbow, splashing to the floor.

I heard a shower running from the back of the suite. Drinking the mimosa in one swallow, I chucked the glass in the sink. It broke with a dainty tinkling. I stomped through the French doors and kneed open the bathroom, intending to throw Ben from the room.

Sipping at my second glass—"Ack, gin"—steam swamped me. Cleo was leaning over the white vanity, her mouth open, her eyes unsteady. She was in the same sweats she'd been wearing when she'd run off this morning.

Tripping toward the shower, I dropped my drink on the bathmat. It didn't break. I rolled it away with my boot.

I found Cleo's eyes in the mirror. Honey. Amber. Gold. Then I found my own reflected eyes. Dirt and moss. Bruised apples.

"How could you?" I whispered to my own face in the mirror.

Neither woman answered. After too much silence, I peeked. She didn't even acknowledge me. Her focus remained solely on her own face. She hadn't acknowledged me, I realized, since last night. "How could you do that to me?"

Her mouth opened and her brows came together. "How could I?"

"Yes."

She turned to face me. "How could *you*?"

She looked at me like I'd wronged her. Like she'd never forgive me. I didn't understand. "It was just a kiss. One kiss. You and Ben did … a lot more than that."

She leaned back against the counter, and I felt insignificant. She'd never looked at me with such disgust. I straightened on my heels. She had hurt me, and I wasn't about to let her forget it.

She spoke slowly, enunciating every syllable. "When it comes to Ben and me, it isn't more. It's not a relationship, it's not wanting. It's not passion, or need, or fantasy, or *craving*. But you and Jessamae consider no one, nothing, but *your* craving. No matter the destruction you cause in your wake."

She took a deep breath and closed her eyes. She was in pain. Why was she so upset by what I'd done? When I'd abandoned the two of them to spend the day with Jessamae over the summer, she'd been the understanding one. She'd played with my hair as I'd fallen asleep.

"I'm not talking about that." My voice shook. "How could *you* do that to *me*? You're like a sister to me. I thought you gave a shit one way or the other. I know you're angry that I hurt Ben, but—"

"It looks like we've disappointed each other then."

"How does my love life affect you? What did I do?" Ben had said they were *both* alone, he and Cleo. That they were *both* sad. "Did Patrick say something to you? Is it because Patrick's been sleeping around? But you hate him." She did … but there was another person who she seemed to get along with from the very beginning. Who she traveled out here to see. Who she dressed up for last night. She'd looked so beautiful. She'd been so eager —to see *her*. "Cleo. Do you—"

"Get out."

"Cleo. Do you have feelings—"

"GET OUUUUT!"

She shrieked at a pitch, frequency, and volume of which I've never known. Her hair lifted from her neck like Medusa's snakes before the mirror burst like an eggshell and the shower door cracked from top to bottom. Glass filled the sink and dusted the grout between the tiles. The light flashed off and on in a strobe-like effect. I crouched down on my ankles and held my fingers to my ears—my hands were sticky with drink. Then I ran from the room at full tilt. The wailing followed me down the hallway.

An old couple was stepping off the elevator and I pushed past them, my fingers still in my ears. I jabbed at the lobby button with my boot, along with a few others.

Promise forgotten—or ignored—I raced through the lobby, through the casino. I ran from the screaming, from the memories, from the destruction. From the hotel.

10

I DIDN'T SLOW until I was two casinos away. I'd never seen Cleo do that, I doubted she had ever seen herself do that. It was a haunting thing, demonic and angelic both.

I was right, and I felt like an imbecile for not seeing it sooner. Cleo had feelings for Jessamae. My only excuse was that Cleo, as a generality, showed about as much vulnerability as Mount Rushmore. Ever since she and Jessamae had worked together to cover the tracks leading to Gabriel's body, they'd gotten along.

I cataloged the evidence in my mind: 1.) The two of them discussing obscure literature, the passion for it, the commonality. 2.) Cleo giving Jessamae one of her blankets. 3.) Cleo casually asking about my feelings for Jessamae, encouraging me to commit to Ben. 4.) I didn't know where Jessamae was for days after our fight with Paimon, but she was at our house along with the others once I finally left my room.

Had the two of them had contact? Had Jessamae been in Cleo's room the entire time I was in mine? I remembered the tension between them when Jessamae left that day. I remembered the way Cleo said Jessamae's name after Paimon ambushed her mind, such concern.

Though I wanted Ben—*had* wanted him—I couldn't ignore the uncomfortable wriggling in my midsection at the thought of Cleo and Jessamae together. How rotten, how egotistical, or unbelievably big-headed was I to believe I had claim to them both? I had driven Ben to pulverize my own heart because of it. And the anger I felt at Cleo, at her having them both when they were both *mine* ... it was real.

How could things have gotten so irrevocably tangled? The answer kneed me in the groin. Because I told Ben I'd be with him but kept Jessamae dangling on the line.

But I had told her what I wanted—Ben—and she ignored it! She called her and me *inevitable*. I took that to mean our connection was deeper than crushes or attraction. It was almost biological. So it didn't have to be romantic. It didn't! I'd made my choice.

And now, it didn't matter ... I'd ruined everything.

My buzz lingered. The number of drinks I'd pounded was a mystery, but I was grateful for the numbness that came with them. Onlookers knew I was drunk—I still wore my tight dress and heeled boots from the night before—but I couldn't spare a drop of insecurity for all these strangers. The drunk would evaporate eventually, just like everyone else.

I was almost out of money, but I could afford a room at Motel 6. There had to be a slew of motels to pick from a stone's throw from the Strip. Or ... I could afford at least five more drinks.

Assuming I could sleep on the floor again if needed, I turned in the direction of The Harvest, wishing I could apport like Jessamae. I felt a twinge of fear at the thought of seeing her at the club, but it didn't last. I wanted to be alone, almost more than anything. But to feel wanted, to feel beautiful, to feel worth something, even if that was only some attention, that was irresistible.

Being a Monday—and midafternoon, judging by the blazing sunlight—the line out front was itty bitty. I still didn't feel much like standing in it, so I shambled between the Greek pillars without a second glance.

"Hey, hey, hey!" The security guard cornered me. He was

clearly B squad—his arms were boneless and stretched out, his gingery mustache patchy and soft. "There's a line! Do you have ID?"

"Do *you* have ID?" I jabbed a finger into his baby chest.

"Who the hell do you think you are?" Rage sparked in his eyes. This was a man who compensated for his lack of muscle tone with hatred and bullying. He wouldn't be made to look weak.

"She's with me." Nicola pushed the guard back with her height alone. Her smile had his tail tucked between his legs. Her dress was simple—long-sleeved, skirt down to the ankle. White, blindingly white. Her lips were as red and juicy as poisoned apples. "Come here, Francesca, let's get you some water." She winked at the rubbery guard who squished his nose at me one last time.

"I don't need water," I muttered, plopping my ass down on a barstool.

"Of course not, sweetie, it's all about de-escalation. You can have whatever you want, provided you've got the cash." I bobbed my head in understanding, reaching into my chest for the last of my money. "Good girl," she said and disappeared behind the bar.

The same handsome bartender from last night appeared before me. "Do you ever get a day off?" I asked. He didn't respond. "Whiskey and Coke." He pulled a tall glass from beneath the counter and poured a dollop of Coke at the bottom, filling the rest with whiskey. He smacked his lips in an air kiss and handed it over.

Even after as much as I'd had today, the gulp of liquor eroded my mouth, and I nearly threw up all over the bar. Telling myself to sip slower, I rested my face in my hands.

"Here, you need to eat something, baby." Something scraped across the bar. I uncovered my eyes to a bowl of fruit. I'd never seen fruit in a bar before, and poked at it, expecting plastic. A mix of berries—blue, rasp, and black—as well as a few dark cherries surrounded two yellow pears.

"You serve this in a bar?" I asked the hand with sharp nails.

"In drinks, yes we do," Nicola answered, taking a seat on the stool next to me.

Feeling exceedingly like one of those sad dogs on TV commercials, I fingered the berries around the bowl. "Thanks." I selected one of the pears and rolled it between my hands. I couldn't block the image of pear juice clinging to Ben's pink lip before we'd kissed in the mountains. An image so inequitably good that it made me squeeze my eyes against the sting.

"Eat it." The demand opened my eyes. "The sun is out, and you are distractingly hammered. It's depressing. And depressing is bad for business."

I belched and lifted my lip, offended by her honesty and her bossiness. Desperate for another taste of what I once had, I brought the pear to my mouth, wishing the sweetness of it came from his lips. It was mushy but delicious. I swallowed too quickly, choking a bit, before pushing it down. The meat of it wasn't pale as expected—there was a periwinkle tinge to it.

Ben moved to the back of my mind as I devoured the pear. I was down to the core in seconds. When I tried to eat that too, Nicola pulled the stem from my hands. "That's better. Something in your stomach. Wash it down." She tipped the remnants of my drink between my lips like you would a baby goat, and I swallowed, unable and uninterested in protesting.

My head dipped on my spine, heavy. I was overcome with fatigue. I tried to shake it off, standing on crooked legs. Nicola raised her hands, her expression alight with surprise. "Where are you going? Sit down."

"To find Jessamae." I pushed her. "We need to talk." My eyelids fell of their own volition, not that I could make sense of what I saw anyway. Blurry. A mess.

I tried to keep hold of consciousness, reaching out for sensory information. I lurched around the outside of the building. There were fewer people than I remembered. They seemed to flicker in and out of existence like lightbulbs in need of replacement. I found the alley, or *an* alley, and toddled down it. Eventually, I'd find the door hidden in the brick wall.

"Smells like … wet garbage … n' … pee. Sounds like …" I strained my ears, working to regain control of my mouth. "Shoes. Feels like …" I closed my eyes as I rounded a corner and conjured my touch receptors, noted the hard asphalt beneath me. "Solid." The chafe of my dress strap against my arm. "Itchy." And something else. Spicy and prickly, it pushed against the back of my legs, my bare neck. I turned around clumsily.

The security guard had followed me down the alley and was practically frothing at the mouth. "Where are you headed? It's still early." His voice was high-pitched with a slight southern drawl, like a Bible Belt mom. He crossed his arms, blocking the exit, though not effectively. Tiny Tim.

The weakness had yet to leave me, so I took my time before speaking. "You think I'm scared of you?" After all, he was only a man, a human. Nothing compared to the nightmares I'd seen.

He kept his arms at his chest but took a few steps in my direction. His anger wrapped around him like a wet, white sheet. "Aren't you?"

I snorted but didn't turn around again. Man or not, exposing my back was not a snub I was willing to make.

"I don't know where you got that fucking attitude." He reached into the pocket of his cargo shorts, and I automatically stepped back. Whatever was in that pocket, it wouldn't be nice. I couldn't see what it was until he triggered the spring. A switchblade. "But I don't want to hurt you." I couldn't remember hearing a bigger lie. "Just follow my instruction, and everything's going to be fine."

I should have seen this coming. He got off on control, and any damage that came to me was my fault for not recognizing his authority. "Leave me alone." I prayed for sobriety.

"Do what you're told, and I'll do just that." He gestured

further down the alley as if he were holding a door open for me, gentlemanly.

I clutched at Betty's pouch, spinning it on its strap until it rested on my tailbone. I didn't want her hurt, and I had nothing to cushion a blow but my own stomach. "Don't think so." He was trying to lead me to a secondary location. At least here, the tourists on the street would hear my screams. If they chose to intervene was anyone's guess.

The guard spun the knife between his fingers, the blade glinting in the sun. "Go on, now," he said, only a foot from me.

I wanted to comply, honestly, but my feet were still disconnected from my brain. When I went to walk in the right direction, I blundered toward the brick wall. Before my body found support in the building, the guard cracked his knuckles into my cheek.

I buckled. The stars did nothing for my disorientation. Though he was a smaller man, he became a skyscraper now. The back of my dress was soaked in water from the floor of the alley. I felt very cold. "You aren't listening. I'd try that if I were you. Now get up."

I flexed my jaw back and forth. The whiskey hadn't numbed the strike and pain lanced my skull. I pulled my ankles beneath me but had even more trouble standing than before. "Need a second." In my mind, I stood, but my body didn't respond.

"You stand when *I* tell you to. Stand!" I lifted my head, looking to the mouth of the alley through the black fog. I saw nothing. And when I remained on the ground, in the shadow of the building beside me, he kicked me. His boot hooked around my rib, the toe at my spine. My bones were all thrown inward and struggled to align again.

The man lowered himself to the balls of his feet. His mouth was in my ear. I couldn't turn my head—the fog had taken me—but I felt his breath on my face. He leaned in close, too close. The blade scratched against the baby hairs of my neck. I wondered if I was still breathing. I couldn't taste the oxygen. "Little girls need to do what they're told." The whisper slithered into me. The sentiment hit with such resentment, such hatred, I wondered if someone, somewhere, had ever said the exact same thing to him. He folded himself in close, poking his knife into the blush of my cheek. Blood welled. I asked the universe to thicken the oncoming darkness, that it would blot out what happened next.

He cupped his hand around my neck viciously, and his peppery wounds exploded under my skin. He was tired—who wasn't? —but there was an illness there, on his spine. As his grip tightened around my throat I could taste it, a tumor. It was small at this stage. I was briefly curious as to whether he knew. Then I realized I couldn't care less.

I turned my head without issue and found his eyes. They were a beautiful sky blue. They widened as I touched. His tumor erased my confusion and his hatred for me swirled around my lungs like the scent of a candle. I was eased, healed, strengthened. I lifted my hands to his bristly chin, breathing him in. I consumed him. His sickness and his ill will. A buffet of flavors and smells, so nasty, so good. I ate until there was almost nothing left of him, until he was nearly empty.

I pressed his shoulders until he lay on his back. Climbing onto his stomach, I leaned down over his blissful face and pressed my lips to his ear. "You should be afraid of *me*." His eyebrows lifted and his mouth gaped open. I smelled his tangy fear before I saw it reach his eyes. I let it electrify my bones as I took the knife from his docile grasp, spun it in the sun, and plunged it into his chest.

I did it again. I did it again. I caused damage faster than I could ever replenish. All the while his blood coated my hands in a familiar wave. It was warmer than a handshake. It welcomed me back. After dozens and dozens of cuts, and dozens more, I stopped. Full.

I folded the knife and slipped it where my cash used to be. I licked the stuff from my fingers—there was so much, I doubted they'd ever be clean again.

Hungry? mocked a death rattle over my shoulder. *Piggy?*

I scrambled off the security guard and backed into the wall, moving without difficulty, sober as a bird. And absolutely petrified.

Swinging Betty forward, I unzipped the bag. Betty's length fell into my lap, and she gave me immediate comfort. I was hurting her, petting her scales too roughly, and I worked to relax my hands.

A void grew in the alley. Without my regenerative skin against his, the security guard had bled to death.

Oh no! Did Piggy take things a little too far?

With Betty cradled in my hands, I got to my knees, then my feet. My breathing was haggard and small. I roved the space, the knot in my stomach pushing against my heart. Sweat dewed my palms, slicking Betty's scales.

"Where are you?" I shouted. Feeling Paimon's stare, knowing it was on me. It never left.

A light blinked on from a low basement window, half of which was exposed above the street line. I looked down into the cloudy glass, beyond afraid—sick.

Two silver eyes watched me from a dark face hiding in that basement. With a smile, the face backed away, further into the underground room. I lowered myself to my ankles, tears stinging my eyes, hating that I needed to see. I always had to see.

"Paimon?"

Miss Hughes. It appears you are in need of my services? Again? The kind voice resounded behind me, near the security guard's body.

I didn't rise from the ground. I didn't pull my attention from the basement. "Stop it," I whispered to the window.

You'll be needing a casket, but please don't fret over details like that. To fit any budget, anything can be a casket! A coffin, a coffee tin … a car. The sound of coals popping, a whispering like clothes blown around on the line. It was coming closer. *Would you like to schedule a wake or funeral? That way his loved ones can pay their final respects. Or you could always leave him here, for the worms and the beetles. You could set him on fire ... You could always set him on fire, Miss Hughes.*

Slipping Betty back into my bag, I rose to stand. This would be so ugly, and I didn't want to subject her to it. The silver eyes once again gleamed from the window, eagerly awaiting the show. I turned and faced the dead funeral director standing in the deepest shadows of the alley.

Gabriel Perez wore his best suit, the one he'd donned for Pamela's funeral. His neck was shaved, though flabby. His hair was gelled, though thinning. His hands were clasped at his rounded belly and his smile was genuine, full of consideration for me.

Then his jowls started to stretch, his jaw dripping down like taffy. His smile was just as sincere as it had always been as the skin of his cheek flopped to the floor. His teeth glimmered like pearls inside an oyster made of bloody, stringy tissue. His gums were crimson, then the coppery brown of a new penny, then black.

His shoulder deflated, getting lower and lower on his torso, the wool of his jacket dimpling. In seconds, the whole of his arm slid to the alley floor, curling around itself like a burst rubber hose. There was no blood. He was already dead. The arm was wrapped in the pale-yellow shirt I'd last seen him in; it was soaked and clinging to his eroding skin.

A flower petal stuck to his eyelid.

Then he burst into flames.

His suit shriveled, flimsy as paper against the fire. His skin curled up into his eye sockets. His eyes began to melt. They dripped down his cheeks like candle wax.

You can always set him on fire, Miss Hughes. The jaw rolled and the teeth fell out as he spoke, littering the asphalt like loose change. He walked forward on burning legs, the soles of his loafers leaving sticky prints behind him.

I screamed and spun around before slamming into a meaty chest.

"Oh, dear. You are in trouble."

And a bag was thrown over my head.

11

I WASN'T THROWN in a trunk, nothing so dramatic. But my hands were zip-tied, and I was now tumbling around a leather seat like a Weeble-Wobble.

"If you weren't so stubborn," Nicola's voice rang throughout the car, "you'd be blissfully snoozing in the liquor closet right now. And my employee would still be alive."

"You're mad?" I held myself steady as the car took a turn. "That drugging me didn't work and your security guard assaulted me? While drugged, I'll add again. For your fucking benefit." I couldn't process the killing. It was not the time to stew, but, regardless, I was grateful for the physical boost the security guard had given me. My voice hardly trembled considering my capture.

"You were not 'drugged.'" Nicola sounded revolted by the word. "You ate an enchanted pear. Fairy-treated fruit. No one forced you."

I didn't mention the fact that she had demanded I eat the pear. I knocked my head against the window, a loud *bonk* radiating in my skull, and let it lie there.

"Why exactly did you show up on my doorstep in such a state?" she asked.

I huffed inside my head bag. "Why exactly would you stuff my body in a liquor closet?"

I heard her sigh through the burlap. "It was an act of mercy. I thought you could use a break from consciousness." I blushed. Must I open my charity case to anyone who stuck around long enough to look inside? "I'm still baffled at how you remained upright as long as you did. Not just upright, but awake enough to stroll about, take a few pictures, murder a man." I couldn't see her, but her eyes burned me like laser beams. "Either you have insurmountable willpower … or you have something else."

Knowledge is power. I remembered Ben's voice with a pang. Nicola had already guessed that my affinity was the culprit, but I wouldn't fill in any blanks for her.

"Nothing? Really? You don't feel like you owe me this?" she asked.

"No! I don't! I'm hogtied! Plus! *He* attacked *me*!" I leaned toward her voice, though my hands were still bound behind my back.

"Alright, alright, Daytime Emmy." Her exhale was ridiculously loud, exasperated at my inability to move past my kidnapping. "Secrets don't stay secret forever, sweetie. Especially not in this city."

We took a vindictive curve and my face smashed into the window. Then we stopped abruptly, and I was tossed to the floor. "Here we are," Nicola sang, as if she expected me to stare out the window like Orphan-fucking-Annie.

"Great, can the bag come off?"

She laughed. Her honking chortles followed her out the car door.

Someone else, a man by the sound of his grunts, wrestled me from the car. He ripped Betty's pouch from around my neck. "Careful with that!"

All he did was blow a bunch of air through his lips like a whoopee cushion.

Once I managed a stable footing, he shoved me forward and ruined all my hard work. Before my knees could touch the ground, he grabbed the wrist ties at my back and lifted me to my feet. The plastic dug into my skin like a knife.

He threw me through three doorways, if I construed the sounds and the motions correctly, and over a stone floor that clicked under my heels. I missed my sneakers.

Nicola didn't speak during the journey through the structure. The only reason I assumed she was still with us was the long stride—another pair of heels—in front of me.

There was no way for Ben to know where we were. Not when I couldn't see.

I was forced to a stop, a rough hand on my arm. A strange buzzing hit my ear. Then my knees bent with the sudden shift in gravity. An elevator. The ride up lasted a lifetime. Or two. Immediately after the ding of the arrival bell, I was shoved from the box and smelled floral cigarettes.

"Welcome," trilled a new voice. Strong like lightning, rough with grit. It wasn't loud, but it carried around the room more effectively than if she'd screamed.

The bag was snatched from my head, catching on my hair and pulling me along with it. The henchman untangled the mess with a scowl and shoved me back in place.

There were at least ten people in the room, which seemed to be an entire floor of the building. Various people in gray suits stood around the space like matching furniture, but there were four people that did not belong. Three men and a woman.

They included a pair of identical Black twins with opposing crooked grins, and big eyes that bulged from their heads; a slender pale person with fidgety hands and hair so dark he had to have dyed it; and her.

It was evident that this was the person who'd spoken. And this person had power. An ocean of it.

I'd never seen a fairy before, but if I were to imagine one … it never would have been the woman before me.

She had a brown, sun-wrinkled face, rippling outward from her mouth like a stone dropped in a muddy pond. The hair surrounding her head and neck was frizzy, curly, and gray as steel wool. She was a smallish person, and wiry, the muscles in her arms falling below the bone like water in a balloon. She wore a white wife-beater—her areolas glared at me through the fabric —and what looked to be a kimono tied around her waist. She held a cigarette between her shriveled fingers, and she sucked on it as she spoke.

"I do apologize for the deplorable conditions in which you arrived. I prefer discretion over infamy. I'm sure you under-stand." She stared and I naturally met her eyes. They were the green of burning emeralds, of clovers in spring—

Thank god I was here, thank god I could see such a woman. I would stuff the bag over my head happily if it meant those eyes looked upon me with approval.

"Your name is?"

"Frankie," I answered quickly, gratified to have any informa-tion she wanted. Her face was smooth as satin, her hair a cascading wave of soft locks. She was the most magical thing I'd ever seen, that had ever breathed.

"Hello, Frankie." I was euphoric that she now knew me by name and could call on me with whatever she might need. "You." She pointed the cigarette at me, the nail of her finger was painted a nuclear green. I wanted to put that finger between my teeth, to kiss her knuckles clean. "Resisted the spell of one of my pears, so I'm told. Weakness, fatigue, confusion. Sleep." She appraised me with mild intrigue, as if I were a sofa on sale. I racked my brain for ways to appear more interesting. I popped out my hip. "And with my enchanted juices pumping through your veins, going in unarmed, you stabbed one of my security agents—" she looked to a stout young man with a buzz cut, a mustache, and light brown skin. He'd been the one who untan-gled the sack from my hair, the one who manhandled me.

"Nineteen," he said.

"Nineteen times," she finished, her eyes returning to my face. "Pity, I might have liked him."

Something tickled my mind, something wrong despite my joy at being in the room. A falsity. I had taken so much pain from the security guard, enough to fight off the fairy fruit completely. It had been more than nineteen times, much more, but some of the wounds had healed and closed before he died.

I'd stabbed him so many times … I lowered my eyes from the woman and stared at my shoes.

The reality of my situation began to pull the gauzy veil from my eyes—I had killed a man. I was a hostage. I was not a guest.

"I brought you here for one reason." The woman folded her arms and leaned against an ornate, garish desk that I hadn't noticed before. It was covered in carved mahogany cherubs and sparkling jewels. Scanning my environment, it dawned on me that I was in an office. Perhaps the most expansive and eclectic office in Vegas. Everything was colorful and mismatched, as if a catalog from each decade of the last century had puked all over the floor. There were candelabras and mod glass tables and ugly tweed sofas surrounded by an abundance of fruit trees, all of which had been potted right inside the floor. Pears and plums and cherries. I was surprised I didn't hear any birds fluttering between them. A butterfly opened and closed its wings inside a fruit flower.

The office was hideous, but bewitching. An antique shop in the middle of an orchard. The air itself smelled sweet. I wanted to lie on the couch, fold myself back over the arm, and relax.

I looked back at the fairy, avoiding her eyes, which were the superstars of her being. There was something about them … they were too much to handle. She was enticing, like Cleo, but in a different way. Cotton candy opioids. Cleo made me crazed, desperate, and unpredictable; this woman made me dreamy, compliant, and unaware. Even now, I struggled to remember why I cared about any of it.

The fairy put her smoke hand to her chin. "You are of magic. I can smell it on you. But the intricacies … I'm dying to know." She flicked ash onto the cement floor, and a suit hurried forward to sweep it up. "How *did* you manage it?"

I dropped my head, a tactic I'd used against Cleo more than once, and tried to concentrate.

"Don't lie. I'll know if you do," she said to my scalp.

Did she mean instinctually or magically? Now there was a talent I wished I possessed.

When I remained silent, a whipping sound filled the room. I straightened my neck, and the tip of a baton pressed into my cheek.

"Not answering is not an option either, I'm afraid." She lifted herself onto the desk and spread her legs, her free hand planted behind her. She was wearing a pair of blue biker shorts under her kimono.

Knowledge is power. I wouldn't lie, but I wouldn't reveal more than necessary. As long as I didn't look directly at her.

"I'm a healer." I cleared my throat. "My affinity is restoration." The fairy nodded a confirmation—she'd already suspected such a thing. "I don't mean to do it. It just happens. When something is hurting me."

"And how did you convince my guard to give you his knife?" She blew smoke rings to the ceiling. They looked closer to hearts than circles.

"I didn't." I thought the words in my head as if they were written on a page, searching for lies within them. "I took it from him. I wasn't out to get him or anything. He attacked me."

She nodded emphatically. "And you don't have any bruises or scrapes, any signs of an altercation, because of your restoration. I see." She had a slight accent, but one that I'd never heard before. Somewhere between southern and Irish. It was hard to tell around the smoker's rasp.

"Yes," I sputtered. "He slapped me, kicked me, pulled out his knife—" I bit my lips shut and looked down once again. The urge to say everything, to please her, was rising in my throat like stomach acid.

The fairy knew I was resisting. Her shrewd eyes narrowed. She stepped away from the desk and approached me. She lifted my chin with an index finger, and I was lost in the green land-scape of her eyes. Rolling summer hills. "Either way. You took something from me and are in my debt. Do you agree?"

I nodded until my neck popped. Her skin rubbed against mine. It was warm syrup, smooth as white sand. I tipped my cheek to feel more of her. "Yes. Yes. I'm sorry."

"Good." She released my face and it rolled to my chest. She turned around and spoke to the back of the room. "The form of your penance will be servitude. You'll work off your debt."

I remembered the sparkly naked cards and my stomach hit the floor. "Um ... I ... Please."

"Oh, you silly." She smacked a hand to her desk, and the black-haired, twitchy man smiled like a lion. "Don't look so scared. Nothing in manual labor or sex work, not for your talent. I feel I can make great use of you." She ground her cigarette butt in a crystal ashtray. "How long since your reveal?"

I searched the room for answers—hoping one might pop out of the art deco music box on the desk—desperate to impress. The twins laughed at me. Their snickers were followed by a ticking sound. The ticking of an actual timer clicked throughout the room as they all waited for me to speak.

The fairy laughed, and clouds of smoke puffed out her mouth that had been hiding in her lungs. "You stop that." She wagged her cigarette at the twins and the ticking stopped instantly. She turned back to me. "Your reveal. When you discov-ered you were a mage."

"Oh! Oh, my reveal. Yeah. Um. A few months."

"Ah! A newbie. Well. Together, I think we might just strike the bottom of the well. Don't you?"

I swallowed my spit. "Yes." She beamed in response, the wrinkles in her cheeks ironing out flat, and held out a hand to shake. I approached the desk with my eyes on her leathery neck. Mustering my courage, I asked. "How long?" The words swayed through the room like telephone lines.

"How long what, dearie?"

"Will I work for you? To pay off my debt?" I wanted the terms now, before years had gone by and I was too deep to walk away. This woman would keep me happy and stupid under her thumb until one of us died.

"Oh." She took a pack of cigarettes from the pocket in her kimono and packed it against her other hand. "Clever woman. Alright." She considered me over the flicker of a purple gas station lighter. "Six months." She inhaled.

I took a shuddering breath. So long. I would be trapped here for so long. "Please. I have a house and a job." I scoured the floor for any mercy she may have hidden down there. "One month?"

"Three months."

It was the best I'd get. I felt her spark of irritation that I had even countered, that I had brought up the length of servitude at all. I reached for her hand, ignoring the constriction in my chest and the speed of my breath. We shook on it. And in doing so, I fell under the rule of the Las Vegas Sovereignty.

She kissed my knuckles and I nearly fainted.

"I am Laisren."

"WHA—WHAT exactly do you need me to do?" I asked. I couldn't feel my toes, I wasn't sure if I was still standing. I orbited around this woman who had become my personal sun.

"Ah, ah, ah!" Laisren admonished with a finger wag. "You shook on it. I'll determine what I need from you at my discretion and my leisure."

"When do I start?"

"You already have." She circled me like a bird of prey. Once behind me, she rubbed my shoulders. Without her eyes on mine, I'd never hated anything so much. Unfamiliar touch, *intimate* unfamiliar touch. Her hands were dry, and I felt the stacks of excess skin roll together in the grooves of her knuckles. "We will need to discover your depths, your use. Come back to this office in two hours' time."

My nausea swelled and it took me a moment to speak. "Okay, I'll just go back to my hotel room—"

"You'll do no such thing. Not after you've seen me, my employees, my workplace. Not until you've proven yourself capable of keeping certain secrets."

Goose pimples bubbled along my back beneath her hands. I breathed a sigh of relief when Laisren stepped into my line of vision with a smile. I watched her browning teeth instead of her eyes.

"Could I at least change my clothes?"

"Why?"

I gave myself a once over. "I'm a little uncomfortable. I haven't bathed since …" Since I'd kissed Jessamae, since Ben slept with Cleo, since I killed a stranger. "Yesterday."

"There are baths here. Most who work for me stay on the lower floors. This building is called The Alcazar, and it will be your home for the next three months." She swept her burning cigarette through the air, nearly igniting my hair, and returned to her desk. I was dismissed.

"Um, wait. Could I please have my bag back? Please?" I gestured to the asshole with the buzz cut clutching my bag in his beefy fists. Betty was very unhappy in there, writhing frantically in the small space.

Laisren sighed in annoyance and asked the man, "You checked it?" He nodded wordlessly. "And?"

"A snake, a phone. Dead. The phone, not the snake. A key to a room at the Bellagio. A credit card. That's it."

That was all I had to my name for the next three months.

Ignoring the fact that I had a snake in my bag, Laisren raised a brow and said, "The Bellagio? Ritzy." She spun her grandma-style armchair around to stare out the window.

I held my hand out to the buzz-cut, my lip twitching. He didn't give Betty to me, instead he threw the strap over his own shoulder, and grabbed hold of my arm, lugging me back to the elevator.

"I can walk without your help, dickbag." I wrenched my arm, but he would not yield. The elevator closed and we were alone.

"You'll sleep on the third floor. You are not permitted to leave without a chaperone. Your apartment includes a kitchenette— any groceries you require will be delivered as needed. Leave a list on your door no later than midnight and they'll arrive in a day or two."

The elevator opened on the third floor and the buzz-cut yanked me down an anorexic hallway with nasty carpet. He stopped in front of room thirty-four and slid a hotel key into its locking mechanism. The "apartment" was a studio with a double bed, a microwave, a beer fridge, and an old television. He fanned out his arm like Vanna White: *Look at what you've won!* "Laisren moves you up a floor as you earn her favor. I am on the ninth floor—"

"Wow, Mr. Big Shot."

He scowled but finally released my arm and begrudgingly extended Betty's pouch to me. I hugged her against my chest. "What about my snake? She'll need to eat soon. A few days."

He shrugged again. "I'm sure there are plenty of mice on these lower levels."

"I'll just put it on the grocery list then."

"You do that." He stepped to the exit. "I patrol these floors. As do my colleagues. But even if that weren't the case, I hope you're as smart as you think you are and you don't run. Running will get you nowhere good. Believe me." He appeared surprisingly uncomfortable at the admission, but before I could read into it further, he adjusted his tie and opened the door. "I'll be back in ninety minutes to fetch you. You'll want to be early. Always. Believe me," he said again before shutting the door.

I did.

I immediately pulled Betty from the pouch. She was

distraught, having been so close to so much stress without being able to see. "I'm sorry." She gave me a spiteful bite, though it lacked efficacy, being so tender and painless. She wrapped herself around my wrist and gave me a squeeze, either in anger or reassurance or both. I lifted her to my face. She wove through my hair, her tongue flicking against my ear. A few fine strands stuck to her skin and ripped from my head.

I didn't have much time for it, but I could finish in the shower if it ran long. So, knowing I only had ninety minutes, I cried.

12

"KNOCK, KNOCK," Buzz-cut said, though he didn't knock and opened the door using his key. I was back in the green dress I now loathed, but my hair was clean and soaking my back. I didn't feel any better. Clean did not equate to better in my book.

Betty waited impatiently on the bed, her eyes following me around the room as I retrieved my boots. I bent to pick her up.

"Leave it," Buzz-cut urged.

I glared at him under my hair and continued to cradle Betty's weight.

"Leave it."

Turning to shout that he wasn't Laisren, he was not my boss, his eyes stopped me. They were earnest and full of emotion. His mouth didn't move but his grief filled the room, smelling of fresh snow.

I unwound Betty from my arms, though she resisted. "I'll be right back." I turned the television on for her. Found a sitcom rerun. She flicked baleful glances at me but couldn't help focusing on the show. It was one of her favorites. I returned my attention to Buzz-cut. "What's your name?"

He assessed me coolly with black eyes. "Anderson."

"That's a last name."

"Yes."

I shoved him and stomped out the door. Serves me right for trying to be friendly.

He raced after me, his hand hovering near my shoulder, but I always kept away from it, until I was running down the hallway and he was chasing after me with one arm extended. When I got to the elevator, I smashed the button repeatedly, hoping to lose him, but it wouldn't light.

"Excuse me," Anderson said, slightly out of breath. He took a thick card from his belt—it was fastened to a cord—and held it up to a black box above the call button. "There you go," he said, happy at reclaiming control.

Curling my lip, I stepped inside. "Am I allowed to add books to my grocery list? Or am I supposed to watch The Food Network twenty-four hours a day?" Now that I'd shed some tears, I felt angry as well as afraid. I thought in time, three months to be exact, I would reassess what I'd done to that security guard and feel remorse, shock, disgust. But for now, I was furious. After all, I could have stopped before it went as far as it did, but *he* could have stopped at the mouth of that alley.

We arrived on the top floor. Laisren was waiting, her three guards stationed around her in a triangle, though we were in fact early.

"Let's get started," she said without preamble. "Come with me." I looked to Anderson for any indication of what my evening might entail. He looked green and his scalp was sweating. He wasn't a witch—otherwise, he would have been used for more than babysitter duty—but he was well-versed in what was about to happen.

Laisren led us employees around the back of the elevator bank, which was constructed in the center of the top floor, the diverse pieces of furniture surrounding its shaft like the petals of a sunflower.

Laisren stopped beside a white door with a simple gold knob. And three deadbolts. One of her low-level guards, a woman, half her pink hair shaved, stepped forward, a key ring in her fist. She found the three correct keys efficiently—though she looked to have at least twenty on her ring—and opened the door.

The sudden sunlight glared hatefully downward, and my eyes sizzled in their sockets. We'd arrived at what was once a rooftop pool, but the pool had been drained. All the sides curved into the bottom without any right angles. It had been painted in a red lacquer glaze, almost plastic in its sheen. It was deep, around ten feet. The two ladders that had originally been submerged remained behind, hanging in the air. The shallow-end stairs had been removed.

The edge of the roof was lined with wire fencing. Scaling it would take a great deal of time. And it would hurt. Though there was no barbed wire, the ends of the metal stuck up from the gate in a spiky barrier.

"Don't worry," Laisren announced, pulling my attention. "You won't be entering The Pool just yet." Her inflection implied it was a title, not a noun. I looked to its depths with new apprehension. "Now, you will simply take hold of my hands, and free your natural abilities." She stood at the head of The Pool, the deep end, and held out her hands. The way the guards surveyed the roof, taut energy shifting between them, I sensed it wouldn't be as simple a task as construed.

I touched Laisren's dehydrated fingers quickly to hide the tremor in my hands. I closed my eyes against the penetrating green stare shining at me like radioactive waste.

Over the past two months, we discovered my affinity was most consistent when I was thinking of something that brought me joy. Thoughts of Ben worked every time. Thinking of him now was paralyzing it inflicted such hurt. With unexpected clarity, I realized that last night was the first night I'd slept without him since Pamela's death. And that tonight would *feel* like the first time, because I knew he wouldn't be there.

"Well?" Laisren pushed.

"Sorry," I stammered, shaking my hands out. "I'm just nervous."

I cleared my mind of Ben, mostly, and instead conjured

thoughts of Betty. Her gooey black eyes, full of trust. Her warm weight in my hands, curled atop my chest as she slept. She didn't hate me just yet. I hadn't let her down. She loved me. And I loved her.

"Interesting," Laisren murmured. I looked up, and gratefully those eyes weren't on me. They stared past me, as if my affinity stood over my shoulder. "Very interesting. I am not injured, however much I'd like to see that practice, but I enjoy this. Uplifting. Like Percocet. Very nice. However, there is more. You aren't telling me something."

I wrapped my arms around myself. "I'm still finding out more every day." Not a lie.

Laisren zhuzhed her hair. "Have you advanced since your reveal?"

I licked my teeth while I thought of my answer. "Some."

"We shall see, won't we?"

She left me at the deep end and walked closer to the building, snapping her fingers as she walked away. In an instant, I was swarmed. Two of Laisren's suited guards pounced on me, grabbing my limbs and hoisting me up.

"Get the fuck off me!" I snapped my jaw at reaching fingers. I kicked my feet wildly, catching the woman with the shaved head in the cheek. She wrapped one arm around my ankles and the other under my calves. They all avoided touching my skin, tucking their hands into their sleeves as if I would stain their fingers.

Despite my resistance, it didn't take long for them to reach the edge of The Pool. And they tossed me in like a Hefty bag.

I LANDED hard on my right shoulder. It felt wrong, tingly, on impact. I rolled onto my back and rubbed my shoulder socket.

There was a new protrusion there. My breathing was labored. The pain hadn't hit yet, but it would. Now that I was at the bottom, I wasn't getting back out on my own. I laid my head back and tried to relax. My body would take care of the bone. I pulled my dress down over my hips and crotch with a groan—it had ridden up to my belly.

Laisren stepped to the edge of the pool and stared down at me like God over man. "The first one is a test only. No permanent damage will come to you, on my honor." I flicked my wide eyes to her without moving my head. She lit another cigarette. Her elbow rested on her hip as she observed me with a clinical focus. "We've found The Pool to be the most efficient means of discovering a mage's individual potential." The twins and the smiling man framed Laisren on either side, their faces eager.

My whole body shook. My hair was still wet, and it chilled my back. I heard a door open past the deep end, a different door than the one we'd used. I knew I should pull myself up, should stand, but I couldn't find the motivation. Part of me, most of me, just wanted to lie here until I dried up like sour fruit.

I tipped my head back and saw Anderson hunched at the shallow end. He jerked his chin upward spastically. When I did nothing with that, he began mouthing words to me. It took three bouts until I read, *Get up*.

Flopping my body to the left, I used that hand to raise myself to my hip. I scooted toward the shallow end, the sweaty skin of my thighs catching on the pool's surface. As I inched closer to the red wall, I realized I couldn't climb out of this end either—the wall was taller than me all around, maybe six feet at its shortest.

"Get up," Anderson stage-whispered above me.

Three new guards appeared above the ladder attached to the deep end. They dispersed outward to reveal a small woman between them. Tiny thing, young too. She had light skin and straight, dark hair. Her mouth was narrow and heart-shaped. Her thighs were miles apart. She wasn't, in any way, restrained.

She appeared bemused, almost as though she were here by coincidence.

Rather than climb down the ladder, she was carried by the armpits over the edge. The man holding her, slid his hands along the girl's arms until he gripped her wrists, then he dropped her the remaining few feet to the bottom. She was wearing a frilly red dress that blended in horribly with our surroundings. She had yet to react. To anything.

She took a silent step forward. She'd weigh 90 pounds soaking wet. With a backpack. And costume jewelry. She considered me with vague interest, her heels touching, toes pointed outward like a ballerina.

A spattering of people now stood around the edge of The Pool, five or six faces that were not in suits and were not Laisren. One had a small notebook, pencil poised for extensive note-taking.

"Stand," Laisren demanded. She and her posse had an entire side of The Pool to themselves, the crowd of strangers standing opposite her. She stood equidistant between the deep and shallow end. The sun sank below the horizon, and the skyline of Vegas glimmered behind her like stage lights. She was a strange spectacle of smoke and sun damage. Still, she was magnificent.

"Why?" I didn't bother mentioning that I was injured. If my well-being were an issue, I wouldn't have been thrown over the side.

"You will face Daiyu." She gestured to the girl.

"How?"

"Stand."

I got to my knees with great difficulty and watched Daiyu, avoiding Laisren's face. "And if I don't?" My energy had evaporated, and with it, any sense of self-preservation or fear or insecurity. I didn't care what happened anymore.

Laisren snapped her explosive fingers, drawing my stare, and extended a hand toward the deep end. One of the girl's—

Daiyu's—keepers briskly approached Laisren's side and offered something to her.

Because he held her like nothing more than a frayed rope, I didn't see until now—I didn't see Betty gripped in the stranger's fist.

I vomited onto the red lacquer.

The mess was sickly brown with globs of purple floating within. When I had sensed Anderson's grief in my room earlier tonight, I'd stupidly assumed he was saddened over the loss of another, or even his own, pet—most likely to the hands of the fairy above me— and wanted to save Betty the same fate. That hadn't been the case. He felt grief over what would happen to her once we left the room.

Leave it, he said. For Laisren.

The guard dropped Betty into Laisren's waiting hands like a bauble, her length nearly tumbling to the ground. My stomach clenched and I bent over, dry heaving. Laisren stroked her scales with adoration. Adoration that I didn't believe.

My stomach clenched again. I had only eaten one unnatural pear on top of all the whiskey I'd tried to drown in today. If I didn't have the affinity I did, I would be in far worse shape than I was. I allowed myself a moment of curiosity—was it even possible for me to starve to death?—before I shoved my ankles beneath me, one at a time. My right arm hung unnaturally at my side.

Laisren didn't reward me with any false praise. She looked to Daiyu, who took another delicate step forward.

"Proceed," Laisren said, using Betty's tail like a conductor's baton. I couldn't remember wanting to hurt someone so badly. I would go crazy from how much I wanted it.

I backed away from Daiyu with one hand at my chest. I'd stored the dead guard's knife under my tits after I'd show-ered earlier, fearing my employment would come to a violent end. But Daiyu stayed far away. She chose to fold herself neatly to her knees before lying flat on her back. Her hands pressed into her thighs, but the dress remained obediently in place.

Nonplussed, I straightened out of my defensive position. My shoulder started to throb, and I held it as I waited for whatever would happen to happen.

Hello, a dainty voice whispered. I whirled around to no one. But the voice wasn't the one I'd grown used to. The voice didn't belong to Paimon. I flipped forward again and nearly lost my balance. *Here I am*, I heard inside my head. I shook it from me like a wasp but soon found I couldn't shake my head at all. I reached up to grab my skull, but instead ran my fingers along the thin straps of my dress. *This feels nice.*

She was here. Daiyu had nested inside my head! Was feeling my dress with my fingers, though I felt it, too. I couldn't use my body. She'd taken control. I would be shaking if I had any advocacy over my skin.

What have you got? she asked me, her voice soft and sweet, as she reached into the cups of my dress. She wedged the knife out from the under the swell of my breast and studied the handle, which was brushed silver.

Get out of my head! Get out of ME! I screamed inwardly. My mouth hung slack. I was imprisoned. If she could hear me, she ignored my fear.

My thumb crept over the silver button near the opening of the knife. I fought with every ounce of fight I had left. But she pressed the button. I pressed the button. The blade flew open avidly, the lights from the Strip sparkling off its surface.

Pretty. My hand twirled the knife between my fingers, admiring the weapon. It then turned the weapon around and cut into the meat of my left forearm. Daiyu giggled as she dragged the blade upward and cut into my bicep. The sting was sharp but fleeting. The wounds were already closing, but there was only so much I could take before my restoration couldn't keep up with the blood loss. Just like the security guard in the alley.

The pain became constant, the blade hardly raising from its

bloody stripes as she continued to scribble in my skin. She hummed a little song in my head while she worked, as if carving or whittling. My eyes skittered to the leaf tattoo on my hand, and I thought of Ben.

Such lovely skin you have, she sang around my brains.

I frantically searched it for a solution, any solution to get myself out of this. Daiyu was clearly a psychopath. She was enjoying herself too much. Though Laisren promised no permanent damage, that left a lot open to Daiyu when it was *my* body she was slicing up. Even without full control of my mind, I could feel. I felt the steel, felt the warm ooze, felt the breeze in my hair.

The breeze. The air. Sacrifice. The elements required sacrifice. Would the cuts Daiyu cause still provide payment? I didn't choose them, but I inflicted them, felt them. My intent was in here, behind the macabre body-snatcher.

The pool drain below my feet gurgled like a thick stew. Cleanup for these events would be easy because of the two drains in the bottom of the tank. I couldn't turn my head, but I assumed there was a hose nearby, and a quick spray would wash any mess away. The water, the blood, my vomit, would flow into the pipes below.

Daiyu pointed the switchblade at my heart, its point digging into the flesh of my sternum, just above my dress. This one would be deep. She pushed with a burst of enthusiasm and carved a crimson diamond into my chest.

I searched for water under the pool, traveling through the building's pipes. I thought I could hear it, as if across a cave, breathing and bubbling. Patient, constant, cold. I channeled the element, shivering as if I'd plunged into a mountain lake— freezing and weighty. A good sign. And as Daiyu continued to etch, rivulets of blood soaking my dress, I had no doubts.

The maw of the water grew louder as it rushed to the surface, working tirelessly. The sound was foreboding, like a cyclone opening, but the work was incremental, one inch at a time.

Steadily, water bloomed from the drain, spreading over the red lacquer in a puddle.

Daiyu's attention was on me, on her art project. If she couldn't sense my efforts, maybe she hadn't heard my pleas after all. It wasn't until the water soaked the soles of my boots that she caught the moon's reflection off the water.

She paused, my knife wedged into the soft skin inside my elbow. She bent down on my ankles to swirl my fingers in the puddle, curious at its appearance.

The water rose faster, gaining momentum and flowing with ease. In Daiyu's distraction, several of my cuts began to close, my reserves of energy able to funnel effectively. My head whipped around The Pool. The water was creeping up Daiyu's small body across the way. It wouldn't take long to swallow her up.

She couldn't pay for any magic herself, not using my body. She couldn't stop the flood. She seemed to try, slashing at me manically and checking the water's level between each slit. In her panic, she flickered in and out of my head like a bad radio transmission. I experienced short clips of control and—jerking, floundering—my body fell to its knees, the two of us battling inside it. "Get—" My right hand thrashed violently from the water, which was almost six inches high. I slammed it back down, dragging myself through the swelling pond of it. "Out!"

`Daiyu's body sputtered around on its back like a beached seal, her sentience flashing between bodies as I pushed against it. The water reached my elbows. Cold as winter.

My knees slid along The Pool's bottom in a four-legged dance. Daiyu used that to her advantage, attempting to stop me rather than take over completely. She could have returned to her body, saved herself from drowning easily, but that would be losing. This was a contest of will as much as craft.

My palm slipped from beneath me and I propelled forward as if through oil until I dropped beneath the surface of the rising waves. She planted my hands on either side of my head and tried to hold my face under, to drown me. I lifted my head for a few moments of precious air before she plunged me back under, time and time again. The constant inhalation of fluids—blood-tinged drain water—was choking me. I coughed below the water, sucking more into my lungs.

I opened my eyes, and everything was purple. My throat burned, my chest ached. I couldn't think of anything other than what was hurting. I was light-headed, painfully light-headed. I'd lose consciousness completely any minute.

My nose smashed into something that sunk to the bottom of The Pool. I pulled my head back as far as she'd let me. The knife.

Daiyu concentrated all her remaining presence on keeping my head down, my hands and feet were outside her control. I grabbed the knife and held my breath. I saw roaming black spots erupt in the water—I was fading. I needed oxygen. I kicked my toes against the red, sliding and fumbling, my face still underwater. A ringing hurt my ears.

When I splashed against Daiyu's little shoe, my body weighed a thousand pounds. I crawled onto her prone form as if it were a life preserver. All her body was submerged, save her nose. She may have floated if I weren't here to stop her. I climbed to her chest, and even with my head held down, my face rose above the water line, my nose smashed into the lace of her dress. Oxygen.

I hacked out enough water to fill a Big Gulp. My innards felt like they'd been rubbed raw with a toilet brush. I held the knife to Daiyu's fragile throat, spitting up pink water all over the blade.

That was it. Daiyu left my mind. I'd never been more grateful to be alone. Air filled my brain readily now, and my strength returned. The blood dripped from my skin, and all but the slice over my heart had closed. As I held the blade to Daiyu's throat, a bead of blood formed, floating into the water in a dark smear. She opened her eyes. Fear. I would eat that fear.

"Enough," Laisren called, but I already used the nick in her neck to seal the opening in my chest. I watched her wound vanish as the water began to recede. The dry air had me shuddering. I didn't pull the knife away. I wanted more from this dainty asshole.

"Enough. Your restoration of self was evident. Though, I admit, I expected more … I enjoyed your creativity. Congratulations." Laisren circled The Pool. She spared Daiyu a look of disdain, then those clover eyes found mine, and I took the knife away from Daiyu's neck. "Move away or someone will move you." I leaped away from her as if she were made of lava, splashing feebly through what water remained. "Until next time," Laisren said. She spun on her heel and headed for the exit with Betty clutched in her fingers.

When the water was nothing but a cold spill, I closed the switchblade. Daiyu watched with apprehension, but her fear was gone—Laisren had made herself perfectly clear. As she rose to her feet, she spat on the ground in front of me. Then she smiled. Though she was forced into this pool just as I was, this girl was batshit insane. She loved what she did.

"What floor you on?" I asked her.

Her eyelids lowered and she lifted her chin in defiance.

I shrugged, kneeling before her. She was so small I could kiss her belly. "You don't have to tell me. I have lots of time to find out." I stood and tapped the handle of the knife against her nose. My legs weren't steady, and I took my time approaching the ladder screwed into the shallow-end wall. Even with the display I just pulled, I was so tired I could barely stand. I refused to let Daiyu see.

I jumped for the lowest rung of the ladder, my knees scraping against the side. Anderson crouched above the ladder, his hand held out in assistance. I had no choice but to take it. My arms twitched in his slimy clutches.

Betty was gone, in Laisren's possession. How long would she keep her hostage to force my compliance? How long until she killed her anyway?

Anderson was silent as he led me back through the white door. There was guilt there, stinking in his gut, and it wasn't enough. He should feel worse than he did for taking Betty from me.

I could take his pain from him, could possibly overpower him, like I did the security guard at The Harvest. But not with my familiar in harm's way. Laisren wouldn't only kill her, *my* punishment would be insufferable.

He opened my door with his key. After I crossed the entry-way, I turned around and held it open. "I need clothes. Anything loose and comfortable. And food. Cereal. And red peppers." His guilt would be enough to get basic necessities for me. I slammed the door.

I kicked off my shoes hard enough to scuff the walls and tore my sopping dress over my head, whipping it to the carpet. My underwear too. Naked, I crawled between the starched white sheets. Not only would a certain man be missing from my bed tonight, I didn't have my Betty either. I felt more than alone, worse than alone. I felt like I was nothing. I wished I'd never met any of them—Ben or Betty or Cleo or Jessamae. Even Patrick. Then I'd have no one to miss but my dead mother.

I stared at the wall, contemplating my ability to decimate my life in so little time.

Smashing a pillow over my head, I blocked out the rest of the word via duck feathers. The TV was still on, mindlessly going through the motions. Which was good. I couldn't be in the dark tonight.

Despite my complete and consuming exhaustion, sleep wouldn't come. I went through every television channel three times. I tried to kickstart my dreams manually, imagining aspen trees and rolling clouds and the soup aisle at work. I counted sheep, but after every dozen, I plummeted back into a pit of self-loathing—sheep quantity be damned. The loneliness was suffo-cating. Gnawing, vicious, and full of teeth.

After hours of deprecation, I drifted into a merciful daze.

Strange and haunting images appeared behind my lids in the greeting of a dream. Or a nightmare. Silver eyes melted into dancing brown irises when I bolted up in bed, the pillow falling to the ground.

It was back. The cords in my chest thrummed. Hard.

Jessamae was in The Alcazar.

13

I KICKED the scratchy beige blanket from me and flopped to the floor. My face smashed into the abrasive carpet and my legs knocked over the lamp. I ran to the door and tugged, still floating just outside of consciousness. It took five too many tries before I realized it was locked from the outside. I was naked.

Hating the green dress as if it had caused this whole mess, I wrapped the top sheet around myself and tied it off above my chest. I bent down to all fours like a goblin, elbows and knees bent dramatically, and crept around the room, following the cords' pull. Jessamae was close. I thought she was below me— the cords led straight into the ground.

Without a shovel or a pickaxe, I was stuck on this floor. I jogged to the bathroom. It was small enough to be called a water closet, the toilet practically inside the shower everything was so close. I closed the toilet lid and climbed the fixture. There was a metal air vent above it, and cool air hit me like an elderly woman blowing out a birthday candle. I yanked at the edges, cracking one pinky nail and not much else. The screws required a flat-head screwdriver. A flat-headed anything.

I went to the kitchen and wrenched open every drawer. A can opener, a spatula. Tin foil, sponges. I found the utensil drawer last. Two spoons, two forks … and two butter knives.

I took them both with me in case one proved somehow defective. I tripped over the bedsheet flapping around my ankles and banged my knee into the toilet. The sheet floated from under my pits and piled on the ground as I reached up to wedge the butter knife into the groove of a corner screw.

It was a tedious process, the knife slipped across the metal repeatedly and I skinned my knuckles against the slats. I'd nearly stripped the screw when it began to turn. Using both hands, my elbows extended above my head, I spun it from the vent. Once one screw was removed, I laced up my heeled boots. They gave me a few extra inches and my arms were grateful for them.

In my boots, on the toilet, nude with a sheet at my feet, I removed six screws from the wall. I had to take a break after two screws, then again after four. I turned on the television to keep time. I worked through a full episode of "Wipeout" and two of "Family Matters" by the time I popped the metal face from the wall, revealing the duct inside.

It would be tight, incomparably tight. In the movies, full-grown men, often with tools, were able to crawl around without trouble, but I worried the duct wouldn't hold my weight. Even if it did, claustrophobia would sink in soon after entry.

The tug of the cords in my chest faded around the fifth screw. Jessamae had made her exit. But there was no way she entered The Alcazar without knowing I was already here, and even if that were ironically the case, she knew now. When she came back, and she would, I needed to find her without being followed.

Just getting into the vent would be a challenge. I needed something to grab. I picked up the security guard's knife, which Anderson never took from me, and I stood atop the toilet tank. I stabbed the blade into the side of the vent, denting it, but not breaking through. I wasn't strong enough.

I remembered Gabriel's burning over the summer, his limp body. I froze as the memories bolted through my head—so fresh after seeing him in the alley—but I was looking for something in my past. Something that existed at the edge of my memory.

Jessamae and Cleo had carried the body from the trunk and into the driver's seat.

Pulling strength from the earth, Jessamae said.

The earth seemed so far away, but there was iron throughout the entire structure of the building, natural earthly minerals. I carefully squatted, still on the toilet, and slashed the blade up my bare thigh. I should have washed it first, but the thought was gone as soon as it came.

I searched for the earth in the walls, in the steel. Solid, nurturing, powerful. The redwoods and the mountains. The soil and the stone. The desert that covered this entire state like a treacherous quilt. I asked for strength. I begged.

Stable on my heels, I stepped to the toilet tank easily and again stabbed the blade of my knife—a bit of my blood along its edge—into the vent's side. The blade broke through, opening a little razor-sharp hole. I punctured the other side while I still could, not knowing how long my strength would last.

I slid the switchblade into the hole on my right, then the butter knife into the hole on my left, and heaved. The vent's edge bit into my chest, but my weight was inside, my legs dangling behind me.

"Knock, knock!"

"Shit!" I smacked my arms into the two handles as I dropped backward. "I'm on the toilet!" I called to the kitchen, rubbing my elbows.

The second I got my feet underneath me I launched from the toilet and slammed the bathroom door. I rinsed the drying blood from my leg and hid the knives under the sink. I wrapped and tied the sheet around my boobs again. "What the hell are you doing here?" I shouted through the door.

"I brought food and clothing. As requested," Anderson said.

I checked my appearance in the mirror. My arms showed angry red lines along their backs. My boots didn't go with my sheet, so I shucked them and left them by the toilet. The dusty grate of the vent leaned against the vanity. Without time to screw it back into the wall, I opened the door.

Anderson leaned on the kitchen counter, two grocery bags and a paper bag at his feet.

"What time is it?" I asked, closing the bathroom behind me and holding my sheet tight.

"Five."

I looked to the lone window in the room—it was still dark outside. I stared, unamused, at Anderson, seeing no need to speak and hating him more by the second. Sweat gummed under my arms when I thought of the open air duct, filling the fibers of my sheet.

"You were awake," was all he said. He picked up the groceries and began unloading them, putting a bag of apples and a quart of skim milk in the fridge. I wrinkled my nose—that shit was nothing but white water.

He put a box of Cheerios in a cabinet, as well as a box of Top Ramen. He left a sleeve of Styrofoam bowls on the counter—there was no dish soap to wash what dishes were here. But he should have just bought soap. Cleo would throw a fit over all this plastic. But Cleo wasn't here.

Anderson offered the paper bag to me, but I walked around him and his bag, pulling a bowl from its sleeve. I was uncomfortable in nothing but a sheet, but I knew it made Anderson even more uncomfortable, and that was an opportunity I refused to miss. I poured some cereal into the bowl before filling it to the rim with the worst kind of milk. The plastic spoon wasn't deep enough, so I piled two or three scoops in my mouth before swallowing. I finished a bowl while standing at the counter, without saying a word. I prepared a second bowl, then moved to sit on the bed.

Anderson sat in the stiff green chair in the corner, his eyes on the television. He looked sharp—his gray suit stiff and free of lint, his white shirt crisp and freshly ironed over his portly torso. He had to have been up for hours.

I knew he harbored shameful feelings about my snake's kidnapping on top of my own, and I savored the scent of it. I wouldn't make this situation any easier on him by speaking or putting on clothes. I went back for a third bowl, and he lifted a dark eyebrow.

Once I was finally satisfied, I crossed my legs on the bed and proceeded to watch TV. The Vegas skyline was an icky pink now, like cat puke, the glow of the sun touching the horizon. Anderson's stare stuck to my face, anticipating rage, annoyance, or speech at the very least. I gave him nothing.

"Well," he groaned, "I brought you a few shirts and a pair of pants. And a book. At your request. If you want anything else, I'll take you to find it."

I didn't look at him. He wanted me to respond with some sort of gratitude, but dressing your prisoner wasn't worthy of a prize. The book gave me a moment's pause, but he still didn't deserve a thank you. "Do you need something?" I asked at last.

Anderson made a rumbly noise. I made him very uncomfortable indeed. "Look. You don't have to stay here all hours of the day. I can take you around. You can get some more books or magazines or something. Get your own shampoos and soaps."

"Wow, I get my own soap?"

"After enough time, you won't need a chaperone. But for now, you just have to play along."

I wondered how long it would be in my three months before I could venture out alone. I doubted I could earn enough trust by then. Laisren was a suspicious leader. Anderson wanted to give me hope, and that was a mean thing to do.

Tired of his eyes on me, I snatched the paper bag off the floor and returned to the bathroom, careful to keep the room's innards from view. I stared at the air duct with longing. I didn't have money or resources or friends, but I wanted to be free of this place, and I couldn't leave without Betty.

Anderson wanted to be cordial. I could do that. I would do

whatever it took to discover her whereabouts. I was working him all wrong. I had to be ... *nice*.

There were three crew-neck t-shirts in the bag—red, yellow, and blue. The pants were gray and a soft canvas material. A thick novel was buried beneath the cotton, an epic fantasy with an orange, horned dragon on the cover. I would have never picked it out myself. I doubted I would like it, but I smiled before I even realized I still could.

I showered in a hurry, the water hot and painful, then piled my hair on my head. I pulled on the red shirt and pants—he hadn't included underwear or a bra, which seemed to pass kindness and skid right into creepy. The fabric was soft.

When I reentered the living space, Anderson had turned the channel to some sort of sports discussion. He watched with rapt attention. I crossed my arms and leaned against the door frame, my new book bumping against my hip.

"I need shoes, and maybe some underwear." Though I wasn't particularly bothered by its absence. "Is anything even open?"

He stood and popped his back. My eyebrows lifted in envy. "This is Las Vegas, everything is open."

ANDERSON OFFERED to take me to several unknown stores as we rode the elevator down.

"Can I see the lobby?" I asked.

He turned, inquisitive but silent.

"Last time we were here, you were busy throwing me around like a bocce ball. And the bag over my head kind of ruined the spectacle. So?" I held out an arm, banking on his guilt.

"I think you mean a bocce ball."

"I don't think I do."

He sighed but switched direction.

The lobby was minimal. There was no check-in counter—

none of the rooms were available to non-prisoners it would seem. It was not a welcoming space, decked out in dark neutral colors, the furniture hard and sharp. The only seats available were stationed around poker and blackjack tables, of which there were five. The visitors were few and far between, and all dressed to the nines, though dawn had just arrived. There were three rows of slot machines, all bland and soundless. No one was using them. This was not a place in which you could escape scrutiny. Not easily.

"It's nice."

"It's not intended for guests. Mages mingle with the magic-less at the bars and casinos Laisren owns elsewhere. They don't take the party home with them. This building is intended to present as commonplace on the Strip. It doesn't draw suspicion." That was quite the speech coming from a boulder like Anderson. This might be easier than I thought.

"You're magicless," I pointed out.

He tipped his head.

"How did you come to work for the reigning fairy of Las Vegas?"

Anderson straightened his tie, and grabbing my arm, dragged me toward a set of glass doors. I scratched at the exposed skin of his hand, and he shoved me forward to the side-walk. The sun was higher now but there was an early morning chill in the air. It smelled like sugar and wine rubbed into a dirty carpet. "No need to touch me." He glowered as if I had no right to dictate his touch. "We both work for Laisren, just because you're on the sixth floor—"

"Ninth."

"Sorry to offend." I rolled my eyes. "But enough with the crony bullshit. We'll both be happier for it." I searched my pockets for my phone before remembering it was dead in my room. "Is there a department store around here?" Not that I had any money. He knew that.

He sighed again as if my every request was as complicated as ritualistic sacrifice. He walked several yards before turning around and beckoning me, then I hustled along beside him. "Why do you need to escort me anyway? I'm not a Hilton."

"It's not for your safety if that's what you're implying. You are a liability, and Laisren is not inclined to waste resources chasing you around the country."

"I doubt I'd get very far anyway."

Anderson led me to a stacked parking garage, then to a simple silver sedan on the third level. "Is this your personal car?" I asked.

"Yes and no. Get in."

I decided not to pursue the subject, and instead devised the steps in conversation necessary to get to Betty. I'd have to be uncomfortably chatty. I'd have to appear to let my guard down. "So. How long have you worked for Laisren?"

Anderson stared ahead, sunlight illuminating his dark irises. I squinted into the same light, wishing I had my gas station shades, and then felt a bud of sadness.

"Okay," I said. "How long do you have to keep working for her?"

His shoulders softened. He was tired. "Eight years."

I balked. I did not care for this man who had handled me so roughly, who had taken part in my familiar's absence, but eight years … that was a very long time to be away from your house, your job. Anyone you were able to care for. "Where are you from?"

"Maryland."

"Ah." He had come to Vegas as a tourist and had made a grievous mistake. He may have had a wife or husband. Children. He didn't have them anymore.

Angry at myself for sympathizing even the tiniest bit toward his situation, I gruffly asked, "Did you have any pets?"

"I had two dogs. A lab and a Chihuahua."

I almost asked their names, but his shame permeated the car like cigar smoke, and I thought I'd done enough for now.

ANDERSON DROVE US TO COSTCO. He showed his member ID at the door, and I found my way to a pair of white Keds, a flannel, a six-pack of Fruit of the Loom underwear, and a sports bra. I hesitated outside of the bath aisle. Anderson tactfully pretended he was interested in an electric toothbrush replacement pack as I snagged some rosemary shampoo and conditioner. He bought us some pizza after checkout.

"What's up with Nicola? What does she have to do with Laisren?" I asked before I sucked on a pepperoni slice.

Anderson swallowed before answering, his Adam's apple dipping with the chunk. He put his elbows down and leaned across the table. "She's Laisren's hand. Runs the various establishments, collects her debts, manages employees. She doesn't work for the personal guard, but while Laisren is at The Alcazar, Nicola keeps the Strip under control." He whispered as if she were right behind him.

"She's Lady to Laisren's Queen. What's so secret about that?"

"Nothing. Forget it." He slurped his soda through a striped straw.

"Okay." I hoovered the grease from my fingers, and he watched, repulsed. "As a new employee, what else is on the schedule for today?" I burped with my mouth closed.

He cleaned his mouth with a napkin. Classy guy. "While you're still new, Laisren's ultimate goal will be discovery. That means she'll be putting you into The Pool every day until she feels like you've reached your current potential."

"My *current* potential?"

"I'm no expert, but my understanding is that a mage will continue to develop as they age. Development only stops with death."

"And The Pool forces the witches, or contestants, to do whatever it takes to survive, unconscious or otherwise?"

"That's the idea. It's effective."

That it was. "You didn't take my knife."

He covered his eyes before raking his hands down his face. "I don't know what you're talking about. But," he peered around at the other tables in the store, "I won't make the same mistake twice."

He couldn't have lied and told Laisren he'd taken it, but perhaps, she just assumed he did. Or Laisren told Anderson to take it, but Anderson somehow escaped from revealing when he would, if at all. Why would he do that? How deep did his guilt run?

He wiped his hands with a napkin. "I suggest you rest—"

"If I needed rest, why did you show up so earl—"

"Then," he said more loudly, "eat. Again. Each round in The Pool is more difficult than the last. Laisren enjoys matching opponents. You won't have a knife this time." His eyes widened in warning.

He had given me more information than I expected, but it didn't relate to Betty. I didn't have time for him to warm up to me. I needed her back now.

"Does Laisren sleep at the Alcazar?"

Anderson rolled his eyes. The intent of the question was obvious and beyond his pity. He knew what I wanted, because it was exactly what he would want in my situation.

"I can't leave my room!" I scoffed. "I was just curious."

I ATE another bowl of cereal after being locked inside my room and even managed to sleep a bit. Since the events over the summer, I found I slept better during the day than at night. I only kept up the nightly practice out of courtesy to Ben.

Angry thoughts pummeled my brain. I felt worse each day since we'd found Jessamae. I was so angry at Ben for being with someone like Cleo, angry at him for making me adore him like I did. I was disgusted with Cleo for taking him away when I'd never been happier. Most of all, I hated myself for rubbing their faces in my relationship with Jessamae. I hated myself for hurting everyone.

What had Jessamae felt? I blamed her too, a lot—she'd given me the shot, she'd kissed me—but I knew that blame was simply to take some of the culpability from my shoulders.

It didn't matter now; our foursome had imploded. And I would be here, in this room, for the next three months. Without them.

I showered again, enjoying the smell of the shampoo though it frizzed my hair out exponentially. I stared glumly at the air vent. There was no point in the venture now. Jessamae was gone. Betty was gone. I watched TV for hours.

Anderson retrieved me after the sun had set. The lights of the Strip glared across my television screen. "You eat?" he asked.

I nodded.

"Come on then."

As I stood to follow, a cord thrummed in my chest, and I stumbled in surprise. I looked anxiously to the bathroom. She was here. She was close. There was no time to search the building. But if not now, when would Jessamae return? How many chances would I get?

"You alright?" Anderson asked.

If I attempted an escape, he'd hear me, he'd catch me. Any kindness he showed me today paled in comparison to his eight-year obligation. His loyalty was to Laisren. "I'm fine," I said, and I walked out the door.

As we rode the elevator, I tapped my fingers against my sternum. The pull was tight in my bones. She was still here. "Why did Laisren have me thrown in The Pool yesterday? One look at Betty and I would have climbed down myself."

"I don't claim to understand Laisren."

"But you've been with her a long time. Rose through the ranks. So …"

I was stroking his ego a bit, which he surely knew, but he answered. "To illustrate her power. And your vulnerability. Never forget it."

The elevator dinged and we entered the top floor. Unlike yesterday, we were alone. We made our way around the elevator shaft in silence, our shoes echoing against the windows until we crossed a series of enormous Afghan rugs. The same guard with the shaved head was stationed at the white door. She speedily unlocked and opened it.

Being late was an impossibility under Anderson's thumb, but there were already even more attendees than last night around the edge of The Pool—a throng. They'd come to watch the show. I forgot about Jessamae and began to tremble.

I climbed down the ladder of the shallow end, shaking the metal against the sides and dropping the last few feet. I felt sturdier than I had in my heels and party dress yesterday, though a t-shirt and Keds was no suit of armor. I'd left my knife under the vanity in my bathroom.

Tying my hair up on my head, I hoped it wouldn't be used to fling me around the red lacquered walls.

Laisren appeared from the second exit, leading a large group of guards circled around a single individual. Daiyu had three escorts. This witch had six.

Laisren returned to the spot between the ends of The Pool, green eyes glittering and alert. Betty was draped over her arm like a beach towel, perfectly still. A seed of despair took root before I realized there was no void on Laisren's person—Betty was alive. She was so limp she must have been drugged. Enchanted fruit. I could hardly see I was so angry.

"Welcome, once again, Frankie Hughes." She'd uncovered my last name. "You're looking well. I wish you the best of luck against your opponent."

The hive of guards buzzed around the opposite ladder before the other contestant was revealed.

He didn't climb down, as I had, and he wasn't lifted, as Daiyu had been. He was shouldered into the arena by the suits who guarded him.

He landed heavily, being a large man, and it took him a long time to stand, as his hands were bound by a cord at his stomach. He was tall, and blonde, and his blue eyes devolved into blackness.

My opponent was Patrick.

14

HE WAS SHIFTING RAPIDLY, either the suits had antagonized him beforehand, or his anger/fear/anxiety caused him to change. The flashing lights of the skyline filtered through the sprouting hair of his knuckles and cheeks.

Laisren knew of our connection, she had to. We'd created a stir the first night we'd gambled together after we'd taken too much money. Had Ben and Patrick gotten caught? There was only the barest possibility Ben hadn't seen that coming. They must have been separated somehow.

There was little time to consider the implications of Patrick here, hands bound and shifting.

I would treat him as a stranger. No matter what Laisren had already guessed, I wouldn't hand her such a valuable weapon as my fondness for Patrick. She'd already used my affection for Betty against me.

Hands up, I said, "Easy." My only options for sacrificing to the elements were hurting Patrick or scratching myself. Useless. Not nearly big enough a payment. I stared down at my hands. I could break a finger if it came to it. My leaf tattoo looked so small.

Confusion and rage rolled off Patrick's growing body like tidal waves. I took several careful steps forward. If I could get my hands on him, I could steal his pain until the shift impulse was gone. I could make him docile.

I needed to be fast. Patrick's shirt shredded audibly with his growth. He backed away from me, leaning into the wall as if afraid of *me*. He extended a hand, halting my progress, the other covering his face. His nails elongated, the claws curved and thick. He must have been hurting the skin of his face. "It's okay. You're okay. I'm okay," I whispered.

Patrick's jaw distended, and his teeth became fangs. I raced to touch him before it was too late. But it already was.

Reaching for him, my fingers splayed, he swiped at my hand with a massive claw. The crunch of my bones echoed off the shining pool walls and our audience awed in appreciation.

I cradled my ugly hand to my chest and backed away from the beast. Two fingers broken, the index and the middle. Bones took a long time to heal under my skin, much too long. Patrick's mind had shifted and he wasn't human anymore. He stood tall enough to climb from The Pool if he were so inclined. But why would he when I—a weak, juicy bunny— was trapped in this arena with him?

He let out a torrential roar and snapped the zip tie from his wrists. The waistband of his jeans held around his hips, but the calves and thighs split open. Drool strung from his morphing muzzle in slimy ropes. His eyes were flooded black, angry obsidian. And even if I had the switchblade, I was no match for such a creature.

It came at me at a sprint, bent forward, arms extended.

"No, no, no!" I uttered stupidly. The red wall pressed against my back. There was no way out. The ground quaked with the beast's charge. I couldn't even cover my face, because if I did, I couldn't see.

When it took a swipe at my head, I barely had room to duck toward its stomach. I planted my foot along the curved edge of The Pool, and using that surface, I pushed off like a swimmer, landing on my chest a foot behind the beast. My Ked slipped against the lacquer, and I only got my feet beneath me in time to flop back down to my stomach further down the line.

The beast whisked around and threw his arm in a wide arc where my legs used to be. I continued kicking off the floor of The Pool, skittering around on my belly. It didn't take long for the beast to form a solution. It bent down on its haunches and sprang through the air. I rolled the other direction like a rolling pin, perpendicular to its path. The beast landed hard on both feet, inches from my ribs.

I latched onto its hairy ankle. Its skin was so thick, I could hardly sense anything within it. The beast balanced all its weight on that ankle and lifted the other high above me. I knew what was coming but had no time to react in those two seconds before the foot came down on my sternum.

The crack of my chest was louder than the wailing of the beast. The force was enough to breach my thorax. I felt dozens of fissures and a rupture in the heart. I coughed up a splash of red juices that vanished into the walls of The Pool.

The beast wobbled, its weight unbalanced between the ankle I still held and the one on the ground. It twisted in the air and crumbled.

I couldn't make sense of the pain. I didn't understand how there was room enough in the world to hold it, let alone in my body, as every pound of the beast's weight came down on top of me, its elbow into my cheek. The pain was blinding, astounding, life-changing. My cheekbone and eye socket fractured, as did three ribs. A vessel in my eye popped. A bone punctured my lung.

The injury the beast sustained from its fall was enough—it sprained an ankle and busted a lip on a fang. It was a taste I could access through its armored exterior. I took without thinking. My body would heal, with or without my consent. The beast offered water in the desert, and I had never tasted something so lovely, so mouthwatering. I drained its physical pain in the blink of an eye, and having gained access to its receptors, stole the buried emotions deep in its primal brain.

It wasn't enough to heal me completely. Patrick's animal fear, his anger, even his shame wasn't enough, not even close. His ankle shrank, the human bones seeming to absorb all the additional armor and cartilage, and became flesh in my hand. The burden of his body on mine lightened. Patrick was convulsing as a man, and his seizing rocked my body beneath him.

After all I'd consumed, all his pain, I had seventeen remaining bone breaks.

"Patrick," I wheezed. My ribcage had been crushed. I struggled to breathe, though my bleeding heart—I thought the term with spite—was fit to pump once again. "I'm safe. Tell Ben. Go home." Sharp painful breath in and out.

Thinking that Ben gave a damn one way or the other, that he had something to do with Patrick being here, was both egotistical and debilitating. But it was true. It almost hurt more to know that it was absolutely true. Ben cared about me very much.

"Can't … he's stuck." Patrick sounded drugged without the beast's dread, the rage. I thought he may have been falling asleep right on top of me.

Suddenly, he grated across my body, the button-fly of his pants catching on my ear. Four suits towed him across the pool. Once they made it to the ladder, after all that tremendous effort, they were stumped. Even all six of them couldn't lift Patrick ten feet.

Laisren chortled at their stupidity. "Please, try. For me, please." She held her hands in prayer, Betty swinging from her elbow.

The guards all looked to one another, desperate to please her. They started pulling at Patrick's arms and feet, his limbs bouncing around as if he were a gargantuan puppet.

Laisren stared at me until I felt it. I turned my head to see Betty dangling loosely in one of her hands. And a knife in the other. I began to hyperventilate. I couldn't get up from my back. I couldn't move. I couldn't save her. Burning tears flooded my eyes. I wondered if I'd ever stop crying after this.

"Calm down!" Laisren belted. "You're no fun at all." She threw my snake over one shoulder and made a small cut in her palm. Very small. The moment the steel left her skin, Patrick began to rise steadily through the air, his limbs swinging at his sides. His head whipped around on his neck as he gained lucidity. His busted lip had closed.

He was four feet above the ground outside of The Pool, when Laisren dropped him. The thud wasn't as loud as when he'd been kicked to my level, but it was loud enough. I watched guards swarm his sore body over the edge of the deep end.

Laisren lost interest in Patrick the moment he lost the fight—though I'm pretty sure we were both losers here—and had only removed him from The Pool as a necessity. Laisren evaluated me for a long while before hopping down into the pit.

When she walked, it was a performance, and she loved the show she put on. She wore leopard print spandex pants, a man's button-up, and kitten heels. She looked like she ruled a trailer park, not the entire city of Las Vegas. But her power was so clear, so evident, she didn't need fancy dresses or suits to be intimidating.

She kneeled beside me, Betty flopping around on her neck, and pressed a cold hand to the exposed skin of my stomach, as my shirt had bunched up beneath me. I sensed Laisren's cut palm, and I'd been right, it was nothing more than a nick. I couldn't resist, not with my body in the state that it was, after all, I hadn't been able to resist Ben's blood when I was perfectly healthy. I took her wound. Her pain tasted so good I nearly licked her fingers. The throbbing in my eye began to fade. Laisren stared at me with gleeful, rapt attention, and I turned to mush in her hands. She was a miracle. An absolute miracle.

I knew as her cut closed and my eye shrank back to human size that Laisren suspected, if she wasn't certain, that I could steal physical pain from others, and that we both benefited from the practice. I could not give away that I'd been sniffing out emotions as well. I could *never* let her know that resurrection was an option—

Her eyes were glowing with love and I forgot all my injuries as I basked in them. I wanted to tell her everything I could do ... Why would I ever keep secrets from someone like Laisren? I could help her, couldn't I? Yes ... I opened my mouth.

"Interesting," she said through teeth that changed from starlight white to smoke-stained brown the moment I broke eye contact. "You don't have to touch me. I can touch you. Instinctual. Inevitable. Interesting." The pain returned all at once and I clamped my teeth to keep the whimpers in. "I'm impressed. A promotion is in order! How does the fourth-floor sound?"

Betty struggled to lift her head from Laisren's shoulder, and my attention adhered to my familiar. Her eyes were barely open, but they met my stare, and I felt such overwhelming failure that I would buckle if I could stand. I swallowed my spit and my need to please this woman. As long as I didn't look into those eyes.

"If I stay on the third floor, could I have Betty back? Please?" It took a piece of me to plead with Laisren from my back, after the second dog fight she'd forced me into ... but I did. And I would again. I'd lift my torso and kiss the hem of her leggings as if they were royal robes.

Laisren watched me lie in misery with a quirk to her mouth.

"Please?" I said again, knowing she enjoyed it.

She dragged Betty from around her shoulders and set her on my stomach. "Deal. You'll have the snake, and you'll stay on the third floor."

I understood the conditions and would not reveal exactly how happy I was with them. I'd already planned to explore the air ducts from my room, and I would never hand Betty over to advance in her ranks. Though I'm sure other employees wanted power, had ambition, ambition is something I never had.

"Thank you." I placed my broken fingers on Betty's scales. She was hungry. Without a thought, I relieved her of the ache and took her hunger pains. I felt my own bones begin to mend in the act—subtly—under my skin.

Was I as good as food, or was I only taking her pain? How far would this go? Would there come a day when I no longer needed to eat, to sleep? I never wanted to reach such a point. I loved eating. I loved tasting the food Ben prepared for me, knowing he put effort into each flavor. I loved to rest. I loved to dream. I'd choose my nightmares over nothing because I loved waking up beside him.

I never wanted to move again. I wanted to lie here until the next opponent squished me like a steamroller. It would seem, a quirk of my magic, that no amount of stolen pain could erase my emotional turmoil. I had to feel each and every bit of it. That was comforting, in a way, to know my mind remained my own.

Laisren climbed out of The Pool and smirked at me one last time before leaving me crushed at the bottom.

Betty seemed content to lie with me. She stretched herself long, aligning with my spine. I stroked her head.

Once the audience dispersed back to hell where they came from, and Patrick had been dragged into the building, Anderson jumped from the ladder and landed low to the ground with a grunt. He trudged toward me, displeasure evident on his face. He watched me watch Betty for a while, before lying down beside us. He intertwined his fingers on his stomach.

I couldn't see the stars here. Just a hazy glow from the hyper-reality I was trapped inside. I wanted to go home.

He said, "You did good."

I snorted and it hurt.

He cleared his throat. I could tell he was fortifying himself, and I let him go about it in silence as I searched the sky for twinkling lights.

"I'm sorry," he whispered. I knew it cost him to say it. It wasn't his job to be sorry to me or sorry for me. "I'm sorry, if I hurt you when I … took you. I think I pulled your hair and um … hurt your wrists. I'm sorry your snake was taken from you, that I knew." He cleared his throat again. "And I'm sorry you have to do this again."

Yes, I did. I would continue until Laisren knew everything. There could be nooks and crannies to my affinity that even I hadn't discovered yet. I dreaded what opponents would befall me before I found out.

"I'm sorry," I said to Anderson. A hitch jolted from my chest. There was so much to apologize for, but not to him. "For your eight years. For your dogs."

He gulped at the air like a strangled man.

I reached tremulously across the gap between us—not because I wanted to console him, no, he deserved the remorse— but because the fissures in my fingers had yet to mend completely. I lay my hand atop the two of his and I took a piece of his turmoil for myself. Just a slice—I couldn't consume emotions like I could bodily harm. Neither of us deserved such healing anyway. But I felt something. A minuscule reprieve from our suffering. A numbness. My bones didn't mend, but their pain dulled the slightest bit.

"Thank you," he said.

IT WAS over an hour before I could stand. My legs were fine, but my thorax had been crushed and I was coughing like crazy. Anderson boosted me over the ledge of the shallow end, my hand too mangled for the ladder. Everything hurt. I needed sleep.

The office of The Alcazar was empty, and I was grateful. I wondered where they'd taken Patrick, if he was somewhere on the third floor with me. Jessamae was gone, the pull eradicated completely. She may have even arrived with Patrick. They'd come to this building for a reason, and I no longer worried I'd missed my chance.

Anderson opened my door. As I walked past, he awkwardly patted my shoulder, unsure of what to do after our moment of camaraderie.

"Night," I said.

"Goodnight, Frankie. I'll pick you up at seven tomorrow night." He looked at his watch before showing me its face. 11:43.

I didn't have a clock, and I appreciated the gesture. He was illustrating some semblance of trust toward me by telling me the time. If he only got a look inside the bathroom, he'd take it right back.

I hated the thought of being away from Betty, even for a moment. So I sat her on the tile of the bathroom floor while I sat on the floor of the shower, letting the water pelt me. She slithered around my feet, slick with the shower's spray, tickling my toes with her forked tongue. She was so beautiful. "Are you okay?" I asked her.

She enjoyed the puddle of warm water, whisking through it like a fish. She dipped her face in, until only her eyes floated. She watched me, a splashy flick to her tail. "Yeah, this is the best we've got."

In bed, I gave Betty her own pillow beside me. She curled into a cinnamon roll, her head balancing atop the rest of her body like a cherry atop a sundae. She was getting so big. The pillow was just wide enough for her. I smiled, knowing that at least one thing had returned to normal. My familiar was back.

I fussed under the covers and watched Betty sleep until my eyelids grew heavy. I closed them, sleep's gracious embrace within reach at last …

Frankie. Ben's voice ricocheted through my skull, hurting my brain.

Why did I do this to myself? Because I deserved it. My subconscious realized Ben would cause more pain than even Paimon, and had created this sick illusion to punish me.

Frankie. His voice made me shiver. Who knew when I would hear it again? Maybe after three months, I'd have nothing to go home to. I relished my name from his imaginary lips, replaying it for myself again and again.

Frank! Ben's voice, crystal clear. Yelling, panicked. His words weren't full of care for me—they were full of fear.

Ben was talking to me. Inside my mind.

15

I WAS SO FAR past exhausted, I couldn't even see *exhausted* on the horizon. I'd officially lost it. I was not hearing Ben inside it. Attributing the voice to my lunacy, I tried to sleep with renewed determination.

Frankie! he shouted again.

My eyes flashed open. Could it be real? It was hard to know anymore; the whole premise of reality was an illusion.

If Ben was in fact calling to me in my mind, that implied two things: First, his affinity had expanded—as all our affinities had seemed to, under the extreme stress of our Vegas vacation; second, he needed me. Patrick was here, Ben could be too. I sensed Jessamae before, and though I had no idea of Cleo's whereabouts, if both Ben and Jessamae were buzzing around The Alcazar, Cleo wouldn't be far behind.

But at this point, my magic couldn't keep up with my body. I'd been surviving on cereal, pizza, and pain. I hadn't slept properly since my last night with Ben three days ago. My bones were still mending, my heart had been punctured. I needed to sleep.

I replayed Ben's voice in my head. I wasn't much good to him now.

But I had to try.

Betty needed her rest, but I refused to leave her. I tucked her into her pouch, and she complied eagerly, feeling the same way about our separation.

I carefully pulled on my blue shirt and pants, ache bursting within me at the smallest trigger. I put on my shoes and, preparing for the worst, tucked my knife in the back pocket of my pants.

Taking the pair of butter knives from the vanity, I climbed onto the toilet tank, and plunged each of them into the rough-cut holes, creating handholds. I threw Betty's pouch into the vent lightly, ensuring I could still reach the strap if I didn't make it in, in case Anderson made another surprise visit. And I climbed.

The bones in my hands screamed with such agony, I let go and fell back to the toilet. I tried again, doing my best to avoid pressure on my broken fingers. It was horrifyingly familiar, like climbing out of a grave. Except this hurt much worse. Sweat decimated my grip on the metal. Betty's black eyes held on me from the confines of her pouch. I was crying when my chest finally slid along the steel shelf.

Pulling my legs inside without any sort of purchase was just as difficult as my chest. I pushed Betty further into the vent as I scrambled, sticking my hands to the metal walls and wiggling my hips until they were inside as well. I had peeled an inch of skin off my stomach.

On my elbows and knees, I made my way through the tunnel like a mole. That's how it felt, like burrowing through earth that could collapse over me and under me at any moment. The vent hooked right only feet from my bathroom. When I came to a fork, I turned left without reason. There were dozens of turns ahead of me, some with squares of light illuminating my path.

I peeked in the first metal window—it was a vent stationed above a toilet in a bathroom just like mine. It could be Patrick's bathroom, he could be on this floor. I knocked my fist against the grate. When nothing happened, I did it again. A young man with bad skin and a nightshirt came into the room to investigate. I moved on as he squinted into the vent at the noise.

If I had a ruler, I knew I could prove that the vent was shrinking, squeezing my sides in toward my spine. Dragging Betty behind me, I inched along like a sweaty worm. My mouth was dry, and I licked the perspiration from my lips. I could die up here and they wouldn't find my body for days, believing the stink of my corpse to be nothing more than an unfortunate raccoon. It was too tight a space to turn around, so I continued forward.

Fran ... kie. Ben's voice had quieted.

The next window proved quite a sight. I wiped the grime from my brow and leaned in closer. The guard who had opened the rooftop door earlier, the one with the pink, shaved head, was vigorously fucking an older gentleman on the bathroom sink. He wasn't a guard I recognized, and being on the third floor, he was likely a trash employee like me. She was very much enjoying herself, squealing like a piglet. Hating her and what they were doing, for their taking pleasure in anything at all, I forced my body into a knot and kicked the vent, propelling myself away.

"The hell was that?" I heard her whisper as I flipped back onto my elbows.

My throat hurt. I breathed in hot dust at every turn. My clothes were grungy and sticking to my sweaty flesh, plus my fingers were killing me. I used the meat of my palms to keep going. But it wasn't until the sixth bathroom vent that I found him.

I banged on the grate, plumb out of finesse, and cut my hand.

Patrick opened the door, conspicuously searching the walls of the bathroom. He was fully dressed in a sweatshirt and jeans, a baseball cap pulled low on his head. "Frankie?"

"What?" I stabbed my fingers into the slats in the grate like the prisoner I was. "How'd you know it was me?"

Patrick looked up at my voice, his eyebrows at his brim. "Oh!"

Pulling my butter knives from Betty's pouch, I slid them through the slats. "Here, use these on the screws."

He grabbed one of the knives and let the other clatter off the toilet seat. He forced the blade between the vent and the wall, using it as a crowbar. One screw instantly exploded from the wall. He grabbed each side of the vent and jerked it free from the duct. The remaining screws plinked to the floor and drywall dust filled the room like airborne spores.

"Jesus." I tried swinging my legs out from under me, but I couldn't raise my body high enough. My arms were shaking and my feet were numb.

Patrick grabbed me under the arms and tugged. I yelped at the stretch, but I was on my feet in no time. I stood tall for less than a breath before I sagged to the floor. He let me flop without interruption, waiting as I coughed and squirmed. "How'd you know it was me?" I wheezed.

"Ben said if I got in, you might find me. And if you did, it'd be through the door or in the bathroom."

"There was a way through the door?" I asked, angry that I hadn't figured out that path. "What else did he say?" There were other more important questions to ask, but I didn't care.

He breathed deeply. I wanted to hit him. "He didn't really have time for much else."

"What the fuck does that mean?"

"He's here, somewhere, I think." Patrick held up his hands when I scrabbled to his feet, clawing at the bare skin beneath his jeans. "God! Stop! I didn't do anything! It was Ben's idea! We hit the high-roller tables. Took too much. He didn't give me as much info as one would hope, but that was the plan! To keep me in the dark so I wouldn't have to lie. Maize gave us away the second she saw us." He pinched his nose. "You'd think she'd be grateful, after the things I did for her. To her. On her."

"Where are Cleo and Jessamae? I know she comes here sometimes. To The Alcazar."

"Who?"

"Jessamae!"

"Will you calm down! Ben didn't want all of us to get taken in. Cleo and Jessamae watched the cuffing in the casino. I don't know what happened after that."

Angst and hope jumped me simultaneously. Everyone knew I was here. Even if he didn't see the actual kidnapping, of course Ben would see, through me, into exactly whose control I'd stumbled. Ben had been apprehended and he was being held in the building. He'd used his affinity to the detriment of the house, and naturally, he was punished.

"Why aren't you with him?"

Patrick waved his stupid arms around. "I don't know. Because *I* didn't win any money? Because they thought I'd be useful as a shifter? Because I was too charming to cage?"

Cage? My insides turned to water. "I think I heard him. Ben. He said my name."

"He was in your room?"

"No, I heard him in my head."

Patrick pursed his lips and chewed on his thumbnail, avoiding my frantic stare. "I see. Well … while I'm sure that's true, how does that help us?"

"You said he was in the building. He needs help. I could tell by his voice he needs help, and we have to find him. We can use the ducts—"

"Frankie, breathe. In, out."

My lip trembled in incredulous fury.

"Do it, woman! You're of no use to anyone if you pass out in here!"

I took one exaggerated breath.

"Very good. Do that more, okay?" He helped me off the ground and set me on the toilet. "We will help him. But I cannot fit inside that thing." He gestured to the air vent. "And I can't change."

"What do you mean?"

He pulled the neck of his sweatshirt down. There was a black collar around his neck. It was made of steel. "If my neck swells, this thing can sense it. It'll *incapacitate* me. I'm thinking something in the lightning strike department."

"Fuck!" That meant his turning into the beast and breaking the doors down was out of the question. "When will they take it off?"

"Probably for my next fight," he said, and his seriousness made me want to cry.

I looked dolefully at the hole in the wall. Did this same duct extend to different floors? Up and down rather than side-to-side? "What's on the second floor?"

"Huh?"

"Did you see the main floor? The next floor? How were you brought in?"

"They cuffed me, threw me in the back of a car."

"Bag on your head? And Ben's?"

He nodded.

"Fuck."

He left the room and came back with a paper cup. He filled it with water from the sink as he asked, "What about the second floor?" He gave me the water.

I sipped at it. It was warm. "The main floor of The Alcazar is the illusion, the machines and the tables. The third floor houses the lowest level employees. Something has to be on the second floor, right? Laisren uses the building as an indication of rank. Prisoners wouldn't be held high in the building. They would be lower on the totem pole. The second floor."

He considered my theory, appearing to have caught most of my rambling, rushed words. "Unless there's a basement."

"Sure, but that only leaves two possibilities in the whole building. And the basement could be maintenance, plumbing."

He crossed his arms. "Alright, baby girl. But if you take the ducts down—" he pointed to his feet and looked at me through his brows.

"I know where down is!"

"Alright! If you take the ducts down, it's going to hurt. That's farther than you think."

Flashing back to my toss into The Pool yesterday, I said, "I've fallen farther."

Patrick nodded solemnly. "How's your chest?" Heady shame filled the room. I smelled its smoke.

He didn't need to feel sorry for me. I knew who was really at fault, and I would get my chance at her one of these days. "I'll heal. I always do. How are you?"

"Couple bruises. I heal pretty fast too, you know."

I beckoned him to the toilet with a hand out. He approached nervously and I took his fingers in mine. We didn't touch much —I'd touched the beast more than I'd touched him. His hip was sore and bruised, and I ate the injury. I needed all the strength I could get.

Patrick was visibly unnerved. "Can you not do that? I feel violated."

"Too late. Do you have a phone?"

He shook his head. "They took it as soon as I got here."

I flipped his wrist to the fancy silver watch. "2:30, shit. That only gives me a couple hours." Anderson might give me more privacy this morning, as his resentment toward me was diminishing. But I couldn't count on it. And if I wasn't in my room, the bathroom was the only option. The vent was still open. All of us would pay.

I didn't have any other choice, so neither did Ben. He'd have to wait another day.

"I'll go tomorrow. As soon as I'm back from The Pool. When's your next match?"

Patrick sighed and leaned against the vanity. "I haven't even spoken with the head asshole here. I was taken to this shit hole immediately. No explanations. Very rude."

She hadn't questioned Patrick, as Ben predicted she might. Is that because she questioned Ben? Was he being interrogated now?

Patrick continued, "Then they bound my hands, not sexy in the least, and dropped me on your doorstep. As if they knew we're best friends."

I tucked my face into my knees and thought of Laisren. I had killed one of her employees, unarmed and drugged. I could heal Laisren, and her goons, without volunteering or consenting to do so.

As a shifter—and a friend of mine—Patrick's utility was simple. He was the perfect booster shot, forcing me to lengths I'd never gone before.

"She wants to dig into my affinity, to use it," I whispered, "in every way possible. That's why I'm going to The Pool every night." I looked around the bathroom, suddenly certain she'd bugged each suite. "She knows there's more to me than restoration."

He stretched his arms out straight in front of him and pantomimed Frankenstein.

If she found out, she'd never let me go. And I could create a thousand Paimon's before I managed to negotiate my way out or jump off the roof. But that wasn't all. I could sense emotions, smell bad feelings as if they were an infected abscess in the heart. If that ability continued to grow ... Could I feed off heartache? Steal someone's feelings?

Patrick bit his lip, his eyebrows low over his blue eyes. "It sounds like you don't have much of a choice here. But, hey." He crouched and jiggled my knee. "You've already made it through two, the second against *me*, I might add. And you haven't revealed everything. And chances are ... you won't have to. That particular ability of yours, Frankenstein, that very *unstable* ability, you won't ever have to use to save yourself. That's good news."

I nodded. He was right. No one would die in The Pool, and even if they did, I would not resurrect them. Laisren may continue sending me, night after night, knowing there was more to my magic. I could live with that. I would keep fighting. And I would find Ben in the meantime. Tomorrow. "Okay."

I stood and climbed on the toilet. "I'm not going to come back tomorrow. I'm going to find Ben."

Patrick helped Betty and I back through the opening. As I slid forward on my belly he asked, "You'll come back before you leave for good though, right? You won't leave me here?"

I looked back over my shoulder. He was tall enough to meet my eyes inside the vent without standing on the toilet.

"No promises," I said as I crawled forward once again.

"That's not funny! You think I won't haunt you like your sweet, old granny?"

It was a joke, but I winced anyway. Nothing would ever haunt me like her.

⁓

BEN'S CALL faded from a whisper to a memory while I trudged back to my bathroom. I hoped he was sleeping, but I had never been lucky.

I dropped Betty to my own tiled floor and had a horrible time getting myself out. After I cracked my elbow on the toilet tank, I picked up Betty and fell on my bed like a rifled duck, desperate for a few hours of sleep. Betty slithered into a ball in the center of my back, reveling in the warmth of my skin. I was asleep in seconds.

When I awoke, the sun was high in the sky and brightening my apartment with an irritating persistence. I woke on my back, Betty nesting on the cushion of my belly. I rubbed her nose before standing, replacing her snoozing form back in the blankets.

It was late afternoon. Anderson had let me sleep all day. Our moment at the bottom of The Pool last night must have convinced him to show a little mercy.

Maybe he would help us. He understood the layout of the building much better than I did after one trip through an air vent. If only Ben was here, he could tell me the odds. But even without precognition, it was an enormous risk. Anderson could turn me in, stop me himself, or face the consequences if my absence were discovered. Though he was the one who'd brought me here, I didn't want to see him punished for my endless bad decisions.

I would drop certain hints, read his emotional pallet, and hope I came back to this room with fewer broken bones than I had last night.

Ripping a sheet from the paper pad for groceries, I wrote, "Frozen mice!!!" and slipped it under the door. I ate two packets of Top Ramen as Betty watched game show reruns, her tail flicking against my foot.

Without any threats on my life, the day passed at a turtle's pace. I read five chapters from my new book. It wasn't bad, but it couldn't keep my attention. My knee bounced erratically each time I sat down. I bit the skin off my lip after each time it grew back. If Ben was being tortured while I was sitting on a hotel bed reading fantasy …

A knock rattled the door. Anderson poked his head in. "Hey."

"Thanks for actually knocking." I grabbed Betty, and instantly paused. I couldn't hide her here. It would take five minutes to search the place and they'd discover what I'd done to the air vent. I couldn't protect her from the bottom of an empty swimming pool.

"I'll hold her. While you're in The Pool." Anderson said.

His remorse made him civil, more than civil, generous. Could I trust this man? Could I take such an enormous leap?

Reading the conflict on my face, he said. "I would keep her safe."

He'd shown me kindness these last few days, and I'd never

trusted anyone who'd been kind to me … I'd give him a test. Much lower stakes.

"Could I take her to someone? A babysitter?"

Anderson searched the sad apartment, frowning. "Who?"

∼∾∽

IT HADN'T TAKEN LONG for him to track down the room number, just a phone call. And he hadn't given our friendship away to Laisren, he didn't sound any alarms. It was promising.

Anderson knocked on the door, then opened it with his keycard. Patrick processed the two of us on his doorstep. "You do not fit the description I requested." He caught the eye of a restless Betty poking out of her bag. "But the snake can stay."

I elbowed past him. "I'm going to leave Betty with you while I'm in The Pool tonight." Setting Betty's pouch on the bed and turning on the TV, I said. "This is Anderson, my escort."

Patrick's mouth quirked. "Very nice."

"Pay attention, Patrick. I'm leaving Betty with you, okay? I'll be back after the match."

He said, "You know I was kidding, right? I don't like snakes, sexually or otherwise."

"Patrick!"

"Fine! Bossy, baby girl." He went to his kitchenette. "How about a drink before you go?" He took tequila from his freezer.

"How did you get liquor?"

Patrick beamed at me. "I can be very persuasive." Anderson cleared his throat and Patrick's smile disappeared. "Okay, okay, I put it on the grocery list. You know how to use it, don't you? Listening has never been a specialty of yours." Patrick poured two shots each into three plastic cups.

Anderson said, "No, thank you."

"Please," Patrick responded, handing the man a cup. And Anderson took it.

He hadn't sold us out. He accepted the drink. I decided in that moment to leap, to trust, for one of the few times in my life. I asked, "What's on the second floor, Anderson?"

He coughed up what little liquid he swallowed. "What? Second floor?"

"Yeah. The casinos are on the first, we're on the third. What's on the second?"

He shrugged like a silent movie mime. "How should I know? And even if I did, it's not your concern." He coughed again into his hand, splashing tequila-spit on his fingers. He rolled the cup back and forth along the countertop, avoiding our eyes. He didn't move to leave, and he didn't puff up at my question. He leaned on his elbows next to Patrick.

There was something to this, this casual act of drinking at a kitchen counter that exuded … normalcy. Anderson seemed reluctant to leave such a commonplace moment, even after I'd disrupted it.

"Anderson, is it?" Patrick asked him. "Do you have a first name, or did your mother do this to you?"

He smiled. *Anderson* smiled. My jaw dropped at the sight of it.

"Last name," he said.

Patrick poured another splash of liquor into his cup and mine. "Where you from, Anderson?"

He took a sip, eyes on Betty. "Maryland."

"Go Ravens."

"Damn right," Anderson said. "Your team?"

"Niners."

Anderson gave a brittle laugh. "So, you're a masochist?"

I marveled at the moment, a *miracle*. Not only had Patrick been met with something other than revulsion, that person was Anderson, who was laughing like a regular, no-stick-up-their-anal-cavity person!

"I'm sure you miss it. Maryland," Patrick said with sincerity.

I sipped my drink to distract from my blatant observation. The liquor burned my insides wonderfully.

Anderson gulped his tequila. "Sure, but ... it's not Maryland as much as just, being out in the world. Off the Strip."

"Well." Patrick finished his drink before slamming it on the counter. "It seems the three of us want the same thing." He moved in closer to Anderson. "But first, I'll ask: are there micro-phones in these rooms?"

16

ANDERSON SURVEYED THE ROOM, both confused and afraid. "I have no idea. But I don't think so. Laisren doesn't need the technology. She can sense if she's being lied to."

"Okay, that's helpful," Patrick continued. "Here's the thing. You want to leave. And we want to leave. You have inside knowledge, we have people outside. Why not help each other out, and get the hell outta' dodge?" He spoke as if he were proposing a new restaurant to try for dinner.

"That's not funny," he said, sipping his drink. Patrick merely shrugged and waited. Realizing Patrick was serious, Anderson sputtered, "That is ... completely insane. Do you have any idea how many people she controls? No, you don't. But it's too many to count, and they are placed all over the country. They'd find us in a heartbeat." He pushed his hands inside the sleeves of his suit, rubbing his arms beneath the fabric.

"That's where this alliance would come in handy, you see. We have a couple of contacts who would help get us out. And help keep us out."

"Who?"

"Ben," I interjected, a cramp developing in my face from grinding my teeth. "Ben. He's a mentalist, and a seer. He could see which paths lead to capture." I held Anderson's eye, imploring the man. "He was taken from a casino last night. For using his affinity to take money from the house."

Anderson's eyes flitted around like fireflies in a jar. "Not a very good seer, I guess." Patrick snorted, but Anderson was nervous. He knew what was in store for Ben, knew where he was, I was certain of it. "And Ben is your gambling partner?" He turned to Patrick.

"Yes. But up until a few days ago, he was also Frankie's lover."

I recoiled. "Shut up, Patrick."

Patrick continued, "Then things got a little ... complicated. Some indiscretions—"

"Shut the fuck up."

"Plus." Patrick plopped a meaty hand on Anderson's shoulder, acting as if he hadn't dropped an enormous TMI bomb. "We have a Jack. Jack is a rune bitch—witch, I apologize—who specializes in being left the hell alone. He'll help us."

"Are we talking about the same man?" I asked, not wanting to lose Anderson's faith, but baffled nonetheless.

"If Jessamae asks, he'll help us," Patrick said with confidence. I sucked my cheeks into my mouth. He might be right, he might be wrong, but I would agree with just about anything if it meant Anderson joined our side.

"Where is Ben, Anderson?" I asked as patiently as I was able.

"This Ben ... he, like, cheat on you?"

"No," I stated calmly. I wasn't sure what to call what happened, on either side. All the lines were blurred, the relationships messy. Plus, we'd been under the influence of ... something. I only knew it hurt terribly, and I needed Anderson's help to save him.

Anderson's eyes were slightly shiny when he finally answered. "I don't know. I don't know who Ben is, what he looks like. But if he is here ... the second floor"—I felt a spark of vindication at the words—"it's for the inmates. Those who have made a grievance against the house and refused to pay the settlement."

"That's why I'm not there?" I asked. "Because I took Laisren's deal?"

Anderson nodded.

"And why wasn't I taken in?" Patrick asked.

"Did you steal from the house?"

Slurping tequila from his finger, Patrick shook his head. Anderson simply stared at him. Patrick had answered his own question.

"Then why am I here at all?" he asked.

"Association," Anderson continued, fidgeting like crazy. "With Ben, or even with Frankie. It's possible Ben was deemed a threat. There are a few mages down there that Laisren works to rehabilitate."

I didn't like that word. "Rehabilitate how?"

He didn't answer me.

"Rehabilitate how! Rehabilitate how!" I shook his lapels and smushed him against the counter.

"I don't know, okay! I'm not assigned to level two!" But he looked sick. Whatever happened to threats on that floor, it wasn't a spa treatment.

"Can you take me there?" I rasped, leaning closer to him.

Anderson's hands shot up like I was wielding a gun. "I'm not agreeing to anything. I haven't! I don't … I don't know if I want to risk it. My life is sort of valuable to me, or I wouldn't be here in the first place."

"We could save you those eight years, Anderson. You'd be free." Or we'd get him killed. But the reward was worth the risk.

Falling silent despite my whims, I gave him time. He needed a moment to think without my roughing him up. Patrick, sensing the same thing, sipped his drink and otherwise kept his mouth shut.

Anderson sighed so hard I thought he might throw up. "There's no time now. The match is in thirty minutes. We need to be early. Just let me—let me think about it. I need to weigh everything. Eight years is a long time … but I'd rather serve them than die. I'd rather serve them than be taken to the second floor."

⬿

JESSAMAE WOULD BE at the match. The pull of the cords was stronger than ever, and they were leading me up to the roof. She'd come to watch, most likely as an attendee and nothing more. But she knew I was a contestant, and that was reassuring. She wouldn't let me die.

"A witch will be at the match, white hair, a scar across one eye, a friend. Talk to her, tell her I sent you," I whispered to Anderson just before the elevator doors slid open.

He didn't answer, smart, now that we were on the top floor, but he swallowed enough saliva that I could hear it slide down his throat. The guard with the shaved head awaited our entrance. I grinned when I saw her, remembering a particularly awkward position with her ass smashed atop the sink's faucet. Water everywhere. I gave her a breathy moan as I passed through the door, eliciting a look of pure disgust. "Right back at you," I muttered.

Her expression melted into one of contempt before opening the door. You'd think her bathroom fixture adventures would have lifted her spirits some.

"What exactly was that about?" Anderson asked, blush tinting his cheeks.

I smirked. That was the first molecule of fun I'd ever had in this place.

The crowd seemed to double each day. I wondered if they, too, wanted to know what it would take to kill me. I understood the appeal, how much was too much until my restoration couldn't keep up. I thought I saw Jessamae's white hair in the crowd before climbing down the ladder and jumping into the red.

Laisren was waiting at the judge's table, as I'd come to think of the spot between the deep and shallow end. She looked down on me, greed seeping from her pores like alcohol. The twins were whispering amongst themselves, and the smiling man crouched down at the edge of The Pool, his eyes fervent and bright. He wanted to see everything.

My opponent was already in The Pool, a first for me. He was small, perhaps smaller than me, except for his gut which was rotund. Distended like an overdue pregnancy past the lips of his trousers. He had a sort of muzzle or bridle over his mouth. It was made of wire and belted around the back of his head. His hands were bound in leather cuffs. He spat and snarled through his teeth. I felt his hunger, smelled his need. His eyes were absolutely deranged.

Nicola appeared at Laisren's elbow—she'd never watched a match before—and pulled an ornate dagger from a thigh sheath beneath her skirt. She beckoned to peculiar young girl standing at the deep end. The girl waved her arms around as if they were too heavy, bending each leg in turn like a drunk water bird. She approached Nicola with a smile, her eyes on the sky, and without a moment's pause, Nicola slid the blade along the girl's throat. I smashed my hands to my mouth to quell my shriek.

Blood dribbled down to the girl's dirty tank top. Her throat opening like a mouth and drooling all over her. Then, before my eyes, fire erupted from Nicola's palms, scalding the blade at the girl's neck. It glowed yellow over the wound, searing it shut. She screamed.

"What the hell are you doing?" I said behind my hand.

As the girl clutched her throat, my opponent cranked his head around like a startled horse. The muzzle was sizzling against his skin. After a spark ignited, the bindings fell from his wrists and face.

The girl had served as a sacrifice to the elements—Nicola had freed him.

He flexed his skinny fingers with a mad gleam in his eye.

When he lifted his head to me, I saw that his mouth was gigantic, the edges rimmed in pink spittle that reached the hinge of his jaw. His mouth took up the entire bottom half of his face.

"Begin," Laisren said from The Pool's edge, and the man came at me, frothing like a rabid dog. I didn't understand his affinity and I didn't know how to defend myself. I covered my face with my arms and ran backward. That was my first mistake.

His smell punched me in the nose. The need, yes, there was so much of it, but then the sour tang of a soiled body. He hadn't washed in a long time. The man spread his jaws and latched onto the flesh of my forearm, his teeth scraping against the bone. I wailed, my hand in his matted hair, and tried to shake his teeth free. When I finally detached the animal, he'd taken a hunk of me with him.

He swallowed it.

I stared at the hole he left in my arm, paralyzed, in the middle of the arena. I couldn't fathom the empty space, the void in me where I used to exist. Blood gushed down to my elbow, dripping and disappearing over the red lacquer of the pool. My pale radius shone through all the torn sinew and capillaries. The colors were striking.

While I watched my heart pump my blood to the ground, my opponent lunged back for seconds.

Though I anticipated his "gift" this time around, I had no way to stop it. I knew to keep my bare skin out of his way and relied on the fabric of my clothes to shield me. I pivoted and hopped out of his reach. The man wasn't a strategist. He was *starving*. My only chance was the same as it was yesterday, to get my hands on him. His gnawing hunger swirled around us, enough to fill this entire pool, and I didn't know if I could take it all from him. I'd burst if I tried.

The man's breath was pungent iron and as loud as a plane engine. He charged and I dropped low. He predicted the move and barreled on top of me. His arms wrapped around my chest and his teeth closed over the curve of my shoulder. I screamed and screamed. The bite was excruciating, but the sight of him hanging onto me by the mouth was worse. I bashed my head into his face with a crunch. The crunch came from my own nose.

I got out from under him as he stumbled. He chortled around the stuff in his throat in sticky blasts as I whirled to face him.

The cannibal was chewing the piece he'd taken from my shoulder, mocking me. I put a hand to the gash in my neck and it was hot, viscous with coagulating blood. He swallowed my meat down and licked his swollen lips.

Lurching forward, his eyes jumped to my bits of exposed skin. Suddenly he paused, then fumbled to one knee, a look of surprise on his face. My opportune moment was small, but I seized it, bolting for the man on the ground.

I lifted my foot as high as I could, and I stomped on the man's kneecap.

He bawled, as human as I'd ever seen him, at the crack that echoed through The Pool. I went to smash the other, raising my foot, and he caught my calf, pulling my leg from under me. I landed on my back and hurried to crawl away from his gaping mouth. I had to steal his hunger, but he'd never let me.

The cannibal grabbed ahold of my foot. I thrashed as he removed my shoe. "No, stop! STOP!" I screamed, fighting to escape. He peeled my sock from my foot and leaned in close. I kicked him hard in the face with my other foot, but as I pulled back for a second strike, he bit down, taking my pinky toe and some of my foot with him. I howled. "NO! NOOO!" Tears and bile soaked my tongue.

He was eating me alive. I caught a single glimpse of my lumpy, broken foot before I rammed my other heel into his mouth.

He fell back, his arms loose at his sides. He was disoriented, almost dazed. I army-crawled closer to him, intending to smash an elbow down onto his broken lip, but I sensed his craving as I drew in close. It was so much smaller than when we began. The meals of me he'd eaten had almost ... satiated him. Almost. I reached out and held his hand. Our jeering onlookers grumbled at the childlike gesture.

His hunger, though lesser, was still enormous to me. I took it as well as the pain from his fractured jaw and his cracked kneecap. Feeling as though he owed me this, and much, much more, I dipped my fingers in the swell of blood on his face. He offered enough to close my open wounds, though they still had a great deal of healing to do. I couldn't see the bones beneath the muscles in my forearm anymore. The skin of my shoulder itched as it pulled together like a patchwork quilt. The opening in my foot clotted. I'd never grow that toe back, and I felt the ridiculous desire to sob over its loss. So much had been taken from me this week, why did I care about the little nub of a toe?

The cannibal's eyes filled with tears. I wondered if there was ever a moment since his reveal that he wasn't a ravenous, insatiable tornado. His magic was a curse. He took vitality from others the hard way. My restoration existed inside my skin, in my blood, as Patrick explained all those months ago. And, having consumed some of my magic, his hunger had finally dulled. I was repulsed by him, but more than that, I pitied him.

I squeezed my foot—the injury hadn't completely shut, and the blood was as thick as oatmeal. My opponent was immobile on his back. I'd won. But Laisren had yet to call the match. The combination of amusement and fury on her face made her look unreal, cartoonish.

Laisren didn't say a word as Nicola strutted to the ladder nearest her. She climbed down, her form-fitting dress bunched around her thighs, and jumped to the bottom, sticking the landing.

I stared at her through my brows. "What?"

She clucked her tongue at my tone. "I'm bored with amateur hour."

I forced myself to stand, with only one shoe, nine toes, and gaping lacerations on my shoulder and arm. My joints and ribs were still healing after Patrick had fallen on me. I needed more time. I needed to eat and sleep and regenerate. Dread and resignation punched through my stomach and stretched my intestines. I was collapsing under their weight, but I would never let Nicola see it. I'd play dumb instead, just to twist her panties. "What the hell does that mean?"

The three witches around Laisren used the fancy dagger to lift the cannibal from the pool. He hadn't stopped crying.

Nicola gave a dazzling smile and held her hands out in display. They lit like torches in a tomb.

At the sight of her fire, I plunged into the past: I was trampled in Ben's kitchen, I was looking up at Jesus in a polo and there was no skin on my legs, I saw Gabriel's teeth through the melting tissue of his face before the funeral director went up in a ball of flames.

I saw silver-dollar eyes reflecting Nicola's yellow glow. Heard flies crawling around in my hair.

I swallowed a bilious burp, vomit rising in my throat. "Bit below your pay grade, isn't it?"

"Tremendously. But you are not infallible, Francesca Hughes—"

"You think I don't know that?"

"—and I'm the perfect person to clarify that for you."

I searched for Jessamae in the crowd. She was here, so close, the vibration briefly overcame my fear. But I couldn't see her, I couldn't find her pale eyes. She wouldn't or couldn't come forward. I was on my own.

"Am I boring you?"

I snapped my head back to Nicola, who was visibly offended by my wandering eye.

"Yes." In the fleeting moment that fear wasn't the most pressing inhabitant of my body, I understood just how much Nicola had contributed to the stupendous ruination of my life. She'd kidnapped me, given me drugged fruit before I lost control, sat Ben in that booth where he'd gotten so drunk. It was *her* giving him drink after drink after drink. And Maize, Maize who normally guarded her club was the one who'd seen and reported Ben's gambling wins. Nicola's crony, Nicola's doing. He was in a cage because of me, but also because of *her*.

I didn't see a dragon. All I saw was a nasty, conniving bitch.

I said, "Well? If you're going to knock me down a peg, then fucking do it." My lip twitched and my teeth chattered in my mouth, but not out of fear. I was so angry I was shaking. I'd lost everything in that goddamn club, and though Laisren was the head of the deformed, heinous body that was Las Vegas, Nicola was the hand. I'd cut off that hand if it was the last thing I lived to do.

Nicola stared at me, suspicious of my mood change, her flames flickering like weak candles.

"DO IT!" I screamed. Blood and spit flew from my mouth and landed on the lacquer.

She kicked into second gear and her face contorted in fury. Her flames stretched higher and higher, nearing the roof of The Alcazar beside us, and her eyes glowed a toxic orange. Good. I was tired of waiting. I would take everything from her. And if she killed me in the process, all the better.

She threw fireballs at me with the insane cackle of a hag. Her nostrils expelled hives of smoke, thick enough to burn my throat as she sprinted toward me on the highest of high heels. I only stepped back once or twice out of instinct, because I knew I wouldn't escape the inferno. I never had before.

My shirt caught fire when a well-aimed cinder hit my stomach and the happy flames danced up my torso, singing the peach fuzz of my belly and destroying patches of skin. Rather than put myself out, I bent forward and hooked my arms around Nicola's knees, tackling her to the ground as she set me ablaze.

The burn was staggering, and I wanted to beat myself against the hard surface of The Pool, but I wouldn't. Nicola would put me out, I'd make sure of it.

She had the size advantage, and my only hope was to keep her on the ground. As we wrestled, my clothes whooshing as the fire spread, her eyes were pits of molten white rock. She was beyond maniacal, beyond diabolical. She was demonic. She opened her mouth and her tongue glowed yellow, hot as a soldering iron. She snapped her alligator jaws, barely missing my face.

"How's the Psychic? Ben?" *BENNY BOY!* "I haven't seen him since your lip lock with the vampire!" Smoke billowed from every orifice in her face, seeping out her tear ducts. As she laughed at me, I was engulfed in the charcoal cloud of it. I couldn't breathe. I hacked, seeing spots. "I watched him, at the club with that pretty thing, the golden siren, touching, breathing … hard." She sighed in ecstasy. "And I was quite the waitress. Every drink they could ask for … and a few that they didn't."

A few that they didn't. She'd given them magical elixirs without telling them what they were. Without telling them what they'd do.

"You …" I got my hands on her throat and her skin scalded me like a cast-iron skillet. She flipped me to my back and was heavy as a tree on my chest. Fire poured from her blinding white sockets and licked her hair like lizard tongues. She smashed her knee on the toes of my foot, on the foot that was missing a toe, and the heat of her welded my wound closed with a bacon-like sizzle. "GAHHHHHHH!" I cried. I didn't want to cry anymore. I hated her. I hated her for hurting me so much.

She held my wrists in one hand and all I knew was heat. The burn charred my marrow and boiled my blood. I hardly heard Nicola over my bleating. "Where is he? Ben? Is he with the beautiful one?" She leaned in, the skin of my wrists black and melting. She whispered in my ear, her words igniting my hair, "Or is he already dead, right under your back?"

Frankie. Ben said in my head, his voice a weak whisper. *I'm … here.*

He was alive. He wanted me to know. And he could see *everything.*

I would not let Ben watch me burn alive. Not again.

I jerked forward and locked my mouth around Nicola's throat. Her skin fused to my lips, burning the delicate membrane away. I bit harder, trying to close my jaw completely. Blood and smoke filled my mouth like lava. She garbled through her torn vocal cords and grabbed my skull, burning more of my hair.

I shook my head, wanting to cause the most damage, wanting to cause the most pain. And there was so much pain in her now, and real fear. It seemed, suddenly, all of Ben's lessons and all my fights in The Pool had paid off. Because I left Nicola's pain right where it was. I ripped her throat open, and I refused to close the wound. I would gladly suffer if it meant she suffered along with me.

Nicola yanked herself back from my teeth and blood drenched her dress, flowing in waves. I spit the burning neck tissue to the walls of the pool, blood splattering over both our faces. It was everywhere and everything. I was afraid to touch my burnt face. The night breeze tickled my slick muscles and cartilage in places. My insides were exposed to the world.

Nicola whined and whined. It was very annoying, but the only distraction from the hell I felt in my body. I didn't know how much skin, hair, or clothes I had left, but I knew it wasn't much.

The dragon writhed on the floor of The Pool, making those noises as she bled out. I dragged myself from her, through the lake of blood. This may have been a dream, or a nightmare, because nothing felt real. Such agony was impossible. Such torment inexplicable.

I folded my leg into my lap—my pants were full of crispy, smoking holes. Where my toe used to be, there was now a black, cracked scab. I saw my pink meat through the fissures.

Pain is an excellent sacrifice.

I stuck my fingernail in the crack, horrified by what I was about to do. I tore. The scab peeled free, and the intensity of the burn burst with a sharp and awful intensity. I was fading out of consciousness. I had to be fast. I stuck my finger in the gouge, breathing through the pain like a wild bull, seizing and twitching.

I asked the wind for help as I dug around inside my foot and began to levitate. I only needed eight feet, and once I passed over the edge of The Pool, I dropped on my hip.

Moaning and gagging, I got to my feet. I was a firework, pain exploding on every surface in colorful displays. The air was abrasive as sandpaper.

Nicola lay flat on her back down below, a hand at the hole in her throat, searing the wound closed herself. It would leave a scar, an ugly one.

I turned to the crowd, their eyes aglow with entertainment, and my hands extended at my sides in red and black claws. Chunks of burnt hair clung to the visible tissue of my chest in black crisscrossing lines. Judging by the chill I felt, one of my nipples was exposed—what was left of my nipple anyway. Much of my outfit lay in The Pool in piles of soot and ash. I was missing most of the skin of my face and stood in a pond of my own blood.

I bared my teeth and waited for another attack. A third, a fourth, however many it would take to prove just how *infallible* I could be.

Laisren watched me with astute eyes but didn't move to stop me as I turned on my heel and limped inside.

17

ANDERSON HAD to let me into the elevator, which dented my pride, but I didn't have much in the first place. I'd felt the thrum of Jessamae's presence long after I rode down to the third floor, but she hadn't revealed herself or our connection. Anderson couldn't find her in the crowd.

Nicola had seen us kissing at The Harvest—how had Jessamae even made it to the top floor without recognition? These questions plagued me as I lay on the bathroom floor of my apartment, unwilling and unable to move. Below the questions, my brain was full of undecipherable keening and growls. The cacophony was deafening.

"How long will it take your hair to grow back?" Anderson sat on the toilet above me, a squeamish set to his brow. I hadn't looked in the mirror, and thank god for that. My cheek left a gummy red-orange smear on the tile.

I couldn't even shrug. Every movement nearly killed me. "Not long."

After I'd been with Ben in the hotel shower, it had nearly grown a foot. My skin had felt so marvelous then, warm and slick with water. I was safe and happy and alive and surrounded by people who cared about me. Ben, who cared about me so much. Too much. Enough to land him one floor below me, dying as I died. More alone even than I was. With my blistered palm on the tile, I thought I could almost feel it, through the floor. His heartache.

Nicola had given him fairy-treated drinks. What I drank —*Joy*, I thought with a sneer—made me drain a man to the point of collapse and kiss Jessamae without a care. What had Nicola given Ben and Cleo? *Lust*? Had to be. And if they hadn't been so crushed at seeing Jessamae and me together, they wouldn't have guzzled so deeply, so thoughtlessly, so blindly. It wouldn't have happened.

But it did.

Tears pooled in my eye until they coated my pupil like a veil. Anderson must have thought it because of my condition, because he clambered up from the toilet. "Hey, don't cry." His hands fluttered over me, afraid to touch anything lest he make things even worse. "Your body will heal fast enough. I've seen what you can do. This is only temporary."

His words pushed more tears out of my face and down my temples. "No, it's not." I turned my head away and spread blood into the gray grout of the floor.

"Can I help? How can I help?"

I coughed up a loogie of red goo and ignored him.

Anderson stood and left.

Unfortunately, it wasn't long until he returned, stepping over my body like I was a piss puddle on the carpet. I wouldn't have bothered acknowledging him, but I heard a hiss come from his hands. He brought me Betty. My Betty.

He set her gently on the bare skin of my belly—which was yellow with angry bubbles—but her smooth scales didn't hurt. She rested her head against my heart.

"Holy. Fucking. Shit."

I groaned and closed my eyes. "Go away, Patrick."

"What. The. Jesus. Fuck."

"Thanks."

He crouched in the bathroom doorway. "You fuck a forest fire?"

"I said go away."

"How long will it take?" Anderson asked him. "Until her skin and hair grow back?"

Patrick's eyes remained on me as he answered, scanning me from tip to tail. "A while, I think, but I haven't seen much of her work."

"Can we help her?"

"No," I croaked.

"Yeah, maybe. From the synopsis Ben gave us before everything went to shit, she can use the injuries of others to heal herself, plus, she heals *them* simultaneously."

Anderson said, "Wow. Lucky woman."

Not at all. "Can you two stop talking about me like I'm not here?" I hacked up more schmutz.

"Do you have a knife?" Patrick asked Anderson.

"No."

Patrick scoured the bathroom for some sort of weapon, but I wouldn't tell him anything. I wanted to be miserable, and they were doing a damn good job of ruining it.

But he opened the vanity and found my switchblade. "Bastard."

He gave it to Anderson and said, "Give yourself a little slice and touch her. I would offer—"

But Anderson hadn't hesitated, he was stripping off his jacket and rolling up his sleeve. He made a long incision along the inside of his forearm. He had a black and gray tattoo of a snake and roses there. It wasn't well done, but it suited him. It gave him a past and solidified him.

He didn't know where to put his hand once he was done. Every inch of my body looked too painful or too intimate. Eventually, he settled for resting the back of his hand on my forehead. It hurt, but not compared to everything else. His arm healed in less than a minute, and I still didn't have skin. "This is going to take a while," he said, bringing the blade to the new scar beneath his elbow.

AFTER A DOZEN ROUNDS, Patrick volunteered to take a turn. The two of them passed the knife back and forth for over an hour, until each had a thick scar on their forearms, plump as an earthworm. Until I could finally stand and bat at their hands.

"That's enough." I was grateful, especially to Anderson, and I hated that. Why couldn't they just let it go? "Thanks."

"You still aren't the right color. You look like a Jolly Rancher," Patrick said.

"It's fine, I'll sleep it off." I turned to Anderson. "Ready?"

He creaked and huffed as he pushed himself to stand. He'd been sitting for a while and his arm was red from leaning on one elbow. "For?"

"To take me to the second floor."

Anderson's eyebrows called me stupid.

"What?" I blurted.

Anderson tapped his temples. "So … in your mind, we walk in, covered in blood, take a prisoner from Laisren, and keep him in your studio apartment? Or did you want to skip out of here, arm in arm?"

"You don't want to try?"

"I told you I needed time!"

"I'm sorry, I thought my being melted like a fucking Barbie might have pushed you closer to a decision!"

"Everyone, just calm down!" Patrick boomed. "I need to eat. And there's half a bottle of tequila calling my name. We're all hitting the hay, and unless someone is offering to hit it with me, I'll see you tomorrow." He sauntered, despite the leaden exhaustion in his shoulders, to the door, and hung his head. "I need you to open my fucking door, kind sir."

Anderson took his jacket and followed him, giving me an unhappy once-over. "I'll be back when I know."

I carried Betty to my bed and folded myself over the covers

insolently as the door shut behind them. She nestled into my lap, nosing the skin of my leg.

Then he spoke.

Frank. So quiet, my name.

I didn't want to do it. I would hate myself for eternity if I gave him a scrap of hope for nothing. But I'd never been a self-less person. "Ben," I said aloud. Then, knowing he couldn't hear me, and he couldn't read my lips from inside my head, I lifted my hand, opening and closing my fingers in a weak wave.

Even softer. *Frank.*

I cried myself to sleep.

"Sorry. But you need to wake up."

The coffee's aroma roused me. I slept in a black void. No toss-ing, no turning. I had no dreams. And gauging from the light, it was either incredibly late or incredibly early.

"Here." Anderson nudged my cheek with the paper cup. Betty slithered inside my elbow, stirring at our visitor. I moved her to the side and took the offered coffee.

I winced at the taste. "Cinnamon."

"I didn't know how you took your coffee, but I thought you might like it. If you don't, I can—"

"No, it's fine. Thank you." I gulped fast without tasting and scratched at the logo on the cup. "What time is it?"

"Almost five."

"In the morning?"

"Yes."

"Are you fucking kidding me?"

He tipped his confused head to his shoulder, taking me more seriously than I'd ever been taken in my life. "No. I've been up all night. I have an idea."

With Ben on the brain, I threw my legs off the bed, leaning forward. "And?"

"First." He chucked a black plastic bag to the bed. Inside was a long, muumuu-style shirt with a glitzy picture of the Las Vegas skyline on its front, as well as a pair of black sandals, which appeared to be covered in dozens of tiny mirrors. "Gift shop next to the coffee cart. I was in a hurry." He gestured to the bathroom door behind him.

The rags that used to be clothes still dangled around me like fringe, murals of bare skin exposed. Only months ago, I was mortified by the sight of my legs, by a sliver of my stomach peeking between my shirt and pants. It was amazing what near-death experiences did for such insecurities. This wasn't the first time people saw more of me than they wanted to in order to save me, and I doubted it would be the last.

Anderson's eyes were on the floor when I came out of the bathroom twenty minutes later. I'd showered prudently—my skin horrendously sensitive and translucent in certain areas—brushed my teeth, and put my uneven, shriveled hair in a bun before donning my new shiny clothes. I was dressed like an eighty-year-old tourist with a glam fetish.

"Samhain," he said. "I've seen four Samhains before, and it's our best chance of getting out. We can try and get your friend off the second floor, but either way, once the effort is made, we have to leave. Immediately."

I chewed on my cheek. He was right. Laisren would know, whether we succeeded or failed in finding Ben. Anderson's eight years could become a death sentence, a death sentence for us all. "Why Samhain?"

"Laisren celebrates rather enthusiastically. There are parties in every club she owns, and Nicola is quite the party planner. But The Harvest is the main event. Laisren attends that party, one of her few annual public appearances. And her personal guard will join her, as will most of her security force. The

Alcazar will be short-staffed. Laisren values her life more than anything else, and that is saying something. Believe me."

I couldn't remember how long it had been since I'd seen The Harvest. The Bellagio. Utah seemed planets away. "What day is it?"

"Halloween."

"No. What day is it today?"

"It's the twenty-ninth. We have two days."

I guzzled more coffee, and it was painful on multiple levels. "What are we supposed to do in the meantime? Hope Ben won't die? Hope *we* won't?"

His body dipped forward, and I feared he might fall, but he set his head on the lid of his coffee and rested his coffee on his knees. "Yes."

I put my empty cup aside. A few flakes of my healing lip clung to the lid. "Okay." I stood and went to the kitchen, pulling two Styrofoam bowls from their sleeve. I filled each with colorful puffs of cereal and dumb skim milk and handed one to Anderson. Without question, he began to eat dutifully. "I'm adding something to our list of tasks," I said. "We need to find Cleo. And we need to find Jessamae."

He tipped his bowl and drained half his milk. "We have to find and save *three* of your friends?"

"Four. Patrick, too."

Anderson was shocked.

"What? Did you want to leave him here?"

"No. Just surprised you have so many friends."

I almost laughed. If anyone had to kidnap me, I was glad it was Anderson.

THERE WERE few clues concerning the whereabouts of Cleo and Jessamae. It was possible they were together, but I doubted Cleo would permit that after everything that had happened. We were all a bit prideful, it seemed. Cleo could be anywhere. She could still be in the Bellagio, having soaked in the bath for the last four days.

There was The Harvest, which we knew Jessamae frequented but generally on Sundays. It was Thursday. And she'd been to The Alcazar, which she wasn't currently, or I'd have known. "Jessamae came to Vegas looking for someone. Are there other places like The Harvest to find witches? A graveyard or a brothel or something?"

Anderson smiled. "Of course. But there are fewer hot spots during the day." Anderson buckled his seatbelt and drove slowly from The Alcazar lot. "But Laisren is expecting us in four hours, so we can't search them all."

"For what?" My stomach turned at the prospect.

He shrugged. "I don't get to ask her questions."

He pulled onto the Strip, which was pulsing with vehicles and bystanders, though the sun was just rising. We went to a shabby diner first, with ripped seats and tacky linoleum floors. I knew she wasn't there before we even opened the door—the cords were quiet—but I wanted a donut. Anderson paid for the pastries while I scoped the restaurant, which at first, I thought was a strange place for magic activity. Until I smelled it.

There was death here. It hung in the air, thick as cobwebs. It was without species or source, it simply was. I fought a sneeze, surprised I hadn't sensed it from the street, from my apartment. Three hairy men in cowboy hats studied me, their scrutiny sharp as skewers at my throat. We left with haste and took a few extra, misleading, turns before our next destination. Just in case.

An antique shop and a piercing studio were on our list, but we drove past both when I felt nothing in my chest.

Finally, I felt a yank at the establishment of "Weller Wellest Wellness."

"What is this place?"

"Sort of a gym and spa. It has a pool and a bath house."

"I didn't know bath houses still existed." I thought of them to be filled with old wrinkly Italian men discussing business and saw no reason for Jessamae to visit.

"There was a time when I didn't know witches existed, but here we are."

It was clean and blue. Everything shimmered to such an extent, it felt like drowning, but in a pleasant way. Several walls weren't walls at all, but tall aquariums reaching the ceiling and squirming with squishy sea life. The floor tiles swirled like a bag of blue marbles, shifting colors under the light like the ocean itself. I'd never been in a building so quiet in all my life. It smelled like chlorine and eucalyptus.

A receptionist sat at a white minimalist desk that was so clean I could see his face in it. He had perfect skin, but no eyebrows or hair. He resembled a mannequin. "How can I help you?" His lack of emotional cues was unsettling. Perhaps he *was* a mannequin, and a witch had breathed life into its plastic.

I had no clue why Jessamae would be drawn to this place, unless she had been an Olympic swimmer in the 1970s or something of the like. I'd need open access to the entire spa to follow the cords. I cleared my throat. "Yes, I'm interested in a membership. Do you provide any sort of tour?"

"No."

"Okay. Uh, what about a day pass?"

"No."

I turned, stumped, to Anderson. He gave a derisive guffaw and stepped up to the desk. He slid a little black card from the inside pocket of his jacket toward the mannequin. I couldn't discern the logo, but it glittered colorfully in the light, like an opal.

Once the card appeared, it just as quickly vanished back into the silk of Anderson's jacket. The receptionist mashed his pointer finger into an intercom button. Instead of making a call, a subtle clicking echoed throughout the blue room. "It's open," he said, gesturing to a glass door at the end of the lobby.

I hesitated. The magical hubs of Las Vegas had not proved

welcoming in the past, and Jessamae circled danger like a vulture. Anderson hooked his arm around mine—making me flinch—and led me through the door.

"Some of these places are invitation only. The cards identify me as Laisren's lackey, and Laisren has free reign, anywhere and everywhere."

Curling my lip, I said, "Thanks for stopping me from asking about day passes and looking like an asshole."

"You got it."

Steam fluffed my hair the moment we crossed the threshold. I drank the air. The humidity gave off a tart flavor—essential oils —and every surface was tiled in a tiny, squared pattern of repetitive white, teal, deep indigo, and crystal clear. Every sound we made seemed to echo forever.

The hallway opened to an enormous room spotted with bodies of water like the Great Lakes. An Olympic-sized pool, though ameba-shaped, dominated the center of the room, and waves curled its waters. The waves were big enough to tide a beach, folding over the heads of witches in varying degrees of nakedness. Jacuzzi tubs, wading pools, and waterfalls circled the lake-like center.

There were several soaked humans gathered in small groups which made me uncomfortable beyond belief. In each grouping, three or four witches circled around the breasts and chests of one person, prodding their sexual organs like a creature in a tide pool. Some of them were fucking with abandon, in the water and out. The ones being groped and penetrated danced as if they hardly noticed, eyes closed, tongues out, laughing or falling. They could drown before they even noticed they were underwater. They were high on the magic. Magicless people put to use by mages ... *however they pleased*.

"It's best not to look at them," Anderson whispered. But it was hard not to, because I was searching for someone. She was here.

Our connection shook my chest, and I was walking without

thinking. I was still so angry at her—we had a *lot* to talk about—but my body took over. I needed close the distance. Now.

In my eccentric attire, I drew the eye of every witch in the bathing pools, pulling their focus and their tongues from whomever they feasted on as my sandals lapped against the wet flooring, the cheap foam of them sliding this way and that.

And there she was. Jessamae floated through the clouds of steam, soaking in a small pool that connected to another with an actual moving river of turquoise water.

Though she was engaged in conversation with three other people, a man and two women, she turned her head in my direction, seeing me despite all the space and water between us.

I was jogging, Anderson whispered words of caution behind me, but I needed to be near her. The need had never been as strong as this. It felt as though our connection would rip me off my feet and drag me through the water. It would rip me in half if I didn't run.

Fear lit Jessamae's glassy eyes once they found me, and the attention of her company shifted my way. I slid through a puddle on my heel and fell into Anderson's chest, my hair filling his mouth and nose. I pushed off him, so close now, when a woman impeded my path.

"Well, looky here! Welcome!" She extended her arms as if to hug me and I backed into Anderson again. He didn't offer comfort but nudged me with his shoulder until I stood upright. The woman embraced me and her arms were like eels on my skin. She smelled salty.

A kelpie. It was the water-witch from The Harvest. And for the first time, I wished for Patrick's presence more than any other.

18

"WHAT ARE you doing out of your cage?" the kelpie asked. I thought her name was Marissa or Melissa. She was the mother of the two creepy blondes, but she hardly appeared older than me. "Did you break the rules? Or are you here on Laisren's orders? You must be climbing the ranks fast, good for you!"

"Are you talking to me?"

"Obviously!" She laughed. "I thought you'd be swimming The Pool for a while. I never imagined seeing you out here! You must be so strong." She squeezed my bicep with a smile. She reminded me of a church lady, trying to get me to join. But this was no church, at least not one I was used to.

I forced my knuckles to pop. "You came to watch me in The Pool?"

"Sadly, I never made it to your events. However, a few of my friends and one of my daughters caught your match with the zombie. And Nicola, of course! Congratulations! She's a toughie." She scanned me from my toes up, a brow raised at my well-being, before tying the sash of her swishy, translucent robe in tighter and twirling around. "I was surprised Laisren let you out for a spa day, but a performance like that does deserve one hell of a reward!" She clapped a few times and laughed. She was nude under that robe, and I had only just gotten used to my own naked body. She strutted across the room, and it was clear we were meant to follow.

Jessamae hadn't bothered to continue conversation with the three strangers. All four of her pool's occupants watched as we crossed the slippery tiled floor toward them. "I moved up a floor, if that's what you mean." I told the kelpie's back, trying to keep things nonchalant.

"I never understood that system, each floor sounds terrible until you hit the Penthouse. But I'm sure it's nicer than I've been made to believe." She reached back to rub my shoulder. I shied away and she narrowed her eyes in offense before that inviting smile, once again, overwhelmed her face.

Witches loved touching people they didn't know. Cuckoo-for-fucking-cocoa-puffs.

She led us around the oceanic landscape, the bodies resuming their grotesque sexual coercion, while the turquoise tide jumped over the glossy edge to touch Marissa/Melissa's painted toes like a reverent cultist. Water was one of my favorite elements, but the elements in general were controlling, not something to be controlled. The kelpie operated at the same levels as Nicola, who sat at Laisren's side. Powerful. Very.

She strutted to Jessamae's group of witches, and without stalling, descended the steps to its depths, robe and all. "What a wild coincidence you're here today," she said to me, "on the same day Jessie stopped by for a dip." Turning to the vampire, she added, "I hope it's alright if we join you."

Jessamae wore a simple white one-piece suit, which contrasted with her skin tone and nightmarish eyes magnificently. Her pale hair was loose around her shoulders, slithering over the surface of the water like alabaster snakes. Her eyes gave away nothing as she shifted her attention to the kelpie. The only sign of her tension was the vicious clasping of her hands under one knee. "Of course, not. Francesca, it's so great to see you," she said with an aloof smile, returning to my formal address. "I heard you were under royal employ, how ..." her jaw trembled before she snapped her teeth together with a clack, "exciting."

The three unknown witches watched me with interest,

ignoring Anderson and even the kelpie. The man in particular stared with such zeal, I crossed my arms to better hide my body.

The man was blonde and frighteningly pale. His eyes were the shade of the weakest tea, diluted with too much water. His mouth opened as he stared, and I shrank away automatically. One of the women was brunette with a strong, curved nose; the other had the thickest black hair I'd ever seen and rosy brown skin.

"Exciting is one way to put it," I said, shaking the silver pool railing and curling my toes in my sandals. Anderson moved to stand at the wall, his hands crossed at his groin in true security parody. I resented his leaving me with so many strangers but straightened my back to their tangible curiosity. The blonde man's eyes clung to me like cat hair, and I hadn't seen him blink once. He was like sour milk in a human suit.

In an attempt at casual questioning, I asked, "I haven't seen any of The Harvest crowd for days. How is everyone?"

Jessamae tickled the surface of the pool and looked at her feet. "I'm sure they're enjoying themselves. Each to their own devices." *Everyone has split up. Cleo is not with me.*

Patrick was at The Alcazar, Ben prison, and Cleo may have been abducted for all I knew. "No shit," I said before I could stop myself, and the man smiled. I glared back. I hadn't been talking to *him*.

"What are you waiting for? Get in here!" Melissa-rissa made a come-hither gesture.

"I don't have my suit."

"Unprepared for a bath house." She grinned and cocked her head. Her eyes were predatory. She oozed gossip. Whatever happened here would get back to The Alcazar. "But suits aren't required here, as you can see!" She waved a hand at all the glistening flesh frolicking through the water. Such a good-humored kelpie. I wondered if she's the one Patrick slept with—he had "motherfucker" written all over him.

I didn't want to bathe naked with them, in front of Jessamae and the intense milkman. My bra had melted last night, and my new sports bra was still in its package. But Melissa/rissa was right, we were acting under the guise that I'd been rewarded with a "spa day." I slid my shoes to the side of the stairs and stepped into the water in my long shirt. It was warm, perfect, with baby currents rushing in every direction against my legs. I held my shirt in close to my thighs to prevent it from rising and sat on an empty bench, though the urge to sit beside Jessamae was almost painful.

"So ... who's excited for Samhain?" I asked.

Why was I such a fucking imbecile?

"You celebrate Samhain where you're from? Utah, was it?" Melissa/rissa asked and Jessamae shifted subtly. The kelpie knew where I lived and announced it to a group of strange witches. I was not safe.

"This is my first time. It's the reason we came to Vegas," I decided on the fly. "To celebrate."

"How fun!" she said with an evil glint in her Caribbean eyes. "Where are your friends? They can't be at The Alcazar with you." *You'd be surprised.* "Will they be joining you for Samhain?"

I pursed my lips and nodded, the currents filling my shirt like a hot air balloon. "We were all going to meet at The Harvest. I barely remember my visit last time." I laughed with real depreciation. "Thought I'd try again. And I hear it's uh ... quite the party. You should join us—" I directed the invitation at Jessamae, but all the pool's inhabitants were listening. "Um, everyone. I hope to see you there."

Jessamae's eyes reflected the motion of the water, and I couldn't read them. I hoped she knew to notify Cleo. "I think I'd like that," she said. "I was going to have a small get-together, but I'll—"

"How kind of you to invite us along," the man said, his voice insubstantial, yet demanding, wind in winter. His attention had become revolting. I brought my knees to my chest, self-conscious that my tits were standing at attention and visible over the skyline of my shirt like twin moons. His eyes loitered around features, making me queasy. "We will have to stop by, provided you two are there." He gestured to Jessamae.

I lifted my lip at the bastard, but Jessamae seemed intrigued by his flattery. She was with this man for one reason: power, political or magical. She'd always been drawn to the stuff, otherwise, we never would have met. Gabriel and Pamela would still be alive.

The man must have been strong—but I wouldn't know, Jessamae would. She could sense vitality and life in a person as I sensed sickness and death.

She hit him with a smile I'd only seen her gift to me. I wanted to slap her.

A part of me wanted her to use her affinity more often. Every witch in Vegas played the villain, and it could use a few eliminations from the board. But she held her hand, killing only when she chose. She enjoyed chatting with the monsters because she was one. We all were.

I forced a smile, positive I looked like a sick dog. "Perfect."

"Pardon me, Miss Hughes." Anderson had crept behind me, and I jumped at the haunting use of my name. He leaned into the steam. "You are expected at The Alcazar at nine-thirty." His formality was incredible. No one would guess we had even spoken before now.

"Right. Right. Um, well, it was nice to meet you. Not Jessamae. I knew her. Marissa—"

"Melissa," piped several voices.

"Right, of course. Super sorry. Nice to see you again—"

"Say hello to Patrick for me."

I paused in my departure, and Melissa's silence grew thick. The only sound was the water streaming from my muumuu and the rhythmic moaning around us. She saw us together at The Harvest, and she knew he'd been taken into custody. No wonder Laisren used him against me. Every witch in Vegas was under her thumb.

"I don't—"

"He's truly beautiful underwater." Melissa's blue eyes darkened from a tropical bay to a frozen mountain lake. My stomach clenched in fear.

"I'll pass along the compliment," I muttered and slid my toes into my sandals. I wrung out my shirt and left a trail of water as I slid after Anderson waiting at the door.

He held it open for me. "Clothes never seem to last long on your back."

"What's that supposed to mean?" My lungs were full of steam, and I was jittery from adrenaline. "You questioning my reputation?"

He shook his head. "Just a statement of fact."

The receptionist eyed us, marinating in disdain, as we walked out the door, without offering us a towel or any assistance. The leather seats of Anderson's sedan burned my skin through my drenched shirt, and I was grateful for the flood of water around my butt. "Jessamae, and hopefully Cleo, will be at The Harvest."

"Jessamae was the one in the white suit, correct? Who's Cleo?"

"She's a friend. She'll be leaving with us." I couldn't consider whether we would all continue to be friends once we were back in Utah. The last few days were cataclysmic to our ragtag band of sad magicians.

"Six people total? We're going to need a bigger car than this one."

"I have a car parked at the Bellagio." If it hadn't been towed or booted by now. "We can all fit if someone sits in the trunk."

"The trunk? Across state lines?"

"It's not really a trunk, it's a space behind the seats! You know what, I'll sit there, okay? Who cares." It would be a fitting justice to get my turn in a trunk.

I was so on edge I felt myself wobbling, slipping further and further over the side. Too many people to transport out of the city safely, four of whom were indebted to the Las Vegas Sovereignty. Ben might need healing. Cleo might not even show. Jack might be unwilling to help us. There were too many possibilities, too many decisions, and we didn't have a psychic to tell us the odds. I was still so mortified by what he and Cleo did, what Jessamae and I did, that a piece of me wanted to forget the whole plan and just stay here. Fighting witches night after night and healing those who belonged to Laisren. It would be a hell of a lot easier.

"I need a beer."

"I'm sure you do, but Laisren is expecting you. Put it on the grocery list."

We parked the car and rode the elevator up to the Penthouse. Anderson wouldn't even let me stop to check on Betty—we were nearly on time rather than early. I was angry and exhausted and hungry and so mind-bendingly terrified, even a moment's rest in my awful apartment sounded like heaven.

We stepped off the elevator to find an understated welcome. Laisren sat at her desk, bent over some paperwork. She scribbled an overtly loopy signature, her fingers stained with nicotine, and handed the folder to a woman in expensive silk clothing. "Thank you." And the woman was excused. "Francesca, how are you faring after your last match?" She took in my appearance with a raised brow. "I'd ask if it's raining out there, but I heard you were just visiting Melissa's bath house. How marvelous!"

A door opened behind me. The smiling man waltzed to Laisren's side, his hands in his pockets. The twins came next, playing an intense game of Rock, Paper, Scissors. And a lion followed the three of them.

A lion.

I stumbled back to the elevator, my wide eyes on its mane that swayed with each thunderous step, its fur that looked so soft for such a killer, on its big, hypnotic yellow eyes. I lost my breath. My muscles turned to stone.

"No," Laisren said, clicking her nails on her desk. "Put it away."

The twins stopped their game with matching disgruntled expressions, then the lion was gone. It didn't walk away. It didn't fall through the floor. It vanished.

"Thank you," she said.

My breaths stabbed in and out of my mouth as if the cat were still here. The guards laughed at me. How fucking hilarious. One of them had done that. One of their affinities conjured a lion out of thin air.

"I'm sorry about that, Frankie. My boys think they're funny." She laughed, clearly agreeing with them. "Before we were so rudely interrupted, I wanted to know how you were doing."

Her eyes were painted in green eyeshadow, which made them seem twice as big as they were. Avoiding all that sparkle, I watched the matte black pen in her hand. It looked like it weighed more than Betty. "I'll let you know as soon as my hair grows back."

She squawked out a macaw-like round of laughter and stood up from the desk. "I'm sure that won't take much time at all. Your talents are im-press-ive." She clapped with each syllable.

Even without taking in her visage, her closeness was incredibly tempting. To know her attention was on me was intoxicating. "Thank you."

"Nicola will be recovering for weeks without your assistance, which …" I waited for the inevitable, the first healing request that would cement me as Laisren Inc.'s personal first aid kit. "I will leave up to you. You don't have to help her if you don't want to." My head cricked around in shock and I looked at her automatically. It was the first offering of control I'd been given since I arrived. And after such a draining twenty-four hours, I was strangely touched by the sentiment. "She decided to get in The Pool. She knew what she was up against." Laisren's gesture made me want to want to help Nicola, but I kept that inclination to myself.

With my eyes on her nose, wanting to be pleasant, I said, "I will consider it, thank you."

"Please." She gestured to a set of metal and leather armchairs facing the window. I looked to Anderson for reassurance, but he seemed just as thrown as I was. I took the invitation and sat.

"It's ugly in the light of day, isn't it?" Laisren asked, indicating the Strip outside. "Its beauty emerges at night." She turned toward me with a grin. "Not unlike most of the people here. Ha!"

I smiled despite my situation, my eyes flicking to her chin, to her forehead.

She took the seat beside me and leaned forward as if the landscape were about to do a tricky fit of magic. "Would you like something to drink, dearie?" My hand, which had been resting on the chair's arm, was suddenly between Laisren's nimble fingers. The pink of my digits looked especially angry between the brown spindles of hers. "Something strong?" Her bedside manner was phenomenal.

"Um." My voice thronged like a springy doorstop. Laisren's touch was soft, softer than satin or velvet or ocean sand, despite the dirty fingernails and the wrinkles. And I couldn't find a single painful feeling in her body. She was perfect. "Okay."

Laisren released me and it was an agonizing, gut-wrenching relief. Her touch was a cocoon of warmth and bliss and gumdrop rain. But it wasn't real. And it was horrible to know I'd gladly imprison myself inside it.

She skipped to a massive mahogany bar. Reaching beneath its polished surface, she retrieved a bottle of gin. I hated gin, and I didn't much care. As Laisren filled a glass with what I thought of as cleaning fluid, tossing in a splash of syrup and some green leaves, it was the most mouth-watering treat this side of the world. "Here you are. I promise it's clean. We don't need another pear fiasco, do we?" She elbowed me in the arm like a couple of chums, chortling so hard that wisps of forgotten cigarette smoke filtered out her nose.

I shook my head in obedience, knowing she wouldn't taint it if she told me she wouldn't. I was almost disappointed. I wanted to taste her magic again.

"You've done very well in The Pool. Your affinity should have worked purely as a defensive mechanism, but you proved just how tenacious, how resourceful you can be. I'm proud"—my heart soared at the words—"and I think you've earned a reprieve. I'd like to offer you a new position. Your three months aren't up, we had a deal, but after those three months, I'd like to offer you a place here. With me."

I sipped my drink because I knew it would please Laisren. It didn't taste like gin, it tasted like candy, like citrus, and like spring water all at once. It was so delicious it nearly erased the fear bubbling inside my intestines. "You want me to live here?"

"Your living situation could be up for discussion, but I'd like to keep you close. I've no interest in lying to you. Your magical affinity is the primary reason I took interest in you. But!" Her smile was gigantic. "It is your mettle, your tooth-and-claw fight that sets you apart! The way you looked at me after you got yourself out of The Pool? Chilling, Francesca. And I mean that as a compliment." Her bouts of eloquence juxtaposed with her general trashiness gave me whiplash.

I was both flattered and insulted. Laisren made me feel special, skilled, things I'd never felt in my life, excluding my unfortunate adventures with Jessamae. But I was insulted at the fact that my big seller was my rage at being forced to fight for my life again and again, that I so desperately didn't want to die.

The insult tried to break through Laisren's Novocain-like attention—it didn't rupture the sack, but it was irritating. Something. I scratched at my own palm, gaining sense from the sting. I took another drink. "I believe you do. And that's very … nice. But I enjoy my freedom."

"You'd have it. Your own suite, a car, a salary. Anderson seems to have taken a shine to you. He could be your personal guard if you'd like." She snapped at him with her loud fingers. "Anderson, would you come here?"

Shit. I glanced over my shoulder at the suit who'd become my ally in hell. Anderson had been watching the conversation and sped to follow Laisren's request. His eyes glistened and his mouth hung open, his lip fluttering with his breath. I wanted his reaction to mean that eight years with me was preferable to eight years with Laisren. No more kidnappings, no more dragging captives to The Pool, to the prison below. A near guilt-free eight years. It came without the life-or-death stakes our escape would create. And it was up to me to decide if he'd have those easy— easier—eight years.

I could ask Laisren for Ben's freedom if I climbed the ladder, but I doubted my employment was worth that much. And if I showed my hand, illustrated that I knew he was here, it would give Laisren all the more power over us both, and she'd keep an even closer eye on us all.

I finished my drink, tucking my tongue to avoid the fantastic taste. "That is so … kind of you to offer. Could I, please, have some time to consider?" I dug through the skin of my palm and drew blood. "When I'm feeling more myself?" I licked the drink from my cheeks.

Laisren's smile held firm, her face like a rainbow hidden in an oil spill. "Of course. It's an opportunity. Not an obligation." She stood and went to her desk. Her guard hadn't moved an inch. The air around them was stale and quiet. "In the meantime, I'd like to treat you to a night of celebration, marking not three but four wins!" She lifted her second cocktail to me in cheers before lighting another smoke. "Samhain approaches," she said out of the corner of her mouth. "I'd love your company at The Harvest. Let the court show you a good time. We're good for it!" She spun her chair around. "I'll see you then." I was excused.

"Thank you," I said again, and unsure of what to do with my glass, set it on the floor. Bending down, I saw Laisren's feet under the desk. She wore white snake-skin boots.

I stumbled to the elevator, feeling drunk already and, for once, unsatisfied by my inebriation. She'd worn those boots on purpose, of course, she had. Of course, she had!

Anderson led me to my room in silence and after he opened my door, he left without a word. He had a lot to think about, too.

With Betty twirling anxiously between my fingers, I ruminated on just how many challenges we'd have to overcome during Samhain if I decided to reject Laisren's offer. Laisren would be at The Harvest, as would her personal guard and Nicola. We'd see the milkman and the kelpie family from the bathhouse, as well as any other witch who bowed to Laisren's rule. We'd have to get in and out of this hotel—with an escaped prisoner—with hives of hammered partygoers celebrating in the streets.

And I didn't even have a costume.

19

ANDERSON DIDN'T COME BACK that day. He didn't come back the next day either. I sat in my room, in my bed, without a terrible amount of fidgeting for hours at a time. Exactly how I'd spend my days full of content and ignorant bliss in Aspen Ridge before all this magic mess started. But now, the last day and a half were up there with the worst days I'd been alive to bear.

My groceries were delivered, as well as some new shorts, a shirt, and some domestic beer after I learned they didn't have Gold Star in Nevada. I gave Betty a frozen mouse. I sensed her hunger, but she wasn't interested. She was unhappy. I smelled it in her as strong as in a human being. She missed the others. She loved me, I knew that, but she missed the others.

Anderson's future sat enormous and sweaty on my shoulders. I could make his employment easier, enjoyable even, without risking his life for four people he didn't know enough to care for. If I went through with our plan for Samhain, I was putting his life on the line for theirs. He'd been nothing but kind to me, kidnapping aside.

Ben stopped speaking to me after the first day of my isolation, and even that had been whispers. He'd said the same thing every time. *Get … others. Get … out.* Until he said nothing at all. He didn't call my name anymore. It made me cry. I was constantly leaking. He knew I was in here, knew that I did nothing but sit on my ass watching shitty day-time cable and repetitive midnight infomercials. I hoped he somehow knew there was a plan. That I would save him. If I could do that to Anderson …

I could. Through it all, guilt sizzled in my guts, because I was merely pretending to battle with myself. I would risk Anderson's life ten times over for Ben's. It was vile and stupid and selfish and deplorable, but it was true.

I didn't know what hurt worse: the haunting pictures of Ben wrapped around Cleo that I invented and obsessed over viciously; or the knowledge that I could die, that Anderson could die, all to bring the two of them into the same room again.

He cared for me. Deeply. I knew that. But I couldn't stop imagining them together. There were more important things to think about, but I had all the time in the world and nothing else to do.

I drank all my beer and was worrying the skin on my lip when Anderson finally returned. He knocked politely and waited a beat before letting himself inside. I didn't say hello to him. I was angry at him for his absence. Turning my back on his reticent form, I tucked Betty into her pouch. My eyes ached.

"New clothes?" he asked.

He didn't deserve an answer to his redundant question. I stalked past him with my arms crossed and waited at the elevator. "Nothing was on the docket yesterday, Frankie. No need to be sore at me."

"I'll be the judge of that." My sandals slipped out from under me in the lobby and I fought the urge to kick them at the poker dealer. "Did you have to buy such ridiculous fucking shoes?"

He didn't answer and walked silently beside me, all the way to the car. It wasn't until we were both buckled in that he turned to face me. "I needed a day to process your meeting with Laisren. I hope you can understand that."

I could. That's why I was so angry. I hated *myself* for his avoidance. Because it didn't matter if he needed time, my decision wouldn't change. "Sure."

"But we're going through with it," he said in a rush, scratching his grizzled cheek. He hadn't shaved in a couple of days. His sleeves were bunched up to the elbow. He was beginning to look like a different person. "You don't want to stay. You won't take the deal. Right?"

I ground my tongue between my teeth. "Right."

"I hope they're worth it."

Whether they were worth it or not was irrelevant. I just couldn't help myself. "I need a costume."

He made a left turn. "Sexy or scary?"

"Um … neither?"

"That's a tall order."

"Either way, I need new shoes. Flame retardant."

～∾∾⌒

PARKING around The Harvest was impossible. Walking around The Harvest was impossible. Bodies swarmed the club like bacteria around a big bloody bite. They seemed to pulse together, as if they all ran on one single monstrous heart. They wiggled like snipped veins free of their organs and I cringed away from their writhing, fearing my skin would come away slimy.

Fortunately, we were given special valet clearance, which was prohibited for anyone not invited by Laisren personally. I stepped out of the sedan and onto a black velvet runner leading between the pillars of the entryway. Plush violet ropes blocked off the runway from the crowd, the masses of which were costumed so lavishly, I may as well have been plopped in the middle of a Broadway production. Goblins and superheroes and lacy dead brides made me stick-out like a sore thumb, offensively underdressed.

I hadn't dressed up for Halloween since I was eight, but I figured the cape and devil horns worked as well as anything.

The leggings were sweltering, but they suited my plans for the night far better than a skirt. The boots had a sole as thick as my arm, and I knew I'd need them.

Holding Betty's pouch close to my stomach, everyone touched me, rubbed me, or grabbed me as we moved through the smoke and flashing lights of the club. I clamped down my hunger for their depression, their heart disease, their cancer. The Pool had truly paid off—I passed through the waves of them like Moses. Their waters barely spritzed me.

The VIP section had been transformed. Garlands of ivy with noxious-colored fruit coated the walls like wallpaper, and dozens—no *hundreds* of flowers coated every dark surface that made up a throne fit for Mother Nature herself. The blossoms fluttered as insidious vines crept by. The plants were alive, and they were moving.

Laisren perched on that throne of flowers, as at home in their stems and petals as Lucifer in brimstone and flame.

"Ah!" Laisren clapped her hands. Cigarette ashes were embedded in the wrinkles of her knuckles. She yelled over the music, "One of my most anticipated guests!"

She looked incredibly ... different, and I didn't know if the effect was good or bad. She wore a spectacular indigo suit over a gossamer blouse, which looked too frilly behind her blunt black tie. Her makeup was extreme, and her eyes were enormous—she wanted everyone to look and risk losing themselves. She wore a silk top hat over it all, looking like a formidable Jiminy Cricket. "And you've brought the prettiest snake this side of the state line!" She drew a finger along Betty's zipper.

I wanted to kill her, and I wanted to hold her, to stare into those unfathomable eyes.

A scary woman with a butt-length ponytail sprouting from the top of her head appeared beside me. She nudged her filigreed tray into my bicep, upon which sat several champagne flutes of cloudy blush liquid. I took a glass for myself—internally screaming a mantra not to drink anything offered freely to me tonight—and a second glass for Anderson.

After a moment's pause, he jolted forward to take it, more out of subservience than actual want. Laisren's mouth turned down in blatant disapproval, but she kept her classist ministrations to herself and turned her frown upside-down. The scary girl handed a glass to Laisren before strutting off to the bar.

Laisren took a hefty sip and licked her mummy lips. Her jade eyes widened in surprise before homing in on me. "Very interesting."

I bobbed my head in agreement without having tried the concoction. I brought the glass closer to my eyes, better to see in the sporadic lighting of the club. Wisps of milky swirls swam to the top as if desperate for air. "What ... *flavor* is this?"

She downed her glass and considered my question before answering. "Intuition."

Her answer almost brought the glass to my lips. What did intuition taste like? I wanted some of that for myself, especially in the presence of this woman. Why would she allow me such a drink? Was this all an effort to get me to trust her, to trust all of them?

Certainly, if she could drink it ... I could drink it. Anderson had already finished his flute, and I hoped he knew what it was. He had to have been offered one, or at least been privy to the secret menu, in the past. But remembering the girl whom Nicola stabbed so callously at The Pool, non-witches seemed worse off than animals in Vegas. Animals were familiars to them after all.

Anderson and Laisren whipped their heads like hunting dogs to the west wall, where moments later, a hole revolved into being via a secret door, the secret door through which I first saw The Harvest. And out of thin air appeared Jessamae and Cleo, each simultaneously frightening and ravishing. Jessamae wore a deep plum vest over her bare torso, ankle-length pants, and heels; Cleo wore thigh-high suede boots, fishnets, and the miniest of mini dresses. I didn't know if her skin or the dress looked softer.

The tension between the two was palpable, and I thought they had just been cut off mid-argument.

I wished I hadn't worn this dumb costume.

Revolving toward the throne, I intended to excuse myself to greet them but found Laisren standing just behind me. "No need, let's go together." She roped her arm in mine and towed me to the secret doorway. I took a sip of my drink to soothe my nerves in a moment of complete panic. The drink lathered my tongue. It was almost smokey, both familiar and strange, heady and electrifying.

I blinked, and we were all together, my group of three having united with Cleo and Jessamae across the room. Laisren reached out to touch my cheek.

I shook away the image, and I was by the throne again, far away from the beautiful duo, Laisren leading me like a pet. The short scene of the four of us together was exactly like a dream. I hadn't felt the ground beneath my feet or the stroke of Laisren's skin. I hadn't heard a sound. But I felt fear in that moment. Raw and sharp.

I'd seen us together when we'd yet to move.

Once we were with Jessamae and Cleo, for real this time, Laisren stroked my cheek and turned to the others. "Happiest of Samhains, ladies. I hope you are in good health. Your lovely friend Francesca is here as my honored guest." She held a hand to my lower back, and I leaned forward until her skin barely brushed my clothes. "As associates of hers, you'll receive the same special attention she does." That was code for we were being watched, all of us, including Anderson hovering nearby, acting twitchy. "So please, eat, drink, and be merry! Sláinte!" She bowed, flipping the top hat upside down in her hand, and left.

I couldn't face Cleo yet, so I downed the rest of my flute, trying to discern why the flavor profile was so familiar to me. It was earthy, almost like whiskey.

Then suddenly, I was standing outside. Anderson spoke with the valet, and I heard nothing, no words. I didn't feel the sweaty people pushing their leather wings and lion's tails into my skin, though they were. The valet shook his head, and suits appeared on all sides of our quartet, obstructing our exit and pulling out their batons.

"Something's happening, something wrong," Anderson whispered into my hair. I was back in the club, standing just as I had, an empty glass dangling from my limp fingers.

Anderson's eyes flickered like old lightbulbs, and his panic tickled my nose. "I'm seeing things. I'm—I'm hallucinating."

I squeezed my flute until the glass cracked. "It's the drink, it'll pass." *Intuition*—more like precognition. We were seeing snippets of possible futures.

When Jessamae bought me drinks from the secret menu last week, the first drink gave me joy, the second adrenaline or energy. Or so I thought. But were they some sort of affinity, the emotions a side-effect to an *affinity*? Anderson had never experienced the sensation before, and he was rightfully freaking. But this was magic.

This was *Ben's* magic.

"I know where Ben is!" I shouted at Jessamae. "And I need your help. Now. And we can't take the car. Laisren's suspicious already. She's going to sic her dogs on us—"

"Slow down, Frankie." Jessamae tried to take my glass. I gripped it harder, and it turned to shards in my hand. I shook them to the floor and Jessamae's ghostly eyes shone with concern. "We just arrived. We have to keep up appearances, and several witches are expecting us, if you recall."

"Who gives a shit! It's Ben, Jessamae! This!" I threw my hands at the glass beneath us. "They've bottled and sold his affinity!" I remembered Patrick's words about me this past summer: *The magic is in her blood.* "She made a drink out of him! She used his blood somehow, some fucking alchemy shit and turned him into a fucking white-wine spritzer! Please, we have to leave. I know where he is." I grabbed her arm and about yanked it from its socket.

A warm hand pressed into my shoulder, and I turned to Cleo's golden eyes. Dropping Jessamae, I felt my pupils dilate. She said, "It's okay. We will find him tonight, but we have to take it easy. Do you understand, Frankie?" Cleo's words were lovely and musical. I stepped into her light and her smile embraced me. Those teeth, that full hypnotic mouth ... on Ben's. Licking fruit juices from his lips.

"Please don't touch me," I sighed without shoving her hand away. But I wanted to. Oh, how I wanted to. I was finally learning to resist her craft.

Cleo was stone. She held me for another moment or more before taking her arm back, as emotionless as a mountain face. That was much better, though my brain was completely scrambled after her influence and my horrible drink. I slapped my cheeks to beat the disorientation away and turned to Jessamae. "Can you apport me? The Alcazar?"

"Not yet. Frankie, there are eyes on you. You must put on a show. Laisren gave you that drink to give you a reason to flee. She's waiting to arrest you."

"No, she isn't. She wants me to work for her. She said ..."

She said she was interested in my magic. And if I were arrested ... she could turn me into another cocktail. Either way, she wins.

Jessamae took advantage of my silence and pulled my cape over my shoulders, leaving her hands by my neck. "Just ... wait. We have no choice. We must keep up appearances."

I turned to leave and said, "Fuck you then." The words felt good. I had a hundred reasons to say them, and they all were laced in.

Jessamae pulled me to a stop by my cape. "For Ben? Can you wait if it will save his life?"

I gnashed my teeth and itched my scalp under the devil horns. I gave a gruff nod and stomped to the bar, dragging Anderson along beside me.

"A beer. Two beers!" I yelled before I realized there was no bartender in front of me. "Eyes on me, my ass," I whispered, as I leaned over the countertop. "Excuse me!" I shouted, smashing my tits to the bar and waving an arm around. "Two beers!" One of the bartenders, a girl dressed like a pornographic Wednesday Addams, saw me and rolled her eyes. She grabbed two glowing yellow beers from under the bar.

I wasn't keeping up pretenses like I should, I knew that, but this was the best I could do. I couldn't hear Ben anymore. For all I knew, he was already dead.

I took our beers, and the woman left without asking me for money. If I drank for free under Laisren's employ, that might be the only employee benefit I'd grieve.

Turning around, I shoved Anderson's beer into his chest. He was jittery as a rat. Then I had another vision.

The sizzling eyes of a dragon. But she wasn't angry, she wasn't leering at me as she normally did. She was scared. I saw true fear in her. Nicola was shaken.

The vision dried up, and after taking a moment to orient myself once again, I searched for her in the club. Obviously, she was here, and I didn't have to look long. Nicola was seated in the VIP section, in a flower-coated booth nearest the bar. She wore a slinky black dress and a witch's hat. What a fucking comedian.

I chugged my beer as I strolled across the floor, towing Anderson like a rolling suitcase.

Witches and non-witches undulated around me like glittery, beached fish—wet and smelly and full of metal barbs. The costumes were covered in spikes and chains that rattled as they danced. One man grabbed me by the shoulders and held me in place. Rings dangled on either side of his torso all the way down his ribs, piercing his skin. They resembled a pregnant dog's nipples. He had a leather collar that connected to straps around his jaw and lips, forcing his mouth into a bared snarl.

"Hey shweetie," he said without full control of his mouth. He had a pair of inch-long canines poking his bottom lip and fake blood on his chin. He was surrounded by similarly clad people who were licking and squeezing one another, or anyone who got too close. His hands on my shoulders were clammy—they made me want to vomit. I wriggled under his touch, trying to free myself, but he thought I was dancing and pushed his erection into my hip, shimmying his shoulders. He leaned in to kiss me, his tongue like a sea slug dripping slime. He yanked the strap of Betty's pouch, and I almost dropped her.

I hooked two of my fingers into the ring beside his belly button and pulled. His skin stretched out like the knot at the end of a balloon, and he squealed in pain. I pulled until it bled, then let go. The piercing snapped back into place. Almost no harm done.

"What the fuck is your problem?" He dipped his finger in the blood on his stomach. And so did I. He sucked in his gut, but I got a swab of the red stuff under my fingernail. I put it in my mouth and felt strong. I wanted more.

"Crazy bitch," he cried, squirreling away.

I sucked the dregs from my nail and turned to Anderson. Disgust marred his face, but after a moment he shrugged. He'd seen me do worse. "He might have a point."

"Yeah," I readjusted Betty on my shoulder. "I know."

Rinsing my mouth with beer, I crossed into the VIP section. Laisren sat on her throne, tickling the neck of a sexy clown. The dark-haired smiling man was with her—he had a Batman in his lap and a butterfly kneeling beside his booth, rubbing his leg. He made eye contact with me across all the costumes and servers, and the moment our eyes met I wanted to scrub my insides clean. Something about that man was incredibly wrong, and he wasn't ashamed of it.

I veered for the dragon. Nicola's neck was wrapped in a thick silk scarf, hiding her wound. I wanted to grab both ends and pull. "Happy Halloween, Nicola. I like your costume. Creative." I drizzled the rest of my beer down my throat and took Anderson's from him.

229

Her lips were painted purple, and when she smiled, the color split, exposing the pale flesh of her lips. "Good Samhain, Francesca." Her voice was shredded paper. I must have damaged her vocal cords.

I sat across from her, a black table between us, and Anderson stood off to the side, his hands crossed in typical security person fashion. "How are you feeling?" I stared at the scarf around her neck. "Probably as good as I'm feeling right now."

Her smile never faltered. "I'm sure you're right. Have you sampled the secret menu tonight, honey? So many delicacies. But you must recognize the special flavor ... delicious."

I would strangle her with my bare hands—the scarf wouldn't be nearly as gratifying.

"What scares you, Nicola?" I was too tired and anxious for pretense. And I wanted to ruin her evening.

"Excuse me?"

"Can't be much, but there has to be something."

"Are you implying that I should be afraid of *you*?" I heard her perfectly despite the violent, thumping music.

"No. I'm not as stupid as I look." I took a moment to consider whether that was, in fact, true. "But there was someone. Once. That scared you. Right? They scared you even more than Laisren does. A man. A witch. A pain junkie."

Her smile dropped to the ground. I heard it go splat. She froze, staring at me. And the fear I'd foreseen overtook her. She raised a finger in the air, signaling a bartender, and covered her mouth. After a moment, she cracked her neck and portrayed some of her earlier composure. "You've seen my written manuscript. I'm surprised. Even a little impressed. As far as I know, there are only five copies of that diary."

Of course, Patrick would have stumbled upon one. He probably sought it out, knowing how exclusive they were. He'd proven how much he enjoyed rare and expensive things.

"Who was he?" There was a reason Jessamae came here, to

the dragon's lair. She hadn't been sneaking into The Alcazar, she'd been coming to The Harvest every week.

Nicola opened her mouth for a snarky rebuttal and paused. She assessed me as the bartender dropped a fizzy, sky-blue drink before her. She brought me another beer and I put it to my lips. Anything to keep from screaming, to keep from breaking the bottle over Nicola's head.

"The pain junkie was a healer … of sorts." She narrowed her eyes at me and sipped her cocktail, the blue foam clinging to her purple lips. "He healed others in that he took their wounds from them, absorbed the damage, and loved doing it. It made him stronger." She dabbed her mouth with a cocktail napkin. "Why do you ask?"

She was suspicious. It wasn't hard to connect the dots between me and such a man. "Did he ever heal *you*?" I asked.

"I don't owe you this information, sweetie. If you remember, you didn't treat me so good the other day."

"I know. Just. Please? We're going to be working together, right? And you didn't exactly give me a choice. You went into The Pool and set my ass ablaze."

She chortled and trailed her sparkling nails up and down her glass. "Yeah. I did."

"And? What'd it feel like?"

"Setting you on fire? Better than sex."

Unamused, I said, "What did it feel like when the man healed you?"

Her eyebrows quirked and she flipped her cranberry hair over her shoulder. "That's an unusual question. It didn't feel like anything other than his hand on me. But I saw my skin come together. I saw him use those wounds to heal himself." She stared at my hands over the rim of her glass. "If you healed me right now, would it feel some sort of way?"

My touch was rejuvenating. Ben told me so on our first date.

I refused to take Nicola's wounds from her in The Pool, so she didn't know what it felt like when I healed physical injuries.

I ate pain, that was sadly true, but I healed my victims too, inside and out. The pain junkie only *removed* injuries, leaving the bodies as they were before their cuts and breaks—no hair growth, no wellness, no strength. The distinction made me feel better. But our affinities, the pain junky's and mine, were incredibly close. They could be directly linked.

"What was his name?"

Please, don't say it. Please. Don't. Say. It. Andrew or Alan. Don't let him be my—

"Aiden."

"Fuck."

Close enough.

20

"WHY ARE you so curious about him, Francesca?" Nicola asked, her fear replaced with vindictive pleasure. But I wouldn't tell her, she already knew. She might not know he was my father, but she knew we were family, to have such closely related affinities. Especially after I asked. I shouldn't have asked, but it was a masochistic compulsion to know who my father was. And now I knew he was a sick, twisted son of a bitch.

How had my mother loved him? Pamela knew him, so they'd been introduced at some point. Did he hurt Allison? Is that why she ran, taking bouncing baby me along for the ride?

Did she know what he was? What I could have been?

"There you are," Jessamae crooned, spilling an arm over the back of my seat. "I've been looking for you," she said, poking at my devil horns. She was putting on a show, but my stomach roiled up into my throat at her proximity. Cleo wasn't far behind, and she draped herself into a booth all her own, crossing her long legs. Not looking at me. At us. I suddenly wanted to push Jessamae onto the floor to save Cleo from further misery.

And a tiny part of me wanted to kiss Jessamae hard on the mouth. The part that felt Cleo owed me for my own dismantled ticker.

"Right, sorry." I tipped back my beer and used the same signal Nicola had for the bartender. She visibly snorted but brought over another round. "I'll take that," I said, grabbing the beer. "But I actually wanted to order something else." I was going to puke. "Intuition. Please."

Both Cleo and Anderson tensed, though Jessamae pushed my hair behind my ear and tickled my neck. Once my deplorable drink arrived, I tossed it back like a shot of motor oil, gagging up the sticky mess over and over. "So lovely to catch up, Nicola, but I just want to … I don't know. Dance or something." I stood and handed my glass to Anderson, whispering in his ear. "Take Cleo and get the car. You won't be as suspicious without Jessamae and me. And Cleo will be able to make the valet comply. Go to Patrick's room, get him. We'll meet you after."

"Where?"

"Ben will see where you are through Cleo." I wouldn't entertain the notion of leaving the hotel without him. I would have him with me by the end of the night.

Without giving Anderson the chance to respond, I grabbed Jessamae and whisked her down to the dance floor, wedging us between a statuesque Barbie doll with drawn-on eyebrows and a woman in a racing jumpsuit. A man in a banana hammock held a bowl filled with little pink pills mixed with candy-colored grapes. Fairy fruit. As much as I could use the blissful slip from consciousness, I pushed the offering away.

"I've waited long enough. I can't be here anymore. I told Anderson the plan. We're leaving—"

Without warning, Jessamae and I were standing beside a slot machine. She picked up a used cigarette slumping inside an ashtray and put it between her lips. I was disgusted. The elevator bank winked at me over her shoulder. The Alcazar. We made it.

"Frankie, slow down," Jessamae said, shaking me. I was back at the Harvest, and I groaned at the lost progress. She grabbed my face to hold my attention. "I can't take you all the way to The Alcazar, even with a sacrifice, which I don't have." Her thumb dipped into my chin dimple, and I jerked my head away.

I gestured to all the inebriated dancers around us. Each

person was more than willing to follow us into a dark corner. "Take your pick."

Jessamae's eerie eyes peeled wide as she considered exactly how far I was willing to go for this. I didn't even have to think about it. It was instinct to use what we had at our disposal. As much as it would haunt me later, just as Gabriel haunted my every breath, I would do it.

Cleo and Anderson appeared behind Jessamae, and shame clumped inside my chest. Cleo's clever gaze held mine as if she heard my every thought. Even if Jessamae agreed, I couldn't do it with Cleo watching. She'd committed horrible deeds of her own, but the fools had always deserved it. She was nobler than me.

"Fine," I said. "I'll heal any wound you cause. How far will pain get us?"

Jessamae said, "Not far enough. But, luckily, I had the mind to invite a few more people to the party."

"Stop being so cryptic!" I was out of time and out of patience.

"Breathe, peach. And wait here." She disappeared between the thrashing bodies.

"Fucking peach bullshit—"

"Frankie, I can drive you to The Alcazar, we can work around the valet," Anderson said, rushing forward, sneaking furtive glances at Cleo's devastating beauty. Her magic was turned all the way down, and she was still painful to look at.

"No, we can't. I saw it. At least not when we're all together. Laisren will stop us." I tried to glean what I'd learned from Ben's visions over the last few months. Changing one thing, one person, could mean the difference between failure and success. "You two go back to the hotel together. And act, you know, sexy together. Like you're hooking up." I dropped my bag over his shoulder, hoping Laisren didn't see. It would make her suspicious, but I couldn't take Betty with me. She'd be safer with him. I trusted him.

Anderson hadn't fully recovered from the magic he'd

ingested. He was blinking along with his heartbeat, his elbow resting on Betty's pouch. He continually leaned in and leaned away from Cleo, both enthralled and afraid of her. With a similar allure to Laisren's, it was no wonder he feared such a witch. "This is Cleo, Anderson. She's a siren, and you've noticed her beauty." I rubbed my face. "And, cold as she may be, she won't use it against you. Right, Cleo?"

Cleo's rocky façade began to smolder. She held my stare until I looked away. "I did wrong by you. I know that. But you are not blameless in this." Never one to beat around the bush, that woman. She took hold of Anderson's arm and dragged him across the club. Playing with his shorn hair and laughing at jokes he never made. He stumbled after her, a look of pleading contorting his face.

I hated how I spoke to her. I wanted to say I was sorry. I wanted to soothe her for once instead of the other way around. But I couldn't help myself. I had such meanness in me.

"Stay safe," I whispered once there was no one left to hear me.

Jessamae marched back into view, two drinks in hand. She handed the liquid over—it was red and glittering. She whispered through a lifeless mouth, "Don't drink. Pretend to drink."

Once the cool glass graced my fingers, she ravished me. Giggling and silly, she huffed hot air against my earlobe, a nimble hand curling around the back of my neck. I put the juice to my mouth, and very nearly swallowed. It smelled wonderful.

"Don't look at her, look near her. Is Laisren watching?" She pressed a kiss to my cheek, only lingering for a moment. Her eyelashes tickled my temple.

I leaned back. As soft as her lips were against the fuzz of my cheek, as much as I wanted to taste the drink lingering on her mouth … my heartache was strong. Gold medal, destroying any and all competition strong. And my self-preservation would never allow my body to put my heart through such torture again.

I glanced over Jessamae's shoulder with a sinful smile, running my fingers over the small of her back. Focusing on the server working the VIP area, I saw that Laisren was indeed paying strict attention to my actions, Nicola chirping in her ear. "Yes."

"Should we find a room? Walk down memory lane?" She asked, much louder than before but as breathy as ever. She kissed the hard line of my jaw, and I felt a vicious stab of both pleasure and pain knowing Ben could see what I was doing. But he was eerily silent. Maybe I was too far away. I hoped so. I nodded against her mouth.

She wound her fingers through mine and went to one of the blank black doors lining one wall, gently pushing strangers out of her way with the hand holding her drink. She opened it, practically shoving me through its threshold, and spun around to turn the dinky lock on the knob. A shadowed figure stood in the corner of the room, and I stumbled back into Jessamae instinctively. "This one's taken!" I yelled, terrified of whoever would lurk in one of these dirty rooms alone.

Jack walked forward into the light. "Fucking fuck fuck!"

"I really don't want to be here," Jack said.

"No one wants to be here," Jessamae assured.

"Why *are* you here? What's the plan?" I whipped back to Jessamae. "We don't have a lot of time. Laisren might have seen, might still see what we're going to do." We were fortunate she didn't have the lifelong experience with visions that Ben did. The drinks caused precognition but they were unpredictable, without focus, and only minutes in the future.

"Jack is a rune witch, he can amplify affinities and spell work." She pulled a pocketknife from her slacks, a pocketknife with which I was achingly familiar.

"Whoa, then why do you need that at all? Can't we just go?"

Jack huffed in exasperation, and I nearly throttled him, shouting, "Keep your little fucking breaths to yourself! I'm still learning!"

"Frankie." My name was cold in Jessamae's mouth, a scold. "Clam. Please. Jack can only enhance, he cannot create. I've always had to pay for the ability to apport and I still do. But it will cost less to travel farther with his help."

"Why did I agree to do this?" Jack asked, appearing painfully regretful. He was paranoid and spasming. He was too close to the queen. Too deep in the hive.

"Because I asked you to come," Jessamae responded seriously. She didn't need precognition—she always had an ace up her sleeve. She told him, "I'll get you out of here, but I can't take you all the way, you understand." Without further ado, she sliced a quick line from her elbow to wrist, and blood welled as I blinked. I stifled my craving for it, rolling my tongue around in my mouth. She held an arm out to both Jack and me. We were both reluctant.

Touching Jessamae had been a gamble since the very beginning, and that hadn't changed.

I launched myself at her, holding her to me, hurting her. I tightened my grip until the dark of the depressing room became the dark of a depressing side street. The lights of The Alcazar emitted a soft glow in the distance, like a candle in a blackout. My cocktail glass was still in my hand, and I dropped it to the asphalt. The alley smelled like hot, wet garbage.

"This is where I get off," Jack said. "I've got work to do out here. Otherwise, you'll never make it out of the city. How uh ... how *precise* are your friend's visions?" he asked me.

Jessamae held me close, and I spoke into her cheek. "Um ... I'm not sure. Some things are clearer than others."

"Whelp, better hope it's clear out tonight with what I've got planned." He seemed a little lost as to what to do next. "Touching works best, I'm afraid." He flapped his hands around like a wounded pelican before finally giving Jessamae a strange and aggressive side hug. "Good luck, blondie. I don't know how long I have till they find the truck, but I doubt I have time for coffee." He continued to hold her, though I was wrapped in her arms.

He tipped his chin in my direction. "Frankenstein. If you live through this, I'll be seeing the two of you soon."

I'd been an asshole to everyone since I took my first sip of the bubbly Ben cocktail, and I knew how much Jack despised being here. He was only here for Jessamae's sake, but I was grateful. "Thanks, Jack."

But we were already gone. Jessamae apported us right out from under him.

The sudden light was painful, and I shielded my eyes. We weren't inside the lobby, but we'd apported to the lip of the alley directly beside The Alcazar.

"Let's go," Jessamae said.

She loped to the sidewalk and turned toward the door. I hurried to follow, but Jessamae stopped me with a hand on my stomach. There was a suited guard stationed at the front doors, a whispering earpiece crammed into his ear. If Laisren knew we were missing, she would have already told him.

"Oh no," I said, yanking Jessamae back into the shadows. "I've never seen a guard outside before … But I saw us in the casino. We can get inside, it's possible, but not with that gorilla out here. How did we do it?" I spoke as if the possibility were in our past, not our ever-shrinking future.

Jessamae's mirror eyes bounced from side to side. She leaned around the building to get a better look. "There's only one. We can get past one."

Scared that Jessamae was banking on my earlier recklessness, I feared we were about to murder someone in the middle of the Vegas Strip. "How?"

"How else? A spell." She rushed me deeper into the alley and grabbed my hand. "I know of something that will work. As long as it's only one guard. It's a mind-addling spell. It will confuse him. But it's costly. Are you willing to pay the price?"

"Yes," I said without understanding the details or asking what it would take. There was no going back now. We'd come too far to return unscathed. I pulled my own knife from my pocket, the one I'd taken from the security guard. Every witch needed one, I figured. It was as essential as a cell phone or a set of car keys. I'd earned this one.

"More than that," she said, and my stomach dropped.

She took a inhaled, clenched her jaw, and grabbed her pointer finger. Without a moment's hesitation, she snapped it to the side, breaking the bone. Her eyes popped and her open mouth shook like a sail, but she didn't cry out, she hardly made a sound. She took three harsh breaths through her nose and then looked back at me. She reached out to touch me and I felt her power flow through me anew. "Now you."

"What?"

"It'll require both of us. You know we're stronger together."

I did know. I remembered Pamela's grave. The thing that started all of this, digging up her corpse and filling it with a demon. A demon we'd killed, or something like it. Together.

"Okay. Okay …" I splayed my fingers far apart like I was afraid of accidentally grabbing four and snapping them all off. I grabbed my index and squeezed until I could read my bone like braille.

"Come on, Frankie. You'll heal."

I nodded. I clenched. I wrenched. And the sound of cracking walnuts echoed against the walls. My finger sat sideways on my hand, crooked at the knuckle.

"OH GOD—"

Jessamae smashed her good hand to my mouth. A tear rolled from my eye and caught in the ditch between her hand and my face. I'd felt worse. But the pain scared me. It always did.

"Shh! Someone will hear. You're okay. You're okay, Frankie."

I nodded under her hand, but the tears kept flowing. Her

hand stayed on my mouth as she hauled me toward the street. We were hidden in shadow, but we could see tourists, gamblers, and hustlers stomping the pavement.

"I'm going to talk to him. I'm going to get him to come to us." She moved her hand to the back of my head, wrestling with my hair. "Don't be afraid."

It was like we'd never left Aspen Ridge. And she scared me just as much as she always did. But even so, she'd become essential to me.

"Okay."

She looked to the wall over my shoulder, and I cradled my broken finger as I waited. I expected her to speak, which she didn't. Not until her eyes, already white in their color, began to roll back in her head. Little by little, they spun into her brain until I saw nothing but the stringy veins holding the orbs inside her skull. She looked like a ghost of herself, and I wanted to shake her.

Her hand slackened on my face, and I held it to my skin, keeping the connection. Then she started talking. "Help, Daniel!" she cried. "Help me, I'm stuck!" Her voice was hers but there was an echo hidden underneath. It was a man's voice. It was the voice the guard heard inside his head. "Help me! Please! I can't breathe!" I heard the guard's feet slapping the sidewalk. Whoever spoke to him now was someone he loved.

He turned the corner, palming his temple like he had a headache. He'd been sprinting, but his legs were gummy worms beneath him, and I was surprised he'd made it this far. He saw the two of us in an almost embrace, confusion twisting his brows.

"Where is he? Simon!" he bellowed down the alley.

Jessamae's irises were sinking back to their expected position, and I pinched her arm to move the process along faster.

"That way," I whispered, tipping my head toward the back of the alley.

He shambled past, calling for Simon and bracing himself against the wall.

Jessamae returned to her body, her head flicking to the man all alone in the dark. In seconds, she ambushed him, the grim reaper herself. He went down beneath her weight, and she clung to his back with her hands around his neck. He was gasping for air, his limbs seizing in their sockets. She was going to kill him, this man who loved someone.

I ran forward and kicked the guard in the head. It was like kicking a bowling ball. Thank god for the boots or I would have broken my toes. His brain shook around on its stem, and he plummeted into unconsciousness.

Jessamae looked up at me, blowing a wisp of hair from her face. "He might wake up."

"I know." But we couldn't kill him. Not after hearing about Simon. We were chasing after my own Simon after all.

She opened his blazer, stripping it from him like a butterfly's wings, and plucked his security badge from the pocket. Then she strode toward the front doors of The Alcazar.

I sprinted after her, my quaking hands hidden under my cape. I wanted to ask Jessamae to set my finger, but she wasn't my mother. My time in Vegas proved that my friends wouldn't always be there to indulge me. I clutched the finger hard and forced it back in place, nearly biting through my tongue to keep from screaming.

The casino was brighter at night, but it was still drab and dull compared to the rest of Last Vegas. Jessamae, walking gracefully in her high heels, veered for the elevator banks past the slot machines. But seeing the banks of them off to the side, the glowing restroom sign above them and the ashtrays beside them, I stopped her. "Wait. I think we need to stop."

"I don't," she said, trying to veer away, but I fisted a handful of her vest.

"I saw something. After I had the cocktail, Ben's cocktail."

"Ben's cocktail?"

"Yeah, didn't you hear me at the club? I know I was rambling but … the drinks have, I don't know, bits of affinities in them. When you drink them, it's like you have another affinity on loan. And Laisren ordered me one that gave me precognition. Just like Ben's."

She stared at the elevators as she considered what I said. Her translucent brows lowered over her eyes until her scar warped her whole face. She hadn't known. That was clear. And judging by the way her lip trembled over her teeth, she was putting everything together much faster than I had. She'd been drinking people. The whole time.

"What did you see?" she whispered. "In the vision?"

I looked back to the bank of slot machines, ensuring the angle was right. "There."

She moved the moment I spoke, exchanging the security card for a five in her pocket. She slid the cash into the machine, then pressed a bunch of buttons without paying attention and lost half her money.

Nothing happened. I waited for something, a signal letting us know it was time to proceed, and was met with nothing but jingling music blaring from the slots. Jessamae pushed more buttons.

I turned to the tables, certain the dealer had been watching us. She kept dropping her eyes whenever I checked. She knew. She recognized me.

Jessamae was out of money and still nothing happened. "Did you see me gambling?" she asked.

"No." I looked down at the ashtrays and remembered what Ben told me—that telling someone what you see can affect how they will in turn behave. It could change the future. But Jessamae noticed my fixation and focused on the cold cigarette curled in the ashtray. She picked it up, and I automatically touched my mouth, fixated on the vision playing out in front of me. Without pause, she put it to her lips. My stomach rolled.

As soon as the stick touched her mouth, a herd of suits

bustled from the elevators, charged through the casino and out the front doors. Jessamae smoked her spitty cigarette as they left, and I pushed every button on the machine in front of me, my eyes on the flashing lights.

How did Ben handle this? It didn't make any sense. If I hadn't had the vision, then I wouldn't have looked at the ashtray and that moment wouldn't have happened. We would have gone into the elevator too soon. But if I hadn't had those visions, then we wouldn't have left The Harvest freely at all, so this entire future was dependent on me having foreseen it …

A headache bloomed in my brain. Jessamae took my hand from my temple and toted me to the elevators the moment the Piss Patrol exited the building. She held the stolen card to the little black box, and with a ding, we were inside.

The button with a big "L" glowed yellow, and above it, the number two. I pressed it, half expecting an alarm to go off, half expecting to die the moment my finger touched down. But I didn't. The doors closed.

21

I EXPECTED blood to trickle down the walls. The wailing of prisoners as they banged their knuckles and mugs against the bars of their cells. Glinting tools of torture, a man in a hood swinging a club covered in bits of hair and brain matter. But we were met with a hotel hallway. It seemed too thin a hallway, even thinner than the third floor in its tight quarters. There were no doors on either side of me, just a stretch of blank, eggshell drywall. Other than that, there was nothing amiss whatsoever.

God … dammit.

Ben's voice was back, and I smiled. He was alive, and angry at me. He was alive, and we were getting closer. Ben couldn't hear anything in his visions, so I didn't bother telling him that being a sourpuss wasn't going to stop me, so he may as well play "Hot or Cold" with us until we found our way.

I marched down the hall, seeing nothing but white on white. Bland as a dentist's office. "There's nowhere to go. Is it a trick?"

"It's not a trick," Jessamae said, pointing ahead to something I couldn't see.

As we shuffled across the carpet, the sound of our padding feet as loud as a tap dance, there was only one doorway on the right side of the hallway. It was white and plain. It didn't have a single scrap of adornment, not even a knob.

There was another black box stationed beside the door. I should have seen it before; it was so stark against everything

245

else. Jessamae held our key against the thing, and the sound of a hatch released, like we were entering a rocket ship.

"That's … ominous."

A set of damp cement stairs led down, but they did not lead up. This was the only way to get to this staircase. The light disappeared after the first flight, just as the steps turned back in the other direction.

"No guards?" Jessamae asked, peering over the first set of stairs.

"Not yet." There was no way our luck would hold. I hadn't had a vision since we left the club, and we were going into an enemy prison blind.

She stepped through the doorway.

"Wait," I said, taking her hand. It wasn't the first time I'd healed her broken bones, and the warmth was familiar, almost comfortable, even when I snapped the finger back into its proper place. She smiled at me as I brought the bits of her together, then she kissed me on the temple.

"We'll find him," she said. And she said it with such confidence, it was almost like having him back.

I wiggled my healthy fingers without pain. We didn't thank each other; we stepped into the dark. Pitch-black dark.

I was terrified, absolutely, but going down into the bowels of the building was no worse than going up to The Pool. My life had teetered on the point of a needle for days. Weeks maybe. I'd stopped keeping track of time when I'd stopped sleeping regular hours. I'd keep moving through the black ichor to get us all out alive. I told myself there were worse things than being lost in the dark.

"If we meet a guard, I will have to take care of them this time. I need to know you understand that," Jessamae said from somewhere in front of me.

My mouth was drying out and I filled it with spit before I spoke. "Yeah. Course." I tried to ignore my thoughts of Anderson. A good man in a bad situation.

We continued down and the dark grew darker, it became a living thing that I felt on my face. My hands shook in front of me. I wanted to turn back. I was afraid of those eyes. Silver dollar eyes that I could feel on my neck like broken red fingers. I heard the cracking of pointed, backward limbs. They would blanket me as dead flies dropped from their open chest cavity ...

Hello, Francesca.

The voice wasn't real. Paimon was dead because of me.

Just like so many others, no? They laughed. The sound crept up from the bottom of the stairwell, their alligator feet scuttled towards us over the porous steps. *And she's so ready to slaughter the guiltless for one sad boy.*

I held a hand to the wall. It was cold, like I was at the bottom of a lake. "Jessamae?" I worked to steady my breathing, to calm my nerves. I couldn't break down, not now. "Jessamae?"

She can't hear you ... Where'd you go? Where'd you go, little peach?

My exhales punched my eardrums, but I didn't hear anything else. I didn't hear Jessamae. I sat down and held my head in my hands. I wouldn't respond. Talking to it made it real.

Am I not real, Miss Hughes?

"No." I spoke without meaning to, denied without thinking.

No? He seemed hurt by it. As if by not acknowledging him, I proved what he knew to be true. That I discarded human lives like bottle caps, cellophane, twist ties.

Something touched my hand, and I froze. If I didn't respond, then it wasn't real. Those were the rules. The thing kept bumping at my hand like the icy nose of a bloodhound, searching for something in my fingers. Instinctually, my hand opened, and the thing curled itself inside. It bloomed, spread, wrapping around me like a squid. Because it was squishy, and cold, but so strong. A dead man's hand, lifting my own up and down in an imitation handshake.

I screamed and threw the thing away from me, crab-walking backward up the steps.

I heard a tinkling at my feet but couldn't see what made the sound. I heard nothing else, saw nothing else. I crawled forward slowly, hoping distance would get me out of this nightmare.

The ground was suddenly wet and sticky, and I couldn't find purchase. My hands and feet slid through the stuff every time. Thicker than water, cold as graveyard soil. My fingertips rolled over something hard, something metal and frozen and covered in goo. A wedding band.

It fell from my fingers, and I crumbled to the floor. I felt it. I held Gabriel's wedding ring and felt it. He was here. He was real. "I'm sorry!" I shouted. "I'm sorry! I'M SORRY!"

"Frankie! Shhh! What do you see? Is it a vision?"

The blood was gone from under me. My ghosts were gone from above. Jessamae gripped me by the shoulders, but I couldn't see her. A part of me feared that Paimon had found their way inside her again, and she was going to pull me down with her. Down the steps, down into the earth, where we kept our dead and our demons.

"No. No, I'm fine. I'm fine."

"Are you?"

I pushed her away from me. "I'm fine. I just slipped." I couldn't see, and Paimon could be everywhere, standing in the corners of the stairwell watching us. Gabriel could be draped over the railing, looking for the wedding band I dropped. Melted and broken and bloody. Dead because of me. "Let's go."

The stairs went down, not one, but two flights without an exit. Then they stopped, and a teaspoon of light slipped into the stairwell from beneath a painted metal door. It was painted black, like it had disguised itself poorly as a shadow.

Frankie. Ben's voice was crystal clear, and I wondered if I'd imagined that too, just like Paimon and Gabriel. But Ben wasn't dead. I wouldn't entertain the thought.

We opened the door, and we weren't in a hotel anymore.

We were in a factory or a boiler room. Everything was made of metal, everything looked like pipes. The concrete walls were brown and black, covered in bruise-like mold. The air filled with steam that clung to my neck and dewed my lips. We could see, but not much. The light was coming from somewhere to our left, deeper in the metal maze. Sound was coming from that light. Clanking and humming. Something being dragged across the floor.

We passed enormous metal cylinders and pipes that glowed red. The sounds got louder, and I wanted to run away.

"What is it?" I asked.

Jessamae didn't answer. I thought she might have been a little afraid of the noises herself. Two steel doors with a push bar stood between us and the sounds, between us and the light. I opened one side slowly, hoping to avoid notice. And the sounds on the other side died in an instant.

The stink was baffling. I stumbled under its heft—it was a physical thing, rubbing its rancid tentacles against the skin of my cheeks, pushed against my nose hairs. It wasn't merely a physical smell, though there was a lot of that—piss and shit and sickly-sweet sweat hid beneath the pungent aroma of bleach. It was the despair, the rotten, festering, misery that leached through the voids of my face and suffocated me. Blood lived here, and only blood.

The prisoners stared at us as if we'd, indeed, stepped off a rocket ship as little green men with probing fingers. They didn't breathe as we moved through the room. Jessamae positioned herself in front of me. It was something Ben would do, and I nudged her out of my way as I searched between the endless steel bars.

Wrecked people stared back with gaping rodent eyes. There were at least ten of them, some old enough to be grandparents and others young enough to be in high school. They wore long white smocks that resembled hospital gowns—the things weren't tied together with strings, but they were papery and rustled as the prisoners squished their faces between the bars. They were dirty, neglected creatures, like dogs in a pound.

"Who are you?

"How … Hey, stop!"

"Help me!"

"Please! I have children! Two little boys!"

"Don't ignore us! Don't leave! PLEASE!"

"FUCK YOU!"

"God. Oh, my god." I was running, desperate to find a pair of dancing brown eyes and was met time and time again with ghostly, angry glares that stole my breath. They screamed at me, spittle flying from their cages and lodging in my hair and clothes. I could smell them on me. I could smell every single one of them. But they weren't Ben. And I couldn't help them.

There was an empty cage, though it reeked as if a family of piglets hid somewhere inside, and that was the cage I tested. Because I couldn't look at the people anymore. I knew what they'd see in my own stare. Disgust and horror and pity. But everyone must look at them like that, and it couldn't sting too badly. The emotion I was ashamed of, that I knew they saw in every line of my face, was disappointment. He wasn't here. They weren't him.

I yanked at the empty cage as if I could break the hinges. These cages weren't locked with little black boxes that we could open with a swipe. Heavy-duty padlocks held those people inside, and no amount of elementally boosted strength would allow me to snap those in half.

He wasn't here. I let myself hope, just as I'd given these unfortunate tourists hope. Losing it might just kill us all.

"Frankie," Jessamae said. I wasn't interested in her condolences, so I ignored her, holding myself up by the tacky cage bars. Maybe I could push myself between them, pulping my bones until I was just a puddle inside a cage. Maybe everyone would leave me alone, ignore me like I ignored the pleading of the others.

"Frankie. Stop it," Jessamae chided, forcing me to stand. Then she turned my head sharply to the left. "There's more."

There it was. The real source of light. Another set of double doors awaited on the other side of the room, a split, billowing, transparent tarp hanging over them, keeping them fresh. Fluorescent, white light spilled into the prison from their edges, but this time, I didn't hear anything on the other side. The tarp made me queasy. It evoked disease, contagion, experimentation. Mess. I ran for it like it held the whole world.

The plastic crinkle sound of the tarp weakened my knees. I pulled at the door as if I were pulling a Redwood from the ground.

Frankie … please no. It wasn't Paimon or Gabriel crushing my spirit now. Ben knew I was close. He didn't want me to see.

I planted my foot on the wall and the door wouldn't give. A strangled animal screeching burst from my throat. I couldn't get to him. Jessamae came forward and pressed the key card to the lock without a sound. The light shone green, and I nearly popped my shoulder in the door's release.

It was a sea of blinding white and I blinked away the glow. It was a hallway lined in Plexiglas boxes, cells as small as cubicles, and each housed a human being. Small metal hoops were drilled into the ceiling of each cage, and holes were cut into the front walls as if they were hamsters or kittens getting shipped overseas. Some of those holes had fingers hooked around them, but only some. I knew immediately that witches were kept in here. Magic crackled in the air like the sky before a hurricane. The ones who hadn't given up were still trying to magic their way out.

I couldn't feel my feet as I lurched forward, inspecting each ravaged face.

A young girl whose hands and feet were wrapped in bandages—blood seeping through the gauze—was biting at her wrappings viscously. The cloth was moving under her mouth; it was gyrating. How many fingers did the woman have? She didn't even look at me. She was crying as she ate the cotton.

A body covered in bruises, the face shrouded in a burlap bag, hovered horizontally above the ground. They couldn't see, and I didn't think they could hear anything either. Their hands and feet were bound, and they floated from corner to corner, ramming their head into the wall. Trying to break through the bullet-proof glass, or trying to die. Blood smeared the walls and the drilled-in hoop above them.

A heavyset man with black eyes watched us through his cell. He didn't move, he didn't try to escape. He didn't seem afraid. He was incensed. His mouth moved as if he were screaming at the pair of us, veins pulsing in his temples, but he was silent other than a mouse-like squeaking. A blood vessel in his eye had burst and the white became glowing crimson. There was a thick bandage around his throat. I thought his voice box or something like it had been surgically removed, and I was grateful for the amputation. Whatever that man could do with his voice that was deemed threatening to the Queen of Las Vegas ... I didn't want to know. He spat at us as we passed.

Ruined person after ruined person. Every room had a drain in the floor. The cleaner the inmates remained, the longer they lived. If the inmates called water into their cells, as I had on the roof, they couldn't even drown, not with the holes cut into the walls.

The doors had no handles, but each cell had two metal slots on either side of the door, and in the metal slots, were circular imprints, as if they were coin operated. I didn't have any change.

An old woman with no hair, scratching at a thick blindfold. A teenage boy that appeared to be praying, or trying to summon something that just wouldn't show. Not Ben, not Ben, not Ben ...

Ben.

Oh, my god. No. "No."

Ben.

He hung from the ceiling. His wrists were bound in leather cuffs that were strung through the steel hoop above. His hands were white with blood loss, his feet were swollen and purple. He was naked, and I wished harder than I'd wished for anything in a very long time, that he would have been clothed. Because I couldn't keep going. I couldn't handle what I saw and keep going. I started to cry. It wouldn't help anything, but I started to cry.

My pain at seeing the crater Paimon clawed through Ben's torso, the scarring that had erased his trademark tattoos, was a dream compared to this moment.

Dozens and dozens of Ben's tattoos had been removed. Not with a laser—with a scalpel. From the outside in, it looked like. A work in progress. The tattoos were removed from his hands and feet, and up his arms and legs. There were only a few drawings left on his neck and chest. Where he'd been covered in beautiful, strange, nonsensical tattoos, he now had exposed splotches of pulsing muscle. Each missing puzzle piece had been cleaned, and his pink tissue looked sticky in the fluorescent lights.

Frankie. He pulled his head back as if it weighed a hundred pounds. His eyes were closed. He wouldn't even look at me. A fraction of a second passed, that or a thousand years, before his head flopped forward to his chest again.

Get … Out.

22

Stop.

The glass was thick, thicker than my finger. My hands couldn't fit through the holes. I couldn't climb it. I couldn't go under it. But I pounded at the barrier until my wrists ached and my skin broke open. It would break. Eventually, *it had to.*

Stop.

"Stop." I was being held, pulled, yanked backward. Away from Ben's prison. I lost my footing and fell, Jessamae going down with me until we spread like mud on the bright white floors. My hands hurt. There was blood on my clothes.

"There's a lock, Frankie. That's the only way we're getting through."

We didn't have the strange key for the coin slot lock. I spun to my back and kicked at the glass imprisoning Ben. I was screaming, howling like an animal.

"Stop it. Stop it!" Jessamae smashed her hand to my mouth again. I spun around and slapped her in the face. She raised a hand to her cheek, stunned at what I'd done. I wouldn't have been surprised. Her constant nagging had gotten old. I burrowed into my pockets, and she didn't move to stop me. I grasped my knife and turned back to the cell.

Scrambling to my feet, and with the closed blade in my fist, I tried bashing the edge of the handle into the Plexiglas. It made no difference. I tried sawing the blade into the steel of the locking mechanism, which was impossible. Then I rammed my shoulder into the barrier. I hadn't stopped the horrible, ear-splitting keening. It hurt my ears.

The *shhck* of a latch opening shut me up. Two suits entered the witches' prison: a scarecrow-looking beanpole of a man and a broad brunette woman whose shoulders were three times as wide as mine. She was as big as a bear. Maybe I shouldn't have slapped Jessamae, because maybe I shouldn't have stirred up such a commotion. But I didn't regret it. These two were our ticket out of here.

Knife poised behind my hip, I walked forward. There was no point in playing coy. We'd broken in, we were caught red-handed. The two guards smiled at me. Looking like I did, they thought I was no challenge, and still, they were eager to hurt me. They weren't like Anderson. I immediately knew it to be true. They'd been assigned to the second floor for a reason.

I bull-rushed the man, springing the blade free.

The scarecrow hollered in shock as I latched onto him, sticking the knife wherever I could. I didn't care where the blade landed, as long as it found a home.

We both hit the ground. He threw me off his chest, surprisingly strong. But I held onto the blade, which was buried in his neck. By hurling me to the side, he ensured I'd drag the knife through his jugular. He did this to himself.

This scarecrow may have been the one to take Ben's skin from him—a gardener clipping his favorite roses. He may have enjoyed doing it. He wasn't sorry for what he'd done to Ben. But I'd make him sorry. My thirst for retribution made me strong, stronger than I'd ever been. I stabbed and stabbed and stabbed. I screamed. He screamed. We all screamed for ice cream.

The bear woman had me by the hair. She dragged me away from the man beneath me. I left my knife sticking out of the scarecrow's chest and was flailing against the rope of my curls. My devil horns fell to the side, and I reached for them, straining my fingers.

"You trying to steal my rats, you little bitch?"

Her rats? She was the one who tortured these people.

I spun around, my hair twisting in her fist, until I was on my stomach. I hooked my toe around the hairband of the devil horns and pulled my knees beneath me. I grabbed them as I climbed to my feet, my hair still in the woman's clutches.

She was too heavy to kick her feet out from under her, so I stopped fighting her. I ran with her, toward her, until she hit the cell behind her. The woman with bandaged hands pressed her face into the glass to watch.

I couldn't move the bear, so I raked five fingernails down her cheeks, digging bloody trenches in her face. Her pain teased my taste buds. "Give it to me," I rasped. The paths in her skin scabbed before my eyes, and I peeled them off like candy cane stickers.

She wrapped her hands around my throat, crushing my airway. I took the devil horns in both hands and smashed one of the plastic cones into her eye. She hardly reacted, only grunting harder as I pressed the tip into her socket. Blood covered my hands like a delicious glaze. The white of the eye pressed into the surrounding walls of bone as my horn ate up the space in her eye socket. Finally, once the entire horn was stuffed into her iris, she shrieked, but she didn't release me.

Something in her pocket stabbed into my stomach, and I went for it, pulling a little black tube from her slacks. I flicked my arm. It was a retractable baton. The stick felt good in my hand, as good as any sword. I swung, breaking its rock-hard surface against the woman's giant head. The crack of bone was a symphony to me. Music, ambrosia, and spice. The flavors erupted from her. I hit her again. CRACK. CRACK. CRACK.

So many bones you have.

CRACK!

NEW HANDS REACHED FORWARD to frame the woman's face between them. And Jessamae took everything, she drained everything I wanted right out from under me in seconds. The guard was dead. I fell to my side, high as a kite. Couldn't feel my feet, didn't know my fingers. "What the fuck are you doing?" I asked.

Jessamae said, "Are you joking, Francesca? Play your cruel little games all you want, but not when we are waist-deep in enemy territory. Killing is one thing. Torture is quite another. We don't have the time. Do you understand me?"

I'd lost control again. But this time, I wasn't sorry. I was over-joyed with what I did to them, their pain sang in my veins. I would do it again. I wished I could. I took my knife from the chest of the scarecrow and laid the baton beside him. His jacket was gone.

Combing my hair with my fingers until I could see, I asked her, "The keys?"

"I've got one," she said. "We need two. Look in the woman's jacket. It looks like this." She held up an Alan-wrench-looking tool with a knob on the end.

The woman with the bandaged hands had crouched down to gaze upon the bearish guard at the foot of her cell. With her eyes on me, I ferreted around in those pockets.

I found the key, as well as another key card and a Taser. I sprinted to Jessamae waiting at Ben's cell. The locks were on either side of the door, requiring two people. We stuck the keys into the slots and turned. A buzzer rang and Ben cringed as if the sound had beat him in the head.

We did it. I made it.

Ben's eyes were yellow and swollen shut. Bruises surrounded each chunk of missing skin across the span of his body. He was a gradient of ever-darkening colors. "Why?" Why remove his tattoos, piece by piece? Skin was skin no matter where you cut it. It was awful because I knew him, because his tattoos represented so much of him. Ben loved them all. I did, too.

"Help me," I told Jessamae. "We have to get him down."

Ben's stomach was level with my head and there was no bed in sight, nothing to stand on. Jessamae was taller than me but not tall enough. We needed Patrick. "Fuck! Ben, can you create a ward beneath you?"

It took him a long time to respond. *No …*

"Shit, shit, shit!"

I was terrified to touch him. Wherever I lay my hand would rub against his insides. I cinched my hands around his ribs, and I nearly collapsed at the rush of torment. His injuries were sweet and salty. Savory and tart. Stolen, bitter candy. Honey drizzled on spiced meat. Delicacies I'd never known. The purple pear that decimated my life could never compare to his taste. Because the pieces that they'd stolen were more than his body, they were a part of who he was, and he was broken over their loss, over seeing me see him like this. He was crushed. I was devastated, and it destroyed him.

Keep it together … Princess.

I cried harder. I'd forgotten how to laugh. We didn't have time to regrow everything, but I could take his pain and begin the process. I wouldn't stop touching him until we were safe.

His cuffs were leather. They could be cut. I carefully leaned into Ben's swaying body, ensuring my skin never left his, and I sliced myself inside my bicep. The blood hardly spilled, my affinity operating in overdrive. A sudden breeze brushed my cheek, supportive and playful, and I rose.

"Thank you," I whispered to the air. I'd never thanked an element out loud before. I took hold of one of Ben's forearms and slid the blade under the leather between his hands. The cuffs were thick, and the knife wouldn't break through. I sawed, flakes of animal skin raining on us both. It was slow work and I whimpered in frustration.

It'll work. Ben continued to speak inside my head rather than aloud.

"I'll slow his fall," Jessamae said. She moved beneath me and scooped up Ben's shins, holding his legs in her arms like she misplaced the top half of her bride. The angle of his legs twisted his hands in the cuffs, and I nicked him.

"Sorry! Sorry!" I said, but he didn't flinch. He couldn't feel his hands anymore.

The leather snapped with a soft *fft* and his weight plummeted into Jessamae. I closed my fist around his arm and grabbed his elbow in my other hand. He grunted at my squishing his many injuries. There were so many bruises, so many open sores.

"Sorry!" I slowly gravitated to the floor, Ben stretched between Jessamae and me. He was tall and we had to keep his bare ass from scraping the floor. "Just a little more, please, please, please," I begged the air, and our burden lightened, if just barely.

Ben's injuries continued to fill me up, and I was losing myself in their intensity. I was drunk on them. High. Paired with my terrified adrenaline, I was overdosing on uppers and downers. I hadn't blinked in a very long time, and my skin crawled with the itching sensation of a million ants.

We carried Ben through the doorway and shuffled down the hall. The prisoners with the capacity to stand ambled to their respective doorways. "Hey. Hey! Let us out! You can't just take one!" The speaker was the praying man. He looked in good health and that helped me ignore him. I couldn't risk freeing them. We didn't have the time.

We continued to scuttle down the macabre hallway like a three-headed turtle, my eyes on the top of Ben's head. He had several lacerations in his scalp. What had they done to his head?

The woman with wrapped hands beat her clubs against the glass. "Hey! DON'T LEAVE US HERE!"

"I'm sorry! I'm sorry, I … Fuck!" I couldn't add their lives to my weighed-down conscience, which was so low to the ground, it was practically plowing fields at this point. "Set him down. Gently!" Jessamae lowered his legs to the ground. Some of the smaller lesions on his limbs had closed, and I couldn't see inside his scalp anymore. "Open the doors. Hurry!" I screamed at her, throwing my key in her general direction. Jessamae sprinted from door to door but needed time to levitate the second key into the opposite lock, as that side of her affinity was only just developing.

Ben shivered on the ground. Buzzers filled the air and Ben flinched at each one.

"It's okay, we're okay, we're okay." I crawled to the dead bear guard and stripped her of her jacket and pants, happy to take the ounce of dignity she had left. I shoved Ben's arms and legs in the right holes, hurting him in my urgency. Newly freed witches sprinted around us, but they didn't give us their attention. I returned the favor.

Once I had him dressed, I grabbed his jaw and tilted his drooping head up. "You're okay. Just … No. They … no." But they had. Ben's eyes were superglued shut. With my touch, the swelling around his face had gone down enough to see it.

"Open!" Jessamae was shouting into the rooms in which the occupants hadn't fled, or they couldn't see.

I'm okay, Ben said inside my mind. I prodded his face, stretching the delicate skin around his eyes. It felt like dying, seeing him like this. It felt like I was dying.

IM OK was still tattooed on his neck, and I thought they'd done it on purpose, his torturers, to impose the worst sort of irony onto their slab of beef.

I cradled his face, as carefully as I was able, and I kissed him. I kissed him to save him. To save myself. Because there was no choice. It was a compulsion, a need. I needed to know he was okay, that he was still Ben. And as I was dying, I wanted this. I wanted his lips on mine before my heart finally gave out.

He moaned, and I knew I was hurting him. I tasted blood on his teeth. I inched away, but he took my head in his hands, pulling me closer. His fingers were icicles on my cheeks, and I covered them with my own as he crushed my mouth to his, as he pulled me onto his black and blue chest. He kissed me like he wanted to eat me. His lips shook against mine at the sting. It only hurt a little knowing he craved my magic more than anything else. Because he was alive.

He pushed me away, and I looked for something I needed in his eyes. But of course, he couldn't open them. I started to cry all over again. He started to cry, too, streaks of water slipping past the glued corners.

Move.

"What?"

We have to. Move. In a cell … Now.

"We have to—Jessamae! Help me!" She'd only opened half the cells but rushed toward the two of us and gathered Ben's legs into her arms. "That cell, let's get him inside." We half carried half dragged Ben over the threshold, the wind having long abandoned us.

The moment Jessamae closed the door behind us, another shrill buzz echoed through the prison, followed by the latch of a door. Someone else had entered this horrible hall.

Ben lifted a finger, which was finally regaining human color, and held it to his lips. With his bruised, crusty eyes and missing skin, I knew the image of him like that, his finger at his swollen mouth, would haunt my dreams for the rest of my life.

Shhhh.

"What the fuck is going on in here?" Came one voice.

"Get back in there! Now!" Came another. Pounding footsteps. Three more guards barreled past the door. The remaining freed prisoners were cornered, and I'd guess the ones who made it past the door didn't get far. We'd condemned them even further. We condemned them to death. I couldn't win. I couldn't take it anymore.

I fortified myself, turning my back to Ben. I would keep them away from him. I would slow them down.

But before I could stand, the imprisoned witches that Jessamae managed to free were on the guards like flying monkeys. Clawing their eyes, biting their fingers, ripping hair from their scalps. The prison sounded like a zoo. And right on cue, the door buzzed again. A new wave of enemies entered the chamber.

Jessamae, tired of sitting on the sidelines, opened the door to our cell and entered the fray. I'd never seen her on the offensive against magicless humans. It didn't seem fair. She raised her hands, stalking each of them silently, and needed only seconds, pouncing on them from behind like a wildcat. She twirled between them like a ballerina, sweeping their legs from under them, caressing their necks like a lover. In less than a minute she'd killed three men. I revered her, envied her. They dropped like puppets at her feet, free of their strings. She didn't give them a second glance, she merely stepped over one and moved on to the next. Her eyes were glacial ice; her hair fell across her pink cheeks like fresh snow. She was magnificent.

But the suits caught on eventually, and as Jessamae lifted her hands, one of the guards whirled to her back and stuck a Taser to her neck. She collapsed in the same fashion as her victims, her body seizing on the floor.

I wanted to help her, but I couldn't stand. I was overdosing on agony. Remembering I had hands, that I had a knife, I pulled it from my pocket and flicked it open in front of me. I would go down fighting.

The prisoner who had a bag on his head was crawling across the ceiling like a cockroach. Then he dropped down onto one of the guards and bashed him in the head with a discarded baton. Brains went everywhere, and a guard ran into our cell to escape them. It was the guard with pink hair, the one I'd seen fucking a witch in his bathroom. Seeing us on the floor was a pleasant surprise for her. She beamed at her luck, at being the one to finish me off when even a dragon couldn't do it.

Unfurling myself over Ben, the knife in my hand, I hoped to spare him even a single minute of continued pain. The guard walked forward, arcing the baton over her head with obscene glee.

Then she skidded back on the heels of her loafers, as if a powerful wind had pushed her away. She whirled around in alarm before charging at us again. This time the shield pushed her all the way back, into the glass wall of the cell. It didn't stop. It kept pushing until we saw her skin flatten, saw her cheek press up into her eye.

I watched, dumfounded, and spread across Ben's chest. His hands lifted on either side of me. Looking back, I saw a version of Ben I didn't know could exist. His face was twisted with loathing. He was sick with it. His jaw trembled under his gnashing teeth. He groaned as he pressed his shield into the woman, seeing her through my eyes.

The guard's skin began to rupture, her organs began to split. She mewled until her lungs popped. Her bones were crushed to shards. The shield kept moving until she was nothing but a rubbery smear on its surface. Nothing but a fly on a windshield. She collapsed and became a spill of a person on the floor. She'd wash down the drain.

Ben's arms flopped to the side, and his head fell away from me. He used every bit of energy I'd given him to save us.

I jammed myself in under one of his arms. My skin tingled wherever he touched me. I was a high-voltage live wire. "Benny."

He lifted his head a few inches from the ground as if he were looking at me.

"Hey, Frank," his words were garbled and slow, but he said them. It was the first time I'd heard his voice out loud since I left.

I reached for his lips. "What's wrong with your mouth?"

He shook me off. "Not now."

"Not now," Jessamae repeated from the cell door. Her foot held the door open, her knife in hand. It was frothy with fresh blood.

Jessamae assessed the pink-haired guard's liquefied body with wide eyes. This might have been the first time she saw Ben as an adversary.

263

Together, Ben and I lurched forward until Jessamae clumsily shifted Ben's other arm over her shoulder. There were two dead witches and seven dead guards. Every cell was open, their escapees loose upon the world—even the mute man with murder in his eyes. We shambled out the set of double doors, and back into the non-magical ward.

"Get me outta' here!" one man screamed at Jessamae, grasping at her skin. Thank his lucky stars he wasn't quite close enough to touch her. The tase she'd suffered surrounded her in a static-filled cloud. She was like a conduit. I felt her charge through Ben's skin. Lightning struck within her irises. If she chose to unleash her affinity now ...

"The way is clear," she said, electric eyes shifting from wall to wall.

"Five. There are five waiting. The second floor." Ben's speech had improved, but he was dead on his feet. We could carry him the rest of the way, but his limp form wasn't the problem. I couldn't make us invisible. I stupidly wondered if one of the imprisoned witches had such an ability—a few of the cells appeared empty in there.

He needed his eyesight. I said, "We need to open Ben's eyes," as his head hung on his shoulders. But I wasn't sure if he wanted his sight back if it meant we had to cut through his eyelids.

"I'll do it," Jessamae said, and both our heads twitched to her.

"Why?" I asked.

"Look at your hands."

I did. They were shaking so violently, I was surprised I hadn't lost my fingernails. "Fine. But be ... please, be careful."

She nodded again and wiped the blade on her vest. There was still blood in its hinges. She stood high on her toes and turned the point toward Ben's face. "I doubt I need to tell you to hold still, Benjamin, but—"

"Got it," he grumbled.

She pulled his eyelid away from his face, stretching it out an inch, and slid the tip between his lashes, in the pocket his tears had escaped through. "Careful," I whispered again.

"Shhh. It's okay," Ben said.

I held his hand and clamped my lips shut. Jessamae slid the knife through the glue, snipping his eyelashes in the process. After a horribly tense thirty seconds, the eye opened. It was clumpy and red, but it survived the blade.

"Don't say anything this time, Frank. You're going to scare her, and she's going to cut me."

I curled my lip. "Okay, okay, just hurry!"

She slit the other eye open, and though time was of the essence, her speed terrified me. But then Ben could see. And I was so grateful to her, I could fall to my knees.

There were guards waiting for us on the next floor, and Jessamae couldn't apport us all without a big payment. "Apport Ben," I told Jessamae. "Get him out of here." I leaned him onto her hard body. Neither of them was happy about it but I didn't much care. They could suffer through a couple of hugs if we all survived Samhain.

"You won't make it alone," Jessamae said.

"We won't make it *together.* I'll get out, I'll get through."

Her face squished in tight as she assessed Ben's condition. He could barely walk, and his muscles had only just started to regrow their dermis. "A cut won't get me far. Maybe outside the building."

"That'll work. Just get him out. Away from the guards. I'll find the others and meet you out front. Ben will know when."

I pulled away but Ben smashed my bicep in his fist, his sudden strength frightening. "The vents," he mumbled. "Remember?" He turned me around as if my arm were a handle and faced me toward the wall.

A vent, just like the one above my apartment toilet, was screwed into the wall above the row of human cages.

"Help me up," I said to Jessamae.

Prisoners' arms and wrists and fingers stuck through the bars of every cage like spiny branches, like the dead inhabitants of the river Styx. I feared them. They were desperate, and we'd all proven what people were capable of when desperate.

Jessamae went to a cage with a single drunk resident—a woman with no pants, her snoring the only signal she lived. Jessamae interlocked her fingers and bent her legs beside the cage. I stepped into those hands, and she heaved me up to the top of the drunkard's cell.

The slats between the bars were big enough to lose my legs to, so I walked on the balls of my feet, tiptoeing over the damned. Some of them could reach me, and their fingers broke through like worms from soil. One man was tall enough to get his wrists through and grab at the laces of my boots. I stomped on those fingers until his arm slithered back through the bars.

I reached the wall and looked back. Jessamae was under Ben's arm again, and he was watching me with a scowl.

He huffed, "Stay safe, Frank. I'm not asking."

"Fine! Just apport!" I slid the blade of my knife into the screw head, glancing over my shoulder. They were both still there and staring at me. "Can I help you?" I called.

"You honestly think we're leaving before I see you crawl through that grate?" he asked.

My hands shook and the blade bounced in and out of the groove. The prisoners beneath me hooted and hollered. "You are making me nervous! Just go! I'll meet you in the alley across the street."

Ben's vermillion lids were freeze rays—I couldn't move with them zeroed on me. Eventually, Jessamae clicked her teeth and hooked her arms around Ben's waist. He didn't shove her off or embrace her in return, he simply faced me as though he could see every emotion I worked to smother.

Hurry.

They were gone.

23

I BEGGED my hands to calm, to steady, as I spun the screws from the wall. The sharks below me called me a cunt and scratched at the soles of my shoes. These people weren't a threat to Laisren, they weren't valuable in expensive elixirs. I didn't care for them.

One screw fell to the floor with a tiny bell's *tink*.

Every screw eventually came loose though I had no idea how much time had passed. Hours it seemed. I should have cut off the fingers wiggling at my feet. I bet they'd fetch a good amount of magic.

I flung the grate to the side and took the cape from my shoulders, draping it over the hard metal edge. I lifted myself into the tube, my muscles still zinging from Ben's wounds, and slithered through the steel sausage casing like ground pig guts. Up. I needed to go up.

Several offshoots and turns led nowhere but maintenance rooms, storage closets, and at one point, what appeared to be an interrogation room. I only surmised as much because of the stream of information pouring from the man's mouth. He was tied to a chair, but he didn't struggle. He laughed. Crazed, high, squeals like a hyena's chortle. And as his legible words tapered into nothing but cotton candy-colored spit bubbles. One of the men standing before him shoved a handful of berries into the man's gaping maw. Their innards smeared his cheeks and entered his nose. He was choking, but still he sought them out with a fervent, worming tongue. "Tomorrow," he sputtered, "we're meeting tomorrow at the corner of ..."

I passed as noiselessly as possible.

It was hot, so hot my hands began to slide along the metal sheet beneath me. Did Laisren know I was in here? How hot could it get before I cooked?

My knees were red and raw. My hands were burned by my own boiling sweat by the time I found a ledge to climb.

Grunting, cursing, I jumped up and splayed my elbows over the ledge above. Heaving my own weight up and onto the next floor would have been the hardest thing I'd ever attempted if I wasn't so high on Ben's injuries. But his pain wouldn't last long. My frenzy was fading. I needed to eat more pain if I was going to get through this.

With a *skeeeeee*, I scraped my body forward, inching like an earthworm until my knees were up and over the edge.

I took the first turn I came across, tired of my metal hamster cage, and the casino sprawled beneath me. It was still inside this horrible building, but this was a better exit than much else. I stalled, searching for any wayward guards, before I realized I was on the wrong side of the grate, and I couldn't remove these screws with my knife.

Ramming my back to one side, I rounded my legs up the vent wall, fumbling like a bloated spider over Vaseline and growling in discomfort. My sweat coated everything like oil, and eventually, I rested on my ass instead of my knees. I braced my feet against the back of the grate. Thinking of Ben, his ink-free skin, his glued eyelids, I hitched up my knees and brought them down with everything I had. I didn't want the elements to help me. I would get out myself.

The bang of my soles on the metal was loud enough to hear over the almost-din of the casino. I kicked again, vying for speed over stealth. Again. The screws were pulling from the wall. Again. One corner came free. Once more. The grate blasted from the wall, and half my body disappeared.

My bottom half was hanging out the vent. My tailbone grated along the edge of the wall, my elbows holding me up. Barely. If I lost my hold, my arms would bend at the wrong angle and snap. I crab-walked forward, my legs dangling down into the casino.

My arms were vibrating, my shoulders about to break through my skin, when my fingers finally curled over the edge of the vent's entrance. With my last bit of strength, I pushed off the beds of my palms and catapulted myself into the open air.

I landed roughly on one ankle, the pokey bone of which rocketed into the business-casual navy carpet. I threw my arms out to regain my balance, the switchblade still clutched in my fist. When I managed to lift my eyes from the floor, the room having steadied itself, every pair of eyes in the room gaped at me, immobile as pinned beetles.

A gratifying pop sounded from my ankle, and I arched my stiff back before hurtling for the glass doors across the desert of slot machines.

It was too quiet. I heard the difference between carpet and sidewalk under my feet. Outside, I found nothing. No guns, no cuffs, no choppers. Tourists continued to mosey, a few stared, but very few. I was one more oddity in a coliseum of oddities.

Frank.

Ben and Jessamae were close, but I couldn't see them. The street was packed tighter than a sardine can, overflowing with cars. I stepped into the road—

EEEEEEEEEEKKKKKKKK!

A nondescript silver sedan rounded the corner, forced itself into traffic, and braked hard enough to lift the back tires from the road. It honked and honked, but of course, the cars would not— could not—budge. The noise stalled for all of three seconds before the car veered sharply to the left and up onto the sidewalk across the street from me. It was wide enough to fit a vehicle, easily, but it couldn't fit a car and the hundreds of costumed flesh bags at once.

Anderson punched the horn, scattering maids and demons

and Super Marios, before barreling forward. I ran into the street, weaving between bumpers and waving my hands in the air.

"Anderson! Anderson, stop!"

Then a glossy black SUV hopped onto the sidewalk after him. Then a second. Then a third.

MONSTERS AND ANGELS flooded the street, crying for safety, screaming, "Fuck you!"

I smashed myself through their mass like a spoon through the meat of a premature cantaloupe. "Anderson!" But he didn't hear me. Between the snarl of the wolf engines in pursuit and the shouts of the tourists, I could hardly hear Ben inside my head.

THE ALLEY THE ALLEY THE ALLEY THE ALLEY!

The ghosts of Jessamae's eyes gleamed through the dark of the alley across the street. I saw her gesturing, summoning me to her side, but she didn't need to. I had nowhere else to go.

A large feather-clad shoulder shoved me into a car. I lost my footing and went down. Folded over a taxi's hood, a stampede of people flooded past. I couldn't straighten, I couldn't move. The car beneath me began to reverse, inch by inch, whatever it could, until I fell to my face in the street. They were trampling me. I sucked in ragged, gravel-packed clouds of air under their feet.

A perfect hand wrapped around my elbow and hoisted me to my knees. It yanked at my arm again and again until I was standing. The river of people had given us a merciful bubble of breathing room, now that Cleo was at my side. They circled around her as if she held a ticking bomb. I could see again.

Anderson's sedan continued down the sidewalk like a salon-bound old woman at fifteen miles an hour, its front passenger door hanging open in a tease. Anderson shouted out his own window, demanding the remaining bystanders to get the hell out of the way.

Cleo moved behind me and shoved me forward. We were running now, trying to catch the friendly car, but they were flying compared to my slow, non-mechanical legs. We'd never reach them, and they couldn't stop.

Ben hobbled into view, into Anderson's direct path from a nearby access road, Jessamae hot on his heels. The sedan stopped on a dime, its grill hitting Ben's shins and forcing his hands down to its hood. Jessamae moved behind Anderson's car, standing between it and the snarling rectangles of metal gaining speed. Her hands glowed, faintly at first, and then like white coals buried beneath fire. I hadn't seen such an act from her since Gabriel had returned. She was evoking fire.

Blood dribbled down her arms and burned up in her hands. She was tragic and stunning.

The first driver in the line of black SUVs slowed and stopped at the sight of her behind our car. But the driver barreling behind the first did not stop, it sped up, veering around the first SUV and scraping its doors against the cars in the road.

Jessamae's hands burned hotter, and the sparks from the SUV's doors and tires turned to shooting wads of flame that soared into the cars behind it. Bystanders screamed and evacuated the streets with renewed urgency. But even amidst the drizzling firestorm, the car didn't stop. It was going to run Jessamae down.

In haste to utilize her distraction, I sprinted faster than I ever had, keeping up with Cleo for the first time in my life and actually outgunning her in the last stretch.

The SUV picked up speed. Jessamae would explode on impact if she didn't move. But she stood her ground, just as she always had. The damage would be extreme, and I wouldn't be able to save her. With a curse and a groan, I flipped away from the open car door awaiting me, bolting for the vampire.

But after mere steps in her direction, Patrick overtook me. His enormous hairy legs shredded his jeans, and the denim slapped against the pavement. His hands were mutating before my eyes, growing extra bones and hair and claws. His torso and head remained human, and he was altogether more frightening than when he transitioned fully into a beast. He was disturbing, like a doll whose limbs had been torn off and replaced with those of a stuffed animal.

"You owe me a window!" he bellowed at Jessamae as he charged the SUV. With the arms of the beast, he ripped the metal collar from his neck as easily as a candy necklace. Flicking an elbow at Jessamae, she sailed across the sidewalk, landing on her side with a gasp of pain. My attention zigzagged between her and Patrick, whose arm was cocked back as if winding up for the punch of a lifetime. From the ground, Jessamae glared at the creature that was Patrick. She bared her teeth as she got to her feet, and I hurried to intervene.

"They'll be fine! The car, get in the car! Now!" Ben pulled me from the oncoming carnage. His speech was clear, if slightly strained. I allowed his escort until I heard the undeniable screech of twisted steel. Ben's hold tightened as he continued to steer me to the backseat of Anderson's car, but I spun my head around to the angry metallic scream.

Patrick did nothing but lean in, he leaned his shoulder into the engine of our enemies and effectively stopped the car in its tracks, crushing the front end in the process. Though one of the three SUVs had stopped, and one was now … ineffective, a third vehicle was coming in hot. Patrick gripped the jagged grill of the car at his side and began to push it backward, without a truck or dinosaur or special effects team to help him.

"Get in the fucking car!" Jack yelled.

Jack?

He jumped out of Anderson's car, his hands extended in front of him. His eyes never met mine—they were on Patrick. Jack was keeping him from shifting completely. I wondered if it was painful, caught between two absolutes like that.

Jessamae stormed Patrick's side, fury lighting her face. She clutched one of his hairy arms in her glowing hot hand.

"Fucking hell! Get off me!" he yelled, shaking her around like a tick. And I saw nothing more.

Ben shoved my head under the roof of the car without apology.

"Wait, wait! We can't leave without them! I promised Patrick!" Sort of.

"He won't let us leave without him. Buckle your seatbelt."

I ignored his suggestion and kneeled on the fuzzy upholstery. Cleo was already in the passenger seat. Ben slid into the backseat after me and I grabbed his chin before he thought to stop me. His lips puckered and he resisted my scrutiny, but I wouldn't let him go. I was stronger than him right now. Holding his head in one hand, I pried his mouth open with the other.

"What … is … what did they do?" I already knew.

He had two tongues, or almost two tongues. I stretched out his cheeks until I could see inside. They'd cut his tongue down the middle, forking it crudely. It was sticky and purple along the seam, and his jaw trembled at the pain I was undeniably inflicting on him. I let go.

"It'll heal okay. I know it will." He tried to smile.

Anderson pressed the gas harder. The roadway was clearing.

"Why?" I asked.

"Why do I know or why did they do it?"

I took a deep breath, trying to remain calm until he continued.

"They said if I act like a snake, and play like a snake, that I should look like one, too." He trailed a finger over one of the new spots of skin on his arm. After all he'd been through, pale, pink, red, and brown patches coated him, and yes, they almost resembled the pattern of snakeskin. I was going to barf. I wanted to murder that bear woman all over again.

"Your eyes?" I asked.

"They thought that's how I saw my visions."

My breathing hitched. I wanted to cover my own eyes, to

pretend this wasn't what he looked like now. This was all my fault.

"Sit down! I'm backing up!" Anderson yelled before doing just that. I was hurled forward into the center console. "You should listen every now and then."

Ben grabbed me by the shoulders and forced me back to the seat just before Anderson slammed on the brakes. I heard shouting outside. Cleo spun around in the passenger seat. "We have *two* arrogant beasts on our hands," she sniped, staring out the back window.

Jessamae launched into our car like a meteor, spitting obscenities in multiple languages. Jack followed closely behind, compressing all of us together, our legs stacking like Lincoln Logs. We were adjusting to such discomfort when Patrick Superman'ed his enormous body through the door on the other side, rolling over all our knees, his legs curled up against the window. His weight was a familiar suffering, I was again crushed beneath a mountain.

"Goddammit!" Ben wheezed, his body still healing under the mass of the beast.

Jessamae continued to curse up a frenzy and Cleo had nothing to say, though she certainly understood.

"Get us the hell out of here, Andy!" Patrick yelled.

"About time," Anderson said as we rocketed forward over the now-empty sidewalk.

"What happened? Where's the third car? The guards?" I asked.

"Who cares? We have a car, and they don't!" Patrick was writhing around on our laps, trying to adjust. He looked like a slug in a straw. His arms and legs were losing their hair, his nails thinning to human proportions.

"There's more. And they're gaining on us," Ben said with a blank face.

"My truck was compromised," Jack said, wiggling around for more room. "But I can still get us out of here. Take a left ahead, through the loading zone."

"I won't fit!" Anderson returned.

"Yes, you will," Jack and Ben said at the same time.

Patrick looked up at the pair. "Creepy."

"Here," Anderson said, lifting Betty's pouch between the two front seats. "She's a little stressed but fit as a fiddle."

"Thank you," I said and hugged her to my chest. She poked her head through the zipper and kissed my cheek. "Hi."

Then we spun into the alley, and I almost bonked her into the window.

"Be careful!" Anderson pointed at me angrily in the rearview mirror and kept driving. Trash bins rolled over the top of us and fornicating couples jumped for cover as we squeezed through the narrow passageway. Another black SUV turned in after us.

Jack leaned over Anderson's headrest. "It's going to open up at the end of this alley. Now I don't know you, but I hope you have the brains to understand this."

"Be nice," Patrick interjected.

Jack continued, "Stay to the right until I tell you. Then veer to the left as hard as you can. Can you do that?"

"I can do that."

"Prove it," he said, his eyes on the road. "Right ... Right ... Almost ..."

The loading zone opened enough to fit two cars. We were almost to the street, and we'd have to turn left or right.

"Stay to the right. The Suburban is almost on us," Jack said.

I heard the rev of its engine. I heard the tires squeal only a foot from our bumper. They were going to nose us off the road.

"Left! Get to the left!" he shouted.

Anderson wrenched the wheel.

"Farther left!" Ben screamed. Anderson whipped the wheel all the way around and we fishtailed to the side, skidding into traffic, and narrowly avoiding an old-fashioned white limo.

An explosion blew out our windows and glass fell like rain. I couldn't hear anything. The heat of it burned my neck. Turning around, I saw the SUV wasn't so lucky. It sat on its side, fire dancing on its corpse.

"I had a couple traps to spare," Jack said, wiping a bucket of sweat from his brow.

"A couple?" I asked. He only shrugged.

⁂

ONCE WE WERE FAR ENOUGH from our pursuers and the sound of sirens filled the air, I asked, "Where are we going?"

We all looked to Anderson, whose eyes spun around as if lubed. "How should I know, I'm from Maryland!"

Cleo put her painted fingers to her temples. "We have to leave the city limits, immediately."

"Can we make it back to Utah?"

"I might die first," Ben said. I wasn't sure if he was serious or joking and I puked a little in my mouth.

"Jack?" Jessamae asked, out of breath from her explicit tirade.

He put his head in his hands, or tried to, one arm was trapped behind my back. "No way, blondie."

"We have nowhere else to go." Jessamae's viper-like focus targeted him, and it was a relief to be free of it for once. "We don't need to go to your workshop or your home. We can rest in Pioche. Find another vehicle."

He made a gargle/snore/retching sound in his throat for half a minute before finally agreeing it was our only option. "Go to the hardware store," he barked before giving Anderson basic directions. "But you can't stay long. In and out. One hour."

"More. We need to eat and sleep," Jessamae held her eyes on him like the beam of a lighthouse. "Jack?"

He didn't answer, he only crossed his arms tight enough to hold water with a simmering glower on his sunburned mug. Jessamae smiled at his apparent fold.

We slipped out of town like a thief in the night. Almost every pair of headlights on the highway faced the city, and only a few lonely vehicles joined us in the other direction. Patrick was entirely human now, but he was still the largest in the car and he smashed everyone stuffed into the backseat with him. He was shaking and sweaty, the salty juices seeping through what remained of his clothes and soaking our legs.

I fought the impulse to stare at Ben. Not only had a few days without him felt like a thousand lifetimes, not only had I last seen him broken on his knees after sleeping with the most beautiful woman in the world ... it felt inconsiderate to stare. To gawk at all his new, transformative wounds. So I pet Betty's silky head, and her hissing was better than any cat's purr.

Cats. Amir. I didn't want to ask Cleo about him. She had to be worried. Even I was worried. A little.

The car was silent throughout our journey, apart from Patrick's bitching as he repositioned again and again. For hours, we all seemed to simply remember what we'd each individually experienced over the last few hours, over the last week. For most of them—and these were the people I was closest with in my whole life—I had no idea what those stories were.

Jessamae watched the nothing-like darkness out the window. Ben picked at the glue over his eyes with his strange new hands. And Cleo didn't look back at us at all.

Anderson pulled into Pioche around six in the morning. The sun was just cresting over the jagged hillside and across the monochrome landscape. It turned the sky into a watercolor of such beautiful smudges I nearly cried. The palest pink, the most vibrant orange. Purple and red and yellow. I'd never felt more awake or more exhausted.

Because we needed a longer bout of recovery time, Jack opted for a different hiding place than the hardware store. And after bumping into town, the car stopped beside a dirty wooden rambler. There was no sign, though it was in the commercial part of Pioche, if you could call it that.

"Thank god!" Patrick yelled as he cannoned from the car and

onto his back in the dirt. He winced and floundered around, pushing his bones back to their rightful places. "Like fitting a stallion into a pet carrier!"

"Be quiet," Jessamae said, grouchy as can be as she stepped from the backseat.

"Might I ask what I did to anger you so? Did I break *your window* or something?"

Jessamae sucked on her teeth. "I had the vehicles under control."

"No, you didn't. But I respect your senseless courage." He applauded, clouds of brown dust puffing from his hands. "Nothing stops a car like a tiny woman … standing. Tell you what, how about we call this incredibly uneven situation, even?" He offered a hand straight up in the air.

Jessamae raised her brows, dimpling her long pale scar. "For now," she said, without taking him up on his offered shake.

"Door's open!" Jack called from the doorway of the nondescript structure, and we all filed inside.

It looked like a diner, if the diner had been abandoned and was haunted by the ghosts of miserable prospectors. There were no shiny leather booths or the enticing aroma of high-octane coffee, there was only a series of small tables, all seating four, and all made of wood shaped in ways that reminded me of a wagon wheel. There was a small bar, laminate and cleaner than anything else I'd seen in this town—which is to say, not clean, but it was perceptible through the dust. Behind that, I spotted a sink, a microwave, and a tower of chipped ivory mugs.

Jack walked past the bar via a square section that lifted on hinges and disappeared into a backroom.

"Feels like home," Patrick said as he took a seat, propping his feet onto the chair beside it. Anderson heaved a bloated sigh and sat across from the werewolf. He appeared unhappy, glaring at Ben and me. Then he crossed his arms on the table and rested his face on the wrinkled elbows of his suit.

Jack reappeared carrying a bulky steel contraption. He

stationed it on the counter and plugged it in. He pulled a glass pot from beneath the bar and sat it in the belly of the machine. Coffee.

I draped Betty on the table and moved to Jack's side as he scrounged up a filter. "Can I help?" I wasn't ready to sit down again after such a quiet ride. Eventually, someone would want to talk about things.

He appraised me and pinched his mouth. "Don't keep much perishables in here. But there's some canned crap in the back."

I dipped my chin and did as he said. The backroom served as a kitchen if this place had ever been fit to open. There were two faded ivory refrigerators sitting side-by-side like malnourished Siamese twins. A long dining table lined one wall, its surface covered in nicks that had filled with greasy dead bugs and debris. A standing sink cowered beside it, cobwebs connecting its faucets. Such a waste. So much of the town seemed to be decoys for Jack and nothing more. It was a lot of empty space for one angry man.

A door faced me, and not having seen any food, I went through it. It was inky black inside the closet, but after the morning light had time to trudge through the kitchen and creep up behind me, I saw it was a pantry. There was no rhyme or reason to the food stock, such levels of disorganization almost seemed intentional. Cans of soup, jars of juices and fruits, and pickled vegetables all existed around hundreds of ketchup bottles that stood tall around the colony like watchful trees. "Jesus." So much ketchup I'd never seen outside a grocery store.

I stepped up to the lines of shelves and picked up a jar. It was dark and viscous inside the glass. I gripped the ring and gave it a good turn, managing to force it free and showering rusty flakes to the floor.

I probed the stuff inside and held my fingers to the light. Seeds. It was jam. Berries. I brought the delicacy to my lips and sucked my skin clean. It was magnificent, the sugar so sharp on my tongue it was almost sour. I crammed all my fingers through the mouth of the jar and scooped out a ball of preserves.

The door shut behind me and I was plunged into darkness, my fingers suctioned between my lips. A glob of jelly fell to my chin as the *tink* of a lightbulb clicked on. I spun around.

Ben stood before me, the snipped string of the overhead light in his fist.

And we were alone for the first time since the last time.

24

"FRANK," he said, clutching that string like it held the sun itself in place. "I think we should talk. Don't you?"

When he pronounced his vowels, his mouth opened enough to see his serpent's tongue. The wound had closed, all his open wounds had, during the car ride. We'd been touching the whole way. But his tongue would always be split, just like I'd never regrow my toe.

I didn't want to talk to him. I wasn't ready to free-fall into that inconsolable pit again, both literal and figurative. Without him, I'd been eaten, flattened, set on fire, and possessed. But this was a different kind of pain. A pain that made me not want to be a person anymore, but instead, a canary or a frog. Something that couldn't process such depths of self-hatred and jealousy and loss. Even now, before we'd started talking, the edges of my heart seemed to shrivel in on themselves like burning paper.

I tried to formulate a reason to skirt past him and ignore him for one more day. Put this off for just one week. But where did I have to go, what did I have to do right now other than continue breathing? How could I tell him my only prior engagement was being terribly afraid of the things he might say?

"Yeah. I do."

He released the string and rubbed his head. He'd been nearly bald when we found him, and he remained so now. His hair hadn't grown, because all my magic had been needed elsewhere.

At least I couldn't see his pulsing muscles anymore. "Thank you. For the rescue."

"Same to you."

He gave me a dejected smile. "I didn't save you. If anything, I put you at risk making you think you needed to save *me*."

"*Think* I needed to?" I gestured to all his disturbing new scars. He sucked his lips into his mouth, and I knew he wanted a cigarette. Smoking calmed his nerves when he felt like yelling.

It might have been true that going after him put my life at risk, but if I hadn't left the Bellagio, I would have never been kidnapped. If I hadn't heard Ben in my head, I might have stayed at The Alcazar for the rest of my lonely life. I preferred this pantry with him, as much as I despised us both. "So ... you can talk to me now. In my head."

He nodded. "I tried with Patrick. But couldn't quite break through that steel-plated gorilla skull of his. But with you ... it was like walking through a door. Like I was lost in the fog of my mind, and your mind was an emergency exit. And each time I went looking, I found the door faster." He leaned back against the pantry door and put his hands in the stolen pockets he wore. "At first, I watched. Then I spoke. I couldn't help myself. I didn't know if you could hear me ... until you waved that night. In your bed."

I reenacted the wave, smearing jam between my fingers. The seeds felt too hard.

"But then my interrogation changed from asking to carving ... and I thought it best if you never found me."

I could almost see it; the horrible picture of Ben's torture was so clear behind my eyes. But where I could *imagine* his week, Ben could *remember* mine. He'd been watching all along, just as I feared. "You saw everything?" He saw the things I'd done, the lows to which I resorted ... the security guard outside The Harvest.

Killing that man had been very different from killing the

guards of his prison. "I didn't … I'm sorry." Why did I say that? I hadn't killed *Ben*.

Ben slid down until he formed a human chair against the door, his legs bent at ninety-degree angles. He watched me smear jam between my hands. "I saw you taken. I couldn't see where. I only had one option. I described your kidnappers to Jessamae, and she gave us the info—"

"Why aren't you talking about it?"

He licked his mouth, the points of his tongues poking two different spots on his lips. "About what, Princess?"

"Don't," I said. "Don't do that."

"I'm not going to stone you, Frank, if that's what you're looking for." He righted himself and grabbed one of the shelves beside him. "You … acted as you had to act given the circumstances—"

"Stop it." I refused to be let off the hook. Refused his attempt to turn this into some little personality quirk that he could forgive, like my manners or my drinking. "I stabbed him. I stabbed him even when I didn't need to. Over and over—"

"And what would he have done if you didn't? I saw the knife, Frank! Not to mention you were drunk, drugged, spiraling. If you hadn't found out about Cleo that morning—"

"Please!" I wailed. Hearing my own voice echo off all the glass and tin around me made me quiet. "Do not say it was somehow your fault."

He didn't. He didn't say anything at all. The light bounced off his brown eyes and I couldn't see any motion in them, any dancing. I wanted to touch him so badly. I wanted to throw up. I whispered, "I crossed the line … I jumped off the cliff. Because I didn't stop myself. I'd beaten him. I knew I'd beaten him. And I didn't stop." Ben didn't look away from me, he held my gaze. It's what I deserved. "And I liked it."

Still, he said nothing. His silence made me furious.

"Am I still your fucking princess now, Benny?"

His hand clutching the shelf started to shake. I thought for a flash that he might even hit me. Because for a flash I wanted him to.

He let go of the shelf and said, "I love you."

Good for him. That stung much more than a backhand would. "Fuck you."

"I love you," he said louder, "every fucking inch of you. I'm not going to throw a parade over what happened, but I will not condemn you for it either! Your affinity is a dangerous one." I scoffed, and berry-colored slobber shot from my mouth. "But we already knew that. It was only a matter of time until it happened to someone else."

My jaw dropped. It was too heavy to pick back up again. "You mean …" I stared at the biggest of his scars, the crater between his lapels. "What I almost did to you? How I almost let you die?"

"I am not going to cry about what happened and I will not feed your guilt! As much as I know you want me to. You are new to this! You need to understand what could happen, and it did happen, and I love you, Frank."

I buckled. I was on the ground, my sticky fingers clinging to the dust beneath me.

"And you love me, too."

I looked up at him in total incredulity.

He wouldn't stop talking. "It might not be romantic love. Not anymore. I accept that. But you cared enough to come find me in that place, didn't you? You're my best friend. Despite what I did, despite what you did, we still love each other, don't we?"

"I …"

Ben kneeled before me. He didn't touch me, but he wanted to. I knew. "Don't we?"

The door flew open, and Anderson held the knob. He looked furious as he took in the two of us on the ground. Ben gradually turned his head, forced to acknowledge him but clearly wanting him to close us inside.

Anderson scowled. "Sorry. I was looking for food. We're hungry."

THE SINK finally flowed clear after a series of phantom clangs beneath the floor. The water felt a little gritty between my fingers, but that could have been the yellow seeds still clinging to the lines of my palms like sweet barnacles. Ben remained in the pantry. I didn't know if he'd ever come out.

Anderson scooped various soups and vegetables into his arms, muttering, and carried them into the dining area, walking around Ben like he was a particularly nasty spot of mold. The thought of soft noodles on my tongue was like worms squirming inside my cheeks. Positively nauseating for whatever reason. I veered for the pantry and stepped over Ben's long legs; he ate alphabet soup with his fingers.

There were so many words I needed to say to him that they formed a ball of gum in my throat. It choked me and I didn't say a thing. I took a jar of tomato juice from a low shelf, its red pulpy clouds looking like blood in vegetable oil, and poured it into a dingy coffee mug. It waltzed around the microwave, bubbling around the edges. It was something my mother used to do for me whenever I was sick or especially apathetic. A part of me recognized that maybe I needed something like that now— comfort—and this was the best I would get.

It burned my throat, but I loved the salt, as it oozed its way to my stomach. Wanting more than anything to avoid Ben, I shuffled into the dining area, where these friends I hated and loved were all spooning a medley of food into their mouths.

"How is our Benjamin?" Patrick asked, his open trap full of beef stew.

"Better," I said, wiping my tomato mustache.

Anderson huffed and I raised my brows at him. He didn't elaborate and continued to munch on mushy potatoes.

"You sure about that?" Patrick asked me.

I kicked the leg of his chair as I moved toward my own, yellow broth splashing the table. I didn't need him making me feel bad. I suspected I held enough bad, enough guilt, to last me well into retirement.

We were spread out, thin as butter, using all four tables between the six of us. Jack sat alone, a glass of clear liquid in one hand and a mug of tar-like coffee in the other. Anderson and Patrick were sitting with me, and though they were focused on their food, their earlier camaraderie had evidently continued. Even their silence seemed shared. Cleo sat alone. She held a glass of water in both hands but hadn't taken a sip since I entered the room. Jessamae sat at the table behind Cleo's, watching her back with the steady magnitude of a storm. When she caught me staring, she gave me a puny smile, then returned her attention to those beautiful, cold shoulders.

I swallowed the rest of my juice and sucked the stuff from my gums before I poured coffee over the red pulp. "You got a shower somewhere in town?"

Jack lifted the glass to his lips, paused, then set it back on the table without drinking. "There's some empty houses. Maybe half the places in town. No beds, but water and power. Help yourselves." He stood and threw his glass in the sink. "But I need you out of Pioche with the moon. This isn't over, and they're going to come for you."

"Then we need your help more than ever," I said.

Jack ignored me and turned to Jessamae. "I've done you plenty of favors, which I did of my own free will. But I can't let them take me. You know that as much as anyone." He slammed his dishes to the counter and hustled to the front door. "East side of town, you'll find some empties." The flimsy door clapped the frame behind him.

"I will be needing my own house. I miss the wide-open

spaces, my voice echoing back at me through the halls." Patrick arched his back like an inverted cat.

I said, "No. Same house, same *room*." Ben watched me from the kitchen doorway, he entered the dining room without making a sound. "I'm not about to break back into that ... place, again, after one of us gets taken." I hooked Betty's pouch over my shoulder and stalked into the dawn. It took a while before I heard feet hit the earth behind me.

I moved fast, fighting constant contradictions. I wanted to be so close to my friends that I burrowed under their clothes, skin, and bones. I also never wanted to look at them again. So, I kept my eyes ahead as I passed rickety shack after rickety shack, but counted their steps as they followed behind me. I walked until I didn't want to anymore, then I tried a door. Locked. I tried another. This door led to a video store.

I hadn't even seen one, let alone been inside of one, since I was a child. Stepping inside gave me a frightening sense of home that I hadn't felt in days and days. My mother used to take me to the local rental place in Aspen Ridge. It was a combination of video rental, CD store, bookstore, plus custom tailoring that they did in the back corner. VHS, DVD, and Beta, each dotted with neon stickers of different colors. I spent hours studying the worn paper covers. My mom took me every week. This dilapidated shack was the first place I could picture her in so long.

There were less than a hundred videos here, each faced out, and there was only one copy of each film. Most didn't even have covers, only stickers and titles in fun fonts. The whole town would have watched the same things, and debate would ensue over each film at the diner.

This place had been lifeless for decades. Maybe that's why I could picture my mother so clearly.

"We sleeping here?" Ben asked. He hadn't come in and stood with the rest of the group on the road.

"No." My inner child got its tomato juice; we didn't have time to coddle it any further.

Expecting a locked door, I fell through the entryway of the fifth house, shouldering the thing with all my strength. It smelled like old bathwater and rodent feces, but it had a lock and I flipped it the moment we were all inside.

The heat was suffocating inside, and moisture instantly beaded between my shoulder blades. The trim along the walls was intricate and formerly beautiful, the floorboards all but rotted through. The staircase railing was curled and dramatic. The kitchen and ceiling were covered in inky stains. It could have been lovely in the right hands. Now it was depressing, like a grandparent sleeping in their own piss, crusty drool flaking in the lines of their cheeks.

A window somewhere had to be broken, because the floor was covered in more dirt and sand than the Sahara. I kicked a pile of it, its shrapnel hitting the wall. "Okay."

"It's nice. Better than most motels I've patronized." Patrick fell to the dirt and promptly lifted his feet in the air. "Someone, please. My arches are howling."

Cleo kicked his feet out of the air with a dirty thigh-high boot. "How high are *your* heels?"

"Would *you* like a foot rub?" he asked.

"Are you uncomfortable?" Jessamae reached for Cleo's shoulder, but Cleo dodged her hand, acting as though she'd suddenly lost her hearing.

Anderson sank to his knees in a corner of what would have been the living room. He watched the floor as if it played movies for him. Maybe it did. Was that regret I tasted in the air? Had I ruined this man's life? I knew I had. I condemned him to die with the rest of us.

Ben searched the floor for a clean space to sleep, and Anderson said, "Maybe you should stay in a private room tonight. Get some peace and quiet."

Ben narrowed his eyes at the newcomer. "I'm alright."

"Don't tell me you expect to sleep next to Frankie."

My palms dripped with sweat as Ben uncrossed his arms. "Is that a problem?"

Blood filled my face. I looked for Cleo and Jessamae, humiliated that they had to see this, but they were gone, whispering in the kitchen.

"It is," Anderson said, folding his legs and leaning against the wall.

Ben licked his teeth behind his lips. "You got a little crush on Frank?"

Anderson interlaced his fingers with an amazing sense of dignity, considering he sat in dirt. "I don't. But I care about her. I don't know you that well, but I know that you don't deserve a girl like her."

"A girl like me? What kind of girl am I?" I asked.

He ignored me and spoke only to Ben. "I know you cheated on her."

I said, "Hey, I already told you that's not what happened." Again, no one cared.

Patrick's eyes were saucers in his head, flying between the three of us.

Ben clenched his fists and stated, "Frankie and I are none of your business."

"The hell you aren't! She's been through enough!"

"I know *exactly* what she's been through," Ben hissed through his teeth. His voice was poison, his knuckles white at his sides. He was so angry, so near boiling over, that I was afraid for Anderson.

Anderson had nothing to say to that, but he studied Ben as if he were a dog shitting in his yard. You'd need more than a knife to cut the tension in here.

I silently excused myself to find a bathroom. I didn't have to pee, but I did need a moment alone, away from those two, so I peed anyway. Tears stung the pockets around my eyes, and I shoved my fingers against them until I saw black. Then I glared at the leaf tattooed on my hand. How unjust it was there on my skin, hardly faded despite what I'd been through this week.

After flushing, I made the mistake of looking at my reflection. Blood dotted my face like freckles, but other than that, I was the poster-girl for wellness and health. Blushed cheeks, bright eyes, most of my hair had filled out again, reaching past my ears in some spots and my shoulders in others. My lips were pink and soft against my grimy teeth.

I hated my face. I hated that I was exempt from carrying my sins and my anguish on my person for all to see like everyone else. This face wasn't mine. It was disgustingly free of all the horrible things I'd suffered, of all the atrocities I'd done.

I never finished any of the assigned readings in high school, but I wished I'd had the gumption to finish *The Picture of Dorian Gray*. Maybe if I had, I would know how Dorian ultimately fell from grace, how his portrait shoved his ugliness back onto him once more. Liars had to fall. In books, on television, in those movies I'd looked at in the rental store. The truth wasn't pretty, but it had to prevail. Otherwise, I'd never know for certain that I'd even lived.

I didn't break the mirror. I didn't scream and punch the walls. I lowered myself to the floor, my back against the door, and held my face in my hands.

I stayed like that for a long time. Until I didn't hear arguing in the other room. Until the sound of snores and rustling snuck under the bathroom door. I stood and rejoined the others.

The sun was high in the sky, but the bright day didn't hinder us one bit. Patrick was the one snoring. He sounded like a rock polisher. Anderson was next to Patrick, his jacket bunched up under his head. I saw Cleo's dark hair beside Jessamae's ashy mop just inside the kitchen. They hadn't stopped whispering. Every moment I saw them together, saw them seek out privacy, felt like a sliver whittled from a tree, another piece cut away from me. I felt small.

Ben faced a windowless wall, his torso bare and his skull on the ground. He crossed his arms tightly over his chest, and he looked cold. His physical pain wasn't an issue, I sucked most of that away like the leech I was. But such sadness I had never known. He was burdened by so much, he needed a second body to help him carry it.

I was confused and scared and angry and lonely. I felt stupid for wanting to forgive him. I was embarrassed that he would so easily forgive me. If it happened again … if he and Cleo happened again, I would never live through the shame of having let it go now just so I could be near him. Ben had been honest with me, loved me, wanted me. I knew it to be true. But what was true now, may not be true tomorrow. He'd always said as much. It was far too easy to change the future.

I didn't know if I could bear his hands on me, if I could bear his whole heart. If I took them back, I could never lose those things again. No …

But tonight, I could bear some things.

I walked across the room and lay behind Ben's back, lining my head up with his. He stilled, holding his breath. I inched my ribs closer, but only just. With trembling wrists, I set my fingers against his bicep, gentle as an exhale. I drew them down his patched skin, the ridges of all his new scars, and was filled with such guilt, I could drown. Until Ben reached over his shoulder, slow, and circled my fingers with his.

I didn't take his grief from him, that would be a violation, however kind. If Vegas had taught me anything, it was that we owned our pain as much as we owned our tongues and our toes. I was in control, holding Ben's hand, when I drifted into a cavernous sleep.

DARK. I was in the dark and my neck was broken. I lifted my head, discovering it only *felt* broken. I swiveled it this way and that, and dragged my arms under my chest, pushing myself up from where I laid.

My face grated against another. I froze, my heart rate spiking, my armpits dewing like morning flowers. A pair of lips dragged against my cheek, a soft breath hitting my face.

Ben.

Ben was asleep. And the entirety of yesterday hit me like a lightning bolt. I killed that woman in the prison. Had I killed someone here? In Pioche? I could smell the stink of death, as if she had followed me all the way from Las Vegas.

A door slammed somewhere in the house. It must have been a door. But we were all here together. Weren't we? My eyes adjusted to the dark and I counted six murky stripes of flesh horizontal in the room with me. We were together. No one had shut any door.

The closest was Ben, the biggest Patrick, and near him was a medium lump I took to be Anderson. The two smaller mounds in the corner were Jessamae and Cleo.

That was everyone … five.

My head whipped to the sixth stripe that lay all alone.

Oh … piggy, piggy. You fell asleep so fast. Such a stupid baby you are.

I scurried back on my tailbone, fumbling over Ben as if he were nothing. The stripe didn't move. "You're not real."

What is real? I'm with you, in you. How could I be there … *When I am right here?*

Paimon spoke of the shape. They knew what it was, and so did I. It was someone else. Someone else was with us in this room.

"Turn on the lights!" I yelled to the group, though I flew on hands and feet to the light switch myself. "Turn on the fucking lights!"

Paimon's laugh faded with the shadows.

The light was worse than the dark. Immeasurably worse.

The shape belonged to Jack.

25

JACK WAS dead and lay motionless in a way neither Pamela nor Gabriel ever did.

Jessamae appeared at dead Jack's side like a specter. She put two fingers to the vein in his throat. I could have told her it was useless, but I wanted to see her try. Sixty seconds of mind-pummeling silence. The only sound was Patrick sitting a little higher on his hips.

She took her finger from dead Jack's neck and covered her mouth with that hand. She blotted her eyes. She took a breath, then another, and turned to me. "Frankie," she said, her pale eyes like a brand, searing me to the bone.

"I … I can't." I backed away from her.

"You will. We are not discussing this. Jack has done nothing but help us and we owe him this. You've practiced. I know you have. Now do it." She pressed her fingertips into the wood until her fingernails turned purple, bending at the knuckle like spider legs.

I looked to the other faces in the room—Cleo, Patrick— expecting some comforting hesitation, some doubt, but no one looked at me. Every pair of eyes was on dead Jack.

She was right, putting up a fight did nothing but strengthen the stench. If I ruined him, I ruined him. But I would take the chance. I couldn't let him go after all he'd done for us.

Would I do it if it were Ben? Would I risk ruining him? It

didn't matter now. It was Jack and I would try. I ignored the sick irony that the only one who could ensure I would succeed was alive Jack. And all I had was a dead one.

His eyes were open and staring straight through the ceiling. They were not dull or empty as I would expect—they were all too bright. The yellow rings around his irises glowed like halos. His mouth twisted down with more muscles than I had in my entire face. He looked begrudging, almost vengeful in death. He'd been a rattlesnake, and none too happy to be found in his burrow. I put my hands on his chest, unsure of where else to put them—

The sound a door closing somewhere in the house. It didn't slam. It eased shut. But I heard it. We all did. Someone else was in this house.

Whoever put Jack here never left.

"Upstairs," Ben whispered, though our volume didn't matter. The person upstairs put Jack in here to scare us, to tell us that we couldn't run and we couldn't hide. If I resurrected Jack now, they'd know what I could do for them. And I'd have to keep doing it as long as they wished.

Footsteps glided along the upper floor. Dust shook from the ceiling and floated down through the air. The steps were deliberate and eased. They didn't walk toward the stairwell, they walked deeper into the house and stopped just above our heads.

Ben slunk to the stairs. Under the foggy, yellow light of the room, he looked sick, jaundiced, and all too thin. But he was moving without difficulty, unwavering as he took the first stair. Then another. He was almost at the top of the staircase. He peeked around the banister when we heard a knock on one of the windows. Ben made it halfway back down when the croak of an old cupboard inching open came from the kitchen.

This little piggy …

"Shut up."

Five heads turned in my direction, eager to know why I'd told off a cabinet. Paimon had been roosting inside my head for months, and only ever spoke to me. How could I explain something like that? I couldn't.

Jessamae crept toward the kitchen to investigate—

"Stop. Don't go in there." Ben had stepped off the stairs, one arm extended as if to stop Jessamae from across the room, but he wasn't looking at her. He wasn't looking at anything.

The rickety screen door clapped against the house, and only once. Was it windy outside? Were the drafts breaking through the walls and spooking us?

I looked to Ben, but he was gone, in his head, seeing things that weren't there, but things that could end up there. We all waited with bated breath to hear the future, to know which path led us to safety. "I don't know," he said. "It's all the same. They all end in the dark."

They were playing with Ben's visions. The Vegas coven had him for days, made fucked up concoctions from his blood, from his brain. They knew how his affinity worked …

But they couldn't see through walls. If I brought Jack back before they pounced, he'd help Ben, help us all.

I crouched, my legs shaking with the incremental movements. I put my hands on the bare skin of his cheeks. It was rough as steel wool, hard as tree bark.

The click of a lock. The slow creak of the front door opening into the room. Everyone around me was silent as death—more so, in my experience—because someone stood in the doorway.

I wouldn't look at them. I wouldn't look in Laisren's eyes.

"Frankie?"

No … *No.* I bowed my head. I couldn't lift it. Even when Jack's facial hair scratched my nose. I would take Laisren or Paimon one hundred times before I'd take this voice.

It wasn't real. I wouldn't look up because this was a trick. I wouldn't entertain the notion that she was here with me.

"Frankie. Please … I haven't seen"—an airy sob—"I haven't seen your face in so long." A woman's voice, lilting and scratched from crying. It sounded like a stranger. But the emotion felt real. Like she was genuinely happy to see me, and a little broken because I wouldn't look up.

"No."

She began to bawl on the front porch, a stereotypical ghost. Sweat stuck my hands to Jack's face. My lip trembled so I smashed my mouth into a fleshy slash. The blubbering carried on quietly, almost a coo. It killed me. I couldn't keep dying like this.

So I looked up, because she wouldn't stop crying until I did.

Her long hair was tied into a knot on her head. She wore clothes like I'd never seen, almost a nurse's uniform. A long teal tunic and matching pants. She wore no jewelry, as she'd been known to do when she was real—gold and beads and long, loud chains. Paler than I remembered, her eyes shone like gasoline puddles, too bright a green inside her face.

"Am I supposed to call you Mom?" I whispered, my voice raspy with rage.

The thing that looked like Allison Hughes stood on the pint-sized porch, illuminated by the living room light. Her eyes were pink and wet. Her hands were clasped at her chest like a bunny's.

Seeing her impersonated like this made me furious to the point of punching my own teeth out. I hadn't seen her in years. And this thing wasn't smiling. She didn't hum her favorite songs. She didn't wear her unreasonable, swishy clothes, and her hair wasn't held together with extra fabric from whatever she was trying to make that week. Her voice was too deep, too clear. A clone. An alien. A changeling. My hands hurt. My nails dug into my palms against Jack's chilling face. I wanted to rip out my hair. I wanted to run and never come back.

The thing was aghast at my question, acting as if I kneed her in the gut. "You always used to."

"You're a dead woman. You're ash. You're scattered some place in the mountains that I can't even find anymore!" Tears filled my eyes, and I ground my teeth until the waterworks stopped. I smelled only one dead body here, and it was under my hands. This woman was no corpse. And though sorrow was evident on its pretty face, I sensed no actual pain.

The thing was an illusion.

Standing, I kept my eyes on the fake, waiting for an attack, for movement. She simply watched me with basset hound eyes and shy hands.

I stormed the doorway. The thing was nothing but smoke, I could almost taste the acrid stuff on my tongue. "Get out!"

The imposter lifted its arms, awaiting a hug. A grand reunion. Discarding the sweet invitation, I backhanded her, hard. And my knuckles met elastic skin and tough bone underneath. The face was real, and sting lanced my knuckles. The curly wisps of hair along her temples were soft where I touched them. She was warm. She was human.

My vision faded in and out. "What are you?"

My mother held a delicate hand to her cheek, where blood flowed hot beneath it.

The hurt she wore moments ago was nothing to how she looked at me now, around her trembling fingers. The first time seeing her daughter again, and I hit her. I hit my mother when I was given the chance to hold her, to know her weight, her freckles and teeth and hair in my arms.

She looked more like me than she ever had before. I couldn't look at her.

I rushed inside the house.

"Frankie!"

I slammed the door on Allison, huddled and crying on the porch. Running for the stairs, I rubbed an arm across my sore eyes.

"Frank—"

"Don't!" How many times did I have to hear my name spoken like that? Like a warning, like a plea, like a dirge.

"It's safer down here!" Ben shouted as I rounded the rotten banister. How could I believe him? How could I believe my eyes, ears, and nose when I just slapped my mother who'd been dead for nearly a year? Had she even died? Were those her ashes I watched Pamela dump to the ground? Had the last three months of magic been a delusion brought on by her loss?

The shadows were thick as winter clouds upstairs, and I couldn't see how many doors there were. I merely flung myself behind one and kicked it shut.

I dropped to my knees and scraped my dirty fingernails over the floorboards, grounding myself in this place. I was here, this wasn't my imagination. I wasn't in a mental ward somewhere, cutting myself into ribbons and swearing up and down there was magic in my blood. A horrible sound poured from my mouth with strings of drool. I beat the ground until my skin turned pink.

Dizzy and numb, I stared into the dark, replaying the scene in my head that I'd avoided since last winter.

'Ma'am, I'm sorry to tell you this ...'

My mother was dead. She drove her car into a snowbank—broken neck, traumatic brain injury, words that danced in my head for days until they became a song—and then they set her on fire. She was nothing but powder. These were facts. As tangible as the woman sobbing on the porch beneath me. Had the others seen her, too? Were they talking to her now? Consoling her?

The moon peeped at me through a dirty square window, and I could make out the dimensions of the room. It was small, a bedroom, with a bumpy shape on one side that I thought could be a radiator. The wallpaper was light with a pattern over it, maybe flowers. The house must have been grateful for the gloom —it hid the cracks, the mold, and the vermin.

Something in my periphery began to grow. My weak eyes darted to the corner as the bloom of obsidian spread throughout the room like ink on paper. It was a door. A closet. And it was opening right in front of me. It moaned like it was in pain. The dark was as thick as black ice on the other side. There could be other worlds hidden in that darkness, nightmares. I too easily imagined fresh, black earth spilling from that void before a casket appeared from the closet's depths.

But that's not what I saw. I saw two silver-dollar eyes, so high they almost touched the ceiling. They watched me for a thousand noiseless moments.

"Looky, looky, looky ..."

I wanted to hide my face, but I couldn't give them the advantage. I stared into those eyes until I couldn't see anything else, like staring at the headlights of an oncoming car.

"I see you," Paimon sang from the closet. "Do you see me?"

I said nothing.

It laughed. "Granny's not trapped in your head anymore, is she?" The door opened further, until it tapped against the wall. "Surprised? But baby knew that Granny followed her, yes she did!" The shining eyes roved up and down, bobbing with Paimon's stilt-like legs. I heard their thick fingernails clicking together, and then a buzzing. The buzzing of flies.

"Frankie!" My mother called from outside the house. She stood beneath the window of this room, calling up like a teenage paramour. I looked at the window as if I could see her from here. Spiders emerged from the crannies around the window frame. Three or four at once.

"Who is it?" Paimon called and I automatically turned back.

Though I couldn't discern the details of their face, Paimon's head spun as if they were on a carousel. Little by little they turned until those eyes passed the window, the closet, the bedroom door, and landed back on me again. Three-hundred-sixty degrees. All the bones in their neck cracked as it turned, one hard *tunk* at a time. "Oh yesssssss. Baby's mommy has crawled out of the ground, hasn't she? Ash made flesh. Survived by Francescally—"

"She's dead!" I yelled, pulling my knees into my body. Spiders skuttled from the window in a mob, dozens of them.

"So am I," Paimon spoke against my neck, their rancid breath spilling over my skin. The demon was real. Paimon was back. And this was somehow my fault, just as I created them.

The Paimon/Pamela hybrid tore through their decaying sack of a carcass. The unnatural red skin was stretched like cobwebs over their bones and yellow teeth. Their stinking tongue rounded their lipless red mouth, looking like a tentacle thrashing above the surface of a crimson sea.

Through it all, in its dripping throat, a node pulsed like a teratoma. The mass squirmed against the constraints of Paimon's larynx. Then it opened. A single green eye blinked at me from inside the demon's neck. Pamela's eye.

A trail of sobs found their way out of the monster's mouth, as hundreds of spiders seethed over my hands.

"How … how could you? Francesca … Get me out. GET ME OUT!"

I ONLY KNEW I was screaming because I couldn't hear Pamela's cries anymore. I scraped the horde of spiders from my skin. They were in my mouth, up my nose. I screamed into my hands until I thought my knuckles would shatter. But I could still smell that breath. I felt that shadow coat me like a dirty sheet. I screamed until I turned and barfed on the floor, drowning a fistful of spiders in the mess.

The bedroom door stabbed into my feet, throwing me forward into my own vomit. There was red gunk on my hands. My eyes twitched. My hands vibrated to the bone. The door beat at my back again and I was forced away from it.

"Goddammit, Frank!" Ben pushed his way into the room. He revolved in circles, searched the closet, and scanned the desert out the window.

Paimon was gone. And so were the spiders.

Ben came to kneel in front of me. He took in my puke, saw it smeared all over me. "Frank. Talk to me. Did they get in? Who was it? Princess. Look at me," He tipped my chin until I saw his eyes.

"Did you see it, too?" I asked.

"I saw what looked like your mom outside, yes. It's still out there. But up here? No, I didn't see anything. I heard you."

"Heard me what?"

He titled his head, and the moon outlined him like an incoming UFO. "Screaming."

Ben rubbed his head, then took my hands in his. "Come on. I'll help you clean up." Then he led me to an upstairs bathroom that smelled like pee and wet clothes. Sitting me on the edge of the tub, he turned on the faucet. "It won't get warm, but it'll clear in a second." He gestured to the brown sludge pouring down the drain.

As it filtered out the garbage, he twirled a strand of my hair between his fingers. It didn't look remotely curly. It was a frazzled nest of tomato juice and dirt and sweat. "Are you okay?" he asked.

Even with him here and Paimon locked back in the closet of my mind, my hands refused to steady. I heard my mother calling me from outside, begging me to love her again. And Ben was as broken on the outside as I was on the inside. "No."

He held my hands under the mostly clear water and washed the regurgitated mess from the crotch between my fingers. Using the cuff of his jacket, he wiped it from my mouth and chin.

"Are you okay?" I asked.

His well-being had always been tied to my own, something I took for granted. But now, he seemed to assess himself, to give himself a moment of thought for the first time. He scoured his hands for a lifetime of tattoos that weren't there anymore. He rubbed his near-nonexistent hair, his scalp covered in sutures. His eyes were loaded with dried superglue and his wrists were scarred from the dig of leather cuffs. He had two tongues, and he was so skinny.

He looked at me, at us, what we were now. Not what we could have been, or what we used to be, but what we were. There were tears in his eyes when he attempted to smile, a grimace breaking through the façade and mangling his mouth. "No."

BEN GUIDED ME DOWNSTAIRS, leading me by the arm as if it were a set of reins. I'd told him about Paimon standing in the bedroom with me, plus the onslaught of spiders, and he nodded, needing no further explanation—he'd seen me after a night terror a hundred times before. And that bothered me, because this time I'd been wide-awake. The closet door was open when Ben found me, wasn't it? I didn't open it. And I'd never seen spiders before.

"Where is she?" I asked.

"Outside, but she keeps moving, so we can't get a good look at her, and she won't talk to any of us."

"Even you?"

He turned on the stairs to appraise me. "It's not her, Frank."

My guilt and confusion spoke for me. "How can you be sure?"

He didn't answer. Jessamae's head appeared beside the railing. "Was someone upstairs?"

Ben's eyes were intent on me, on my hysterical hands and my uncertain footsteps. I said, "No. Just a bad dream."

She nodded, accepting the fact without question. "It's time, Frankie. We can't let Jack decay any further."

Ben pushed out a sigh. "Can you leave her alone for five fucking seconds?"

"Can you?" she retorted, her focus latching to his hand on my arm.

I shook Ben off me. How was this still happening? After all we'd been through, nothing had changed. Nothing would ever change. We would, again and again, find ourselves jealous and bickering atop the putrid mountain of corpses we would eventually attain. Villain after villain would murder our friends and our families and we would crawl over the rot of them like cannibalistic worms, hissing at each other all the while.

Two deaths were more than enough. Jack almost looked like him—Gabriel. But maybe everyone looked the same when they were dead.

Even if it led to Laisren discovering what hid in the crevices of my affinity, I wouldn't leave him like this.

I lumbered down the last steps and shoved Patrick out of my way. He'd been staring out the window, mumbling something inconsequential. I crashed to my knees beside the body and wrapped my hands around Jack's throat. There was no pain, no fear. Nothing appetizing, nothing at all. It wasn't merely the absence of something, it was the inverse. A void having a corporeal, tangible presence all its own. It existed inside him like an egg ready to hatch. It was the thing I smelled in the dead, its seeds finding home in sickness, and injury, and pain.

The void scared me. Touching it was so unbelievably intimate, like I'd exposed myself to the shadow under a tree. And it saw me just like that—exposed. It saw my dirty teeth and my bruised spine. The hair under my arms, on my legs, between my thighs. It saw the blood crusting beneath my fingernails and the scab where my toe used to be. It saw all my confusion and attraction and greed. It saw all of me packed into a condom of the newest skin, none of which had been mine three days ago. And it asked me to share it. To share my utter nakedness, everything I'd stolen and ate and felt. To share just a morsel of what I'd used to build the body I currently wore.

So I did.

Jack's neck burned under my hands. I offered the void a piece of me, and it took a chunk; ripped it from me like a starving animal. Still, I held on, and Jack grew hotter. With each degree, it felt as if a rope strung from my teeth to my bowels was being yanked out of me, catching on guts, blood, and bone on its way out. It hurt a little, and then more. I was afraid. It would take too much.

Something warm tickled my scalp. Hands. Hands wove expertly through my hair, and they eased my dread. They continued to play, and the bits of me I offered penetrated Jack's brain, his heart. I thought of the hands combing through my hair —the hands of a friend—and felt something good. We were all here, together. And as horrible as things were for every one of us, I'd take that over being without them every day of the week.

The void shrank and shrank, as if its only purpose was to consume a slice of me, and then it could rest. It was the size of a bird, the size of a pin. It was nothing. We were all suspended, hanged men, in the quiet for several missing heartbeats.

Jack drew a violent, hacking breath into his lungs and lived.

26

FOR A LONG TIME, there was only his frantic, clattering breaths, and then I flumped to the dust. I was conscious. I knew that, because I kept thinking about how tired I was. There should be a way to measure exhaustion, in ounces or feet. I had too much.

"Frankie? Can you hear me?" There were hands at the back of my head as the voice spoke to me. She leaned over me, her face brighter than the rings of Saturn. It had been Cleo's hands to steady me when I nearly lost it. She kept me together. Again. "Can you hear me?"

"Yea … Yeah, yes. I can hear you."

"Okay. I'm going to help you up now." She moved her hands to my shoulders and rolled me to my backside. I wobbled on my butt and held her elbow for support. Once upright, I found Ben's face in the group. He'd been across Jack's corpse from me, and he was helping Jack sit up. When he looked at me, he appeared unsure and unhappy.

"What? Did something go wrong?"

Ben opened his mouth, but Jack started seizing in his arms. I sensed Jack's fear, it smelled like citrus, and I reached out to take it from him. Emotions were coming in clearer every day, and that fact smelled like an orange grove to me.

Cleo curled her hands around mine and pushed them into my chest. "Just give him a second. He'll be alright."

I licked my teeth—they were sticky and strange. My mouth was too loose, like a deflated balloon. I wanted a toothbrush.

Patrick bent down to better glimpse my face. He exhaled through his lips, a sound he'd make if he was looking at extensive car damage. "You don't look so hot, baby girl." Cleo whacked him in the head.

Running my fingers over my cheek, I checked for blood, for soreness, but I didn't feel anything. I turned to find Jessamae watching me closely. Her eyes were like mirrors on me, but she was too far away, keeping her distance. She was worried. Something *had* gone wrong.

I gripped Cleo tighter and baby-giraffed my way across the room. My bones were soft as silicone. I teetered around Jack, who was regaining control of his lungs now, and Ben, who was tracking me like a hound dog. My hands grated along the heinous wallpaper, making a neck-twinging noise, until I found myself in another bathroom attached to the kitchen. This house was bigger than it looked.

There was no way anyone had used this toilet in decades. It smelled like a dead raccoon—a pack of dead raccoons—floating inside a Port-O-Potty. Black crud circled the water of the toilet bowl and yellow powder circled the toilet itself. The shower was full of pellet turds and mold had covered the tile to the ceiling. The sink was littered with little dark nuggets, like fungus rolled between two fingers.

Had the other bathrooms been so disgusting? I couldn't remember. I looked in the mirror.

It was dirty, but not dirty enough. I saw my tired face, my folded neck above my newly dipping chest. My mouth was covered in tiny branching lines, like tar-striped asphalt, and some flyaway hairs that floofed around my head, they were gray.

Reviving Jack had aged me. It had aged me at least twenty years.

I REJOINED THE OTHERS, and now that Jack was standing—woozy and nervous but standing—everyone stared at me. They were horrified. Jessamae was chewing her cheek bloody. Ben looked like he was about to faint.

"I don't know," I said.

"Has it happened before? Like that?" Anderson asked. His face was grim and the pallor in his hands made me think that he was a terrified man pretending he wasn't. As the only magicless person here, it couldn't have been an easy thing to watch.

"Of course not," Cleo answered with disdain.

"Then what's wrong with her?" His fingers were spasming.

"She's only done small animals. There was one try with a human but it … failed," Ben said. "She hasn't tried another in months."

"I'm standing right here!"

"Obviously, or we wouldn't have anything to talk about," Patrick contributed. Cleo charged toward him, and he ducked away.

Jessamae took my hands in hers. She was much more afraid than she was letting on. The orange stink was overwhelming. "It's okay." She was talking to herself as much as to me. "Your affinity will most likely counteract these side effects—"

"Side effects?" Ben growled. He blamed her for what happened to me. He always did. "Like she took some fucking Viagra?"

"It's not her fault," I said. "I didn't want to lose Jack either. I made the choice."

He smashed his lips together and put a hand to the back of my neck, and then with a flinch—feeling all the new wrinkles back there—moved his fingers to my bicep. He looked away, scrutinizing possible futures. "You'll change back. I think. In your reflection … but *I* can't see you. Not every time … It's Allison, or whatever she is, and whoever's controlling her. The Knights of the Blackjack Table. They're convoluting my sight."

"Jack can help you," Jessamae said.

Ben lifted his head and I thought he might just spit in her face. After a tense pause, he said, "You need to back off and give everyone *time*. Jack is—"

"Jack is just fine, thank you very much," Jack wheezed. His voice was thick and scratchy, like he just puffed on a pipe. He had one hand on his chest and the other braced against the wall. I knew I looked bad, but Jack somehow looked worse. The yellow ring around his eyes had amplified, taking up much more of the white than they should—inhuman and afraid. His tongue licked around his lips and poked out at nothing, catching invisible flies. His knees knocked against each other, though he tried to hide it. It was as if he were trying to remember how to be human again but kept getting the species confused with other creatures.

Working to keep the guilt and pity from my voice, I asked, "Do you, you know, want to talk about what happened?"

A mournful howl called to the absent moon, pained enough to shake the stars. "Frankieeeeeee!" My mother cried, just on the other side of the wall. "Frankie, please! Please come out! PLEASE!"

"Maybe later," Jack grunted, his grizzly eyes locked on the wall as if he could see right through it, like he could see my mother out there waiting.

Anderson moved to one of the dust-caked windows. He rubbed his forearm over the glass in an effort to clean it. When the stubborn stain refused to budge, he stepped back with a frustrated grimace.

"Don't," Ben said. "Don't break it. You'll hurt yourself, and they'll see us inside."

"Don't tell me what to do … Why don't we want them to see us?" Anderson worried the skin on the back of his neck, like he was trying to burst a seam along his spine. We were driving him insane, literally. I assumed the Vegas coven had hardened him to witchcraft, but then again, he'd never had to fight in The Pool before. Magic looked different from above the water line.

"So what? We just leave her out there all night?" I asked.

"Yes," Ben answered.

"And then what? The next day? The next night? Two weeks?" I stared through the window. I thought I could see her in the gray glass, wandering the desert. "Is she a danger to us?"

"I don't know. I already told you, they're messing with my sight. If she's not a direct danger, then going outside to talk to her *triggers a danger*. You have to stay here, Frank. Too many futures go black."

"So ... if she isn't a direct source of harm ... it could—could it really be her?" I shoved a hand to my mouth to cover my shameful hope, wiping at something that wasn't there.

Ben's voice dropped an octave or two, and it came out horribly gentle. "No."

"But I just brought Jack back, didn't I?"

"Yes, but Jack had a body, Frankie. One that hadn't even hit rigor yet. Your mom was cremated. Almost a year ago. You can't honestly believe—"

"But what if those weren't her ashes? What if ... Pamela tricked me, or Allison went into hiding or—"

"She's dead. I'm sure of it." That's when I felt it—the punch of dreadful anticipation. Something was coming. He was going to say something, and it was going to knock me silly.

"I spoke with her," he said. "Allison. After her accident."

I was ready to blow my brains all over these ugly walls. They were swollen, much too big for my skull anyway. I didn't want them anymore and I hoped for detonation. "You spoke with my mother. After she died."

He picked at a button on his blazer before he ripped it off and chucked it across the room with a glower. "Yes."

"And you never told me that in the last ten months."

His split tongue made an appearance as he tore another button from his jacket. "That's true."

My brain was ticking. I could hear it counting down. I wished it would just fucking burst already. "You have a bad habit of keeping things from me."

Ben's cheeks reddened, defensive and angry. "Not anymore, if you recall."

"This is my mother we're talking about."

"I'm fully aware."

I wanted to hit him, to hurt him. I wanted to break down. "How?"

We had an audience, and despite the personal nature of this argument, I didn't care if they were uncomfortable. They could try the feeling on for once.

Ben pulled the remaining buttons from his jacket before he spoke to me. "Remember, after Pamela came back?" He shot a venomous glare at Jessamae. "I told you that there were other ways to speak to the dead than to bring them back to life?"

Jessamae's face pinched, a wolf's quivering muzzle.

I did remember. I remembered every second of that summer. Every second, awake or asleep. "You said you'd only done it once."

He didn't respond. He looked at me through his eyebrows and waited.

"You called my mom? Beyond the grave? What did she say? What did you ask that just couldn't wait until *you* were dead, Ben?"

A thousand-pound silence followed my question, and every moment he didn't answer me was like another dumbbell of weight. Patrick tiptoed backward toward the stairs. "Maybe we should give you some pri—" when everyone else in the room stayed exactly where they were, he leaned against the wall and finished with a whisper, "vacy."

We were safer together. And they all had a stake in this now.

"Frankieeeeeeee!" Allison called from behind the house. Her voice was beginning to tear, she'd been screeching for so long.

"Why, Ben?"

He was actively resisting rubbing his head. His arms swung and his fingers wriggled like centipedes. "I just … I just wanted to know why. I saw her crash, but I couldn't see why, what made her swerve. She'd been acting weird for months. I just wanted to ask her what happened."

I bit clean through my lip, and blood dribbled down my chin. I lapped at the stuff. "Tell me."

He stepped closer. I didn't move because I wanted to hear this. I've wanted to know why she swerved on that road for almost a year. And he knew. All this time.

"She looked different. Younger. She wore a dress even though it was the middle of winter. Blue and silver with these—" he opened and closed his hand.

"Lilies."

"Yeah. She was happy and sad to see me. She knew what I was. That I was a seer, that I was a witch. She was relieved you weren't there, that you weren't involved."

My chest was paper, and the image ripped it in half. I couldn't take this anymore. How many more punches until I keeled over and never got up again?

My mother, appearing younger than I did now, happy that she didn't have to see me there, with Ben. Happy that I hadn't turned out exactly as she feared I would. A dirtbag. A witch. A murderer. "How did she know what you were?"

He stretched the skin of his face toward his ears, looking helpless. "She said she always knew. I asked her what happened, and she … she said, 'I crashed.'

'How did you crash?'

'I lost control.'

'Lost control of the car?'

'I lost control, I lost. Lost, lost, lost. And it's all my fault.'"

It was like watching another person take control of Ben. His hands fluttered and his voice changed. He took on a certain melancholy that hurt in my toes.

"So you knew? You knew she wanted to die?" *It's all my fault.* The apple doesn't fall far from the tree.

"No. She never said whether it was intentional or an accident. She was flighty, distracted. She seemed more dazed than present, like she was only half there. If she gave me any answers, I would have told you."

"These *are* answers." I couldn't look at him. I stared past him. "Did she say anything else?"

He did rub his head now. "Just something about me. It's not important."

"IT'S MY MOM!"

My shout was a black hole, and everything was lost to it. It sat on the floor and continued to pull everything within reach inside it.

"Frankie?" my mother whispered outside. She was so close to the wall, I thought I could feel her breath. She spoke to me and only to me. My name was cold on my back, the most tender violation. "Frankie, it's me. It's your mom."

She said it wrong. She didn't say it like she used to in her voicemails.

"Keep her close," Ben said, pulling my attention from the wall, "Keep her safe."

I struggled to make sense of it until I realized he wasn't speaking as Ben, he was speaking as Allison.

"She didn't say anything else. I promise you."

To picture her, in his house, maybe in Ben's backyard where we evoked the third eye, in the very spot I rested in the cool grass, speaking those words. "Was she ... like a ghost? See-through? Or could you touch her?"

312

He took a step toward me, dropping his defenses. "She wasn't like a ghost."

"You mean—" I swallowed whatever was trying to jump out of my stomach. "You mean you could have slapped her?"

Ben's confusion lasted the blink of an eye before he lunged for me, arms out. But he wasn't fast enough. He wasn't prepared for my split decision because I didn't realize I was about to make it. I got to the door before he could catch me, before the others in the room even understood my intentions. Then I was outside the house, crying for my mother.

"Mom!" The air was dry and acrid. The world was black and blue, and the ground was rock-hard beneath me. There were no slender aspens, no tall yellow grass, but I may as well have been home, circling the house and begging my mom to appear from the dark. I was desperate to apologize for not understanding, for not loving her enough when she was alive. "Mom!"

Feet beat the earth behind me. Ben. He was faster than me now that he regained some of his strength. I didn't have long. Pushing myself farther, faster, I lost my balance and my chest tilted forward until I was running like an upside-down L. I scrabbled on my toes. If I fell, I'd lose my chance. I smelled a dead rabbit nearby. My spit tasted like blood.

A yellow light beamed ahead, illuminating the toes of my shoes and the cracks in the ground underfoot. I slowed just enough to regain my height. Then I veered for that light. It came from the window of the house next door to ours, which was a hundred yards away.

"Mom!" I was almost to the backdoor. It would be open. She wanted to see me. She wanted to see me cry and tell her that I should have appreciated having a mom while I did so she could forgive me. She wanted to forgive me almost as much as I did.

I staggered up the back-porch steps, one foot catching on the lip and smashing my hands to the splintered wood. Ben was a hairsbreadth away. I could hear his quick strides over my shoulder. I pulled the door open. My knees hit tile and I could feel the grease and dust through my jeans. "Mom?"

I was kneeling in a kitchen. The tiles beneath me were a checkerboard of white and pale blue. The kitchen was old enough to be my grandmother, and the sink was surrounded in lines of brown that was either rust or excrement. The window over the sink was strung with cobwebs, and the countertops were lined with the bellies of black bugs.

The light was coming from the living room. "Mom?"

My question brought a figure into the kitchen with me, so tall she ducked through the doorway. Her shadow hit me like ice water, but I refused to shudder under her russet stare. "Hey girl."

I turned around and tried to stand, but the door behind me was blocked. My mother stood in its frame, her sun-spotted arms like wings at her sides.

"I've always wanted a daughter," she said.

And gunshots rang through the air.

They weren't in the house with me, they were in the house I'd just left.

27

I CLIMBED to my feet as bullets shredded the house next door, my heart in my throat, my lungs in my shoes. I couldn't breathe. I couldn't speak. I couldn't do anything at all.

Trying to wrestle my mother aside, my eyes on the flashing lights of those windows, Nicola's hands came down hard on me and she forced me into a dining chair that looked haunted from a mile away. "Hold your horses, sweet cheeks."

We sat and listened to the gunfire next door. Hundreds of bullets. Hundreds.

My mom bent down with a smile I'd never seen her wear. Her outfit had changed from the one I saw before. The teal ensemble was now a pair of dingy department store sweats. They were layered in dirt and her hair was knotted around her face. I searched for a mark on her apple cheek where I'd slapped her, for any semblance of the pitiful creature I witnessed fall to her knees, but she was gone. My mother—as wild, as beatific, as sure as she was—had never carried this frightening arrogance.

"What did you say to me earlier?" I asked, my voice as small as a kitten's. The words tumbled from my mouth without inflection. I was full of dead aspen leaves. Maybe she'd never been dead. Maybe *I* died in that car crash. I didn't feel alive now, and hell was only a hop, skip, and a jump away. Just next door as a matter of fact.

"I've always wanted a daughter. And now I have one." She

cocked her head. Her voice shifted in pitch, like she was going through puberty. "She's older than she used to be. But that's okay." She pinched the extra skin on my neck, pulling it away from me until it hurt. "Call me Mom again, would you?"

I shoved her, and she only giggled at my fight. Nicola draped her arm around me. "You must really miss her to run away from all your friends like that." Her silky hair fell over my shoulder and my insides curdled at the contact. The gun shots were few and far between now, but they weren't over. The Las Vegas security detail had grown tired of batons and Tasers it would seem. They weren't working to control us anymore. They wanted us dead.

I said, "Yeah. Maybe." But it wasn't missing my mother that drove me out here alone. It was the opportunity to relieve myself of the guilt I carried around every day. More than I wanted to see her, I wanted her forgiveness. "How do you two know each other? Church?"

My mother thumped the top of my head hard enough to clap my teeth together. When I looked up, rubbing my scalp, Nicola had moved in closer, like an imminent storm cloud. Her neck was wrapped in a chiffon crimson scarf. She looked like a guillotine victim. Or a high school drama teacher. I wanted to pull the ends until she turned purple, until her head popped off like a cork. Surely, she would set me on fire if I did. I reached for it.

"Warm for a scarf," I said.

Her smile shook, held up with strings. She whipped the long end over her shoulder. "I like the heat."

Without warning, Mom took the back of my chair and slammed it to the floor. I hit the ground, the wooden slats beneath my ribs, and the air was knocked out of me.

Nicola lifted me from the ground and squeezed me like an overbearing aunt, smelling of scorched meat and apples. "Things have changed, haven't they?" She clicked her tongue. "Well, now that the gun show is wrapping up, let's adjourn the living room." She dragged me through the dingy kitchen, my mother too close behind us. Her eyes were on my neck. Her fingers tickled my back. I felt them too much. I wanted to take off my skin.

Nicola pushed me to my knees in what would have been the living room if it held a single soda cap of life, of furniture even. The dead rabbit I smelled running through the desert was rumpled like a rag in the corner. Even the coyotes didn't bother with the thing if they had to creep through this building to get to the meat.

"You've got a pair of balls on you, I'll give you that," Nicola said, looming above me.

A hand with curious fingers trailed its way up my thigh. My mom's. She was missing all her rings and store-bought nail polish. "Do you?" she moaned into my ear.

I slapped the hand away, and if I hadn't already voided my guts, I would have blown chunks in her lap. "What the fuck is wrong with you?"

"You're one to talk, little one." Mom bent in close and fondled the wrinkles of my cheeks. "Daughter mine, what happened to you?" She didn't smell like a corpse. She smelled like salt and perfume. The resin so strong it stung my nose.

My lip lifted in repugnance. "Stress." If this was what truly became of my mother's wayward soul, then I didn't want it. Maybe death ruined every person that tasted it. And I fed off it like a parasite, let it fill me like a resigned virgin on her wedding night. Maybe that was why I was so broken. Like mother, like daughter.

Mom braced herself, one leg in front of me and one behind, and slid her body down beside mine, her crotch an inch from my arm. She leaned in so close to my face, I was sure she could see my skin cells splitting. Her breath hit me in hot blasts. Before I could stop her, she raked her nails down my cheek and took a layer of skin off my face.

"Christ!" I pitched to the side.

She looked at the skin under her fingernails, then she rubbed them on her own face like war paint. She turned to Nicola, "Is it working? Am I young again?" she sang the words to the ceiling, throwing her hands out.

Nicola raised a brow and smirked. "I'm sure it would take more skin than that. You'd need a Francesca-infused facial."

My mother wrenched my head around and coated the scratches in wet kisses. "Mmmm, a facial would be nice." She leaned into my ear, and when she spoke, her tongue flicked against my earlobe. "Call me Mommy first."

My gag reflex kicked at my tonsils, and I started to dry heave. I tasted tomato juice.

Two doors slammed upstairs, and I rolled my eyes back instinctually, looking for the ghosts of Pioche. "Frankiiiieeeeeee!" My mother cried in my ear. I looked up to her, but her mouth never moved. She beamed like a clown as the screams filled the room. "Frankiiieeee! This is your fault. THIS IS YOUR FAULT!"

I tried to run away, away from my mother's body and her disembodied shrieking. But then the world went dark. I couldn't see anything. I smacked myself in the face, feeling my eyes open and close. I had eyes, but I couldn't see a thing. It wasn't even darkness, it was nothing.

Why did I run from Ben? Why was I so fucking moronic! I'd run toward death. He'd never find my body. I didn't even know where I was. I only heard my mother's continued bleating.

"*This lady* beat you in The Pool?" It was a new voice, someone I didn't recognize. My sight had yet to return.

"She cheated," Nicola snapped.

"Sure she did. They always do."

Something touched me, or someone. I squealed and floundered, completely blind, until my back hit something I hoped was a wall and not a person. I shielded my face. "Don't fucking touch me!"

"Aw, you scared her."

"*You* scared her. All that screaming?"

Someone was arguing with themself … but their voice came

from multiple locations. Nothing made sense and I was so terrified I couldn't function. I couldn't even question it. I just slid down the slope and waited for the splat.

"That's enough. No more games."

If I was in deep shit before, I would never break the surface now.

Laisren's smoker's rasp entered this dump, the front door closing with a repetitive clack behind her. "Frankie. Wonderful to see you. Particularly because I should have never lost you to begin with."

I pushed myself into the wall, working to disappear somewhere inside it.

"Take the veil off her, Omar."

He sighed somewhere in the room, disappointed, but then I could see again.

A gaggle of people stood over me, all in different states of delight. The two bug-eyed twins from Laisren's personal guard stood on opposite ends of the group, shooting each other meaningful expressions.

Nicola stood at the back of the group, tall enough to see over everyone and still look down on me. Laisren had a cigar in her mouth, having upgraded for Samhain, her top hat pulled low over her brow. Without looking into her clover green eyes, I still craved her attention, her love.

My mother straddled my legs. A savage thrill lit her features and scared me to death.

"Francesca Hughes, you've met my friends, though I don't think you were properly introduced. Omar and Mo, tricksters. One tricks the ears, the other, the eyes. Very valuable players in games such as these!" She laughed until she started coughing and I thought she might spit up a lung. The twins were the ones who took my sight. They conjured the screams. The spiders, the ticking, the lion … they'd been in my head all night.

A great boom shook the ground beneath us, and the light

fixture above rocked with its tremors. The quake went far underground. It came from next door.

Laisren shook her head and patted her hat. "Would you two go over there please? It sounds like your assistance is needed."

"You betcha' boss," they said in unison, bowing at the waist. They laughed as they jogged out the back door, looking like a pair of reflections rather than real people.

"And, Frankie, you know—" she leaned over my mother and flicked her in the forehead. "Drop the face, please. We need to move this along and I find honesty to be the best policy."

I flattened myself into the wall until my shoulder blades ached. "Drop … the—"

My mother finally got off me. She gave me a half-assed curtsy, then she collapsed in on herself like a bendy straw.

All her bones crumbled toward the center of her. They crunched and cracked under the thick slabs of her skin. It sounded like a shark munching on river rocks as her arms and legs bent and folded. When she expanded to human shape again, looking like a shriveled sponge beneath water, her skin was paler, her arms thicker. Her breasts inverted into her body as if popped and her red hair curled its way into her brain.

My mother disappeared back into the underworld, and the smiling man with black hair stood in her place.

"Hello, Francesca," he said with a grin, his newly dark hair falling over one eye.

"You remember Billy," Laisren said with a wave of her arm.

Billy. It was a child's name, and a mean one at that. I didn't like the way he looked at me, even with my potential incarceration and torture on the horizon. His *elation* over our mother-daughter relationship was vile beyond belief.

I was fighting my own wooziness. With as much as I'd witnessed this year, I could not handle seeing this perverted psychopath where my dead mother stood only moments before. To think of him inside her skin, even if it was an illusion, was almost as bad as a demon making camp inside my dead grandmother.

My mother had never been here. I'd never touched her, and I'd never slapped her. I slapped Billy, and he was probably excited by the violence.

"I apologize for that. But it must have been quite nostalgic, seeing your mother again." Laisren stepped into my line of vision, puffing her cigar and tapping the ash to the ground. It sprinkled on my shoe in what I knew to be a disrespectful gesture, but I didn't care.

"How ... How?" *How did you find us? How did you know my mother? How did your receptionist steal her visage?*

I wouldn't ask something stupid like, *how could you?* I thought our stunt tonight, as much as it annoyed her, excited Laisren as well. So much drama. So much opportunity.

"Did you think I would take a mage into my employ without minimum investigation? Francesca Lee Hughes, twenty-three, former bagger at Jim's Family Grocery?"

"I was a *cashier*."

I hadn't had a phone in days, but I wasn't surprised to learn I'd been fired.

"Graduated with a 2.7 GPA, no college applications, no car registration, no memberships of any kind, no continuing education classes, no clubs."

She was trying to insult me. And it was working. Not because I was bothered by my lifestyle; I relished it. But I didn't have the few things I'd been proud of anymore. I didn't have anything. I didn't even have Jim's Family Grocery.

"The sole surviving Hughes member after both her mother and grandmother died in the same year. Bad spot of luck."

"You could say that."

She bent down on her haunches, her elbows on her knees and her fingers wrapped around that fat cigar. "I have your address. I know all about your friends. And you thought it wise to steal not one, not two, but four of my employees right out from under me? You didn't even make it across the state line."

"Ben was a prisoner. And Patrick never—"

Nicola hocked a wad of snot and saliva into my face. It stuck my eyelashes to my cheek. I dragged the back of my hand through the slime until I could open my eye again. "Okay."

"Get off your moral high ground. You're in the trenches now," Nicola hissed, unwrapping her scarf and revealing what I'd done when I tore into her jugular. The scar across her throat was a puckered, pulsing mess. The stitch job was decent, but the skin didn't line up just right after her emergency soldering and it looked like she had a zipper in her neck.

"Settle down," Laisren said in the voice of an apathetic babysitter. She sucked the stogie until her cheeks pinked and the cigar was nothing but a wrinkly nub between her lips. She faced Nicola standing behind her. "What I do with those who steal from me is far above your concern. Please keep your tantrums and your fluids to yourself."

Nicola didn't say anything, but the room warmed around her. I began to sweat and dropped my eyes to Laisren's shoes. Polished loafers.

She noticed my attention and said, "Look at me."

I did before she finished speaking. She was magic incarnate. Her skin was perfect, so smooth. Thorns and roses. Her eyes were the Northern Lights. Her hair was soft and shone brighter than a diamond could ever dream. Her very presence turned this place from a dump to a palace. I was honored to look at her. She said, "We had a deal. Three months' employment. With negotiations for permanent placement. You remember?"

"Yes."

"That's how I tracked you down, you know. Once you shake, there is no going back. There is no escaping a deal with me." She winked and I laughed. She was so funny and so kind. She didn't want to kill me. And if she did, I didn't want my life anyway. Not if she wanted it more.

"Now. You are a greater thief than one Mister Benjamin Bowen. He only took cash. You stole prisoners as well as a long-time guard who wasn't even halfway through his own contract." She placed her polished loafers on the knuckles of my right hand and slowly transferred her weight to my bones. "What to do, what to do."

Her pounds crushed my hand one at a time. The veins criss-crossing my knuckles would burst, the meat would tenderize. It hurt very much. And I loved it. I wanted Laisren to break me. "Please," I said.

Her eyes flicked away, and I hated that they weren't looking at me anymore. It was then I noticed a scream piercing the night air. How long had there been screaming? My ears rang with the sound, but I didn't cover them—one of my hands was unavailable, and I couldn't be bothered. Laisren was here. I needed her more than I needed water. More than I needed not to hurt. I wanted to bite her, to eat her. To have something of her become something of me. I whispered, "Please, please look at me." She didn't hear me. She didn't react.

Leaning forward a pinch, I opened my mouth. A sliver of her ankle was exposed, the tendons so delicate, the skin so smooth.

She was talking to the others, and I couldn't hear what they said anymore, because my lips were an inch from her skin. She smelled sweeter than candy. Sweeter than blood.

The front door banged open as I closed my lips over that soft skin. I held the protruding ankle bone between my teeth and bit down. I tasted her. Spun sugar and pink sores. I moaned at the revelation that was her body and went back for more.

Laisren kicked me like a dog, and I was free from her shoe, my hand throbbing at the release.

I couldn't lift my head. My hair was caught on a loose nail in the floorboards. Someone had opened the front door, but I couldn't see. "What ... what happened?" I pecked my head forward and ripped a tuft of curls from my scalp with a curse. I was dizzy. There was blood on my tongue.

"Can I help you?" Laisren asked politely.

The world was fuzzy and so were my gums. The fuzz spread to my teeth. I was drunk on fairy blood. I sent a word of thanks to my dead mother—and my atrocious, but very alive father—for what I was. I would sober quickly because of my magic. And I needed to kick every bit of the fairy from my system immediately, because I knew who was at the door. The cords in my chest knew, too.

"I doubt that," Jessamae said, her voice calm, solid as a tree. She appeared in control of herself but wasn't looking Laisren in the eye. I hoped she could get her hands on all of them before they spit on me again. If Laisren were to hock a loogie, I'd surely lap it up like a house cat.

"Well then, if you would excuse us," Laisren said.

I risked a squint through my hair at the Queen. She gestured to the door and then buttoned a button on her overly buttony blazer.

Jessamae said, "I won't."

Nicola waved a hand at Jessamae, her face contorting in angry swirls. "Jessamae, get the hell out of here. You haven't crossed the line. Yet."

Did they not know her part in this? That she killed so many of their suits back at The Alcazar?

"That, Nicola," Laisren said, steepling her fingers, "is actually not your judgement to make."

"Good." Jessamae stepped forward. "If I haven't established my position when it comes to this 'line,' I'd like to clarify things." I heard her smile before I saw it, but when I did, I shuddered on the floor. It had been a long while since I feared Jessamae like this, as a mystery, as a hunter who took pleasure in what she did.

"Why did you crawl through my door in the first place?" Nicola asked, playing with the thread poking out of her neck. "What do you have to do with any of this?"

"That is not your concern."

"Wrong." Nicola's quick response earned a glower from Lais-ren, but she held Jessamae's glass gaze. Billy watched her with a focus that made the back of my knees prickle. I hated him the very most.

Jessamae looked away first and her attention settled on me. Goosebumps spread over my back. "I was searching for someone."

"Her?" Billy kicked me in the thigh, drawing an embar-rassing whimper out of me. He was a violent motherfucker.

Jessamae dropped her smile. "No."

I wanted her to attack, now, so we could get back to the others. But I knew the moment I did, all hell would break loose. This was a chess match, not a sword fight.

"No, our friend Frankie here, found *you*. In fact, she did more than that," Nicola said. She tossed her bright hair, and it splayed over her ample chest. "So what is she to you, if she's not the reason you're here?"

Laisren observed the conversation as if it were an exhibit in a museum, and she was more than ready to move on to the dinosaurs. Billy crouched slowly beside me, while the others were preoccupied. His fingers fiddled through the air as if playing a flute, closer and closer to my skin.

Jessamae was not afraid. If I had her talent, I didn't know if I would be either. But her brain was as valuable as the rest of her. There was a reason she'd yet to kill anyone. She kicked dirt over the floor and knocked her boots together. She beat her heels as if the soles were covered in dog shit. Jessamae was a soundless creature, and she was making an awful lot of noise.

She approached my body, which I'd yet to move, and bent down opposite a leering Billy, who seemed more than eager she'd joined in his games.

Brushing a thumb across my eyebrow, she gave my head the tiniest nudge in the other direction. I followed her lead and turned my face until I saw the kitchen.

Ben was standing inside the doorway, silent as a dead mouse, with Betty draped over his shoulders. Blood trickled from his lip and both his ears. He tucked my snake under the collar of his jacket, so she rested against his bare skin.

Jessamae chose that moment to answer Nicola's question, and I forgot about Ben and Betty completely.

"She's family."

28

I DIDN'T MOVE SO AS NOT to expose the lie, but to lie in front of Laisren ... Jessamae had to know better. Unless it wasn't a lie if it was an expression? She felt like family to me. Everyone back at that ramshackle rat's nest did.

"Family?" Nicola barked. "Kissing cousins?"

She'd seen us together at The Harvest. Laisren saw us go into a private room together last night. Had Ben told her to do this? Would spinning tales save our skins?

Jessamae pressed her palm to my cheek before standing. "You are very funny, Nicola. However, we are not closely related. Entirely separate branches on our family tree."

I stopped breathing. Her response was no expression, but a stark and blatant lie. It was very quiet now. Ben stopped moving amidst the hush, which buried all of us, heavy as snow. He'd almost made it to the living room behind the coven's ignorant backs.

Laisren's tongue slid over her top lip, which had returned to its thin, bumpy self. Now that her effects were wearing off, I saw her as she was.

"Interesting," she said. She traced the line of spit she'd made with a bony finger and ducked, slightly taller than Jessamae, trying to find her eyes. "Your affinity is quite literally in the same vein as hers?"

"That's how it works," I yapped from the floor, desperate to stop Jessamae from saying anything else.

Laisren turned her head to me, her body stiff as bone otherwise, and I closed my eyes. "Manners, Frankie. Bite your tongue lest I keep my offer all to myself."

I crossed my elbows over my eyes, all the better to not see her with. Under my limbs, I watched Ben sneak along the wall at the back of the room. His eyes were vacant; he was using his sight to steer his body. Oh my god, one wrong step …

I cleared my throat. "Shot in the dark—you'd like to extend my enslavement?"

"Ha!" Laisren slapped her knee. "Shit. That is good!" She took Jessamae's arm as she spoke to me. "That is good. But that wouldn't be an offer—that's *penance*. If you refuse what I have to say, then of course your contract will be extended. However, my *offer* involves your lovelorn cousin, here." She tucked Jessamae's bleached locks behind her ear and caressed her jaw. "Leave her," Laisren said to me. "Leave her and go. Lord knows you have been a prickly pear toward my staff."

"A prickly pear?"

"A bitch, dearie."

I snorted. "Yeah, I've been completely unreasonable since you kidnapped me off the street—"

"You killed a man, Francesca."

I had no rebuttal for that.

"What do you say? Leave this one." She ran her fingers up Jessamae's arm. "She's got fireworks inside her. I can feel them exploding in there! Sweet Jesus, she's got the goods!" She turned back to me. "And you're free to go."

"No fucking—"

"Deal."

Jessamae's word sank into me like the world's slowest bullet, but it hurt as if it blasted through my kneecap. I clambered off my back, not bothering to hide my eyes from Laisren. "What? Are you kidding? No."

"It's my decision, Frankie." She stood tall in Laisren's grip, retaining more composure in that position than I ever could.

"Shut up, Jessamae, it's *my* offer!"

"She's right." Laisren smiled. "The offer belongs to Frankie. And if that's the final decision, would you please join me?" She stepped to the door, getting alarmingly close to Jessamae and leeching over her like ink. The question was for me, but it fluttered that white hair.

The jig was up. And when I arrived back at The Alcazar, there would be much more than an extended contract waiting for me. Someone had to fill the newly emptied glass prison. And my blood would be taken from me in brutal, traumatizing ways. The suits would drink the bits of me and be healed, satisfied, would maybe even become younger before their own jolly, jiggling faces. They would never stop.

There was a small drop of relief, that I had at least gotten my friends out of the city. Ben would heal and be safer in Aspen Ridge without me. Jessamae could go about whatever she was doing before she ever met me ... maybe with Cleo. If I could ensure Patrick and Anderson and Jack could walk away scot-free, then it was a win. A bigger jackpot than I could have ever realistically hoped for.

Wasn't it?

Though my blood had stopped moving through my veins, though my hands shook as I pushed myself to my feet and my eyes burned like fire, this was a win. Hip hip hooray.

"I offer another offer," Ben said. I'd forgotten about him in the room with us. I'd forgotten everyone but myself as I walked toward destiny. But he was here. He was wrapped around Billy, Jessamae's knife tucked tenderly under the smiling man's chin.

Ben scared me. He looked like a crazy person—covered in blush-colored lesions, donning an oversized, blood-speckled blazer, and slacks that barely reached his ankles. But he held the blade steady over Billy's bouncing Adam's apple.

Nikola rounded on Ben and her eyes glowed orange. Her

dragon's fire would never stop Ben before he slit Billy's throat, all it would do was push him into action. I doubted she cared for Billy, but she cared for her station enough to hold her attack. Smoke plumed from her pouting lips as she waited.

Ben poked at the insides of his cheeks with his double tongue. "You fire Frank and let us all walk out of here *alive*, including your little Animorph here." He gave Billy a shake, sawing the blade across the thin skin of his neck. Billy was enthralled by the turn of events. His exhilaration was obvious and gross.

Laisren turned to the threat slowly and without an ounce of surprise. "Benjamin Marshal Bowen. I'm impressed by your resilience." She continued to pet Jessamae, and when she stepped closer to Ben, so did Jessamae. "But you of all people know what's in store for you if you don't stay out of this. And *this* is between your ladylove"—she gestured to me—"and myself. No one else."

"I've always been nosy," he responded with his hallmark grin. "And I see us all coming to an agreement at the end of this. Everyone goes home happy. But mostly, they just go home."

Laisren cackled, bending over in her jackass hilarity. "Your affinity could prove useful. I enjoyed it myself at The Harvest last night. Though I admit, fifteen seconds of foresight leaves much to be desired. Exactly how farsighted are you?" Jessamae's knees were shaking, and her eyes had glazed over. Laisren gave her a ravishing smile and stroked her scarred brow before turning back to Ben.

He asked, "Do you have an eye chart on you?"

She wagged a finger at him, Jessamae clinging to her other arm. "Aren't you fresh? But you've been nothing else since your apprehension." She air-kissed Jessamae softly on the cheek, whose forehead was visibly dewing with sweat. "We all know why you're here, and if you care about Frankie like I think you do, then you will put your pocketknife away, and come with us back to Las Vegas."

Ben tucked his face into the back of Billy's head. Because of the height difference, Ben might have been smelling Billy's shampoo. He knew better than to look Laisren in the eye.

He was actually considering it. After all we'd done to get him free. "No! Ben, you can't seriously think you're being there will help me? Will help anything! I can't see you like that again ... please. Don't make me."

Laisren addressed Ben without doubt, acting as if I hadn't said a word. "Ben. You are not a killer—"

Ben ripped the steel across Billy's scrawny throat, and blood squirted across the room.

✺

BILLY DROPPED like he had no bones, and Ben wiped the blade on his sleeve.

Laisren all but tackled me to my back, Jessamae loitering around her like a toddler. Those emerald irises hit me like two sulfuric comets. "Heal him. Quickly. Now!" I was being dragged across the fungal floor, but only because I couldn't get my knees beneath me fast enough. I feared for Billy. Laisren needed me to heal him, and I would do anything to keep her eyes and her hands on me.

I would kill Ben for this.

But Nicola got to him first. Ben's suit jacket caught fire in a wink, but he'd already freed one arm from its sleeve when the flames hit. He moved incredibly fast. Once he had the jacket off, he threw it at Laisren, and it shrouded her in fire. She struggled to free herself from the burning fabric, the dancing tongues of flame spread over her hat, hair, and shoulders like an army of rats.

Billy, the twisted humor finally erased from his face, cupped his throat in both hands.

I was groggy. Laisren was distracted by her own engulfment,

and I was dipping back into my senses. Slowly, I charged for Nicola, but again, was beaten. Jessamae, freed from her own fairy-tinged haze, stood up on her toes like a child reaching for the kitchen faucet, placed her hands around either side of Nicola's temples, and the dragon dropped dead. Just like that.

She looked like she'd never been alive to begin with, like she'd always been a pile of large limbs and skin and eyes. She smelled terrible in seconds.

Billy was writhing on the floor, kicking up dust like a wild horse and clutching the streaming slit in his neck. His body was morphing, changing shapes every few seconds. His head was an oversized bubble, then as small as a grapefruit, as young as a baby then as old as the sea. His hands were shrinking and stretching, changing color faster than a chameleon. He was afraid now. Every face he wore was terrified, because each one of them was bleeding out, and he couldn't stop it. No matter who he changed into, they all had open throats.

A strong hand wrapped around the back of my skull. "Heal … him."

Laisren's eyes were cherry tomatoes ready to burst. The green in them so vibrant against the red, I thought the irises might slide forward and drop away from the eyeball, like a cutout in a jack-o-lantern. Her hair hadn't stopped smoking. The flames burned their way through her shoulder pads and her shiny skin poked through the singed fabric. Her face was all the tones of a sunset, but not because of the fire. Her airway was closing …

Betty was coiled around Laisren's throat, a scarf of muscle and scales. She was closing around that neck, thicker than a belt.

"Heal … him!" She thrust me into the shapeshifter's face. Inches from my nose and mouth, I tasted it. A mortal wound. The most delicious thing to ever grace my tongue. I realized at that moment that death itself did not taste very good at all. But this, this was everything.

I dipped my fingers between his flaps of skin and smeared it across my lips, glossing them in the most exquisite berry.

"Wow." I fell forward and sealed my mouth to the wound. It painted my tongue, danced in my stomach. I'd never tasted food before. I'd never tasted anything before now.

A terrible racket filled the building and the hand on my head disappeared, but I didn't need it. I continued to suck the juice from the fruit, slurping it up as if through a straw as the opening shrank smaller.

"Hey, I think that's enough, okay?"

Hands covered my shoulders and pulled. I fought them until I couldn't.

"Frankie! We have to move!" Anderson. Anderson's petrified voice lifted my face from the throbbing throat.

"Yeah … yeah. I'm done." I raked my arm across my mouth, leaving a red skid mark. Anderson's nose streamed blood down his lips. His jacket was gone, and his shirt was missing a sleeve. "What's happening?" I turned to the noise, ignoring Billy, who was sputtering guttural frothy words.

Ben had rammed Laisren around the middle and bulldozed her off me. The two fought over the little knife, their arms shaking between them. Ben's eyes were closed against Laisren's visage, he couldn't see in real-time as he fought. Betty was tangled around Laisren's neck and half smashed beneath her shoulders.

Using Anderson as a support beam, I propelled myself into the brawl. "Jessamae! Help him!" If she could simply touch Laisren then all of this would be over. Killing them all would leave no witnesses, no vengeful visits next season. "Jessamae?" I turned back to the stack of Nicola flesh, but Jessamae was gone. Anderson limped to the back door, a gun in one hand.

A single minute had passed since I feasted on Billy, who hadn't stopped leaking. My touch had helped, but I didn't finish the job and he'd continued to die. Ben and Laisren grappled over the knife, but I could tell Ben was flagging. Laisren's touch was pulling him under. He could smell her, feel her.

I slapped a hand over Laisren's eyes and twisted her head around, lifting her off Betty's length.

Parts of Betty were crushed. She suffered several broken ribs and her body looked flattened because of it. Still, she used what she could to squeeze Laisren's windpipe. The bulging skin on either side of the snake had turned a sickly shade of violet. But Betty would die if she didn't stop. She was bleeding inside.

"Come on, sweet lady. Come on," I coaxed, stroking her head with my thumb as I pulled. But without my hands, Laisren could see again, and she whisked her face around in my direction. As she opened her mouth, her beautiful mouth with perfect little teeth that I wanted so much to reach in and steal, Ben clocked Laisren right in the nose.

"Hurry, Frank!" He pushed and pulled the knife as if the two of them were working a double-sided saw.

Betty yielded to my touch, softening in my hand. I began to unwrap her.

"Stop!" Laisren hissed, her throat kinked and bruised. I did. I stopped. "Get the—"

Ben clapped a hand over her mouth. "Get Betty!" He was losing the fight for the knife, Laisren had both hands around its handle.

No matter which way I forced Laisren's head, I was squishing Betty. Around and around I pulled her. She was so much longer now. I had one more ring of snake left when we heard the roar. It was a sound I was all too familiar with, and my insides turned to soup.

In the battle next door, a very different attack than the one I experienced here, Patrick's beast had broken free.

My hands quivered as I concentrated on my snake. She was almost free when the window beside us shattered and a human head entered the room. I screamed, seeing the yellow glow of Jack's eyes glaring at me over the glass in his face. He was alive, just very bloody and impaled by a lot of window.

"Can you fuckers keep me out of the grave for one fuckin'

night!" Blood and glass fell from his face before he was ripped backward with a wet wheeze. The beast had hold of him.

"Ja ... J—Jack ck?" Billy spit through the hole in his throat. The Vegas coven had killed him and seeing him alive had surprised Billy so much that Jack's name was the last word Billy ever spoke. He released his throat, and his head slumped to the side. Dead.

Laisren took advantage of our distraction and finally pulled the knife from Ben's white knuckles.

And swinging it around like an axe, she chopped Betty in half.

29

I FAILED HER. I failed my Betty. Just as I always suspected I would. Her blood poured to the floor, and it felt like mine. But it wasn't mine and that truth made me so angry, so disgusted, so hideous that I couldn't even say it. I couldn't even scream.

Laisren sawed through the last bits of muscle until it was as stringy and thin as chapped-lip skin. Betty's tail flopped to the ground.

I couldn't remember moving. I couldn't sense Laisren's bulbous skull in my hands. I couldn't feel the reverberations from the floorboards, the vibration of sun-damaged skin under my fingers, as I beat her head into the floor. The hands must have been mine, I recognized the tiny leaf tattooed above my wrist, and they bashed the head into the ground until it opened like a melon. Until it bled all over Betty's severed half.

Then I did feel something, something pinching around my ribs and hips. Nothing but ant bites. Let them devour me. The hands wouldn't stop.

"Frankie, take it easy. Take it easy!"

I didn't stop.

If you kill them, there will be others. Someone else will take the throne.

I ignored the voice in my head. How could he be calm? How could he think rationally after what she'd done?

I healed the flappy gash in the back of Laisren's head, closing the ugly wound faster than I ever had before. Once a thin layer of skin sealed over her skull, I rammed her crown back into the ground and created a new gash. Chunks of her brain splattered the floor and then regrew, her skull cracked and mended. She never fully healed, and I wouldn't let her die.

Those green eyes rolled like marbles until they found me. I shouted, "No! No more." My fingers crawled up her face until they reached the eye sockets. I pushed my fingers around them like sticky, plum pits.

"Stop!" Laisren gasped, her hands around my wrists. She was struggling to breathe, the streams of air sounding like they filtered through a cheese grater. Because Betty was alive, and she hadn't stopped constricting around Laisren's throat.

Her beautiful head turned, and the glossy black globe of her eye shone like a midnight pool. She was trying her damnedest to finish off Laisren. Her tail was a hose of innards, spilling her blood and stuffing over the floor. The more she squeezed, the more she emptied. But she wouldn't quit.

Laisren was turning blue, but she didn't pull at the snake. She protected her eyes from my probing fingers. Her power was more important to her than her life.

I squeezed the skin of Betty's open tail together, keeping her alive and strong enough to finish the job.

Frankie … our freedom is more important than revenge. Please, Ben said in my head.

He was right. If I killed her, we'd all be doing this again when the next ruler of Las Vegas tracked us down. But pulling my fingers away from her eyes was the hardest thing I'd ever done.

"Free us," I told Laisren. "Every single one of us. Let us out of our contracts, Anderson too. No prisoners, no payments, no hunting Jack down in his home. Vow that no Las Vegas employee ever comes back for us."

She said nothing, but I wouldn't look at her eyes. I wouldn't risk it. I'd never felt more in control of my affinity, enchantment be damned.

Death was closing in on the fairy. I smelled it. "Swear it," I said.

She struggled beneath me, but I'd never let her go. She couldn't even spit on me, white slobber merely bubbled down her lip and pooled in the corners.

Digging her chin into Betty's scales, she gave a half-hearted nod. I swung my leg off her stomach, kneeled at her side, and rolled her onto her hip, Betty tight around her airway. "Write it." I slapped one of her veiny hands in the lake of blood that flowed from Billy's neck. Then I tossed it to a dry patch of wood like a stamp. "Write it!"

I didn't trust a nod to get us out of here without ramifications. If she could find me in the middle of the desert because I shook her hand, I knew she could wiggle her way out of this if I didn't have proof.

Laisren drew dark shapes on the floorboards with twitching fingers. I thought she would certainly die by the time she spelled out *U R FREE*.

I didn't recognize my voice when I growled, "Sign it."

She wanted to look at me, to show her derision, but her eyes were cloudy with blood. Pink spit hung from her tongue. She could hardly see when she wrote out a sloppy, lopsided *L*.

"Phone?" I asked Ben without turning around. He was the only one left. Everyone else was dead or fighting a beast out in the dark.

"No. But." As I watched the sheen shrink in Laisren's eyes, I heard Ben shuffling around in the room behind me until he presented a cell phone. A sticky thing that was warm to the touch. Billy's, I'd guess.

I handed it back to him. "Take a picture. And get Laisren's face in it."

Ben took a step back to accommodate Laisren's willowy frame. "Say cheese."

I looked to the camera over my shoulder, a dying woman beneath me, a mutilated snake in my hand, and two dead bodies splayed in the background. It was quite the Christmas Card. "Cheese."

Ben gave a stiff nod and slipped the phone into the pocket of his suit pants.

I unraveled Laisren's snakeskin boa, who was once again undulating and flicking her tongue. Where Betty's tail used to be was all translucent tubes, rib bones, and moving muscle, but the blood was congealing, and the skin was filling in fast. I cradled her halved weight in my arms and stared at the rubbery white tail that used to be hers.

Laisren's life was strobing. It was an irritant, but nothing more.

Ben said, "Frank … you made a deal—"

"I never offered shit."

Ben took a few flighty inhalations before giving the same strained nod as before.

What emotion was left in Laisren's face shifted toward twinkling outrage. The burst blood vessels looked like watercolor flowers around her eyes. Then the outrage became loss. A sadness overwhelming enough to push through the veil of death.

A foot. An inch. An eyelash away from lifelessness.

Finally, I draped Betty over my elbow, and touched my fingers to the ugly bruising on Laisren's throat.

"You taste like artificial sugar," I informed her as she healed.

My hands were smooth, the last of the wrinkles ironed out by Laisren's heady damage and flavorful lifeline, when another body flew through the open door.

It was one of the trickster twins, Omar or Mo, but as if he'd gone through a paper shredder. His skin hung like tassels off his muscles, and he was dead as a doornail.

A roar followed the smell, as ear-splitting and heart-stopping as an oncoming train.

Outside, the beast was twirling in circles. Its enormous set of shoulders were tipping toward the house like a top loose on its axis, its hands at its ears. Its colossal figure would certainly break through the living room wall, smashing us and the bodies to gelatinous smithereens.

Cleo was singing to it. Thank god her voice didn't reach us in here.

Something bumped my bicep. Betty. Betty was trying to lift herself and wrap around my arm, but she was too tired to achieve it. I circled her around my neck and tried not to think about how much lighter she felt. "You crazy serpent." I kissed her head.

The wall shook but it didn't break. The beast had shouldered the house like a plywood door, but somehow it didn't break.

"Let's go, Frankie. You spared one life. The rest are on their own." Ben's hands were extended in front of him. His breath was strained. He bit into the tissue of his lip as sweat spread through his brow. He'd made another force field in front of the house, and it was costing him dearly.

I stepped into him without a thought, his arms brushing my arms, my crown tucking beneath his bristly chin. The moment his warmth hit me, tears filled my eyes. It was so familiar. So beautifully, terribly familiar. His skin on mine. The veins branching from the inside of his elbow and over the bones of his wrists. The pressure of his stomach on my chest was like home.

A home in which my favorite chair had been moved two inches to the left. A hairbrush was webbed in strands of hair that didn't belong to me. An uncanny house. An almost home.

But I didn't step away. I cried while Ben's breathing evened out, while he regained his strength. Betty seemed content to lie squished between our bodies, and she warmed with us.

"What now?" I asked.

Before Ben could answer, a body clapped into Ben's force-field. Jessamae's eyes blared through the night. Her arms bent at unnatural angles above her head, her hands flat against the air,

340

PARED

against Ben's ward. Then she was sucked back, as if by a vacuum. She was flung forward and back. And again. And again. Finally, she froze, flat against the air. Patrick's beastly black eyes appeared like oil slicks behind her.

The beast was beckoning us outside. It knew exactly what it was doing.

∽

BEN DROPPED the shield and Jessamae fell to her knees. The beast towered behind her. It curled its claws around the edges of the doorway. It punched at the wood until the frame turned to woodchips, and the beast wedged its way inside—

Gunshots tore the night in half. The beast wailed and bucked forward, nearly collapsing over Jessamae. The bullets infuriated the creature, but they did nothing to slow it down. Patrick's own Mr. Hyde bellowed like King Kong, spittle glistening in the starlight, and spun on his callused heels. His back was full of dark, oozing holes as he barreled into the night.

I ran to Jessamae, Ben close behind me. I tried to lift her by the arms, but she'd gone limp. Ben hooked an elbow under her armpit and propped her against the wall of the house. I held her face—she had a broken wrist and a cheek fracture. "Jessamae, Jessamae. Wake up! What's happening? Where's Jack?"

Her leaden head lolled on her neck, her pale hair thick with dust.

"Where is Jack? Can he stop Patrick?"

"Jack," she slurred. "No. Shot. Jack was shot."

"Goddammit," Ben muttered.

I asked, "Where's Anderson? Cleo?"

Her eyes were as big as the stars when she looked into my face. "I don't know."

Together we limped away from the house, Jessamae cascading from side to side, barely keeping her balance.

341

The ground was littered with ant hills and shrubs comprised of meat and fabric. The dark landscape was empty of life, but full of death. The moonlight was too feeble to shape identities other than suits and not-suits. All I knew was that there were nine of them outside the house. Nine deaths.

Coughing. Wet, phlegmy coughing.

Ben took off after the sound and fell beside a lump of a person on the cracked earth. It was alive. And it was Jack.

"Fuck ... I can't. I can't keep dying. Or living." He hacked black goo onto Ben's arms. "Just pick one!" He screamed at the apathetic sky. "Fucking pick one already!"

"Do you want me to pick?" Ben asked as he brushed Jack's eyelids shut with his palm.

Jack kicked his legs and punched Ben's arm from his head. "What the hell is the matter with you!"

"Thought so," Ben said with a smirk.

I rushed forward and got to work. I was high on all the pain in my body, high on everything I'd stolen time and time again. I could feel my pupils outgrowing my eyeballs. My hands were covered in diamonds, sluicing like water down my wrists. It felt wonderful. Until it felt like I was covered in bugs. Spiders. Ben would tell me if I was.

"Easy," Jack whispered. His hands covered mine. "You're overflowing."

"Over ... flowing?"

"Overdosing, really," Ben added. "It's okay. Jack will keep things under control. Except in Patrick's case."

Jack grunted, sparkles in his eyes. "I couldn't. I tried. I just fuckin' died if you recall. It's taking some getting used to. Some bodily recognition. But Frankenstein brought me back. I remember her hands." He gave my hands a pat, like you would a good horse.

"But you're okay?" I asked.

"Course," he huffed, but there was a twitch in his cheek, a nervous smack to his mouth.

He was not okay. He was very un-okay. He'd died, been dead, and was forced to return to his cold, stiff body, where he was thrown back to death's door like the Sunday paper. But we didn't have time to discuss our feelings. We needed Jack in this fight, and he would deal with the trauma of it later, just like the rest of us.

With my hands on Jack's neck, a scream stabbed my brain like an icepick. I covered my ears and howled at the pain. Blood pushed against my fingers, desperate to get out. Even as far as we stood from Cleo, her siren shriek split my eardrums and blurred my vision. The scream cut off as if with a blade. It stopped in a way that scared me to the bone.

I tugged Betty from my shoulders and laid her on Jack's chest. Without time for anything else, I ran. Ben ran. Jessamae vanished into the surrounding fog, apporting. Jack pet Betty's head as he sprawled on the ground. I'd given him some magic, enough to keep him alive, I told myself as we flew.

I tracked Ben, who was faster than I was despite all the pain I'd swallowed. He ran for Cleo because he loved her. He would always love her. And I loved her too. My anger and humiliation and sorrow hadn't gone anywhere, but I couldn't lose them.

They were all in the house we'd slept in—how long ago? An hour? Less? The bangs and the snarls were beastly. I didn't hear Cleo.

Ben made it inside the tattered doorway first. More bodies. So many dead suits covered the floor like cockroaches.

A gunshot blasted from the kitchen, then a grunt, then a clank. "Patrick!" Ben shouted as he raced through the house.

"Anderson!" I called, I hadn't seen him since he pulled me from Billy. "Anderson!" He didn't answer. I hurried to the kitchen, dread lurking behind my sternum.

The second twin, Omar or Moe, flumped in a dark stain on the floor, leaving bloody mud pies—blood pies—beneath him. His brother was kneeling over him, trying to hold his hand but he couldn't clasp those reaching fingers. Because he wasn't corporeal, he wasn't real. This was the visual trickster, and he didn't want to die alone, so he tricked his own mind into believing his brother was here with him in the end.

I felt an unwelcome sadness. I didn't have the capacity to care for more people than I did. He wasn't mine and I would not mourn for him as if he were. I left him there and followed the noise to the bathroom.

Patrick was the centerpiece of the room, and he was surrounded by three cracked, bleeding, and dangerous women. The beast held Jessamae by the scruff and was smashing her face in the mirror above the moldy sink. Once the beast pushed her through the glass, Jessamae's head grated against the wooden shelves on the other side.

Cleo was hooked around the beast's thick neck, her fists full of pale fur that wouldn't pull free from the thick, reptilian skin. Her lips trembled against the monster's folded ears, singing softly to his brain. The music was driving it insane. Dried blood striped his neck from her earlier scream. Its head sprung from side to side while it roared in agony, swatting at her like a pesky bee.

And Daiyu, the woman who possessed people like a certain mad demon I've come to know, was unconscious in the claw-foot tub. She was naked other than a pair of ballet slippers that poked from the porcelain like rabbit ears.

Reevaluating its biggest threat, the beast chucked Jessamae to the side. She knocked a sconced light fixture from the wall and folded beside the toilet, her hands coated in crispy roach shells and dirt. The scar over her eyebrow was hidden beneath new deep slashes marring her face.

The beast clapped its jaws with a snarl only an inch from Cleo's cheek. She continued to sing, and the beast began pummeling her with its oversized fist. It only got one good hit in before Ben erected a shield around her skull.

They're too close, I can't cover all of her.

I jumped at the beast's feet, wrapping an arm around one

naked calf. He'd been shot over and over, he'd been beaten and tackled. I tried to pull the wounds from him, to take the beast from him like a sickness. Before I even got a taste, he kicked me in the head. My vision blurred and my hearing faded away to nothing. It felt like my bones were burning.

"I can't get in his head!" Ben yelled, and he left the bathroom.

"Ben!" I screamed. He left us. Me. With Patrick's other half.

Without Ben, Cleo was completely vulnerable. The beast flipped her to the floor. It ravaged her with a mammoth claw, raking the nails down her stomach, opening her up. She screamed. It was a human scream. A terrified, human scream. And it hurt so much more than her siren wailing.

The beast opened its mouth wide as a hippo's and brought it down over Cleo's forehead, her temples between his teeth—

Then he began to change. Not back to a man. He began to age; he began to shrink. The flesh of his face and his hands and his chest collapsed in on themselves like hot plastic, leaving dozens of folds and crevices in their place. As his body shifted and lessened, he didn't crush Cleo's head between his jaws, but he didn't release her either.

Patrick was withering away. And in his animal face I saw a dead dog, sizzling in the summer heat like jerky ...

Jessamae's strong hands circled the beast's head like a crown. Her eyes blazed with blue fire and her lip trembled against her teeth.

I was a struck by conversation I had with Jessamae when I was just beginning to understand what she was:

Can you hurt people, like I heal them?

Yes, but I don't see the point.

"Jessamae! That's enough!"

She didn't react to my voice. I finally understood what it was like for her, to watch me lose control to my affinity, to not *want* to stop.

Patrick's skin stuck to his gargantuan bones as if there was no meat between them. "Jessamae! You'll kill him!"

"You will," Ben confirmed.

His shadow blanketed me as he appeared outside the bathroom. I smelled him. So much blood that wasn't his. And something else that wasn't his. As my gaze roved up his lanky frame, my eyes locked on the pistol in his hand. It belonged to one of the guards littering the living room floor.

"Take your hands off Patrick, Jessamae."

Her returning hiss put Amir to shame. "This isn't Patrick."

"It is, and you're killing him." His hand was so steady it was frightening. He was ready to kill her. He would kill her to save Patrick.

Patrick's beast continued to mummify around Cleo's head, her hair pouring from his throat like black vomit. Her hands gripped his snout, one palm smothering his nostrils. She pried his jaw open further and further, and his fangs dislodged slowly from her scalp, pulling from the skin like carrots from the earth.

As Cleo forced the fangs away from her, taking a deep breath through the ropey slobber, Jessamae didn't budge. Her eyes darted from the back of Patrick's head to Ben like a tiger protecting its kill.

Ben didn't blink. "I won't ask again."

I whispered, "Ben—"

She hasn't stopped. He said inside my head.

Cleo's head emerged from the wilting mouth like a disturbing, backward birth. Drool clung to her hair in a viscous shower cap. She forced the snout away until there was a foot of space between them. Patrick was too weak. Too sick.

"I'm okay," Cleo said, her voice astoundingly clear.

Jessamae told her, "He would have pulverized your skull if I hadn't intervened. If I hadn't been the only one willing to do *something*." She turned to Ben. "He would have killed her. And I know this isn't the first time he's tried. He tore her shoulder open as if she were made of twigs and leaves, didn't he?"

Jessamae and Cleo talked much more than I ever realized. How had I been so stupid?

"I'm sure you know what he did to Frankie at The Alcazar. If she hadn't been forced to face this creature once before, what would have happened? How many times will you allow this to happen? I understand you are fond of Patrick, but he is a *threat*. To you. To those you love. Every day."

"Jessamae," I whispered. "He helped us—"

"He hurt us." With her face full of mirrored glass, I couldn't argue with her. "It's irresponsible."

"Just get off him!"

"Irrational."

Cleo dragged herself from beneath Patrick's diminishing weight. He was vanishing before my eyes. His body was here, but Patrick was disappearing.

"Jessamae!"

"No. I can't allow this to happen again. Over and over. He can't control it. It's the only way."

I got to my knees and pulled at her wrists. Red filled my eyes. "Stop it! It's not his fault."

"I know." She leaned forward and rested her chin on the bones of Patrick's head. "I'm sorry I have to do this to you. Again."

Ben fired.

30

"I HOPE one day you can forgive me."

Ben helped Patrick into a nasty gray jacket and a pair of slacks that matched his own. He gave a tiny smile to the man, who tried to return the gesture, however feeble. The most disconcerting thing about bringing Patrick back from that place between life and death, the place so many of us had been in before now, was his wounded spirit. If the soul was a real thing, something tangible, I feared he had just lost his. And if he didn't find it again, it would snap my heart in two.

Maybe time is the only medicine that would take when it came to mending a soul. Jack—though I didn't know him as well as the others—was some shade of shell-shocked, too. Everything made him twitch—loud noises, soft noises, light, darkness, movement, a sharp look. His eyes, which had been peculiar before, were more cat-like than human now. Though he stifled my magical overdose when I tried to heal him outside, he was struggling to sense affinities like he used to before he died, and he couldn't change Patrick back after he'd shifted into the beast.

Time. They just needed time.

"I need to check on the shop. Make sure they didn't get in the vault, though I guess it doesn't matter now." Jack scanned the bodies around him. "They must have blown half my mines to hell." He pulled at the neck of his shirt. "It was her. Daiyu." He visibly shuddered and I knew this wasn't the first time he'd met the girl. "She only needed to get close enough. Then she got in my head and … all she needed was the pillow beneath me … I don't know what happened at the shop after that." He gave us an awkward wave and was out the door, pulling at the collar of his shirt as he left.

Anderson was outside, identifying the bodies. He'd been the one to shoot Patrick when the beast was breaking into the house next door, and the beast had in turn, knocked him unconscious. Anderson had a concussion, a broken nose, and had been shot in the leg by a security guard. He'd used his sleeve to make a tourniquet.

If Cleo hadn't been here, Anderson would certainly be dead. She'd conjured Cleo illusions all over the property, distracting the guards and wasting half their bullets.

Though I saw them as mere suits, even villains after my kidnapping, I knew they had partners and children and friends somewhere in the world. Anderson knew them, had cared for a few, or at least had grown used to their company. He'd worked against them tonight and had maybe even killed a few. I gave him time to grieve.

Laisren was gone. The only evidence we had that she'd been in the town at all, were the damp cigar butt resting between a set of floorboards and one dented top hat. We had the photo, we had our freedom, but I doubted we'd seen the last of her. Monsters always came back for me.

The bodies of Nicola, Billy, and the twins would go into the mass grave with the others. I would have left them where they were, hoping the coyotes would sniff them out sooner rather than later, if it weren't for what I'd seen in the kitchen: that twin clutching to the image of his brother as he died. I couldn't leave town knowing they weren't together, as much as I hated them.

"Hey. I mean it," Ben said, patting Patrick hard on the shoulder. "Taking the shot was the only way to get her off you."

Patrick rubbed his left pec, needling the dent where the bullet kicked through. Jessamae thought her words had spurred Ben on, had convinced him that she was the righteous one in all of this, and he chose to kill Patrick himself. And after he buried a bullet in the beast, just above his heart, she took her hands away, and blinked up at Ben in surprise. In that split second, Cleo and I wrestled her into the bathtub, smashing Daiyu's corpse into the brown porcelain.

Patrick told us that Daiyu tried to possess the beast, tried to take over his mind. But the beast wasn't human. His brain was a combination of primitive instincts and rage bordering on insanity. Even a moment inside such a head fractured the woman, and once she fled back into her own body, she didn't act right. She stripped the dress from her back after biting some of the fabric off and swallowing it. She scratched the skin from her arms and face and tried to pull her own tongue out while looking in the bathroom mirror before Jessamae put her out of her misery.

Healing Patrick had been easy. Too easy. It was positively invigorating. I was getting faster, much faster, at my craft. Compared to Ben's stomach wound over the summer, this felt over in the time needed to take a photograph, though they tell me it took longer. After that, I hovered from person to person, drinking their injuries. Eating their pain. The whole building smelled like Pine Sol, drenched in their fear and sadness.

Cleo had been quiet as I healed her, but my hands on her stomach didn't feel as awkward as I thought it would. She was a hero. And it wasn't her fault I was so devastatingly jealous of her. I was the bad guy.

Jessamae and Cleo had ventured off to dig a hole, or maybe a quarry, big enough to function as the mass grave, taking only our switchblades with them.

Patrick wasn't upset with Jessamae. As he was healing and she excused herself from the small bathroom, he offered her the only genuine smile I'd seen from him since he changed back. Patrick was angry at Ben for stopping her.

"Yeah. Yeah, I know, Benjamin," he said, straightening the lapels over his bare chest.

He didn't react much to my stealing his numerous bullet wounds and his exponential dehydration. He'd been helpful, holding still and moving as needed. He never said a word. But the shame on his face and in the limp sway of his arms illustrated just how much he agreed with Jessamae.

But just because his body count was the highest of the coven, didn't mean he was worse than anyone else. None of us were innocent.

"Cuffs are a little bloody. But we're just grateful it fits, right?" Ben asked.

Patrick stared at the stains beneath his hands for a long time before responding. "Yeah. Maybe I should … wash up. Give me a minute?" He went to the bathroom and shut the door behind him. The bath water sounded lighter than spring rain—the faucet was probably clogged. I pictured the black and brown water swirling like sewage at the bottom of the tub. But he'd probably feel cleaner underneath it than he did now.

I guess anything can be a grave, right piggy?

"Fuck you," I told Paimon, exhausted of their constant companionship.

"Guess I deserve that," Ben said.

He leaned against the stinking, cobweb-covered refrigerator, watching me talk to someone who wasn't there.

"Uh, no. No. I was talking to myself." I crossed my arms on the counter, feeling the tacky grease and dust adhere to my arm hair. The sink was layered in grime, its texture inexplicable. But the sink itself was beautiful. Enormous and sturdy underneath all that dirt. The sort of sink rich ladies with bad haircuts paid extra to own.

"Do *you* deserve it?" he asked, making me jump.

He'd moved closer to me, his steps light.

I snorted. "It's one of the few things I do deserve."

"We're all culpable here, Frank … Princess. Frankie?"

Ben had only ever called me Frankie when the situation was serious, and I didn't like hearing it. "You can call me whatever you want." I stared at the tattoo on my hand, picking at scabs that weren't there.

I didn't want to do this today. I didn't want to do anything today but drink until I blacked out. But maybe tomorrow would be better if I just got the bad parts over with now.

I whispered. "I care about you, Benny. More than anyone. And ... you're right. I ..." I couldn't say it. I wouldn't let the first time I said those words be tonight, standing in the blood of a stranger. "And that's why I can't be anything but your friend. At least right now."

"I said I was sorry, and I meant it—"

"I know. It's not just that. *I* started all of this." Bitter tears scalded my eyes as I remembered the picnic he'd taken me on over the summer. "When I told you ... when I said I was shit—that I was bad—I meant that. And I was right. Look what I did to us."

"Frank, I'm in love with you, shit or no shit. And I'm not holding any of this against you. I can move past it! We were both drunk on that fairy's sick elix—"

"I still think about it. I picture you and Cleo together whenever I'm alone." I covered my eyes to it. "Have you stopped thinking about Jessamae and me?"

I remembered kissing her. I remembered the twist of Ben's face as he watched. And those things, those horrible facets of me, felt like nothing compared to the rest. I lied to Ben on the day of my grandmother's funeral. I nearly let him die in my need to consume ... and I'd killed a man. I killed again and again. I scared myself. Because it felt like the beginning of something.

"I can move past it," he said with eyes like iron.

"I think I can too." I trailed a finger through the muck of the sink, drawing a circle in the gunk to avoid seeing what my words would do to him. "But not yet."

He cleared his throat, and he was in so much pain, it was crippling to witness. "Right. Okay, Frank. I'll just ..." his pauses were worse than his words. "Go find Jack." And he was gone.

I was curb-stomping my heart as I broke his. But I needed to think I was worthy of his love, or I'd never trust him. I needed to *like* myself before I would allow myself to love him.

Or some other bullshit like that.

✺

I DIDN'T KNOW what to do with myself, but sitting in the house all alone—like I very much wanted—while everyone else recouped or covered up our grizzly night, seemed like a good way to get myself left behind. So, dragging my feet, I caught up to Anderson, who was sitting in the dirt with his head in his hands.

"Hey."

He noted me over his shoulder and went back to his hands.

I said, "Bet you're regretting taking me for pizza now."

He chuffed but didn't look up.

I folded myself down beside him. "Laisren's gone, back to Vegas I think. But you're free. I hope that's what you wanted." Betty flowed left and right across the desert, her tail ending in a strange stub. But she lived, and she didn't hurt anymore. She slithered into my hands and coiled around my wrist.

"I heard," he spoke to his fingers. "Thanks."

I pictured some form of celebration, balloons and streamers and a fat little pony, because we wouldn't get one here. "Will you go back to Maryland?"

He looked up to the horizon. The stars were beautiful. How they must hate us for how ugly things were down below. "Yeah, I suppose I will. But my dogs are dead or in a shelter. I haven't spoken to my girlfriend in years. Am I just supposed to tell her, 'I missed you, baby, I've been working for a coven of witches and ghouls. I wanted to come back all along, I swear it, sweetheart.'" His sigh shook his frame. "It's going to be hard. Going home without any piece of home left."

"Yeah. I know." I reached a hesitant hand forward and touched the fabric of his sleeve. He and I rarely touched, but he was my friend. And I hated the defeated sag of his shoulders. It was almost enough to stay here and watch the sun rise over and over until *this place* became home for us.

"You need somewhere to go?"

Still numb from the last few hours, the new voice didn't make me jump like it did Anderson. I rotated gradually until I saw a slightly damp Patrick standing barefoot in the sand.

"I have a place," Patrick added when Anderson kept quiet. "There's room."

Anderson didn't speak. He swallowed hard and turned away from Patrick, his eyes on Betty who hissed in conversation.

"Yeah. I heard you caught the show." Patrick smiled a very un-Patrick smile. "I wouldn't want to live with me eith—"

Anderson rolled to his feet with a grunt and brushed the dirt from his ass. "How much room?"

Patrick froze for a beat. "Enough to house you and your single suit." He smiled for real. It was little, but it was sincere.

They walked together back to the house, and I trailed behind them. Betty slithered up to my shoulders and stuck her tongue in my ear.

"Do I get my own room?" Anderson asked.

"Let me guess, you wanted to sleep with me? William, you are forward."

"William?" I blurted, stumbling to catch up.

"Oh, yeah," Anderson said, with spots of blush on his neck. "That's my name."

I stifled the irritation that he told Patrick his first name before me. "Can I call you Will?"

"No."

"Only I can," Patrick said.

I envied them terribly, but I had my mother's house, and a cat that must be dead by now. I had no job, no money, and no romantic partner. Was I supposed to return to Aspen Ridge, arm and arm with Cleo? Did she still want to live anywhere near me?

We helped gather the bodies, mostly Patrick, and moved them into the fresh grave behind the house with a hole blown through it. Jessamae hunted down a skinny brown rabbit and used its sacrifice to move a good chunk of the corpses herself. The sun was rising by the time we packed the earth down over their curling hands and empty eyes.

As we trudged back to the house full of bullet holes, a black crossover crunched down the dirt road toward us, Ben in the driver seat and Jack riding shotgun. Dirt sprayed from their tires like a boat in water.

"Car's gone," Ben called out as he slammed the door. "Jack was gracious enough to lend us this one." We'd left Pamela's car in Vegas, but I'd die before I'd go back.

"I'll be needing it returned in one piece." Jack shot a finger at Patrick and Ben, ignoring the rest of us. "Now that Daiyu is dead," he paused to glare at the memory of the tiny girl, "and Laisren vowed to keep her lackeys off my ass—not that I trust 'em—I should be safe to rebuild here. Don't want to let all the land go to waste."

"Yeah, I bet it cost … a lot," Patrick said with a somber expression and Anderson—William—rumbled out a laugh.

"I need to bury more mines and burn the old map." He pulled a shovel from the backseat and scowled before he turned to Jessamae. The scowl morphed into a grim frown. "I'll still help you find Eliza. But nothing more. Do you understand me?"

She nodded and touched his sun-beaten jowl. "Of course. Thank you, Jack." She patted his chest, and he squeezed her bicep before turning on his heel and stalking back to the main street of town.

"I'll drive," Ben said.

Patrick shouted, "Shotgun."

"Frankie gets shotgun. She needs the room for Betty." Even without the end of her tail, she'd continued to grow over the last week, and she almost reached my wrists on either side while hanging from my neck.

"I propose that I need the most room," Patrick said with a hand around his chin.

"That's why you're sitting behind the back seat."

Jessamae, after an awkward sweep of her arm, opened the back door for Cleo, who sat in the middle with William—no, I preferred Anderson—on her other side. Ben slammed the back hatch over Patrick, who hugged his knees in what was, essentially, the trunk of the car. Betty fell into a doze the moment I buckled my seatbelt. And Ben didn't play any music for the entire duration of our journey home.

PATRICK AND ANDERSON raced off in the Tesla collecting dust in front of the house after a clumsy, but somehow nice, side-hug from Anderson and a gentle knock to the jaw from Patrick.

I unlocked the front door and was hit with a wall of stale air. I didn't smell a cat, but I didn't smell death either.

"Amir!" Cleo called as she pushed past me into the house. All her stuff was here, and she had a key to the door. That might be enough to get her to stay.

Jessamae's steps were timid, as much as she was capable, as she entered the kitchen and sat at the table. Ben's plates were stacked in the dishrack. His art hung on the walls. His fancy meats were rotting in the fridge. "God," I whispered.

"My house is ready. The renovation's all done … Now's as good a time as any," Ben said before pulling a produce box out of the garage and stacking his dry dishes inside.

I didn't speak as I followed his lead, grabbing a garbage bag from the pantry. I set Betty in her wardrobe—she zipped from chamber to chamber, thrilled to be home. I wish I felt the same, but this didn't feel like home anymore. Not without Ben. But I needed time. Otherwise, resentment would build and build until every moment I was with him would feel like lying.

One splash of color at a time, I tossed Ben's clothes into the trash bag, sinking in his smell, suffocating in it. I thought a few of my organs, maybe a rib or two, was packed away with all that fabric.

After the bag was full, I tied it off and turned back to the closet, noting one last piece of clothing on the floor. Purple. I fingered his "Mama Needs Some Wine," sweatshirt, overwhelmingly grateful for not having washed it before we left. I brought it to my face and rubbed it over my cheek, even pulling it between my lips, leaving a small spit spot on the arm.

I tucked it between my mattress and my box spring.

"Amir!" Cleo shouted for a cat that was no longer here.

THE TRUNK SLAMMED over the few boxes Ben brought with him when he moved in. He was taking his car and the crossover would stay here until we could get it back to Jack. I would report Pamela's car stolen, under the advisement of Ben.

"Well," he said. Cleo had already waved her goodbye and returned to the kitchen, leaving us alone on the front lawn. I wanted to ask him to stay, to take my room and stay with Cleo in this house. I should be alone across town, if anyone should.

But I was too afraid to say it. Too afraid that he'd say yes. Too afraid that if I lost my physical connection to Cleo, I would lose Ben and everyone else so gradually that I wouldn't notice until I had no one left. "Time to hit the dusty trail."

"Literally." As fall rolled in, the drought had yet to disperse. Everything had been yellow and brown, dead for so long, that if I didn't have a calendar, I wouldn't have seen the season change. But it was November now, and death would be replaced with snow soon enough.

"We need to get you a new phone, Frank. But if you need anything in the meantime, email me. Send me a smoke signal." He smiled.

"A letter?"

"I could use a love letter or two." I either laughed or cried. Or both. He reached out and tugged on a dirty curl spilling out from my bun. I wanted to run, I wanted to lean in. Had the last three months even happened? Had it all been a dream?

Ben left. I watched his car bounce down the road as if it were nothing but a mirage.

When I entered the sweltering house, Jessamae was still sitting at the table. She hadn't moved. The cords in my chest were happy to see her, but I felt a stronger pull lead out the door. This was going to be rough. I rubbed my painful heart.

"We need to talk," she said.

"Of course, we do." I went to the fridge and pulled a dented Gold Star from the vegetable crisper. At least one thing would never change. I put it to my lips and smiled.

EPILOGUE

Cleo

"Amir!" I cried for the four-thousandth time. I couldn't stay in this house without him. He was the only creature around who I knew would be happy to see me, and, silver lining, searching for the animal gave me an excuse to leave Jessamae's constant pestering. She'd yet to cease filling my head with excuses and reasoning and any other words that might sway me back into her waffling arms.

She was happy to have me alright—for an hour. For the night.

Looking under my bed, flipping my hair from my eyes, a knock came at the door. It had to be Ben, unable to spend even an hour away from Frankie after their long separation. A separation that was no one's fault, and everyone's fault. Reasoning told me there was nothing else to be done, but whenever Frankie looked at me, the fear, the betrayal in her eyes ... reasoning couldn't fix that. And god, how I missed her.

I regretted it. So much so that I wish I could cut the memories away with a scalpel.

Cancerous things. But I'd never known such hurt, such loneliness, until I saw that kiss between Frankie and Jessamae. They were bound, we all knew it ... but I thought—

The door creaked open, and a strained silence filled the house. It wasn't Ben.

I hurried to the living room to greet whatever had come for us now.

He was familiar, but I couldn't speak, I was so thrown to see him. It was the blonde man I'd seen outside The Harvest as Anderson and I waited for the car. He hadn't approached me, but his eyes were like hands on my body. He looked at me as one looks at a hunting trophy, a rhino's horn. The attention was something I was used to, but he had the power to back it up. He was no average man, and no average witch.

He was pale despite the Nevada sun, and his hair was nearly transparent. He was handsome in an unseemly way, his cheek-bones too sharp, his teeth too white.

He held a hissing, spitting Amir by the scruff of the neck.

"Francesca! Or … Frankie, right? So good to be back in Aspen Ridge. It has been years!" Amir squirmed like a trout, sharp little teeth poised for shredding. The man paid my kitten no mind, though it fought his arachnid hands savagely. Good boy.

The man noticed Jessamae poised at the table. "Wonderful! Jessamae is here, too. Looks like we'll be having a little family reunion."

He walked into the living room without proper invitation, Amir swinging his claws closer to his face. He appraised our home with unhinged delight. "It looks so different! It suits you. Both of you."

He hadn't bothered to address me at all.

Before I could lead him out of the house, all I'd need was a glance, Frankie asked suddenly, "What's your name?"

He turned with a jovial grin and squeezed Amir so hard that the poor baby began to yowl. "Aiden." He offered a chalk-white hand. "But you can call me Dad."

ACKNOWLEDGMENTS

I am so grateful to my publisher, Lake Country Press, for believing in the PEACHY trilogy, despite all the tragedy I've stuffed into it. This book wouldn't exist without you.

A huge thank you to my friends and the first readers of PARED, Kat and Beka. Your feedback was invaluable and your love for these characters is everything. I am so lucky to have such a phenomenal agent in Helen Lane, who gave her time and energy to read both PEACHY and PARED, provide feedback, and fall in love with these books, which I wrote before we ever met. Thank you all for your honest opinions on such a controversial chapter.

Thank you to my family, especially my dad who is my biggest fan and the character inspiration for Jack. Thank you to Shay, Tan, Maddie, and Mom for being four powerful, breathtaking women, in the book and out. Max, I swear you'll be in the next one, but I couldn't have too many people who looked like family in the same club, okay!

Thank you to my friends, especially Brittany, Chris, and Nicole who listen to my endless prattle of fictional worlds. Thank you to Whitey and Deb who make me feel worthy of compliments.

I acknowledge my husband Dylon, who has always championed my dream of being an author and every single one of my books, whether he's read them or not. I love you, Pook.

Thank you to my readers who came back for seconds! Frankie's last desserts are coming soon!

ABOUT THE AUTHOR

Raised by a welder and a Jack Mormon in the small town of Wallsburg, Camri Kohler worked her way to the grid city, Salt Lake. Camri earned her BA in English from the University of Utah before completing her MLIS at the University of Illinois. Camri is an archivist at PBS and spends her free time with her partner, her dogs, or her tomatoes. She is a mess of unresolved issues which are the primary inspiration for her writing.

X ◎ ♪

ALSO BY CAMRI KOHLER